THE FATHERS
and Other Fiction

THE
FATHERS

AND

OTHER FICTION

Allen Tate

Introduction by
Thomas Daniel Young

LOUISIANA STATE UNIVERSITY PRESS

Baton Rouge and London

LIBRARY OF CONGRESS CATALOGING IN PUBLICATION DATA

Tate, Allen, 1899–
  The fathers, and other fiction.

  (Library of Southern civilization)
  Contains a revision of the author's The fathers,
originally published in 1938, and two short stories.
  CONTENTS: The fathers.—The migration.—The immortal
woman.
  I. Title.
PZ3.T183Fau [PS3539.A74] 813'.5'2   77–22617
ISBN 0–8071–0381–0
ISBN 0–8071–0359–4 pbk.

A Dream

At nine years a sickly boy lay down
At bedtime on a cot by mother's bed
And as the two darks merged the room became
So strange it left the boy half dead:

The boy-man on the Ox Road walked along
The man he was to be and yet another,
It seemed the grandfather of his mother,
In knee-breeches silver-buckled like a song,
His hair long and a cocked hat on his head,
A straight back and slow dignity for stride;
The road, red clay sun-cracked and baked,
Led fearlessly through scrub pines on each side
Hour after hour—the old road cracked and burbned,
The trees countless, and his thirst unslaked.
Yet steadily with discipline like fate
Without memory, too ancient to be learned.
The man walked on and as if it were yesterday
Came easily to a two-barred gate
And stopped, and peering over a little way
He saw a dog-run country store fallen-in,
Deserted, but he said, "Who's there?"
And then a tall fat man with stringy hair
And a manner that was innocent of sin,
His galluses greasy, his eyes coldly gray,
Appeared, and with a gravely learned air
Spoke from the deep coherence of hell—
The pines thundered, the sky blacked away,
The man in breeches, all knowledge in his stare,
A moment shuddered as the world fell.
                                    —Allen Tate

CONTENTS

INTRODUCTION

by THOMAS DANIEL YOUNG

The Fathers was completed while Allen Tate was deeply involved in the Agrarian movement. In addition to the essays he contributed to the Agrarian symposia, *I'll Take My Stand* in 1930 and *Who Owns America?* in 1938 (of the latter he was co-editor), he published eight or ten perceptive, influential essays on the unique nature of southern society and the hazards awaiting those who would not meet the extreme dangers confronting them.

In the late twenties he had written biographies of Stonewall Jackson and Jefferson Davis; even before he completed these books, he began to think of an interpretative life of Robert E. Lee, to many the greatest southerner and one of the few genuine heroes in American history. Almost immediately, however, he began to run into problems with the character of Lee. As he wrote John Peale Bishop on October 19, 1932: "The whole Southern incapacity for action since 1865 is rationalized in the popular conception of Lee. . . . Lee did not love power; my thesis about him, stated in these terms is that he didn't love it because he was profoundly cynical of all action for the public good." Tate goes on to argue that Lee was unable to "see beyond the needs of his own salvation" and that he was not willing "to risk soiling his military cloak for the doubtful salvation of others."

This biography was never finished. Radcliffe Squires believes Tate came to see that the attitudes he had given Lee
concerning "action for the public good" were really his own.
For whatever reason, Tate put aside the biography in early
1932 and began working on a long piece of prose—a piece he
was at that time calling *Ancestors of Exile*. Thinly disguised
autobiography, this work intended to point up the differences
between the two basic strains that had developed the South—
the Tidewater Virginia aristocrats and the energetic south-
western pioneers. After more than a year of hard work, Tate
abandoned this project, too, because it contained a problem
he could not solve. This problem, he wrote Bishop on October 30, 1933, was that "the discrepancy between the outward
significance and the private was so enormous that I decided
I could not handle the material in that form at all, without
faking either the significance or the material."

Although the material could not be handled in the autobio-
graphical *Ancestors of Exile*, it could be used in fiction, and it
found its way into two short stories—"The Immortal Woman"
(1933) and "The Migration" (1934)—and into the novel *The
Fathers* (1938). During the time Tate was struggling with the
two divergent strains—the aristocrat and the pioneer—that
were fused to produce the southern character, he was writing
some of his best poetry and some of his most influential social
criticism. Some of the poems from this period are "Ode to the
Confederate Dead," "Aeneas at New York," "Aeneas at Washington," "The Mediterranean," and "Sonnets of the Blood."
The poems, the essays, and the novel complement each other
with great emphasis, because together they comprise Tate's
several efforts to provide the form necessary to encompass
the southern myth. Before we examine the novel at some
length—surely the most remarkable first novel in American
literature—it would be helpful, I think, to look briefly at some
of the ideas in the essays and the poems.

2

In an introduction to Faulkner's *Sanctuary*, Tate points out that before the 1920s southern writers wrote, not a "literature of introspection" but one of "romantic illusion." Its mode, as he described it in "A Southern Mode of the Imagination," was rhetorical. It presupposed "somebody at the other end silently listening." But this silent and courteous listener was never expected to respond. The rival mode of the imagination, the dialectical, which presupposes "the give and take of two minds, even if one mind, like the mind of Socrates, prevail in the end," was not the kind of creative imagination that shaped southern literature until the 1920s. This shift from one mode of imagination to another accounts in large part, according to Tate, for the renascence in southern letters; and this change occurred in a most unusual manner, at least in the South where far too often the production of literature was not regarded as a pursuit significant enough to require the serious attention of a gifted man, particularly if he were a gentleman.

But, as Tate remarks in "The New Provincialism," at the end of World War I, the "South reentered the world—but gave a backward glance as it stepped over the border." This backward glance successfully innoculated the modern southern writer against the disease that innundated some of his contemporaries in other sections of the country. It made him aware of and interested in his traditional heritage; unlike some of his contemporaries from the North and East, he was able to see "the past in the present"; he was not "locked in the present" and therefore was not forced to live by chance. This double-focus, this looking both ways—glancing at the past as they gazed into the future, made the writers of Tate's generation aware of what he calls the southern myth, "which informed the sensibility and thought, at varying conscious levels, of the defeated South." This myth is true, Tate insists, as the

Oedipus myth is true, and it was not invented, as Malcolm Cowley once implied, by William Faulkner. This southern myth informs Faulkner's greatest novels: *Absalom, Absalom!*, *The Sound and the Fury, Light in August,* and *Go Down, Moses*, among others, as it does—with significant variations—Tate's *The Fathers*. Although this myth varies with one's degree of self-consciousness, it fostered much of the best writing done in the South between 1925 and 1950. Tate describes this myth generally as follows:

> The South, afflicted with the curse of slavery—a curse, like that of Original Sin, for which no single person is responsible—had to be destroyed, the good along with the evil. The old order had a great deal of good, one of the "goods" being a result of the evil; for slavery itself entailed a certain moral responsibility which the capitalist employer in free societies did not need to exercise if it was not his will to do so. This old order, in which the good could not be salvaged from the bad, was replaced by a new order which was in many ways worse than the old. The Negro, legally free, was not prepared for freedom; nobody was trying to prepare him. The carpetbaggers, "foreign" exploiters, and their collaborators, the native rascals called "scalawags," gave the Old South its final agonies. The cynical materialism of the new order brought to the South the American standard of living, but it also brought about a society similiar to that which Matthew Arnold saw in the North in the Eighties and called vigorous and uninteresting.
>
> The evil of slavery was twofold, for the "peculiar institution" not only used human beings for a purpose for which God had not intended them; it made it possible for the white man to misuse and exploit nature herself for his own power and glory. ("Introduction" to William Faulkner, *Sanctuary* [New York: New American Library, Inc., 1968], xi.)

This southern myth, Tate concludes, did not merely decline gradually, die of its own inertia, as Hawthorne suggests that its counterpart in New England did; it was destroyed by "a great action in which the entire society was involved . . . by outsiders in a Trojan War."

This myth, although it will surely appear inadequate to

most outsiders, has allowed many modern southern writers, Tate among them, to dramatize much of southern historical reality. A recurring theme in Tate's poetry is the attempt to see the "past in the present," to find not only one's personal past but the "past that lies behind that personal past." In "Message from Abroad," written in 1929, while Tate was in Paris on a Guggenheim grant, and dedicated to Andrew Lytle, the poet ponders the means, the process through which a culture is maintained, how tradition is passed from one generation to the next. Some cultures, the speaker in the poem points out, "Provence/The Renascence, the Age of Pericles," are clearly preserved. Others pass into oblivion, are lost because they have no poetry. From his European vantage point Tate has difficulty seeing the faces of his ancestors who were "bony and sharp but very red." In "Ode to the Confederate Dead," the man at the gate of the Confederate cemetery cannot make himself see charging soldiers in the falling leaves; thus the protagonist of this poem fears he is losing his awareness of the tradition out of which he comes. In a poem written a few years later, "The Mediterranean," Tate was able to move out of "time's monotone," to reverse the process of Western expansion and recover his ancestral home, his spiritual roots; and he made this discovery through the use of myth and great art. This search for a meaningful relationship between his present circumstances and the traditions to which he belonged continued to dominate Tate's writings in the 1930s. In 1936 he described the traditional man:

> Man has never achieved a perfect unity of his moral nature and his economics; yet he has never failed quite so dismally in that greatest of all human tasks as he is failing now. Ante-bellum man, insofar as he achieved a unity between his moral nature and his livelihood, was a traditional man. He dominated the means of life; he was not dominated by it. I think that the distinguishing feature of a traditional society is simply that. In order to make a livelihood men do not have to put aside their moral natures. Traditional

men are never quite making their living, and they never quite
cease to make it. . . . The whole economic basis of life is closely
bound up with moral behavior, and it is possible to behave morally
all the time. (*Essays of Four Decades*, 556)

It is easy, and quite proper I believe, to see that the traditional society, one which can allow the existence of the kind of
men Tate described above, is very similar to the myth encom-
passing the society that existed in the South before the Civil
War. In his description of this southern myth Tate emphasizes,
as I have said, that, unlike its counterpart in New England,
this society was destroyed by a single, catastrophic action, "by
outsiders in a Trojan War." Many readers accept Andrew
Lytle's argument that William Faulkner's *The Unvanquished*
demonstrates how such a society may be destroyed. Since any
social order includes the imperfections of the fallible men
who developed it, the society may exist only so long as it can
contain "by rules and orders, accepted habits and the convention of property," the involvements, disgressions, those destructive aspects of man's inheritance which would destroy it
(*The Hero with the Private Parts*, 122). For Faulkner the Civil
War, Malcolm Cowley believes, represents a kind of retributive justice, the strong arm of God punishing man for his sins:
his cheating the Indians out of the land and his forcing his
fellowman into servitude. Lytle believes *The Unvanquished*
demonstrates how the Civil War, the first unrestricted war in
modern history, destroyed the concept of order upon which
that society was based.

However, as I read Allen Tate's *The Fathers*, his most exten-
sive treatment of this traditional society, I do not believe his
interpretation of this southern myth is quite the same as his
explanation of this myth in Faulkner. For it seems to me that
The Fathers will support the suggestion that the antebellum society had within it the elements that would have destroyed it
even if the Civil War had never occurred. To *I'll Take My*

Stand Tate contributed an essay in which he argued that the
pre–Civil War South did not have the proper form of religion
to support the kind of civilization it was developing. Its Prot-
estantism was appropriate for a mercantile and technological
order, but it would not support the section's traditional Agrarian culture. He had argued, too, that the enslaved black man
did not form a proper peasantry for an agrarian society.

3

The story of *The Fathers* is told by Lacy Buchan, a man of sixty-
five, living as a retired doctor in Georgetown. But the story he
tells is centered in events that occurred just before and during
the Civil War, in which he served as a common soldier. His
story concerns two families—the Buchans and the Poseys—
and he tells us not only what he experienced and his attitude
toward those experiences but, he says, "in my feelings of that
time there is a new element—my feelings now about that time:
There is not an old man living who can recover the feelings of
the past." Lacy Buchan's account includes his feelings now toward those events that happened fifty years before, as well as
his remembrance of his feelings and attitudes as the events
occurred.

The occasion for *The Fathers*, as Arthur Mizener has pointed
out, is a "public one, the achievement and destruction of Virginia antebellum civilization." At the outset Tate presents the
"terrible conflict between two fundamental and irreconcilable
modes of existence," a conflict firmly embedded within the
civilization and one that would inevitably destroy it. The cen-
tral tension in the novel is between these two forces, both of
which are integral parts of the social order. This tension is
succinctly stated by Mizener: It "is a tension between the public and private life, between the order of civilization, always
artificial, imposed by discipline, and at the mercy of its own
imperfections, and the disorder of the private life, always sincere, imposed upon by circumstances, and at the mercy of its

own impulses." (*"The Fathers* and Realistic Fiction," 606) Both elements of the conflict are presented within the first few pages. Pleasant Hill, the setting of the opening section of the novel, is a microcosm of antebellum southern society, as its owner Major Buchan would seem to be a true representative of this social order. The society is tightly structured, agrarian, and obviously tainted by slavery; furthermore it operates under the terms of a highly developed social code. As Lacy expresses it: "Our lives were eternally balanced upon a pedestal below which lay an abyss I could not name. Within that invisible tension my father knew the moves of an intricate game he expected everyone else to play." Any society made by postlapsarian men, Tate is suggesting, bears the imperfections of its makers. These imperfections, disgressions, sins (if that word is not too old-fashioned to have a meaning) forever threaten to destroy the social order, for they can never be solved. There will be no utopias, but these destructive elements, those intent upon destroying the social system, may be held in abeyance by rules, rites, ceremonies, conventions, and rituals. Through forms such as these, as John Crowe Ransom has argued, man's animalistic nature is transformed into civilized behavior. "Is not civilization," Lacy Buchan asks, "the agreement, slowly arrived at, to let the abyss alone?"

The stability and order, represented by Major Buchan, is opposed by his son-in-law—George Posey, whose family has long since given up the land and moved into Georgetown, where all semblances of family ties have disappeared. All members of the family never appear for a meal together. Uncle Jarman Posey wanted to be a man of letters, but no one else wanted him to be, so he became a recluse. He "had had so long an assured living that he no longer knew it had a natural source in human activity." Thus he viewed life as it appeared from his dormer window and came downstairs only once a year. George's mother "was a gentlewoman who became in the common sense more and more 'gentle' as she grew older, and ended up by not being able to entertain longer than a minute any thought that did not concern her health and feelings." George's Aunt Milly never ate anything except overripe bananas, and she would vaguely sniff if such concrete subjects as money, childbirth, or poverty were brought into the conversation. She and her sister could never admit that common people were real, for "it is just too painful that they should exist."

It is a family which communicates only through its infirmities, and its head is George Posey, who can be contrasted at every point with his father-in-law Major Buchan. George Posey is the traditionless man, one who construes the world's actions to be intended for his private reaction and consumption. He is a man, Lacy says, "who received the shock of the world at the end of his nerves." Because Posey is unable to objectify his feelings, all action becomes intensely personal to him; thus he is terribly embarrassed when he sees the little bull about his proper business on the Buchan plantation. Similarly, he cannot remain for his mother-in-law's funeral because the rites and ceremonies of the religious community do not exist for him; thus there is nothing to divert his attention from the corrupt body. He cannot participate in the pageantry of the religious community; therefore he is preoccupied with the putrefying corpse. He is forever flirting with the abyss, because he is unaware of the agreement—made up of ritual, manners, customs, and ceremonies—to leave the abyss alone.

But the imperfections that will destroy the antebellum southern society are unalterably at work even before the Civil War begins. This force is represented by the inevitable clash between the Buchans and the Poseys. The southern society has become so static that all personal feelings are automatically channeled through custom and ritual; an individual has no existence apart from the family or the society to which he belongs. Major Buchan's refusal to recognize the fact that disunion is possible, not to say inevitable, forces his two older sons to join the Confederate army against their father's wishes. And the Major's inability to face concrete facts—much like that of the Posey women—allows Lacy to see his father in a true light:

> That was the first time, I suppose, that Papa had seemed to me to speak from a great distance, as if he were a man preoccupied with some private mystery that could not be connected with what was going on in the world. . . . Where in his mind were the vast hordes of young men who were rushing to village and country town, from river bottoms and the hills, coming with squirrel rifles, shot-guns, bowie knives, to "form military companies" in Georgia, Alabama, Mississippi, by the banks of the James, the Chatahoochee, the Tennessee. For Papa, these young men did not exist; all that country from below the James to the Rio Grande was a map, and the "war" was about to be fought between the "government" and the sons of his neighbors and kin in the old Northern neck of Virginia.

At another level Tate presents the contrast between the private and the public domains in his views of the two ministers who preside at the funeral of Lacy's mother. Mr. McBean, the Presbyterian minister who is obviously moved by the death of a loyal member of his congregation, reacts personally and spontaneously as he moves among the mourners or says his "Amens" at the funeral service. But, Lacy wonders, why does Dr. Cartwright, the Episcopal rector, talk differently from Mr. McBean: "His words were different, he seemed to be just a voice, in the *ore rotundo* of impersonality, no feeling but in the words themselves."

Like the Reverend Dr. Cartwright, Major Buchan embodies perfectly the tradition to which he belongs. If he has any personal warmth and feeling for his son Lacy, he conceals it behind the impervious mask of his formal manner. The relationship between father and son is impersonal, ceremonious. The same ritual is enacted at the beginning of each day:

> As I came in [Lacy says] he laid the box on the small table by his

chair, rose to his feet, and as I stood before him he leaned over
and kissed me on the forehead. Then he shook hands as he said:
   "God bless you, my son, in your labors of this day."
   "God bless you, Papa," I said.

All their days, the reader is told, began in this way, almost as if
the manner in which father will meet son each morning is set
forth as a service in *The Book of Common Prayer*.

Tate's myth of the antebellum southern civilization, then,
varies somewhat from that which he suggests as the one from
which Faulkner and other southerners wrote. This society was
not destroyed by the Civil War, as that retributive justice for
the white man's cheating the Indian out of the land and in-
stituting the barbarous system of human slavery. In Major
Buchan we can see that this society had already become ossified
so that the rituals of society express all the feelings that the
individual possesses. The person who reacts against the discipline of this formal society—that is, George Posey—destroys
the fundamentals of its civilizing influences and is left naked
and alone. Somewhere between these two extremes—that represented by George Posey and that of which Major Buchan is
an emblem—is the position of a vital, strong, and permanent
social order.

Thomas Daniel Young

Selected Essays on *The Fathers*

Carpenter, Lynette. "The Battle Within: The Beleaguered Con-
   sciousness in Allen Tate's *The Fathers*," *Southern Literary Journal*,
   VIII (Spring, 1976), 3–24.
Kane, Patricia. "An Irrepressible Conflict: Allen Tate's *The Fathers*,"
   Critique, X (1968), 9–16.
Kermode, Frank. "Old Orders Changing," *Encounter*, XV (August,
   1960), 72–76.
Mizener, Arthur. "*The Fathers* and Realistic Fiction," *Sewanee Review*,

LXVII (Autumn, 1959), 604–13; also printed in *Accent*, VII (Winter, 1947), 101–109.

O'Dea, Richard J. "*The Fathers*, A Revaluation," *Twentieth Century Literature*, XII (July, 1966), 87–95.

Smith, Janet. "The End of the Old Dominion," *New Statesman*, LIX (May 14, 1960), 718–19.

Squires, Radcliffe. *Allen Tate: A Literary Biography*. New York: Pegasus, 1971. Pp. 123–46.

Sullivan, Walter. "Southern Novelists and the Civil War," *Hopkins Review*, VI (Winter, 1953), 133–46.

————. "*The Fathers* and the Failure of Tradition," *Southern Review*, XII (Fall, 1976), 758–67.

[Tate, Allen, on *The Fathers*], *Partisan Review*, VI (Winter, 1939), 125–26

PREFACE
Caveat Lector

The Victorian reader quite reasonably wanted to know what happened to the characters in a novel following its completion. My chief revision in this new edition of *The Fathers* tells the reader in a few words what George Posey did after he rode away into the dark. This revision gives the novel two heroes: Major Buchan, the classical hero, whose *hubris* destroys him; George Posey, who may have seemed to some readers a villain, is now clearly a modern romantic hero.

A. T.
1975

THE FATHERS

Part I

PLEASANT HILL

I T WAS ONLY TODAY as I was walking down Fayette Street towards the river that I got a whiff of salt fish, and I remembered the day I stood at Pleasant Hill, under the dogwood tree. It was late April and the blossoms shot into the air like spray. My mother was dead. Crowds of the connection had arrived the night before; and I had come, a boy of fifteen, after breakfast, out into the yard. Under the tree I could still taste the salt of the roe herring that Aunt Myra Parrish had kept serving to the kin and friends from Washington and Alexandria. There was old Uncle Armistead, my father's brother and twenty years his elder, born at the end of the Revolution and older than even his eighty years: who deaf and half blind said only "Hanh?" to remarks directed to him, and he never asked a question. My mind now echoes *Hanh?* to the smell of the herring and I can see the black coffin of my mother lying in the hush of the front parlor, a white, long room.

My name is Lacy Gore Buchan, the third son and the last child of my parents. My father was the late Major Lewis Buchan, a native of Spotsylvania County, Virginia, who died as I shall relate, at the beginning of the War, in Fairfax County at Pleasant Hill, a "place" that came to us through his mother, who was a Lewis of Spotsylvania. My

3

father, through his father Dr. John Buchan, was the grandson of the "immigrant," Benjamin Buchan, a Scots adventurer who ordinarily must have followed his compatriots west of the Blue Ridge had he not won the hand of Mary Armistead the very year of his landing, I think 1741; Mary Armistead thus became my great-grandmother, and by means of certain dower properties to which she fell heir — after her father's displeasure with the adventurer had been conquered by the grave — the name of Buchan, obscure in origin, became assimilated to that unique order of society known latterly as the Virginian aristocracy. Of my mother's people I know, first-hand, much less. She was Sarah Semmes Gore of the Valley of Virginia; on the Gore side, Scotch-Irish; on the Semmes, of Maryland stock that had migrated to the Valley around 1800. My mother might have said of my father, "Thy people are my people," for she became a pure Buchan — in all but religion; she could not have added, "and thy God my God." She remained a Presbyterian.

The death of my mother is a suitable beginning for my story. There, for the last time, I saw our whole family assembled from that region, down to the fifth and sixth degree of kin, besides three or four of the Poseys, the family of my remarkable brother-in-law, George Posey from Georgetown, who had the year before married my lovely sister Susan. A year later came the war; we were uprooted from Pleasant Hill, and were never together again.

Of the Poseys I shall have a good deal to say hereafter. They were a respectable family of Anne Arundel County, Maryland, quiet, presentable, and at one time, in the day of old Samuel Posey, George's grandfather, possessed of considerable landed property and servants; but otherwise, like the Buchans, undistinguished. Mr. Rozier Posey, George's father, moved down to Charles County, and in

George's boyhood the family left the land and settled permanently in Georgetown, in a tall red brick house on Vista Avenue, overlooking the Potomac. The family, I say, was unexceptional. I cannot understand why they came out, in the old phrase, "at the little end of the horn," as they grievously did.

That, perhaps more than anything else, is the reason why an unmarried old man, having nothing else to do, with a competence saved from the practice of medicine, thinks he has a story to tell. Is it not something to tell, when a score of people whom I knew and loved, people beyond whose lives I could imagine no other life, either out of violence in themselves or the times, or out of some misery or shame, scattered into the new life of the modern age where they cannot even find themselves? Why cannot life change without tangling the lives of innocent persons? Why do innocent persons cease their innocence and become violent and evil in themselves that such great changes may take place?

These questions must go unanswered. I have a story to tell but I cannot explain the story. I cannot say: if Susan had not married George Posey then Susan could not have known Jane Posey and influenced her. But of course I might not have known Jane either. Could I have known her without Susan, I might have married her, for I loved her. That no doubt was the life I wanted. But what I wanted and did not get would not have changed the events by which all these people were tortured. It would have all happened in some other way.

I see figures on the lawn that morning at Pleasant Hill, I hear voices. Of that large company I remember the ordinary tone of the conversation, the hospitable anxiety of the nearer connection for the comfort of the more distant kin and friends; it was like a family infare but that my sister sat in the back parlor with my poor father and the kindly smiles never broke into laughter. Only Uncle Armistead sat all day in the front parlor by the coffin. Aunt Myra — his sister and my father's — went in to him, or took the kin in to the presence of the dead: a small decisive woman, Aunt Myra, with deep eyes and a long straight nose: she would say to Uncle Armistead: "Brother, go into the chamber and lie down." The "chamber" was my own mother's bedroom where the family sat informally. But Uncle Armistead only replied, "Hanh?" and took another toddy from Sam, the little colored boy he had brought with him from Falls Church.

But as I went aimlessly about the lawn, a mysterious exile from the other children, I seemed to see the home of my childhood with new eyes. I could feel that people were waiting, waiting; but it was different from our waiting for my mother, over many days, to die. The waiting was hurried; there was hurried deliberation in Aunt Myra's managing everything. Out of this changed tempo trivial incidents emerged, and were fixed in my memory: and changed even was the air of the place.

I remember George Posey coming out into the yard, not restlessly but inquiringly, swinging a riding crop and looking from tree to tree and off into the slanting fields. How big and mature he was! He was actually only eleven years older than I was — a man of twenty-six, married a year to my sister and the father of a baby girl in whom I took no interest. He was a good six feet three, and standing he always rested squarely though easily on both feet, his head back, his arms limp at his sides: he seemed taller than he was because he looked at you from the angle of his backward tilted head. He stood looking at the long gallery, two stories, on slender square posts, across the whole front of the house; and his lips moved. I thought he had spoken to me. I ran nearer.

"Brother George!" I cried.

He motioned me to him, put his hand on my head, and smiled down at me.

"You're my friend, Lacy boy."

He resumed his gaze. I too looked up at the gallery sagging at one end, at the cracked paint on the weatherboarding, at the wisps of smoke struggling out of the big red end-chimneys, then off up the ridge towards the Negro cabins, a pink brick row, and towards the stables and, back of them, near the woods, the big unpainted tobacco barn. I looked at Brother George but he was as fixed as a marble in Mr. Corcoran's gallery. A phrase of my father's comes to mind, for at that moment Brother George's face was a "study." His eyes roved to my mother's garden, down towards the lower end of the ridge by the side of the house: the garden was a big square bordered by box, the inside a tangle of shrubs from which now I saw the first shoots of April green. And on the hither side of the garden I saw the horseblock, an old millstone standing on edge and half buried in the ground: there began the long line of gnarled cedars winding with the muddy lane along the side of the ridge, the half-mile to the old Ox Road, the "big road" that led into the great world — Fairfax, Occoquan, Pohick, Alexandria, then down the Potomac by salt water to the cities beyond the main!

Then for the first time in the wonder of death I saw the whole place all together. Looking back through the cloud of George Posey's life and my sister Susan's, I think that he too saw as a world, as a strange place, the home of his wife's family, as if he had never seen it before. How handsome he was! How strong! His hand on my head, I glanced from the gray homespun of my trousers and jacket to the rich broadcloth of his black double-breasted coat with the big square lapels. It fitted him like a glove, and the silver buttons glistened in the sunlight. He turned my head and looked down into my eyes.

"Son, I've got to go." Putting on his black silk hat, he glanced at the front door where people were still going in and out. "Go tell Coriolanus to saddle my horse!"

I was off like a shot towards the side of the house to the path that led to the stable; then I slowed to a walk, in doubt that a boy should be running on the day his mother was dead. Round the corner of the house, out of sight of the porch, there was little Jane Posey, Brother George's sister, just my age, stooping in a bed of new violets. She looked stiffly dressed up, in poke bonnet, blue velvet jacket, with the pantalettes showing white at the hem of her dress. She looked up with doe-like eyes and said, "Hello!" I paused, but she picked violets as if I had passed on. I suppose it was out of the wonderful loneliness of that day that I wished to say something, or rather to plead for the chance to say something later, at some certain moment, in a world in which nothing could be counted on, it was so quietly bustling and strange. I said, "Wait for me."

I ran again, as if being out of sight made it proper, and vaulted the rail fence into the stable lot. I shouted, "Uncle Lanus!" Then I saw him, his white wool first, and the faded brushed broadcloth above the tallow-grease on his boots. He sat on a stool, his hands folded; he raised his eyes gently, with the polite attention of an old gentleman whom nothing can surprise.

"Brother George says saddle his horse." Then, as if I suddenly knew something important: "Quick!"

The old man placed his hands on his knees and rose. He

vanished into the stalls, and I looked at the back of the
house. One of the Negro girls was hanging a red quilt over
the rail of the upper back gallery: it had come from my
mother's bed. Over to the right beyond the out-kitchen,
by the smokehouse, Henry Jackson, the yard boy, now
that the severe old Coriolanus was out of sight, was whis-
tling; one of the young wenches passed and he laughed
and slapped her; she giggled. I felt an almost uncontrol-
lable desire to laugh. I looked down at the pawed earth.
There was a piece of old strap. If I wanted it I knew I
had better get it into my pocket before the old Negro came
out again. With one motion I had it and it was in my
pants pocket. I looked again towards the smokehouse. The
Negroes had gone. I lifted my gaze beyond the smokehouse
to the rear of my mother's garden down the ridge towards
the three big chestnut trees. By a low wall I could see Mr.
Higgins, the overseer, squatting on his heels and smoking;
just below him two Negro men with shovels were scarring
the red earth with the new grave.

Coriolanus was talking to the big bay mare, and now
he led her out. But he did not lead her to the gate; he
stopped. There was anxiety in his weathered face, as if
he did not know what he was expected to do. "Come here,
Lacy," he said, and when he said it, his anxiety left him.
I came nearer. He handed me the bridle and turned away
as if he would have nothing to do with this business. He
sat down on his stool, folded his hands, and looked me
calmly in the eyes.

"I knowed he'd do it," he said.

He couldn't have known anything of the kind, but there
it was; I actually got a little comfort out of the fact that
someone imagined he had predicted Brother George's
impulse, which had surprised and excited me. And I was
more excited than ever now that I was leading Queen

Susie, the fine mare Brother George had bought from Colonel Tayloe the day before he had become engaged to my sister; I led her through the stable-lot gate, down the short lane by the side of the house and into the front yard. There was Brother George on the far side by the horse-block, one foot on the block, holding his elbow on his knee, his chin in his hand. I pressed right on, but all the way I admired him all over again: the frank, open face, the careless, cold blue eyes, the cheerful mouth with the corners curving upward in a kindly smile. He never looked any other way — only even more that way sometimes, when he broke into a sudden laugh that startled you at first; yet in the end you laughed too, without reason, and you felt you were only waiting for him to tell you what to do. I had heard my father say that George could make anybody do anything. In my boyish delight I would have any day followed him over a precipice, just for his bidding. I know distinctly that I thought of him always boldly riding somewhere, and because I couldn't see where, I suppose I thought of a precipice. Yet I am sure he had never done anything crudely bold that would arrest the attention of a boy.

I was at the block, the mare whinnied, and Brother George noticed me. I held the bridle out to him, but he ignored it. He took his foot off the block and stood erect. I followed his eyes to the front gallery, where Sister Susan was coming rapidly down the steps. He advanced to meet her, pausing to flick a spot of mud off his knee with his whip, for the world as if he were walking towards some natural object, like a gnarled tree, that had engaged his curiosity. The permanent smile was on his face. They met about fifty feet from where I stood holding the mare, halfway between the block and the steps.

My sister was not beautiful, but she was lovely; the hazel

eyes, set deep in their sockets under a wide low brow, dominated her face. Her hair was like an acorn, her skin fair
almost to monotony, not pale but without trace of color;
she was like pear blossoms against a lingering winter landscape. Her face was all structure, with just enough smooth
surface to bring all the strong lines together into design. I
know now, what I could not have known or cared about
then, that she had got that face from papa, who had got
it through his mother Margaret Lewis from her people, the
Washburns, a family greatly distinguished in the Revolution, whom recent members of our own family are proud
of being descended from: in the old days the Washburns
were unlike other people for their saying so. Some of them
over in the Valley of Virginia had always said that if only
Mr. Jefferson had not been so perversely democratic they
would be the royal family. Well, papa — who had been a
fine horseman in his youth — used to say that perhaps he
could have qualified as Master of the Horse; but he was
not sure, he was perversely democratic too: he was only
Major Lewis Buchan by grace of the county militia that
had not fought since 1812.

George was taking off his beaver hat, smiling, while
Susan, speaking in a low tone, looked him gravely in the
eye. For an instant Brother George hung his head as if
he were impressed by her earnest words, whatever they
were, and she smiled at him and placed the tips of her
fingers on his forearm. Standing so, she raised her voice
and I heard the one word — "papa." That must have been
too much for Brother George. He said — raising his head,
the permanent smile a little tighter on his lips — he said:
"No, damn it"

Her fingers lingered on his sleeve. She withdrew them,
clenched them at her side, and turned so quickly that I
heard her hoops swish under the heavy black silk of her

skirt. Ladies did not run in those days, but she very nearly ran, with the rigid plunging and dipping of the hoops, until she sailed up the steps and with the same motion went through the front door. Not until the door had closed behind her did I see Brother George. He was smiling, not after the vanished figure of his wife, but at Mr. Higgins, who had slid noiselessly into the scene, and was squatting on his heels (he never stood up, he only walked or squatted) not ten feet away from Brother George, a little to one side. He was a hatchet-faced, impassive young man, quite honest — said my father — of the small-farming class for generations: if he never entered our front door, we never entered his simply because we were not wanted. Mr. Higgins, squatting there in his black store clothes, did not smile. Brother George turned on his heel and approached Queen Susie. He looked a little surprised when he saw me; he had forgotten that I was there. He must have forgotten Mr. Higgins, who shifted his balance a little, took his pipe out of his mouth, and said:

"I like the mar' better ever' time I see her."

Brother George had heard no words but only a voice. He looked off over my head as he took the bridle from my hand.

"No, God damn it!" he said. He put his foot into the stirrup as he threw the bridle over the mare's head, and he was off before he was well seated, down the lane under the broken cedars.

Mr. Higgins' expression had not changed, nor did it change when he spoke to me.

"Boy," he said, "hit ain't right fer a man to gallivant off on a day like this."

I remember, of the minutes before he spoke, a suspicion that I should not have been present, that I did not want to be there in the midst of things that I could not understand; perhaps I went far enough with Mr. Higgins to appreciate the correct sentiment that he had expressed. But now that he had expressed it I resented it.

"You can't say nothin' against Brother George." I burst into tears.

The next thing I knew I was running to the house by way of the dogwood tree, towards the crape myrtles under the windows of mother's bedroom. Then I was around the side of the house. There was Jane Posey, a large bunch of sweet violets in her hand, sitting on a root of the big sugar maple that went up the side of the house and canopied the roof. She was not "little Jane" any longer since the birth of Susan's and George's even smaller Jane: both were named for Brother George's mother whom I knew later as Aunt Jane Anne, after the families became intimate. So the Jane there under the tree I had never thought of as little, only as Jane, a large child for her fifteen years, with mournful brown eyes and, as I look back, a docility of nature that made her a joy to her family. I suppose my face was wet, but before I could feel my shame Jane said, "Hello," exactly as she had said it before. "I waited," she said. Now I felt ashamed; so I said, "Let's go around back and play." The meek round eyes fixed me in wonder. "We can't play," she said.

I was blushing as I heard: "Mercy, child, where you been all this time?" It was Aunt Myra, severe but kind, looking round the end of the house from the upper gallery. "I've looked for you high and low," she said. Jane got up and walked slowly round the house towards the steps, and when Aunt Myra disappeared I knew that she had not been looking for me. I looked about me; the yard was deserted, I could hear only the plunk of an ax in the distance and a calf bawling over the hill in the cuppen. I was alone in a world that had been created by George

Posey, out of the dead world of my mother: an emotion that the years alone can enlighten, for a child, expecting nothing of people, is shocked only when what happens has not happened before. It was the first time anything could happen at my mother's death! Yet the savage sense of propriety so acute in children told me that I had witnessed an event extraordinary and violent, more violent even than the death which had not happened to me till now but which could always happen in the world in which I lived. I thought: Suppose papa should die? I could understand it, and I went round to the back gallery and up the gallery stairs, thinking that George Posey could never have anything to do with death.

*   *   *

Upstairs, in the back room that I occupied with my brother Semmes, the trundle bed on which I slept was standing, unmade, in the middle of the floor. It was the dark side of the house. A dull light came through the small panes, and the charcoal fire in the brazier, for there was no fireplace, had gone out since early morning. I stared stupidly at the dirty water, still unpoured, in the blue china bowl on the washstand. I looked at my hands; they were dirty. I moved to the big bed and looked over the footboard. There lay Brother Semmes, in his shirt sleeves, on his back, his hands under his head. He did not move. He had the most expressionless face I have ever seen, and he looked me up and down with a neutral gaze.

"I'll go down in a minute," he said. He threw one leg over the side of the bed, and out of the deep feathers he brought himself with a wrench to his feet. He stood, in his black satin waistcoat, rubbing his arms and swaying a little to get his balance: he looked older than his twenty-three years. I was immensely fond of Semmes, and when I think of the end he came to I remember the long, mask-like face, which never acquired any of the lines of his ordeal, the high sloping forehead, the bushy, Scotch black hair, and the long nose with the Washburn button on the end of it. He was a humorous-looking fellow without humor; the slight puff of flesh over each eye gave him a meditative look which accounted no doubt for his having written at the age of sixteen some romantic verses which had found their way into the first issue of the *Washington Star* in 1852. But he hadn't continued this talent, and he was now a medical student in Washington. He and Brother George were devoted friends; it was through him, of course, that Brother George knew our family in the first place; and I wondered if he would ask me, now, where George was.

"You didn't clean my boots this morning, sir!" A shy look came into his drooping eyes that told me he was saying that life went on, we had to go on as we had lived, without mother. Semmes was the most sympathetic brother a small boy ever had, the most temperate, the most perfect in consideration. I suppose he did lack imagination; he had rather a quality of mind that runs things down in a bee-line of logic, that was misunderstood.

He had not said enough about the boots.

"I brushed them myself. How do you ever expect to amount to anything?"

He put on his coat and straightened his collar; he moved his eyelids, which was his version of a smile.

"Did George go away?"

I said nothing.

"He said he might go. They don't understand George," he said.

He went over to the tall dark wardrobe, opened one of the doors, and took out a round bottle which I knew was his favorite, apple brandy. He found a small glass on the dresser, poured a little brandy into the bottom of the glass, held it up, saying, "Have a drink, Lacy?" and then drank it off. He corked the bottle and put it back into the wardrobe.

He took a step towards the door, hesitated, came back and sat on the bed. "Lacy," he said, "I hope papa will move to town." I had thought of "town" as a far-off place where other people lived, kinfolks mostly, whom one visited in the winter, but town was for those other people, and I recalled that older members of the family had said more than once, with peculiar emphasis, that Brother George after all had been raised in town.

"Aunt Myra said she'd stay here with papa," I said. "Said she wasn't going to tell papa — she'd just stay on." Aunt Myra, a widow, had been living with her husband's people in Maryland; now, I thought with delight, she would live with us. I saw her sitting in mother's low rocking-chair in the bedroom downstairs, hearing my prayers at night — "Now I lay me down . . . Now I lay me" — but I couldn't finish it, for I wondered if Aunt Myra, an Episcopalian, would make me learn new prayers with big words, like the Catholics, such as Jane Posey had to say at night. I couldn't look at Aunt Myra in mother's chair — there were the gray curls under her cap where mother's golden brown hair had been. I went to the dresser and fingered a hairbrush. "That's all right, son," Semmes said. "Don't take it hard. Why, you'd probably go to Alexandria where you could see all the boats and eat oysters in all the months with r! You'd have somebody to play with besides darkies."

I thought of the time we were in Alexandria when I was a mere child, going into the grandest hotel I had ever seen, The Marshall House, with the long front porch and

the row of split-bottom rockers where bearded men sat
languidly in the sun. We walked into the lobby, as we
always did in public, single file — at least mother followed
close after papa, who marched to the desk in a distinctly
military style, as if he were about to report something or
were leading a parade: the children came after them, and
at the end old Lucy Lewis, my mother's maid. At the
clerk's greeting papa said, "We need rain, sir!" "We do
that, Major," said Mr. Jackson pleasantly. After papa had
signed the register, and had begun leading his procession
towards the dining-room, I looked at what he had written: *L. Buchan Wife & 4 Family—1 serv't: Burkes Sta. Va.*
One day I asked him why he wrote Burke's instead of
Pleasant Hill where we lived, and he said, "Ain't* that
where we get our mail?" Then, looking at Susan — it was
during her betrothal — "Susie lives at the post office, don't
she?" But we ought to have been *5 Family,* and I remembered a sister dead before I was born, who came between
Susan and Semmes and died of croup in her first winter
because old Lucy had let a draft into the room through a
window that she had raised to let out the smoke from
a windy fire. Papa was a great reader of history — Gibbon
and Doctor Robertson's *History of Scotland,* where our
ancestors had lived, and the campaigns of the Swedish
hero whose word portrait in *The Vanity of Human Wishes*

* I may as well say here that my father did not speak dialect but the
standard English of the eighteenth century. In pronunciation the criteri-
on was the oral tradition, not the way the word looked in print to an un-
educated school-teacher. For example, although he wrote *ate,* he pronounced it *et,* as if it were the old past tense, *eat.* He used the double
negative in conversation, as well as *ain't,* and he spoke the language with
great ease at four levels: first, the level just described, conversation
among family and friends; second, the speech of the "plain people"
abounding in many archaisms; third, the speech of the Negroes, which
was merely late seventeenth or early eighteenth century English ossified;
and, fourth, the Johnsonian diction appropriate to formal occasions, a
style that he could wield in perfect sentences four hundred words long.
He would not have understood our conception of "correct English."
Speech was like manners, an expression of sensibility and taste.

papa thought the "most moving in English poetry, sir." So he passed over his father and named his eldest son Charles Twelfth and Charlie had vainly tried to make a secret of his middle name.

But all this time, as I stood there with Semmes, I was staring at a picture on the back wall but it was some time before I saw it: a black and white silhouette of mother and papa in a small walnut frame. The two figures were black paper pasted on white, cut out with scissors by an armless man who glanced at passersby and then, in less than a minute, gave them their silhouettes. He had cut them out with his toes. This very picture — papa in marching posture, chin drawn in and coattails flying; mother just behind him, hands clasped and head inclined — had been made as we went into the Marshall House on that day, and the artist handed it to papa as we came out. And mother said something like "Mr. Buchan, purchase it, it will amuse the children," and he handed the man four-bits.

Whether I felt it then I do not know; yet I see the silhouettes, mother and papa together for the last time; for afterwards the picture became lifeless; the small black surfaces were all edge and outline; the black bodies retreated in the next year into the hard shade of the past. What Semmes had just said — Alexandria and the boats — had ended a time in my life, had I but known it; and I suppose I did know it, for I asked him: "What school could I go to?" And Semmes said, "A better school with maps and blackboards on the wall. To old Mr. Leary, where papa went to school." I remembered Mr. Leary, hearing about his great age and his Latin, and I didn't want to study Latin any harder than Mr. McGovern taught it down at Langton's Cross Roads, in the log house on the

triangle of land given to the school by Mr. Langton,
papa's friend.

Semmes rose, put his hands in his pockets, and walked
to the window. I followed, and looking down on the
brick walk between the house and the garden I saw
Henry Jackson going round the end of the house with
an armful of wood.

"He's carrying it to the front door," I said.

Semmes seemed not to hear me but followed the Negro
with his eyes. "It don't make any difference where he totes
it." He turned away from the window. "Twenty Negroes
are too many for this place."

That was the beginning of my introduction to the world
where people counted and added things, the first intru-
sion of change into my consciousness, and I only dimly
knew what it meant. I had heard it said that it wasn't
much worse to sell Negroes than to buy them: I suppose I
thought that some people had Negroes as naturally as
others did not, that it was all chance, and nothing could
be done about it. In the resentment of boyish perplexity,
I said:

"Anyway, papa didn't buy the Niggers. He freed Jack
Lewis and give him a horse and he freed Agnes too. And
all their little Niggers. And sent 'em to Pennsylvania."

I saw in Semmes eyes a momentary agitation as he
returned to the bed, sat down, put his hands on the bed
rail, and leaned forward in thought. I said defiantly:

"Used to be more'n twenty!"

He said nothing until I came over to the foot of the bed
and sat in the straight chair.

"Papa *thinks* those Negroes are free." He rose and taking
off his coat laid it on the bed. "Good God, boy, look
around you — there hasn't been any tobacco in the barns

for nearly ten years. And how much corn do you think papa makes? Fifteen bushels to the acre!"

The image of papa rose up before me, strange for the first time—his head bowed in humiliation as if he had been accused of wrong; that at least was the role I thought in my ignorance that Semmes had put him in. It struck me that I ought to hurt Semmes' feelings if I could; I sulked in my chair, and the double wrong, the criticism of my father by my brother, the violent behavior of George Posey on the day of my mother's funeral, came out in —

"Brother George swore at Sister and rode off."

He jumped up and walked across the room; he turned to face me.

"Are you sure he swore at her?" He looked more solemn than I had ever seen him. "Didn't he just swear?"

"Yes, brother," I said, and he came over and patted me on the shoulder. He began to pace back and forth between the bed and the window. I knew that he was excited, for he was holding his left forefinger against his nose — an invariable sign, in Semmes, of unusual agitation.

"Lacy, they don't understand George Posey."

There was a knock at the door. Semmes halted, then reached for his coat, while I went to the door. It was Henry Jackson, cap in hand.

"Miss Myra say is Marse George goin' to be here for dinner?" She say hit's twelve o'clock now."

I started to speak, then looked at Semmes, who was looking at me. He laid his coat on the footboard and thrust his hands into his pockets.

"Henry, did you see Miss Susie?"

"Naw, sir, I ain't seen Miss Susie, I ain't seen nobody but Miss Myra. She done call me from the yard."

"Well, Henry, tell Miss Myra that I don't think Mr. George will be here for dinner."

Henry said "Yassir" and started down the gallery steps. I listened to his deliberate feet until they were silent. I went to the window and looked down into the yard. Old Coriolanus was leading a horse and buggy down the lane towards the front of the house. Somebody else was leaving. For no reason he stopped and just held the horse's rein. Henry Jackson, a dozen paces away, seemed unaware of Coriolanus. With a slow, sidling gait he approached the older Negro, and the two of them stood, as if they were each alone on a mountain top. Henry said a few words, which I could not hear, into the general air. Coriolanus, ignoring Henry, talked as if to himself, but angrily, and I could hear his words. "I knowed he would, I knowed hit yestiddy!" The two Negroes separated as if they had never met.

Semmes was speaking.

"The Negroes are talking about it," he said. He put on his coat and stood at the dresser before the looking-glass. He picked up his hair brush, glanced down at the sleeve of his coat in the glass, and put the brush down.

"Lacy," he said, "it's all right." He went to the door. "I'm going down to sit with papa." And he was gone.

I flung myself upon the bed, Semmes' big bed, as I was not permitted to do, and put my hands behind my head, lying motionless in the deep hush. I could hear no sound. The house seemed empty, and I thought how deserted it would be if we went away to live in a town. I thought of myself now as all alone, the halls empty and no life inside the closed doors. The dead coals in the brazier smelled damp in the chilled air. Across the room, hanging on two wooden pegs driven into the plaster, the greased blue barrels of my gun held a ray of the western light. I could see myself taking the gun down, and lifting the rawhide strings that held to the pegs my powder horn, that I had made myself two springs ago after papa had had a steer butchered, and the brass shot pouch that papa had passed on to me the day after I got the gun. I didn't go hunting that day because I played soldier in the Revolution. The pouch had come down from my grandfather, Dr. John Buchan, who had not fought but who had saved the pouch as a souvenir of his brother Ben, my grand-uncle, a private in Daniel Morgan's Virginia riflemen, who had been killed at the Cowpens in 1781.

In my feelings of that time there is a new element — my feelings now about that time: there is not an old man living who can recover the emotions of the past; he can only bring back the objects about which, secretly, the emotions have ordered themselves in memory, and that memory is not what happened in the year 1860 but is rather a few symbols, a voice, a tree, a gun shining on the wall — symbols that will preserve only so much of the old life as they may, in their own mysterious history, consent to bear.

I thought of the grandfather that I had never seen, whose portrait hung downstairs in the front parlor, looking down out of a long face upon the scene of death. The puffy bold eyes and the big mouth told me that he had never known fear; the set of the shoulders in the bottle-green coat, the buff waistcoat with one button unfastened, and the high stock a little askew bespoke what papa always said about his father: "Dr. Buchan was an elegant gentleman." I didn't quite know what that meant, yet I fancied that the old man was examining the people in our house that day with astonishment, as if his elegance meant that people didn't ride suddenly away from places where they were expected to be. My new brother George had needed

intensely to leave, to escape from the forms of death which
were, to us, only the completion of life, and in which there
could be nothing personal, but in which what we were
deep inside found a sufficient expression.

Was Brother George an elegant gentleman? Only a
simple boy could have thought of the question. He was
the handsomest, most affable young man I had ever seen.
My eye went back to the shotgun on the wall. The sun
had moved and the metal no longer shone. But I saw it
shining in my mind, with the light that had made it the
most fascinating gift that a little boy ever received, and
the light spread until it was a brilliant day in May. That
had been nearly two years ago, and George Posey had come
riding up in a new gig right after dinner. Mother had
gone in for her nap, papa was abroad in the neighborhood,
and Sister Susan, whom of course he had come to see,
would not appear until she had been asked for. George
Posey tied his horse to the rail down by the horseblock.
He looked around the yard, and when he lifted out of
his buggy a large carpetbag I knew that he had been
looking for a servant. Did he not know that in the country
Negroes disappeared every "evening," the time of day that
began for us at dinner, to return to the big house only a
little before dark? He set the bag down, and reaching to
the seat of his gig picked up a gun. I remember my surprise. Men didn't hunt that time of the year, though little
boys might shoot squirrels the year round. The carpetbag
in one hand, the gun in the other, he walked towards the
gallery. I didn't know him very well, and I didn't greet
him. But as he came to the steps he said, "Howdy, Lacy."
I said, "Good evening, sir." He saw that I was looking at
the gun.

George Posey laughed with all his face but his eyes.
They remained cold and motionless. "Would you like to

see the new gun?" he said. Before I could say yes he handed
it to me, stock first, and the polished walnut glimmered;
I could see my face in it. I held the gun in both hands; it
was a muzzle-loader, breechless, the front sight a round
silver bead; and the ramrod fitted snugly under the two
blue barrels. I opened the side of the stock; bright brass
percussion caps fell into my hands. George said, "Here,"
and he handed me a tin box of powder and a cotton sack
of shot. "Number eight," he said. I couldn't take it in,
and I said, "It's a mighty nice gun." He stood smiling at
me. I looked at the top of the barrels: *Duckworth and
Simmons, London, Established 1761.* I moved the gun
towards him to give it back.

"No," he said, "it's yours."

That was the way George Posey did everything — by surprise. I was embarrased, and I said not a word of thanks,
but kept looking at the gun. He too was silent but smiling,
as I stared at him in wonder. He said, "Has Semmes come
back?" "No, sir," I said, and looked at his heavy carpetbag. He had come to stay with us awhile, and I remembered tomorrow. "You want to go to your room," I said,
"I'll tote it." I reached for the bag, but he said no, he'd
take it, it was too big for me. He led the way round the
house to the back gallery steps, up the steps, to the door
of the room next to mine and Brother Semmes: you
could only get to those rooms from the outside, they were
cut off from the rest of the house — the "boys' rooms" they
were called. He hesitated at the door; I opened it and he
walked in. I didn't know how to leave him; so I stood
at the threshold, unconsciously holding the gun at "order
arms." George Posey laughed and said, "You'll be a soldier!" I blushed and started to go away.

But he called me and said, "What time did Semmes
leave?" I said that he had left before dinner, with Jim

Mason who had come for him, and they ought to be back from the Court House long before dark. I could see that he wanted to know something, yet after some hesitation decided not to ask about it, and he looked down at his boots, which were muddied at the heels. I thought, out of gratitude for the gun: I'll offer to clean them, as I did my big brother's and of course he'll say no, but it'll please him. Then I thought: he might not say no. And I decided to let Jack Lewis do it. I said — with my back half turned, I was so embarrassed, in the kind of rudeness that my mother took almost as seriously as lying — I said: "Well, good-by, Mr. George." He answered in a low voice, "Good-by, son. Be careful you don't shoot anybody."

I thought how lucky it was that mother was asleep: I wouldn't have to show her the gun and overcome her scruples about my accepting it. Hadn't I already accepted it? I went off towards the woods beyond the field back of the garden. The lane was dusty for the time of year; the ground was warm; soon I would be going barefoot.

When I got to the woods I crawled through the snake fence, and advancing with dramatic caution owing to the gun and the mysterious enemies it had suddenly created, I came, after about fifty yards to a little clearing, where the first thing I saw was the toothlike ribs of a steer picked whitely clean by the buzzards and carrion crows. At that moment a rustle in the new leaves revealed wide struggling wings, high up, and a giant bird clumsily got under way. I saw the skinny red neck vanish in the leaves. I looked down at the bones scattered over the ground. I saw a big white skull with, sticking straight up, a short, thick, mouse-colored horn.

It was the work of a minute to open my Barlow knife and to cut and pry the horn loose. Why hadn't the Negroes beaten me to it? Old Lucy kept a little powdered cow-horn in a box and took it in water for her rheumatism. I trimmed the big end of the horn, admired it, then felt defeated because I couldn't plug it up — I should have to wait and get Henry Jackson to cut me a plug of white oak; but I cut off the tip and rounded out a small hole for the powder to trickle through; and that was all I could do for awhile.

I had almost forgotten the gun. I had laid it across a rotten stump. Grasping the muzzle, I threw it to "right shoulder rest," and said: The British are coming! I shoved the horn into my jeans, felt for the powder box in my hip pocket, and carrying the sack of shot in my left hand and the gun on my right shoulder I ran towards the fence and the lane. The faster I ran the more I felt afraid, for the running made the fear. I decided that the British were really in the lane and that I was not running away, but going to meet them. I lay down behind the fence. I took out the tin box. How much powder was a charge for a twenty-gauge gun? I opened the box and poured into the right-hand barrel what I thought was a charge, and from the sack I poured into my hand about a dram of shot, then tied the shot into a small rag torn from the corner of my red handkerchief. I rammed it home, adjusted the cap, and I was ready for the enemy.

A chicken hawk flew out of the woods at my back, pursued by a flock of crows. The crows had him surrounded; he couldn't get away from the leader, who savagely gored the back of his neck. I pitied the hawk but I raised the gun and aimed it about six inches ahead of him on his path of flight. I pulled the trigger, and found myself lying ten feet from the fence, the smoking gun beyond reach at my side.

The wind was knocked clean out of me; I lay panting, looking up into the sky where neither crow nor hawk was visible, but only the sudden blue stillness. I thought of the British in red coats but they were not coming, unless a redcoat were mounted on the horse now approaching at a rapid canter that I recognized: I knew that the rider would not be dressed in red but in a short jacket of homespun, a grayish brown. I had to face the music. I scrambled to my feet, rubbing a sore collar-bone; picked up the gun and leaned it against a fence rail; and put my elbows on the top rail, trying to look unconcerned.

The rider had slowed down. Directly in front of me he stopped and looked me over, not speaking. There was a light film of dust on his black jack-boots; his jacket was open at the top button, where his black satin neckerchief hung loose, partly untied. He removed the gray gauntlet from his right hand, took out a red handkerchief, like mine, lifted with his left hand his wide-brimmed black felt hat, and mopped his brow. My father's long, iron-gray hair and his long drooping mustache had been disheveled by the brisk canter. He looked severe, as he lowered the handkerchief, out of deep brown eyes, but I could see under the mustache the wide mobile mouth, which began to move, and the deep vertical lines of his face, which were about to break into a smile.

"General," he said, "I moved my troops to the sound of the cannon." He pulled his mustache. "The celerity of the movement has somewhat fatigued the troops."

I began to feel uncomfortable. I said nothing, but looked solemn.

"Where is your artillery, general?" he said. I moved my head vaguely towards the gun which I knew he could barely see behind the rails of the fence. He changed his tone. "Now, son, did your brother tell you you might use his gun?"

"No, sir."

"Why then did you take it?" His color mounted and I looked for squalls.

"I didn't take it, sir." He looked puzzled and then said impatiently: "Come, sir, don't trifle with me!"

"Yes, sir. I didn't take it, sir. It ain't Brother Semmes' gun. It's my gun!"

I had never seen my father astonished, nor was he astonished now. Every muscle of his face kept its place.

"Let me see it," he said. I vaulted the fence, reached back for the gun, and took it to him as fast as I could, handing it to him by the grip. "It's new," he said. He ran his eye along the barrels. "A handsome fowling-piece." He looked at me shrewdly. "Where did you get it?"

"Well, papa," I said, "Mr. George give it to me."

"Mr. George?" he said. "Mr. George . . . I don't know a Mr. George, son!" He was getting red in the face again.

"Well, Mr. George Posey, papa. You know Mr. George Posey."

"I know Mr. Posey, if that is what you mean." He was silent for a moment while he seemed to be thinking through something. As he handed me the gun, he saw the big end of the horn sticking out of my jeans pocket. He glanced towards the woods, then back at the horn. He smiled. "So that's it," he said in his kindest tone. He wheeled his horse, but checked him, and turned his head towards me as he adjusted the brim of his hat.

"Son, did Mr. Posey ask for your mother?"

I hadn't thought of that, but he certainly hadn't; I couldn't think what to say for I didn't want to say the truth.

"I thought not," he said. "He comes in and settles down!"

With that, papa spurred his horse to a gentle canter,

and I watched him till he turned with the lane a hundred yards away. Getting my gear in order for the homeward march, I began at a walk that quickly became a trot towards a scene that promised excitement to a small boy. What would papa say? Had Brother Semmes come back and would he let me go with them tomorrow? The gun became heavier as I ran.

*   *   *

When I came into the back yard papa was walking slowly along the path from the stable lot, and the look of his face would have led a stranger to think that he had just eaten a good dinner or greeted an old and valuable friend. But somehow his composure did not satisfy me; so instead of running to meet him I walked as casually as I could up the back stairs, and went into my room. I listened. Mr. George was moving about, perhaps dressing; I left my door ajar and peered through the crack by the hinges. Papa had not gone round to the front of the house. At that moment he set foot upon the gallery stairs. But that was as far as he got. He stepped down, and looking about him he called in a low voice, "Lacy!" I went out on the gallery. "Yes, sir," I said. He was staring benignly into space. "Go," he said, "and tell John I want to see him. I shall be in the back parlor."

I went, and I found Jack in the out-kitchen. "Lacy," he said, "what you talkin' about? You know the major don't never send for me till nigh on about sun." Jack looked uneasy, and I felt uneasy for a different reason, for I too was astonished by my father's unprecedented request which violated all the rules of a rigid life. But Jack was my friend, and I did not care to remain and be questioned. I darted out of the kitchen door and glided at the trot which, for a boy, is half walk and half run, towards the gallery; in three seconds I was upstairs and in my room, and I had closed the door. On the bed, where I had hastily dropped it, lay the gun. I stared at it dully, and without thinking, I jerked out my handkerchief and rubbed a spot of red mud off the butt. How beautiful it was! I caressed the smooth barrels. Then I heard footsteps on the lower gallery. It was Jack. I dropped the handkerchief and plunged through the door and down the stairs, and ran after Jack who had just gone into the back hall through the door under the gallery stairs. Inside the hall I sat down on the low chair that Lucy Lewis would come to occupy at five o'clock, after she had helped mother dress. I heard papa move in the back parlor but he couldn't see me for I was almost behind the door. Jack was just inside the door. "Yassir, marster," he said, "could I do something?" Again I looked through a door crack, this time at Jack who had thrown on his old broadcloth coat, above his dirty blue pants, and from the rear he looked like a cross between a field-hand and a decayed gentleman. "John," said papa—he never addressed servants by diminutives or nicknames—"John, I want you to go up to the gentlemen's guest room and ask Mr. . . ." He paused, then began: "If you please, tell the gentleman there that I will be glad to see him here at his convenience."

I knew that when papa spoke that way, so formally and in a low tone, something was about to happen, and I thought that I should be ordered to give back the gun. As Jack Lewis backed out of the room and slid by me with a serious face, I entered, and stood on one foot by the tall "secretary" just to the right inside the door. Papa glanced at me over his steel-rimmed spectacles with the square lenses, then continued with his book, the "Helper book" as he called it, which he kept locked up in the secretary so that no other member of the family could read it: a dangerous book, I had heard him say, with the little truth in it that slavery was an evil, but not in the sense that Hinton Helper thought, for slavery was a great evil only to the slaveowners themselves, who were depicted by Helper as prosperous barons grinding down not only the Negroes but the slaveless whites. He continued placidly with the book, and I noticed that he had changed to his long coat, but he still wore his boots. Why had he pretended to Jack that he didn't know who the man upstairs was? And why did he wish to see him when he could have ordered me to return the gun?

I moved from the secretary to the end of the room by a small deal table where lay last Saturday's *Alexandria Gazette*. My eye fell upon *Intelligence from the West,* and I turned to the heading: CONGRESS—*Speech Concerning the Relations of the States by the Senator from Mississippi: Mr. Davis Attacks Mr. Douglas, Who Replies.* I recalled that papa liked Senator Douglas and knew him well, but disliked Mr. Davis who, he said, had learned from John C. Calhoun the lesson of secession and would have led the South into ruin long ago if moderate men like Douglas had not forestalled him. I didn't know much about this matter, and I dropped the paper and tried to think of some way to appeal to papa about the gun. Then I knew that if I stayed in the room after Mr. George came I should have the advantage: papa would be under the restraint of my presence and of the kindness of feeling that never failed where his children were concerned. I took up the paper again. In the right-hand corner of the first page I saw words that turned my mind from the gun into even brighter fields:

☞ *NOTICE: Members of the Gentleman's Tournament Association of Fairfax County are hereby notified that the Annual Contest will be held on next Saturday, May 6th, at two o'clock, at the west meadow of Henry Broadacre, Esq., near Fairfax Court House. Members expecting to attend are respectfully requested to communicate with the undersigned so that colors may be distributed to them in good time.*

The Committee:
William Lewis, Chairman
Semmes Buchan
John Langton
James Mason

I put the paper down. Upstairs the girls were stirring from their afternoon rest: I heard footsteps at the ceiling and looking up I gazed idly at the starry heavens depicted in tinsel and azure, and my eye followed the long thin streak of the late sun where it struck the molding running round the wall in the angle of the ceiling — a yellowish white, the Wall of Troy design that one found in nearly every house. I began counting the little blocks, beginning at one end, but they were so small they ran together and I gave it up. Would mother let me go to the Court House tomorrow? I had never been to a tournament and I saw knights riding in armor, with feutered lances, clashing in mortal combat before pavilions gaily colored, in which lay beautiful ladies swooning in the anxiety of their delight. I saw the Black Knight charging down a dusty course, and I rose and walked a few steps to the high bookcase with the glass doors that stood in the far corner of the room. Opening the doors I tiptoed on the red ottoman to the tall brown volume of *Ivanhoe,* which then I sat down with on the ottoman, turning pages and staring with half-awareness at the pattern of the paper on the opposite wall.

There, ever since I could remember, Sappho had been reclining with her lute while Alcaeus listened with rapt adoration, in the midst of lovely girls, against an impossibly blue sky that enclosed a landscape in the eighteenth century taste. The broken column in the distance I had always wanted to pick up and restore to its place. I felt the book in my hands, but it no longer interested me. I looked at papa who was still reading in a low mumble that rose at intervals to "Damn!" as he came to a passage that irritated him, and shifted his body in the old Windsor chair.

My mind must have been wool-gathering, for the next thing I knew I was looking at George Posey standing in the door at his ease. If papa saw him — he was nearer the door than I — he gave no sign. George Posey surveyed the room with his opaque blue eyes, the smile barely perceptible round his lips. He said in a loud voice:

"Good evening, Major Buchan!"

My father, not looking at him, leaned forward, gently removed his spectacles and placed them between the leaves of his book, laid the book on the table, and with, to me, painful deliberation, rose to his feet. For the first time he glanced at his visitor.

"Good evening, sir," he said, and lowered his head. "Oh, yes," he said, "it's Mr. Posey." But he made no gesture towards shaking hands. "You've been here for some hours, I believe."

"Not long, sir, not long."

"Well, Mr. Posey, I am sorry that we had no opportunity to make you comfortable." Getting no reply to this, he sat down, and vaguely indicated a chair on the far side of the room. George Posey sat down. My father pulled a linen handkerchief, almost as big as a sheet, out of his sleeve, and blew a long and, in the silence, ominous blast on his nose. Replacing the handkerchief, he took from his waistcoat pocket a small mother-of-pearl box, and opening it he inserted his thumb and forefinger; throwing his head back he put thumb and forefinger to his nose and sniffed. After a few seconds that bore upon me as an hour, he sneezed, and I thought to myself: he is primed for action. I began to feel sorry for George Posey.

"Mr. Posey, it wa'n't so much the gift itself. No. It wa'n't that. It was the kind intention of the gift, your good feeling for our family. I don't know that we are entitled to your kindness — no, sir, I don't know that we are."

He considered it, and reaching for his black felt hat which lay by him on the floor carefully adjusted it to his head. He helped himself to another pinch of snuff. After the sneeze, which seemed to give him great satisfaction, he put his left hand on his knee and began tapping it with his forefinger. The long hand was a claw. I looked at George Posey with increasing apprehension.

"Major Buchan, it goes without saying that I have the most respectful feelings for your family." Papa's finger stopped in the air. George Posey smiled. I felt that this talk about family was dangerous. Why hadn't papa inquired after George's family, the first thing he always did when he met anybody, black or white? And why hadn't George asked about our folks? I didn't understand all this then, but I soon did, in a few minutes; I knew that papa was telling George Posey in a roundabout way, the way he always told unpleasant things, that young men from distant places, like Georgetown, twenty-five miles away, who happened to become acquainted with one of his sons, had no claim upon any other member of his family. I suddenly became aware of the silence that had engulfed George Posey's remark. I looked at papa. If, a few

minutes before, the addition of his hat had framed his
mustache in such a way as to make him resemble a benev-
olent tiger, he now, as he took in the remark, looked
like a tiger without the benevolence. Momently his ears
were getting redder — that shade of high pink that one
sees in a winter sunset, burning heat in an atmosphere
of intense cold. I shivered in the warm air of early May.
The old gentleman's nose exhibited a premonitory quiver.

"Now that's kind of you, Mr. Posey. I tell you, sir, that
we do not deserve your kindness—why, we've done nothing
to deserve it . . ." He waited for a reply but none came.
George Posey, cool as a cucumber, sat with his hands
folded before him, and complacently surveyed "the
major's" fierce mustaches as if they adorned a kitten.

"Major Buchan," he said, "I have expressed only my
feeling of respect for your family, sir. I have said nothing
about kindness. If you refer to the gun, why, the boy
would have had one sooner or later." He leaned forward.
"I didn't buy it for him. I took pleasure in just buying it;
a new shipment had just come in; then I thought who
I'd give it to, I didn't need it myself. I was coming here
and I thought I'd just give it to Lacy. He's a right smart
boy, sir." And he smiled at me over the major's head.

I winced a little: what papa had said to him would
have blasted off the earth most of the people I knew,
yet George Posey was affected not at all, and sat imper-
turbable at what I felt now was the end of the storm.
Papa just looked bewildered. He could do no more — he
had fired his heaviest charge short of. insulting his son's
invited guest. He coughed, and covered his mouth with
his handkerchief, a little too long I thought, and I wondered what he would do next, since I could see that
George Posey did not intend to leave. Papa replaced the
handkerchief, stuffing it a little at a time into his sleeve.

When it was all done, he leaned back in the chair, then took off his hat and put it down on the floor, heaving a short sigh as he raised his eyes in astonishment. George Posey sat against the back of his uncomfortable chair, his arms folded.

"Major Buchan," he said.

He was speaking, he had actually said those words. Papa looked as if someone entitled to know all about it had denied the heliocentric theory or argued that there were no Abolitionists in Boston. That was the first time I knew the meaning of the word aghast; he was aghast. But George Posey was calm. When I thought about it later I saw that there was nothing papa could do; his visitor hadn't been rude in any sense that papa knew rudeness; he had, as a matter of fact, been courteous. He had simply refused to recognize the only danger-signals that papa knew how to give, and he, George Posey, ought to have been the guardian of his own safety. That is what he was; but he sensed no danger. That papa was aghast was only due to his never having seen anybody like this young man. Papa had run into a panther, and he had fired a charge that had hitherto been good enough for his game; but the game had been rabbits.

"Major Buchan, I came here early in order to speak to you." He rose and walked to the window, as if it were his own house; but he had no feeling of victory or of assertion in doing it. The man was incredibly at his ease, the way a man is at ease when he is alone. "As I tied my horse to the rack I saw you riding away from the house." He faced papa. "Therefore I did not disturb the ladies."

He walked back to his chair and sat down. If he had only said that at first! Then I knew why he hadn't said it, for he was not now saying it by way of apology; he had saved it until he could use it to press an advantage. That my father had no inkling of this I saw in his still puzzled eyes; that he could have no warning that his amazing guest was pressing an advantage I knew from the whole tenor of his life; he did not live among people who pressed advantages and he just couldn't take it in. I looked at George Posey again. He was silent, waiting for further bewilderment in his host, not waiting, as it had seemed for an instant, for his own next words to come to him. He was never at loss for speech! I heard the echo of his last words — *Therefore I did not disturb the ladies . . .* When George Posey spoke you couldn't think what you were going to say, you were dominated by what he had said, by the sound of his voice, by a resonance that hung, like the cry of wild geese at night, in your memory of the highest air. "That young man is well-spoken," my mother had said; and when no one had agreed with her she said: "You know, Myra, as well as I do, that Jane Gibson is a lady." She was George Posey's mother. *Therefore I did not disturb . . .* It was like a logical deduction, a step in a set purpose, not consideration for the repose of the ladies.

"Ah, yes — I see, sir, I see." was all that papa said.

It was plain that George Posey was taking his time for a purpose, for he now did a remarkable thing — he took out his watch and not merely looked at it but studied it, this, too, as if he were alone. In place of the watch dangling on its bright chain, I saw a bass flipping on the surface of a creek pool, and I looked at papa. He was breathing a little hard, and as he gazed at the watch his breath rose to a gasp. George Posey's head was cocked towards the window; he was listening. As I began to listen I heard the increasing clatter of hooves on the cedared lane. Even papa listened. We all listened for the relief of it, all but George Posey, who put his watch into his waistcoat pocket and sitting back in his chair absently appraised the toe of his boot. When the horsemen rode across the front yard, George Posey got up again and folded his arms.

"Major Buchan," he said in an even voice, "I intend to marry your daughter."

Papa tossed his head. Big man that he was, he was on his feet like an acrobat. He threw his head back and opened his mouth, but no words came. A look of innocent wonder spread over his face, the incredulity he might have felt on first contemplating the flying-machine.

George Posey had not moved an inch: I was afraid to look at him but the edge of his shadow still marked the exact line on the folding door to the front parlor that it had marked when he had risen. Then I looked at him. He backed towards his chair and sat down! His host, attracted by the movement, glared at him; then he too, I thought a little wearily, dropped into his chair. George Posey spoke.

"Well, major," he said, as if explaining a fox hunt, "you see why I thought that propriety required that I see you first." Then in a lower tone: "It wasn't necessary."

Papa had mastered himself, but at this last remark he looked at George Posey uneasily. Has this fellow actually won my daughter, was the thought that I could see in his face. But I knew it wasn't that. George Posey was bluffing, or at best he was saying arrogantly that it didn't matter whether the old man gave his consent or not. The "old man" didn't know what to say. He crossed his legs and folded his hands, and suddenly was speaking to George Posey in his most courteous tone.

"Well, sir, you young men ought to be flyin' high this time tomorrow. Perhaps you would like to join them. I believe they are here."

George Posey made no reply to that, but smiled his

tremendous well-being into the room, until at last even papa was affected by it, and smiled too.

"Major," and I noticed the lapse of the surname, "I bought me the prettiest mare you ever laid eyes on; bought her yesterday, a big bay, fourteen hands high, from Colonel Tayloe in Prince William. I'm riding her to-morrow."

"Colonel Tayloe is a friend of mine," said papa, "a little my senior I believe. I was a private in his company at the battle of White House Landing. That's a long time ago, Mr. Posey, a long time."

Semmes came in from the hall, followed by Jim Mason and Will Lewis.

"Good evening, papa. Oh, there's George. I'm sorry we're late, George."

"Good evening, son. Why, Jim, how are you? Come here, Will, I want to see you. Did you bring what you promised?"

"I did, Cousin Lewis. Pa said it's the best he's ever had." And he handed papa a dusty bottle of madeira.

"Being late's no matter," said George Posey. His voice slid into the talk like a razor. Everybody stopped to look at him. Semmes looked at Will Lewis.

"Will, you know Mr. Posey? My cousin, Mr. Lewis."

George Posey advanced across the room and held out his hand. Will Lewis took it and bowed.

"I don't know the other gentleman," said George Posey, looking at Jim Mason.

"Well, then," Semmes said, "you'll have to excuse me. Mr. Mason, Mr. Posey."

Mason bowed stiffly from the waist without uttering a word.

"Be seated, young gentlemen," papa said.

"Major Buchan," said George Posey, "I must ask you

to excuse me. With your permission I'd like to see the ladies. I hear them in the front parlor." He nodded to papa and walked past the boys into the hall.

They all looked at each other. Semmes addressed papa: "I'll be back directly." And he left.

"Howdy, Cousin Will," I said. "Howdy, Mr. Jim. Have you all seen Mr. George's new mare?"

"I'll see her soon, Lacy," said Will Lewis.

"Will, I've been wanting to ask after your poor mother. Is she better?"

"A little, not much."

"Bad, bad," and he shook his head. He fixed them with a stern eye, and they waited in respectful silence. "Now, boys, Mr. Posey is here, he's a fine young man — why, you should have seen the light in his eyes when he told me about that mare of his." He paused to look into their faces, which were still respectful. "Ain't a better judge of horseflesh in this country." And then he said in a measured voice: "He has the instincts of a gentleman!"

*   *   *

With a leap I was off the bed and on my feet. I stood on the floor, wondering why I had got up and looked around for something to do. I looked at the closed door and I decided that I could go downstairs now, if only I did not have to open the door. Of my own will I could not enter the world of death that already demanded of me unknown actions, the creation of strange desires, and I felt the ache in my arms and legs, and I was tired. I saw in the mind's eye, sitting sweetly in a corner, Jane Posey, and I remembered what I had told her; but even then I could not open the door. I saw her holding the big bunch of violets in her hand. I suddenly wanted to seize them and trample them to the ground. I went to the big drawer at the bottom of the wardrobe and grabbed the glass knobs, which were loose, and yanked the drawer open about an inch; it stuck. I jerked first one knob, then the other, with a see-saw motion that at last brought the drawer with a rattle upon the floor.

I cast my eye stupidly over the array of useless objects that lay scattered in the drawer. I picked up a brass bullet-mold and looked at its two chambers and at the little hole at the top made by clamping the arms together like a nut-cracker. Stamped on the side of one of the arms was *.51 cal.*, too big for any gun we had in the house. I laid it down. I saw a faded white ribbon with a brass pin at one end of it, *Polk for President* in black letters. I ran my hands down into the mass of old shirts and papers to see what they would fish up. In one hand I held *Liebig's Agricultural Chemistry*. I tossed it back. In the other I held a thick roll of papers, tied with a string; I untied it. The first page, a little dog-eared, showed at the top in the left-hand corner: *To Maj. Lewis Buchan with the compliments of his friend the Author, G. W. P. Custis. Arlington December 8, 1850.* The writing was a legible scrawl. Below the inscription was written in a neater, clerkly hand the title of the work and the opening passages. I could tell by the way the lines were arranged that it was a poetic drama. I glanced at the title: *Cincinnatus Americanus: or, The Triumphs of General G. Washington.* I could see papa's face a few wears before vaguely smiling as he said, "Custis has written a great many dramas and they are all about his foster-father under different names, all Latin." Then he added: "Custis is a most accomplished gentleman. A very fine artist, sir! In the heroic style. And an elegant speaker." When we went to Arlington every Fourth of July to hear Mr. Custis' annual eulogy of the General I noticed that papa was always fidgety. "The tropes

get a little more tropical every year," he would say to
mother. I shuffled the papers and started to roll them up
when a small folded sheet fell out upon the floor. I un-
folded it and read the heading: *Woodstock Va. Jan. 21 '55.*
And under that: *Dear Niece.* It was to my mother, who was
dead. Mr. Custis was dead too. We should all be dead. I
read the letter. *Dear Niece: The sad intelligence of your
uncle Michael's death has I trust reached you ere this, but
I write you on this date of a less melancholy event, as I am
wont to do. I need not remind you and Lewis of the occasion, which is your birthday, dear niece, adding to your
store of years the fifty-first of your blessings to yourself and
loved ones. Today is your 51st Birthday. The day you were
born it snowed in the morning; this morning the snow fell
thick and fast. This afternoon the sun is shining bright and
beautiful; in Woodstock 51 years ago when our dear Sally
was born, in the afternoon, the sun shone bright and beautiful as it is now. The soldiers of Woodstock were on
parade with a Band of Music, and your Uncle Henry
Semmes had the whole company march down to your
Father's house and the Band played and the soldiers presented arms to the New Born Girl. When your father—alas
for my dear Brother, I would he were here — found out
about it he was very angry and your Uncle Henry was as
proud as he was angry and said Tom was a fool. Do you
remember this old tale, my dear Sally? Your Uncle Michael,
in case you have not been so informed, died a great sufferer
after three weeks of the bloody flux. We are very well here.
Tell Lewis I send him by Ed Brooks who departs tomorrow
for Washington 3 of my choice hams. The Johnsons have
set out for Mississippi, the whole family lock stock and
barrel. Yr. aff. Uncle James Gore.*—Uncle Jeems, the short
fat man with the red face and pear-shaped head whom I
had seen only twice, whom I hated a little for being so at

his ease between the mysterious realms of birth and death!
Uncle Jeems, who lived among the "Dutch" over in the
valley where my mother had come from. I had heard papa
rally her about it—"I committed a matrimonial indiscre-
tion in the Valley, I reckon," he said, and mother raised her
head with a gentle expression. "Well, Mr. Buchan, I tried
to prevent it." And he laughed and came over and kissed
her hand.

The letter also became a dead thing. I threw it into the
drawer, and tied the string around Mr. Custis' drama. I
looked at the letter where it lay and I could barely recall
after five minutes what I had read in it. I was suspended
nowhere, in a world without time. Ahead of me downstairs where I could not escape it, was death, and if I went
back in any direction I arrived at birth, my own birth, a
shameful and terrible thing that I could not reconcile with
the perfection of my father's character, nor could I forgive
my mother her sorrowful inconvenience before I was born.
Do you remember this old tale, my dear Sally? That alone
compelled me to face her dread possession of the physical
body that I had concealed from realization, and now that
body was dead. What was being dead? An image came up
in my mind that I had seen in sleep the night before — a
face of wax below which a sour mortality had turned everything cold. The little boy's fiction, that grown women were
only neck and head set above a mysterious region that did
not exist, was a fiction of death, and in the conviction of
guilt that harasses children I saw myself responsible for
my mother's death.

I saw myself walking up and down her bedroom, ten
times, the daily command, with a book on my head — "so
that you will carry yourself straight and when you look at
people you will turn your whole presence to them." Our
lives were eternally balanced upon a pedestal below which

lay an abyss that I could not name. Within that invisible tension my father knew the moves of an intricate game that he expected everybody else to play. That, I think, was because everything he was and felt was in the game itself; he had no life apart from it and he was baffled, as he had been baffled by George Posey, by the threat of some untamed force that did not recognize the rules of his game. I admired George Posey even when I did not understand him, for I shared his impatience with the world as it was, as indeed every child must whose discipline is incomplete. He could do the things that I should lose the desire to do by the time I was grown and my own master. I remembered the only time I had seen my father blush; somebody had tried to tell him his private affairs, beginning, "If you will allow me to be personal," and papa blushed because he could never allow anybody to be personal. Uncle Jeems' letter was emotional and affectionate — that I knew in an obscure way, but it was not something that Uncle Jeems had burst out with, it was only a habit that he adhered to once a year, a kind of minor rite that he had to perform.

I could see George Posey two years ago, the next morning after the presentation of the gun, walking with papa out to the stable to show him the new bay mare that his servant had brought in late the night before. I had taken the gun to show it to Coriolanus after a promise to papa not to load it. I had then gone off into the pasture behind the stable to join Mr. Higgins, who was watching the behavior of a young red Durham Bull that he had turned into papa's fine herd of cows. The bull was a little fellow, hardly more than a calf, but he felt no inferiority in his size; he pawed the ground and stared at us with an appealing ferocity. Papa and George Posey were approaching, and the bull at that moment mounted one of the old cows. Papa smiled and said to Mr. Higgins, "He's a little young for it, but I reckon he is equal to the occasion." Mr. Higgins cocked an eye knowingly. "Now, major," he said in an injured tone, "that 'ar little male cow shore is a cat." With the sudden loss of interest so inexplicable in cattle the bull dropped to the ground, unsuccessful, and gazed stupidly at the spectators.

I looked at George Posey. He was blushing to the roots of his hair. He looked helpless and betrayed. I saw papa give him a sharp, critical glance, and then he said, "Mr. Posey, excuse me, I have some business with Mr. Higgins. I will ask Lacy here to take you back to the house." Papa's eyes were on the ground while George Posey mastered himself. Papa said, "I hope you young folks enjoy yourselves. We had nothing like these tournaments when I was a boy. . . . Good morning, Mr. Posey." George Posey looked his host in the face and his eye conveyed its coldness. He lifted his hat. "Good morning, major," he said. He raised his head towards me, and I led the way back to the stable and on into the yard.

When we came to the side of the house I didn't know how to leave him, so I said, "Mr. George, I'm obliged to you for the gun." He patted my head and tousled my hair. "You better hurry," he said, "if you're going with the big white folks."

I was going, all right, and I hastened to my room to put on my new butternut jeans and blue soldier's blouse with the brass buttons that had American eagles on them. By the time I got downstairs and round to the front of the house the party were assembled.

George Posey was rubbing the neck of his mare and talking earnestly to his Negro man, a little to one side of the three young ladies, the Langton girls and Sister Susan, who stood in their finery by the carriage. Jim Mason and Will Lewis were coming rapidly from the house. Before they reached us the Negro man mounted the mare and with a grin at old Coriolanus, who sat on the driver's seat under his frayed gray beaver hat, turned the mare down the drive at a fast walk. Will Lewis had seen the grin too, for as he came to us he spoke to George Posey. "Posey," he said, "you certainly had it all planned out." And he grinned at him. George Posey offered no reply, and merely looked handsome in the brown beaver hat, the sky blue coat, and the tight fawn riding breeches strapped under the instep of his boots. As he moved towards the ladies there was a clink from the rowels of his silver spurs.

There was a pause that I didn't understand till later, for I, a mere boy, was so concerned with my own embarrassment, not knowing where I was to ride, that I could think of nothing but Brother Semmes, who had gone off to escort our cousin, Araminta Lewis, or Minta as we called her, to the tournament. I didn't have him to lean upon. George Posey was waiting for one of the other boys to tell him to ride in the carriage, the only place he could ride, for that matter, his horse having been sent on ahead. But I could see that neither Jim Mason nor Will Lewis intended to do it. Jim laughed and with extreme bows and nods proceeded to hand the girls into the low door of the old closed carriage. He backed away and he and Will, smiling at George Posey, left him high and dry, as it were, and mounted their horses.

Sister Susan put her head to the window. "Lacy," she said, "you get on top with Uncle Lanus." I put my foot on the front hub and sprang up to the seat. "Mr. Posey," she spoke in a lower voice, "you will ride with us." He took off his hat and got in. Coriolanus spoke to the horses, and we were off.

There was laughter inside, and I could hear voices, but I could not, in the rattle and squeak of the old carriage, distinguish what was being said. I turned in the seat to listen. Coriolanus spoke irritably. "Set still, boy, set still. Ain't nothin' you can do about hit." I couldn't imagine what "hit" was, and as we bumped and rolled down the drive I looked back towards the house and saw mother going to the garden. She wore a slatted bonnet, a wide dark apron and black gloves, and in her hand she carried her garden trowel. I had never gone off in the carriage without her, and she herself rode in it only two or three times a year — the round of calls in the neighborhood in early spring and early fall, and the annual trip to Alexandria, or perhaps every three or four years, when papa had made money on the farm, we drove to the Virginia springs in the mountains, the White Sulphur or the Old Sweet, but I didn't like it because I had to wear a velvet suit and get dressed up every day at four o'clock.

Will and Jim were a hundred yards ahead of us, like outriders, their long linen cloaks trailing round their spurs. When they came to the Ox Road they turned left towards the Court House, six miles away, and we followed. The country was almost in full leaf. The scrub oaks and maples showed a thin light green, with here and there a field newly turned and steam rising from the wet red clods. The carriage dropped into the mudholes remaining from the winter rain, and lurched out again with a groan from the leather springs. I was lost in this monotony. I watched the rump muscles of the straining grays as we rounded the top of a hill and came to a few small wooden houses; down the road I saw a dozen horsemen and farther still the white cupola of the Court House rising above the Roman arches of a red brick colonnade.

Coriolanus whipped up our horses and we passed the mounted men with a flourish. I saw Will Lewis and Jim among them. They lifted their hats, and the other young men, following their example, held their hats above their heads until we had passed. Will and Jim spurred their horses and followed us. We went at a trot past the Court House, then turned down a side lane towards a big clump of trees a little way from the road, where I knew Mr. Broadacre's house lay.

In the big yard of oaks and chestnuts there was no grass. The sun sifted weakly through the high leaves. There was a babble of voices from the house as we drove up to the front door. Surveying the yard I saw twenty or more vehicles of all kinds, from sulkeys to family coaches with four horses. Negro men lolled near them on the ground or sat dozing in the seats. As we stopped, I looked across the yard towards a big meadow, green as the sea, where a small pavilion stood gaily draped with bunting of every imaginable color; even the mounting tiers of benches showed red and white. At a long rail in front of the pavilion were tied bunches of three and four saddled horses switching the flies.

I jumped down off the box. The door of the carriage opened and lithe as a cat, a big cat, George Posey stepped to the ground, turned and held a gloved hand to each of the girls as they emerged in their swaying hoops through the narrow door. Sister Susan came last, and as the Langton girls moved towards the porch to speak to the Broadacre ladies, she lingered a moment, her hand on his arm, while he whispered, bending his great height over her bonneted head. She colored and her hazel eyes flashed, then she smiled directly into his face. He handed her two long ribbons. They were orange and black. She nodded her head, removed her hand but held it over his arm for just an instant. I saw George Posey gradually resume his full height and take a quick breath through his teeth, his cold blue eyes fixed upon Susan's poised hand. It came over

me that they were unaware of the place, that they were
suddenly alone. Susan recovered her hand, quickly rolled
up the ribbons and dropped them into her bosom. As she
moved away she kept her eyes on him, then she stopped
and, without giving me a glance even, said: "Lacy, you
must speak to the ladies. You know Winston is here for
you to play with." She tripped across the porch and
entering the door was gone.

I followed. Mr. Broadacre, a fat man with a pale sagging
face, came out on to the porch. He was dressed, from head
to foot, in blue broadcloth, with a white stock around his
neck. There was new mud on his black boots. He looked
at me absently. "Howdy, feller," he said. "What's your
name?" "Lacy Buchan, sir." "God-a-mighty, last time I
saw you you wa'n't dry behind the ears." He said *years*.
He gave me one finger of his left hand, so hard that I
winced. "How are you all?" he said. I said we were well.
"Where's your pa? I see he didn't come. I reckon your ma
didn't either." He looked at me solemnly. "A fine Christian
character, sir, a fine Christian character. You must give
her my compliments." He sputtered and wheezed, and
I caught with each breath the fragrance of Bourbon. He
was looking over my head. He shouted: "Winston, come
here, sir!" I glanced over my shoulder and saw a skinny
boy, dressed like a young man in boots and breeches,
walking slowly with a disjointed gait. When he reached
us he stood looking haughtily at the floor. So I was to
"play" with Winston. He was about sixteen, and I hadn't
seen him since the difference of age had begun to count.
"This is Lacy Buchan—why, you know him, son. Show
him around." He walked into the house with the absent
look completely restored to his face. Winston didn't move.
I said, "Well, I'll go in now." I went into the house, and

that was the last I saw of Winston until late in the afternoon.

After I had got through reporting to the ladies I slipped out into the yard. There was George Posey talking to Coriolanus, giving him instructions that brought into the old Negro's face that expression of respectful obstinacy I knew so well. "Yassir," Coriolanus was saying, "yassir, I reckon I kin." George Posey, seeing me, turned on his heel and started for the front door. "Don't get into any meanness," he said, smiling. I watched him disappear into the house.

"I kin, but I ain't," said Coriolanus to me.

"You ain't what?" I said.

"I ain't goin' to leave Miss Susie. Marse George say he git her home, and t'other young ladies too, but I say ain't I in chyarge?" Before I could object, he said confidentially, "Boy, you ain't et, has you?"

"No," I said. The ladies had offered me ham and beaten biscuit but I didn't want to eat with the grown people. I was hungry. "Uncle Lanus, can you get us something to eat?"

"Course I kin," he said. " I knows these yere Broadacre Niggers." He drew himself up importantly and marched off towards the back of the low rambling house.

I squatted against one of the carriage hubs. The guests were coming out into the yard, the young couples going off in different directions like cards slowly cast from a hand. A young man in a long green coat took out a big gold watch and looked at it. "It's stopped," he said to his girl, a powder-head in lavender bombazine. I recognized her—one of the Sterrett girls, a friend of sister's. Her squire called to another man: "Lumpkin, what time is it?" The man said it was one o'clock. "Just an hour," said the beau, and he opened the back of his watch case. He inserted a

key from the end of his chain and began winding. "It was
natural that I should forget everything today," he said in
a low voice. "You goose!" she said. She looked at me. "Oh!"
she cried. "There's little Lacy Buchan!" She dragged her
beau over to me, and seizing my hand said, "Why, Lacy,
you remember Lucy Sterret." I said, "Yes'm," and took off
my cap. I was in for it. She put her arms around me and
pressed my head against her breast, simpering, I was sure,
for the benefit of the beau, who looked on with a sour
face. "When you grow up, Lacy, just propose to me and
I'll marry you and we'll go to Niagara Falls on our wedding journey." She held me tighter and I grew hot in the
eyes. I could smell the perfume and the flesh of her arms,
together. She let me go and as she simpered away without
another word, on the arm of the beau, my hand shook, and
I felt a little sick; I could smell the odor of rank walnut
juice, only it was sweet — walnut juice sugared.

Coriolanus appeared in the distance, a parcel in his
hand. I saw Sister Susan coming down the front steps on
the arm of George Posey, slowly, looking about her with
her lovely smile. When she saw me she freed herself and
walked rapidly towards me. "Lacy," she said. I waited. "If
you don't want to go with Coriolanus, you may wait for
us." She drew me to her, as she had a thousand times. I
pushed her away. I felt the grievous humiliation of a child.
I couldn't think of anything to say. "Now, Lacy," she said.
I burst out — "I ain't going and Uncle Lanus ain't going
either." I could still feel the softness of her bosom against
my cheek. She turned to George Posey and took his arm,
and I hated him with an illumination of jealousy that I
had never before known.

Coriolanus stood by me with the parcel. "Lacy, you look
lak something done bit you." The hand that he put on my
shoulder was like a polished brown glove. "Me and you

is leavin' this place." I was staring at the backs of Susan and George. When I looked at Coriolanus he too was following them, with a sad eye. He said: "Ain't I told you you can't do nothin' about hit? Ain't nobody kin stop that young gentleman, nobody. The major can't stop him. Old Mistis can't stop him. How you stop him?"

We got up on the driver's seat, the old Negro pulled the reins, and we drove slowly down the driveway to the road. When we were within a hundred yards of the Court House Coriolanus drew up under the shade of an elm. He opened the parcel and handed it to me. I took a handful of beaten biscuits and two big slices of ham. I gave him the rest. We sat there eating our lunch. Down by the Court House a small crowd was gathering; men walked to and fro between the portico and the pump in the Court House yard. I said, "Uncle Lanus, drive down there." We went to a wide place in the street by the side of the Court House, and swerving to one side we stopped by a covered wagon full of Negroes.

The Negroes were laughing and a couple of them crawled out through the opening in the back of the wagon hood. Others followed until four or five stood in a row, watching us eat. A fat wench said, "Ain't that a nice some'm t'eat they got." She called to Coriolanus in a high treble. "We's hongry." Coriolanus threw a piece of ham into their midst. A stout buck Negro pounced on it and lay flat on the ground until he had gorged it all. The wench looked at him scornfully, and shouted to Coriolanus: "That ain't no way to do!"

Coriolanus said in a severe tone: "Well, ain't I throwed you something to eat?" He threw two biscuits, and they scrambled for them. The fat woman was still without food. She leaned against the wagon, dropped her lower lip, and sulked. Coriolanus eyed her disapprovingly until he had swallowed the last morsel of his lunch. He rubbed his hands to shake off the crumbs, then cocked an eye judiciously at the group.

"Ain't that a ornery passel of Niggers?" he said to me in an undertone. Then louder, as if he were asking somebody's opinion of the weather: "Whose Niggers is you all anyway?"

The fat Negress came out of her stupor and giggled. "Yeah, whose Niggers *is* we?"

The buck said sullenly, "We ain't nobody's Niggers. We just befo' bein' somebody's Niggers."

"Yeah," said the wench, "and we just after bein' somebody's Niggers."

Coriolanus drew himself up haughtily.

"Plumb eboe," he said to me. He said to the crowd: "Is you Niggers perchance done been sold down the river?" It was like a polite inquiry.

A tall, well-made yellow man stepped from the back of the wagon and addressed Coriolanus with an assurance that had in it no trace of servility or insolence.

"I reckon you mought know me. I reckon you mought because I knows you. You Marster Major Buchan's keeriage driver, I knowed you all along." He glanced at the other Negroes. "I was sold by myself. I didn't come with these yere Niggers." He looked about him. "I ain't no Virginia Nigger."

Coriolanus looked at him contemptuously. "What kind of Nigger is you?"

"I been mostly raised by ole Marster Rozier Posey in Charles County, him that's daid, but I been sold day befo' yestiddy by the young marster, Marse George. I been raised in Maryland, that's whar. I seen you last Christmas when I come with Marse George when he come to see yo young mistis."

"I disremembers a heap of things," said Coriolanus. He

squinted at the man. "I got to disremember 'em. I knows you, all right." He folded his hands and looked away.

"Yas," the man said, "I'm Yaller Jim." His eyes suddenly bulged white. He held out a hand as if he were about to receive something. "Joe, Blind Joe, he's with Marse George now — you seen him this morning."

"Yas, rabbit-eyed Nigger, I seen him."

"Marse George sold me, he sold me 'cause Blind Joe ain't no 'count, ain't worth five hunnerd dollars. He can't see good outen them rabbit eyes. Why, I'm the likeliest Nigger he had. I brung fifteen hunnerd dollars." He dropped his hand and looked Coriolanus in the eye. "I'm liquid capital, that's what I is, that's what Marse George say when he say he got to sell me. 'Yaller Jim,' he say, 'Yaller Jim. I hate to do it but I got to. I got to have money. I got to sell you.'" He raised his eyebrows in new astonishment. "What you got to sell me for, Marse George? What I done? He say, 'Yaller Jim, you ain't done nothin'. You're liquid capital, I got to have money. I ain't sellin' you fer. I'm selling you to Colonel Tayloe,' he say." Then politely, as if he had seen me for the first time: "I reckon the young marster knows the colonel."

Coriolanus spoke for me. "Course he do. We all does." He looked at Yellow Jim. "You ain't a bad lookin' Nigger."

Yellow Jim bowed his recognition of the compliment, then reflected upon it; his eyes bulged again, a cotton-white, and his patient, thin mouth tightened. I was fascinated by the change in him. And then I heard the cutting blast of a bugle from the direction of Broadacre's meadow. I said excitedly to Coriolanus.

"It's about to start. We'll be late, Uncle Lanus."

"Late nothin'," he said. "That ain't nothin' but the first call. Hit's half past one."

Yellow Jim, when I glanced at him, was straining his ear

for another sound of the bugle. He relaxed, with a smile in his eyes that meant a kind of satisfaction.

"You seen Marse George's mar?" he said. "The colonel give Marse George six hundred dollars boot. That mar's wuth any man's nine hundred dollars."

"Why you with these yere common Niggers?" said Coriolanus.

"Yassir, the colonel's Nigger say the colonel shore hated to sell that mar, but he's got too many horses so he done it. But he ain't got too many Niggers." He looked at Coriolanus. "Marse George ain't got no time to 'liver me, so he done turn me over to Mister Benning, and the colonel's overseer meet me here to go down to Prince William."

Coriolanus nodded his understanding of this convenient arrangement, and I remembered hearing our people at Pleasant Hill speak of "Mister Benning," the slave trader from Alexandria. A dusty buggy drawn by a tired horse drew up at our side. A middle-aged moon-faced man glanced at us, and let his eyes rove over the group of Negroes. The young buck Negro had withdrawn a little from the others, and lay fast asleep against the tree. Yellow Jim took a few steps to the wagon, and pulled out a small bundle, holding it under his arm. He moved quickly to the side of the carriage.

"Yeah," he said in a whisper to Coriolanus. "Yeah, *you* ain't liquid." He backed off and put his hands on his hips. He glared at the ground. "You'd just pour out like piss outen a boot." He stretched his lips and his teeth flashed in the sunlight.

The white man rested his eye upon Yellow Jim. "Air you Colonel Tayloe's new Nigger man?" His thin, mild voice languished in the air. "I reckon you air," he said to himself. "The colonel allowed I'd find you here." He pursed his lips as if he were about to whistle a tune. "This

yere must be the colonel's new Nigger man." He addressed
Yellow Jim. "Air you the colonel's new Nigger man?"
Yellow Jim went over and stood by the buggy. "Git in,"
said the moon-faced man. Yellow Jim got in beside him.
"I reckon I ought to find Mister Benning. I don't want to
make no trouble." He said "Git up" to the horse and
drove off.

"Uncle Lanus," I said. "I want a drink of water."

I climbed down into the road and ran towards the Court
House yard where the crowd I had seen forming was now
a motionless unit. From somewhere in its midst I could
hear a high clear voice. I stopped at the edge of the crowd
by an old man who leaned upon a sassafras stick. He spat
out a quid of tobacco, ground it into the dirt with his stick,
and with his free hand stuffed, from his jeans pocket, a few
broken pieces of tobacco into his mouth. "A smart feller,"
he said to me, nodding in the direction of the voice. He
rolled his lower jaw. I stooped a little and wormed my way
through the crowd. The voice was distinct . . . "no provision
in the sacred document which is the legacy of our fathers
and the charter of our liberties—I refer to the Constitution
of the United States — I say, gentlemen, that, in this safe-
guard of our democracy, there is no palliation of the ex-
cesses and usurpations now being practiced against our
rights in the territories, by zealots and fanatics who no
longer affect the guise of friendship but who, in overt hos-
tility, flout the bonds of amity and openly nullify their
obligations to the Federal compact. We seek redress for
this increasing violation of the Fugitive Slave Law which
our erstwhile brethern of the North were bound, by every
tie of honor and protestation, to uphold. In electing me
as your representative to Congress from this district you
will send to those precincts" he paused on a high quaver
— "those *hallowed* precincts an uncompromising de-

fender of Southern Rights. Gentlemen, I thank you."

As he sat down I squeezed between two men, and saw that the speaker was our cousin John Semmes. I had not seen him for several years. He looked older, a little grayer at the ends of his long hair, a little redder around the eyes, and his dewlap hung loose upon his black stock. He was wiping his mouth with a white silk handkerchief, and I noticed how perfectly the immaculate broadcloth of his trousers and long coat set off his giant frame. He looked at his auditors with abstract complacency, mingled deference and pride; there was no ire in his face but I thought it conveyed a kind of anger recollected in composure. A phrase ran in my mind—"I can't get along with her as it is, sir." Years ago, it seemed years, I had heard papa ask Cousin John why he didn't "go on and marry the woman." The woman mother never mentioned, and she was never more than civil to Cousin John — the woman being, as I knew by the grapevine telegraph (an institution of the public service conducted by the darkies), a certain "Miss Maggie," a person of no connections who pretended to be a semptress but who was my bachelor cousin's mistress in Alexandria. Cousin John had replied, "Good God, Lew, I can't get along with her as it is!" . . . The chairman was on his feet, but before he could speak a voice from the crowd shouted:

"You going to take Miss Maggie to them hallowed precincts?"

There was subdued laughter, then deep silence. Cousin John vaguely waved his handkerchief towards the chairman, who quickly sat down. Cousin John slowly rose, slowly folded the handkerchief, slowly put it into an inside pocket; he dropped one hand to his side, the other he held across his chest. He stepped forward and raised his head.

"My friends, there has been an allusion to my private

life. It would be as contemptible of me to evade that allusion as it was of my fellow citizen to make it." He looked blandly over the crowd. "I am a man," he said. "I hope that every person here is a man." He paused and gazed severely into space. "Gentlemen, I did not enter this race as a gelding."

The crowd receded like a wave; the loud buzz of talk rose to a cry. "Hurray for Johnnie Semmes!" A roar went up as a man rushed to the platform and seized his hand. The crowd near me had ebbed away. I wanted to speak to Cousin John but he was surrounded by his admirers. I saw men and boys running towards the pump. I too ran and, ducking into the crowd, I saw a "plain" man, his nose white with fear, held by two other men, one of them jabbing the hatless head with the palm of his hand. They dragged him to the pump, and a man running up from behind pulled the victim's feet from under him while the others forced his head under the water, which was already flowing. The man howled. "Lemme go!"

The old man with the sassafras stick was at my side. "Hit sarves him right. One of them Yankees that's moved into the county."

A young man broke in: "No, Mr. Regan, he ain't a Yankee, he's one of the Richard's boys."

The water was still flowing over the man's head: he had ceased to struggle and he gave forth low sputtering sounds. The sallow-faced pumper stood up. "He's about drownded, I reckon," he said. The wet man, hanging his dripping head, stumbled away from the pump. The man at the pump laughed. "Well, now, ain't he clean. But he's got a fer piece to go befo' he'll be warshed in the Blood o' the Lamb." The bystanders laughed at the wit.

The young fellow spoke again to Mr. Regan. "You raisin' a big crop of tobacco this year?"

Mr. Regan meditated. "Jest enough fer my own chawin," he said.

The victim was running towards the back of the Court House but a small boy threw a rock at him and he turned in defiance. He resumed his retreat more slowly, casting an eye every few steps over his shoulder. He disappeared.

Mr. Regan sucked at his new quid and glanced at me. "Son, the times is bad." He fixed me with his watering eye. "The idea of hollerin' out about Miss Maggie. Why, she ain't nobody's business but the jedge's." He spat a stream of ambeer that wavered elastically as it settled in the dust. "That ain't nothin' but women's politics. Durn if hit won't be a purty sight when the men-folks gits to votin' on wether the candeedate messes with women or wether he don't. Durn if hit won't," he said without emphasis. He looked around vaguely to see whom he had been talking to.

I slipped behind him and ran to the pump. One push on the handle filled the rusted tin cup. As I drank thirstily I looked up the road and saw the top of our carriage, now facing the direction of the meadow, over the heads of a long single file of horsemen moving at a slow walk.

I reached the carriage in time to pass around the rear of the last horseman in the line. Coriolanus raised his whip as the distant bugle sounded once more. The riders far up the road had increased their pace to a trot which was taken up by every man in turn until the line stretched like a rubber band. Coriolanus moved the grays into the road behind the last horseman. The leader turned to the right into the meadow, and I heard another blast from the bugle.

"Uncle Lanus," I said, "I'm going to cut through the field." I looked at him and I was aware that he had not spoken. "Ain't you going to see it?"

"These critters," he nodded at the horses, "they ain't been fed." He tapped me on the arm with the back of his hand. "I be waitin' fer you. Whar I left the young mistis. Nowhars else."

"Well," I said. Coriolanus stopped the horses and I leaped to the ground. I vaulted the stake and rider fence; my feet sank deep into the soft clover; as I ran I felt the breeze cooling the sun in my face. Ahead of me, off to the left, the long line of riders had come to a halt about fifty yards from the pavilion which lay directly in my front. At the back of the pavilion a tall pole, supported by the structure, rose into the air, from which flew gently the flag of the sovereign State of Virginia. I came to the end of the pavilion into the midst of a group of Negroes who were standing or lolling upon the ground by the rope that, dividing them from the track, ran along the whole front of the pavilion. I went along the rope, below the bunting, and sat on the ground. I looked up at the front row. There was Lucy Sterrett waving a handkerchief in her bold way at somebody across the track. Sister Susan was with her, and the Langton girls, and I heard the too hearty laughter of Minta Lewis.

A little Negro boy and a half-grown mulatto girl with kinky red hair and muddy green eyes in a pretty, Caucasian face, had crawled under the pavilion from the rear and were peeping through the draped bunting.

"Who you all belong to?" I said.

"We b'longs to Marse Henry," said the girl, giggling. She put her hand on the boy's head and held up between thumb and forefinger a small gray object that upon pressure yielded a faint popping sound.

"You got lice?" I said.

"Co'se I is," he said. "Ever'body do. Don't dey, sis?"

"*I* ain't," said Sis sulkily. I looked away.

Across the track stood a low wooden platform upon which, seated around a rough table, five or six men were consulting a long sheet of paper. At the head of the table was Mr. Broadacre, a tall brown beaver tilted back on his head. Brother Semmes sat next to him. He was not going to ride. "It's enough to take her," he had said. I knew that he didn't mind bringing her to the tournament because everybody knew that Minta Lewis was his cousin, not his choice; but he'd be damned if he'd ride, win the prize, and crown her queen—he'd act as judge. I stood up and looked at the girls. Sister Susan smiled at me, and Lucy Sterrett said, "Oh, Lacy, come sit with us," but I said no, I'd stay where I was. Cousin John Semmes was bowing over Minta's hand, more gallant to her than he would have been to a reigning belle, and I thought how nice he was, as I inspected Minta's coarse mouth, the small, pig-like eyes, and the stiff black hair showing under her bonnet.

Mr. Broadacre was on his feet, looking down the track where the riders were lined up awaiting the final blast of the bugle. The bugler sat upon a stool at one end of the platform. At the other end there was a tall cedar post with an arm running from the top out over the middle of the track. It looked like a gallows. From the end of the arm depended an iron hook and upon the hook hung a red wooden ring about eight inches in diameter. Under the "gallows" a stout Negro held a pole upon whose small hook he was ready to lift rings into place from the pile that lay at his feet. Down the track, at the end, fifty yards away, I saw a huddle of little Negroes, the runners who would take the rings from the riders and bring them back to be used again. The bugler was on his feet and all eyes were upon him in the sudden hush.

The blast lasted long, till I thought the blood in the "herald's" face would spurt out upon the ground. He removed the trumpet from his lips and stood in a kind of boiled self-consciousness. The judges on the platform lined up and, as if a drill sergeant had ordered "eyes right!" turned their eyes up the track. The horsemen were approaching at a prancing walk, the bridles held tight over the horses' necks, the horses' heads high as they strained at the bits. Each rider carried in his right hand a slender lance and wore on his sleeve his colors.

This was the Parade of Chivalry and I was not surprised to see John Langton at the head of it. Decorous applause arose from the pavilion, swelling into loud clapping that increased and subsided intermittently during the parade. When John Langton came opposite the pavilion he looked over the crowd with vacant eyes, his hard mouth withdrawn in a cruel curve; his face was darkly red. He had led every tournament since the custom of having them had begun; when that was I couldn't remember, but he was the oldest young man on the field, a perpetual bachelor and sportsman who, it was said, had never read a book and could hardly write a letter, who knew nothing but whisky, horses and fox-hounds, speaking on all occasions the only language he knew—the jargon, heightened by oaths, of the paddock and the kennel. He was a bold and insolent man who deemed himself an aristocrat beyond any consideration for other people. I knew that his father, the squire and our neighbor, had paid out, according to gossip, nearly his whole estate to keep him out of trouble. As he passed the lower end of the pavilion, Cousin John Semmes said, "Jack Langton is under the influence, but he'll outride anybody here."

"He's not as drunk as he was this morning. I saw him, he was tight as a tick," said Minta Lewis. "Oh, Minta," said Susan in a shocked tone. But a hush had come over the crowd.

A big bay mare was giving trouble: she wouldn't stay in line. Her rider was trying to control her, talking to her in an undertone. The hush of the crowd was giving way to a whispered mumble, for even more remarkable than the beautiful mare was her rider, a large man with a tight hooded mask of satin over the entire head, one side orange, the other black, with slits for the eyes. He wore a tight velvet jacket with white pearl buttons. I saw his buff pants tight over his boots, and the silver spurs. In my excitement I looked cautiously at Sister Susan. She was staring straight ahead, and I noticed that, unlike the other girls, she wore no colors.

The whole line of horsemen had passed before the spectators and was doubling round behind the judge's platform. They were lining up for the contest. The bugler blew three short notes. Mr. Broadacre looked up the track and raised his hand. John Langton settled himself in the saddle, dug in his spurs, and as his roan gelding shot out into a lightning gallop, he leveled his lance. When he came to the scaffold he was going at a terrific speed, but his eyes held the vacant look, and I could see him sitting on a fence carelessly gazing into space. He tilted the lance and lifted the ring off the hook as if it had been a hat on a hatrack. There was a crash of applause. Brother Semmes among the judges raised both arms — the signal that John Langton had won two points; he had not only removed the ring, he had done it with perfect form. Mr. Broadacre made a mark on his long sheet of paper.

I was so absorbed in John Langton's spectacular performance that I did not realize that the second rider had failed to take off the ring. The next rider took it off but the ring scraped the hook and he was given one point. The four or five riders that followed all got one point, though I thought that one of them should have had two until Mr. Broadacre held up the proceedings to announce that Blue and Green had approached the hook out of line and had leaned so far to the side, in order to reach the ring, that he had removed one foot from the stirrup. It all looked easy but now I knew why the young men practiced for the tournament the year round. Blue and Green looked a little dejected as he trotted his horse round into line again. He was Lucy Sterrett's romantic beau. I lost sight of him, and followed idly the succession of riders who performed with indifferent success, watching from the corner of my eye the hooded man on the bay mare who awaited his turn far down the line.

At last it came; I saw the glint of his spur as he turned his heel into the mare's flank. The light wind had died, and the silence that fell upon the gathering was so deep that the creak of the new saddle reached my ears. My heart leaped into my mouth: the mare, instead of going forward, shied to one side. I knew that I wanted George Posey to perform better than anybody else, but I didn't know why nor did I even ask myself why that was so. He turned his left wrist down, and the mare responded to the cruel curb of the bit. There was no other curb bit on the field — another difference between this mysterious rider and the members of the Gentlemen's Tournament Association. The mare at last jumped forward with a speed that would have unseated a poor rider. George Posey never lost a fraction of his balance. He was glued to the saddle as if he had grown from it as the hard gallop brought him towards the ring.

Again I was afraid. He was out of line and I was sure that he, like Blue and Green, would have to lean so far that he would lose a stirrup. What happened flashed before me in less time than the intake of a breath. Instead of tilting his lance upward, the butt under his elbow as a fulcrum—for the lance was heavy bowdock* ten feet long —he held it at arm's length, perfectly balanced, and lifted

*Bois d'arc.

the ring off the hook so gently, going at that headlong speed, that the hook was not disturbed the fraction of an inch: it was as if the ring had melted into invisibility except that the rider visibly carried it, his arm stretched out full length, near the point of the lance.

It was not only a great exhibition of skill, it was a feat of strength. But there was no applause. The crowd sat stunned. Mr. Broadacre raised both arms to signal the two points. Brother Semmes at Mr. Broadacre's side was staring directly over my head, a smile traced faintly upon his mouth; I knew that the scene just enacted had given him great satisfaction; but I couldn't look up to see how Sister Susan had taken it. I was afraid.

I haven't said that every rider had five chances at the ring. There were, as the afternoon wore away, some beautiful performances, but nobody showed the unerring skill of John Langton and George Posey, and they alone of the thirty-odd contestants received two points every time. John Langton repeated his first tilt five times to the last detail, his eyes becoming increasingly vacant and his cheeks a little redder. George Posey never varied a hair from first to last. I suppose I only mirrored the excitement of the crowd, which was too well-behaved to shout and cheer but which shifted on the benches and talked rapidly in low voices. I had forgotten my jealousy of George Posey and I wanted him, my friend and Brother Semmes', to receive the prize as the contestants lined up before the judges.

Their backs were presented to the audience, John Langton at the extreme right, George Posey, still concealed in his hood, at the left near the other end of the line. The people in the pavilion could look over the heads of the horsemen, but to see the judges, who were now about to do their part, I had to look between the horsemen who were in front of me.

Mr. Broadacre stood out a little from the others at the edge of the platform, a megaphone in one hand and in the other a handkerchief with which he wiped his brow. He looked pale and nervous and he turned for a whispered moment to Brother Semmes, who shook his head emphatically; Mr. Broadacre, more ill at ease than ever, prepared to address the crowd.

"Ladies and gentlemen," he said. He closed his lips and clamped his jaws to rearrange the tobacco juice in his mouth. He had evidently, in his anxiety, forgotten to spit before he rose. "Ladies and gentlemen." He pronounced the *gen* in the antique way as if it were *jane*. "It has been my high privilege since the inauguration of these ceremonies some years past to act as principal arbiter of the contest. But first I desire to express my gratitude to you all for consenting to be my guests. It is beyond disputation that the chivalry of this County is unsurpassed in our State, which in turn is unsurpassed in the world for cultivation of the manly arts of Nimrod and of Mars — the hunting field and the field of war, those two great" — he paused, he gulped, and I knew he had swallowed it — "those great and ancient preoccupations of manhood handed on by our English sires as eminently befitting the notice of janetlemen." He paused again. There was the absent look in his face. The sound of his own voice had restored his equanimity. "But if this is true of you, young janetlemen," and he bowed to the riders, "where shall I find the eloquence to praise the ladies, without whom your efforts here today in this contest were in vain? It is the ladies alone who are the repositories, nay, the gyuardians of our virtues, it is they, it is for them that you have achieved this brilliant performance." He looked uneasy for an instant, then he shouted: "The ladies! God bless the ladies!" The men in the pavilion applauded and the horsemen cheered.

The speaker was now paler than he had ever been. I wondered what the tobacco juice was doing in his stomach. Gazing up the line, I saw John Langton. He had tossed his lance to the ground, and sitting with one leg thrown over his horse's neck he was talking to a Negro man, in insolent contempt of the ceremonies. Mr. Broadacre gestured to the crowd for their attention, moving the palm of his raised hand before him.

"I now come to the decision of the judges." There was that complete hush again. "It has been a most difficult decision, one that has taxed our judgment to the utmost. The contest, on the part of two of the knights, has been the most brilliant ever witnessed on this field. In the number of points these two knights have achieved a tie in winning the maximum. Since, in this anomaly, it is a part of our duty to decide the tie, we have considered some of the finer points of the respective performances of the Orange and Black rider and the Purple and Gold." He stopped and surveyed the riders. "Will the Orange and Black knight please approach the platform!"

There was a burst of applause while in the upper rows of the pavilion people stood up to see who the Orange and Black knight would reveal himself to be. Mr. Broadacre took advantage of the interval to mop his forehead and to drink from a long glass some liquid that I thought was colored a slight amber.

George Posey had ridden round back of the line. As he came to the center the riders parted and swung back upon a broken half-circle; he stood alone before the judges.

"Dismount!" said Mr. Broadacre in a military voice.

The Negro man who had fixed the rings on the hook stepped forward and took George Posey's lance, holding the mare as, with one swing of his right leg, he gently dropped his big frame to the turf.

Another man had dismounted next to George Posey. He had moved up the line when the shifting of position had taken place. Something like a gasp rose from the pavilion as he moved forward directly in the path of the Orange and Black knight. He didn't walk around him. He raised his hand and pushed him out of the way. With a quick turn of his head George Posey tried to see what had happened, but his hood must have obstructed his vision. He pulled the hood off.

John Langton was addressing the judges.

"You goin' to give this feller the prize?"

Mr. Broadacre's sleepy eyes were popping out of his head as Brother Semmes leaned to him and whispered. If he was whispering advice, I do not know; it was not carried out. George Posey took one stride towards John Langton, his right arm extended, the palm out; he reached around Langton's neck and grabbed his shirt-front. He jerked him to him, stooped, and with that one arm raised him off the ground. Then, as if he were pitching a sack of meal, he tossed him away into a heap. John Langton lay on his back and I saw in his dazed face, as he tried to rise, that he was drunk.

Scattered applause came from a few persons in the pavilion but it had no conviction in it, and it died away. Sister Susan was holding her handkerchief over her eyes. Lucy Sterrett giggled, and Minta Lewis, with her tongue as usual too big for her mouth, was mumbling in Susan's ear, until Susan turned impatiently and said, "Be quiet, Minta." I felt a hand on my shoulder. Cousin John Semmes was leaning over the rail. "Son, there's goin' to be trouble. You better tell Semmes I'll see the girls home."

I had no time to answer him. John Langton lay in mortified isolation. In the sullen droop of his mouth I could see his humiliation at being prone on the ground; but he could not get up; there was nothing he could do once he had regained his feet. George Posey gazed at him a moment out of his cold, bland eyes, then turned and bowed to Mr. Broadacre.

Mr. Broadacre gulped. A galvanic jerk of his Adam's apple signaled the swallowing of his quid. But it was no loss of dignity. He clutched his megaphone and raised his hand whilst John Langton got to his feet and disappeared in a small group of men who were dismounting; they led him around behind the judges.

"It is my privilege, sir," began Mr. Broadacre, then he glanced over his shoulder at Brother Semmes, who whispered in his ear. "It is my privilege to announce the winner of the Fairfax tournament for the year 1858. That fortunate gentleman stands now before me—Mr. George Posey of Georgetown who has been with us today as the guest of our friend Mr. Semmes Buchan. I place the crown of laurel in his hand."

From somewhere in his rear he brought forth a small wreath of laurel that somebody must have made a trip to the Bull Run Mountains to get. He held it before him triumphantly, as if it were a rabbit out of a hat. He handed it to George Posey, who bowed again.

"We now await the winning knight's pleasure. We are ready to hear the name of the lady with whom he intends to share his honors."

George Posey moved to the edge of the platform and spoke in a low voice. Mr. Broadacre nodded.

"Miss Susie Buchan will please rise."

I looked around. She had not yet risen but everybody near her had, and amid the growing applause Cousin John Semmes stepped forward and taking her hand brought her to her feet. She looked pale and inscrutable, and I thought: Sister Susan is not blushing, as any other girl would, and

I have never seen her blush. Cousin John, holding the tips of her fingers, led her along the narrow aisle to the end of the pavilion, down the steps, and across the track where with a flourish of his hat he delivered the fingers into the hand of Mr. Broadacre. That harassed gentleman gracefully drew her up on the low platform into a chair that had been pushed forward. With the floating motion imparted to the female figure by the hoop skirt, she glided backward as if she were on roller skates, and as she sat down the expanse of the white flowered poplin collapsed about her like a tent. Every curl of the vast cluster at the back of her neck was in place and a white rose dangled artfully from the crown of her hair.

George Posey, his face in profile, had not moved a muscle during this ceremony: it was composure, not control. There was the vague smile about his mouth and the too narrow eyes moved in his motionless head in order to see, I thought, what these antic people would do next. He lifted the wreath and stared at it as if he had not seen it before.

Cousin John had backed off; he stood watching George Posey. Everybody was watching him. He did not move. Mr. Broadacre gazed at him and his mouth sagged into that look of astonished indigestion which seemed to be his sole emotion. He looked like a family portrait. Susan raised her eyes casually and George Posey looked again at the wreath, a little ruefully, and I felt that he was about to do something ridiculous, and I think he felt it too.

He stood before her and bowed, and lifting the wreath as Susan leaned forward to receive it, according to custom, on her head, he hesitated, looked around him, and then dropped the wreath into her lap. He drew himself up to his full height and laughed!

Susan sat a moment holding the wreath, her eyebrows lifted, gazing at nothing. She turned her head to Mr. Broadacre and I saw her lips move, and Mr. Broadacre's mouth fell open as he stood again erect. He raised his hand for the attention of the crowd, which had been amazed and silent, but his gesture broke the tension, and a loud murmur filled the air. He looked frantic and at last he shouted in a voice that everybody heard.

"Ladies and gentlemen, ladies and gentlemen! Miss Susie Buchan has been crowned—" he stopped to wet his lips—"has been—Miss Susie Buchan has been *designated* the Queen of Love and Beauty! She will receive the homage of her subjects!"

He faded away into the rear of the platform. Sister Susan smiled and held her hand out to George Posey who took it and led her to the ground. The crowd broke in all directions. Cousin John shook hands with George Posey and kissed sister's hand. By the time I had got across the track a small group had gathered round them. I stood a little to one side. But Susan saw me. She looked very happy as she motioned me to her.

"Lacy, there won't be room for you with us. You go find Uncle Lanus."

A few steps away Will Lewis and Jim Mason were talking in low tones. Before I could answer Sister, Will addressed her.

"Susie," he said, "the girls say they must go now. You must excuse them." The girls were the Langton girls, John's sisters; I saw them over by the pavilion talking to Brother Semmes. "They can't wait for you."

"Very well, Will, and I shall excuse you too." Her lips tightened and the lids of her eyes flickered as the blood left her face.

Brother Semmes came over and was standing by Susan, and he had opened his mouth to address George Posey when Jim Mason said:

"Mr. Posey, I am sorry to say to you that John Langton has asked me to deliver a message. He will meet you immediately at any place you choose."

Sister was gazing at George and he returned her look with a glance.

"Miss Susie," he said, "if Mr. Semmes will stay with you for a few minutes . . ."

"Of course he will." She looked at Cousin John, then at Jim Mason. "Jim Mason, you ought to be ashamed of yourself."

Brother Semmes was speaking. "Jim, you leave us a minute. I'll bring you George's answer."

"It won't be necessary, Semmes," George Posey said. "I'll meet Langton at the upper end of the pavilion as soon as I can get there." I looked towards the upper end; it was deserted; only a few people remained near the lower end and they were leaving. Susan was paler than the handkerchief she held to her mouth. She spoke to Jim Mason again.

"Jim Mason, you know that John Langton is a scoundrel, he always has been." She looked him in the eye. "It's because Mr. Posey is a stranger."

Mason hung his head and ignored her. "Mr. Posey," he said, "the challenger, you know, does not choose the weapon."

"I don't choose any," said George Posey. "Let him bring the whole government arsenal." I was aware of a change in him: his tone was casual and remote. Mason was staring at him. "Well, Mr. Mason, are you waiting for something?" George asked.

Jim Mason was rubbing his hands uneasily. "I only thought," he said, "that you might care to choose some less public place."

"I don't want a less public place," said George Posey. "I'd prefer the Court House yard." Jim Mason left them. George Posey bowed to sister, walked a few paces to his Negro, Joe, who was holding his horse, and taking from him his hat and his blue coat started for the upper end of the pavilion. Without a word Semmes followed, and I backed off against the judges' platform, slid around it and ran, out of sight of Susan and Cousin John, up the track where I met Brother Semmes at the end of the pavilion.

"Get away from here," he said, but he went on and I trailed him around the end of the pavilion. I ducked under the scaffolding and lay on the ground out of sight. George Posey was standing not twenty paces away, his hands on his hips, staring at two men who were talking earnestly just out of earshot down towards the lower end of the pavilion.

I smelt the acrid smell of tobacco smoke. I turned and saw Winston Broadacre, so near I could almost touch him, lying on his side smoking a long cigar. Then he saw me. "God damn," he said. "Son of a bitch. Bastard. Say, Buchan, cain't you cuss? Jesus Christ." He lay on his elbow gazing at me with a smirk. "You want some of it?" "Some of what," I said. There was a stir farther back under the pavilion. I saw the mulatto wench I had seen earlier with the small Negro; she was lying on her back and the boy, crouching in the grass, his eyes like fried eggs, was grinning. "She'll let you have it," Winston said. " I don't want none," I said.

Winston was gazing at me curiously. "Say, what you doin' here?" he said.

"You'll see in a minute," I said. "Look!" and I pointed at George Posey, who had moved farther away but retained his former posture. The two men had separated, one of them, John Langton, remaining alone about thirty paces from George Posey; he was slashing the clover with his crop. The declining sun was full in his twitching, bloodless face.

The other man, Jim Mason, was gesticulating to Brother Semmes midway between the two enemies. "I know it, Semmes," he said, "it's John's fault, he started it. But why didn't Posey wait and challenge him?"

"Every man must do as he thinks best," Semmes said.

"He oughtn't t'have put Langton in a position to do the challenging. He oughn't t'have embarrassed Susan by throwing him down."

"Jim," said Semmes, "we're old friends. But I'll be the judge of that."

"Excuse me, Semmes." He paused. "Won't Posey apologize? It's going to be mighty serious."

"No. He won't apologize. Langton started it and the apology is due from him."

Jim Mason took from under his coat a flat black leather case. "We might as well get them started." He walked towards Langton. Semmes called George Posey, and all four of them met for the parley. They talked in undertones, then Mason stepped off ten paces and with his heel drew a line in the turf. He came back and opened the case, producing two pistols with long blue barrels. Langton stared at them sullenly and taking one of them examined the priming; he dropped it to his side and glared at the turf.

George Posey as he took his weapon bowed as if he were acknowledging a glass of water. He looked at Jim Mason. "Do we get a practice shot?" he said. "It's not my pistol."

"If you demand it," said Mason. "It'll bring a crowd." George Posey removed his hat, stooped and picked up some dirt between his fingers, and smudged the side of the hat. "Semmes," he said, "put it down on the line, please." Semmes put it on the line that Mason had marked off, and stepped aside. George Posey raised the pistol and taking instantaneous aim, fired. The bullet drilled a hole in the hat and the smudge disappeared.

"I'll reload," said Mason.

George Posey looked at him. He moved the pistol towards him, the smile on his mouth, but he suddenly drew back. The smile vanished, his eyes narrowed. He raised the pistol and tossed it in our direction. It hit the scaffolding and bounced over my head; it lay within reach, under the pavilion. I saw the powder stain at the muzzle.

George Posey raised his right arm and fingered his lapel. The arm went rigid, the fingers became a fist that shot out like a catapult. It caught John Langton on the chin. I heard the crack like the limb of a pine breaking in the wind. Langton fell back and as he rolled over on his face I saw that it was covered with blood.

I looked at the pistol lying by me in the grass, then at Winston. "We better get away from here," I said. The Negroes had gone. Winston grabbed the pistol and crawled under the front of the pavilion. I didn't see him again.

"Is he all right?" said Brother Semmes to Jim Mason who, leaning over John Langton, was wiping the blood from his face.

"He'll be all right," said Mason. He stood up and looked George Posey in the eye. "Mr. Posey, I did not in the least approve of Langton's rudeness to you and it was equally insulting to the judges." He glanced at the prone figure. "I never did like Langton, from the time we were boys. But that ain't the point." He turned to Semmes. "Mr.

Posey agreed to come out here and there was only one thing to come for. Not for this." He grimaced at the still unconscious man, who began to flex his arms. He opened his eyes, forced himself to a sitting posture, and stared unseeingly at the three men. Mason seized him by the arm and pulled him to his feet. "I'll get him home," Mason said. "Where's that other pistol?" he said suddenly.

George Posey looked directly towards me and but for the fading light he must have seen me through the tall grass and clover. He looked at Semmes, his head back, the glance falling at an angle from his great height. That was the first time I ever saw George Posey look at anybody that way, and I wanted to ask him if there was something I could do, some errand for him, something I might perform that would lift me out of ordinary life. Brother Semmes had caught his glance and stood irresolute. I thought: he ought to be helping Mason with John Langton. He turned on his heel and walked rapidly in my direction. I crawled farther under the pavilion and got out on the other side.

There was rabbit-eyed Joe. He was holding the bay mare just where George Posey had left him.

"Who's kilt?" he asked.

"Nobody," I said. "Where's Miss Susie?"

The Negro did not reply but drew his lips back like a bad dog. At the upper end of the pavilion Brother Semmes and George Posey had just appeared. Blind Joe led the horse towards them, and when we were all together we started, without a word, across the meadow towards the Broadacre house. Our walk was soundless, only the faint thud of the mare's feet in the clover giving us a kind of fixture round which our senses could become regular again. The sun was high on the distant trees of the yard.

Around me the even light glowed in the green and I felt it as the late chill of spring.

We went through a side gate into the yard where, of the many vehicles that I had seen earlier, only four or five remained. Coriolanus was sitting in his place on top of our carriage which was drawn up by the front door. I said, "Uncle Lanus!" He turned his head and looked away through the trees. George Posey and Brother Semmes were walking towards the steps, but Semmes touched George Posey's arm and said: "Maybe your Joe could tell the girls we're ready."

George Posey nodded and they came to a halt at the foot of the steps, as Joe went towards the door. The door opened and Mr. Broadacre, followed by Cousin John, emerged, and stood on the top step. Neither of them spoke, but Mr. Broadacre gazed at us one after another till at last his eye rested upon Semmes.

"Well?" he said.

There was no time for Semmes to answer. Mrs. Broadacre came out, a white cap and faded blonde curls above an immense middle-aged body: Sister Susan was on her arm. They stopped just behind Mr. Broadacre, to the side, Susan looking curiously at him, at Semmes, then at George Posey, and I saw her take a quick breath. Cousin John looked back at the door and I saw three girls come hurriedly out on to the porch and take their places on the other side of Mr. Broadacre who now looked uneasily about him, I thought, as if he might need to escape. These newcomers had upset him and he lowered his eyes from the excited faces of the two Langton girls who were each grasping an arm of Araminta Lewis.

Mrs. Broadacre sniffled. "Henry," she said weakly. "Henry, get my smelling salts!"

Mr. Broadacre went over to her and took her hand,

patting it and looking at her kindly. "Madam, I will do nothing of the sort!" His own firmness had frightened him, for he backed away from her and distractedly ran his hand through his rumpled hair. He spoke in a low, pleading tone. "Semmes, for God's sake, relieve the anxiety of all these people."

Sister Susan pulled herself away from her hostess who was left swaying and neglected. She clenched both hands before her, the deep eyes lighting the pale strong face so brightly that I thought she had a fever.

"Before anybody says anything," she said. "Before I know what happened, I wish to say something." She fixed her burning eyes on George Posey. "I want you all to know that I shall ask papa to announce my engagement to Mr. Posey."

It was getting dark. A light breeze rustled the leaves and I wanted to cry, but the fixed figures before me held my eyes and I can still see them in that *tableau* — a group of ladies and gentlemen on a porch about to take leave of one another. George Posey was the first to move. He walked slowly up the steps to Susan and took her hand, and still holding it led her down to where we stood, by the carriage. He said, "My dear!" and took both her hands and held them to his breast. He released her and turned to Mr. Broadacre.

"I didn't kill John Langton. I didn't even shoot him." He ran up the steps and bowed to Mrs. Broadacre, and looking at her astonished husband he said, "I must thank you for the happiest day of my life, sir!"

He turned on his heel like a soldier and walked evenly down the steps where he stopped and looked at Semmes who came forward to meet him, removing his hat, and the two men shook hands. They separated. George Posey opened the carriage door and handed Susan in. Semmes looked at Minta.

"I'll just wait and come home with Will," she said, and led the Langton girls back into the house.

Everybody had forgotten me and I waited till the carriage door had closed upon Semmes, and I clambered up on top with Coriolanus. He pointed his whip in the twilight towards a large coach with four horses, that I had not noticed before.

"He's plumb forgot that hired coach and the fancy free Nigger on top of it."

"Yes," I said. The gay party had been lost in the quarrel. Coriolanus threw the whip over the heads of the grays and we started briskly down the drive. When we came to the gate, rabbit-eyed Joe, mounted on the mare, closed in behind us, leading Semmes' black gelding. I heard the tap of the hooves on the pike as we turned towards the Court House. We passed the big elm where we had begun to eat our lunch, we came to the wide place in the street where the Negroes had been and where, again, I saw the moon-faced man and the flash of Yellow Jim's teeth; we passed the Court House and turning left to the edge of the village we passed the last house. Then it was dark, and we plunged into it.

*   *   *

A knock at the door opened my eyes to the light. I could neither go to the door nor say come in, for two whole years had been canceled out, and I was rising from bed the next morning after the tournament until the knock had sounded a second time and I felt in my pocket the strap that I had found in the stable lot: those two years came back with the image of Brother George riding away under the cedars, and I knew all over again that my mother was

dead. There was the crowd of people downstairs but there
was deep silence. I heard the tall clock on the landing in
the front part of the house strike two, through the floors
and partitions; I hated the sound and I wished I too had
ridden away, and I remembered, if not the words, the
meaning, then, of the motto to one of Poe's tales: *No man
need succumb to death utterly except by his own feeble
will.* I felt in me a surge of immense well-being and the
desire to go to unknown realms, and then I was frightened, for I had come out of the dark.

The door was open and two men stood before me.
Brother Charles came over and held out his hand. I took
it and burst into tears. He pushed me back and I sat on
the bed. Cousin John Semmes was still standing in the
door. He closed it and came forward, speaking to me
kindly, and moved over to the window and gazed out into
the yard. Brother Charles spoke.

"Lacy, it's our duty. Why, son, they've left you all by
yourself." He took me by the arm and led me to the washstand. "Wash your face," he said.

Cousin John turned. "It's a damned outrage," he said
quietly.

I changed the water and dipped my face into the bowl.
Brother Charles handed me a towel. "There!" he said. He
walked over to the window and folded his arms. I had not
seen him for more than a year and I had never known
him very well, nor did anybody else: he was too much like
papa. The handsomest young officer in the United States
army, everybody said, and outdone in looks only by
Colonel Lee. For some reason that was still talked about in
the family he had married Lucy Sterrett last summer after
a courtship of three weeks. At that time I saw him but
little, and before that he had been away in the West at an
army post for years; he was twenty-eight and like an

uncle. It was Lucy's vivacity that had captivated him, and
that was all that mother, while papa was saying nothing,
ever said about her. I suppose she had been too easily
swept off her feet, and there were people who said that
she had done the sweeping, for Brother Charles, like all
the Buchans, was conventional and unimaginative, and
could not have thought of anything so dashing as a three
weeks' courtship. I noted his attire, a black informal coat
without waistcoat, and a low collar with a large black bow
tie—Lucy's notion, I was sure, for all the other men would
be in dress coats. It gave him a kind of frivolous dis-
tinction, as if he had stepped out of the pages of Murger,
but it didn't suit his formal face whose eyes alone were
sometimes capable of a smile.

"Cousin John," he said, "we mustn't judge him too
harshly."

"I ain't judging him," said Cousin John. He walked
over to the slop-jar and spat out his quid. He poured a
glass of water, rinsed out his mouth, and spat the water
into the slop-jar. "No, I ain't judging him, but I do say
that his conduct has been outrageous."

"Susie ought to have made him stay."

"She tried but couldn't. I asked her and she didn't answer, and I knew he'd disregyarded her wishes."

Brother Charles accepted this, indeed seemed not to
have heard it. "George Posey has done a great deal for our
family. Papa don't know it yet. Look at what he's done
for Semmes."

Cousin John pursed his lips, sucking them against his
teeth; his flaccid dewlap hung lower than it had two years
ago, his eyes were redder, his hair longer and whiter, and
I wondered if his defeat in the race for Congress had aged
him, and whether Miss Maggie had anything to do with
the defeat; but I supposed not, for everywhere in Virginia

the Union men had been elected, the Southern Rights party having been discredited as too extreme. Cousin John had resumed his law practice in Alexandria. His lips still pursed, he moved his jaw up and down: I decided that he was exercising his false teeth.

"Has it ever occurred to you," Cousin John said, "that George Posey makes himself felt in this family when we make mistakes? Ain't any question about his generosity. He'd give the shirt off his back."

"That's true, Cousin John, very true. That's what I meant about Semmes."

"What's he been up to?" Cousin John sat down in a straight chair by the window and folded his arms. "I can't figger that feller out — no, sir. I just can't figger him out." He raised his eyelids towards Brother Charles. "I mean George Posey, Charlie. Why, he gave a beggar ten dollars one day this winter, old woman with starvation sores all over her face, and he was embarrassed when he did it! Now what do you think of that? But he won't pay his free labor enough to buy bacon and meal. Cap'n Corse told me so only last week. I can't figger him out." He paused as if he were about to make one more effort. "He don't think it's right to own Negroes. I don't either." He slapped his leg. "By God, I don't own any. And I didn't sell the Negroes I had."

"Has George sold any Negroes?" Brother Charles spoke in a low voice.

"He rode away from here today on the back of a bay Negro." He watched for the effect of this on Charlie's literal mind; but it had none. He gazed through the window. "We were coming over here. Last summer. We passed the prettiest stand of tobacco you ever saw, in Cyarter's big field. Why, man, every leaf was pea-green and the light played on it like it does on a tropical sea. I called George's attention to it. 'Yes,' he says, 'old Cyarter's got it over his whole damn farm.' Charlie, it ain't natural for a man not to like to see a fine stand of tobacco."

"Cousin John, you do George an injustice. Semmes says that George thinks tobacco is the ruination of everybody around here, that papa showed unusual judgment in giving it up."

"Yes. And George showed remarkable judgment last year in buying Cyarter's tobacco and a lot more, for a profit of twenty thousand dollars!"

"I never knew anything about his business."

"A Buchan understand business? You are all gentlemen." He laughed and leaned forward in his chair. "You may as well say what he's done for Semmes."

Charlie got up and put his hands in his pockets. "I thought you'd heard, Cousin John." There was no reply. Charlie looked down into the yard. "He bought those letters from the Stacy woman."

Cousin John's serene face did not move. "What Stacy woman? Where?"

"You'd never think it of Semmes, now would you?" Brother Charles asked it curiously as if he couldn't believe it. "In Washington. A widow of good connections, from New York. Not more than twenty-five, mighty pretty and very presentable. Why, Cousin John, Semmes wanted to marry her, if she'd had sense enough to see it; but after she demanded money for the letters he just couldn't, though I believe he still wanted to. If George hadn't put up the money papa would have heard about it. I can't understand it, Cousin John."

"Why can't you?" the older man said. "So you don't see why she wouldn't marry the boy? My God. Of course,

any woman would break her neck to marry any Buchan!"
He stared at Brother Charles. "Tell me, did he have relations with the Stacy?"

"No, Cousin John, no, he never said, but I doubt if he
did."

"I thought not." He raised his voice. "Ain't that a hell
of a thing for a gentleman to get into?" By God, Charlie,
even John Langton would have more sense, and he ain't
got half the sense Semmes has."

He rose and walked past me towards the door.

"Let's take the boy downstairs." As Brother Charlie
left the window, Cousin John opened the door and held
the tarnished brass door-knob. He emitted one word:
"Letters!" He glanced at Charles who was arranging his
tie, then he addressed me.

"Lacy, I'm going to tell you a story."

"Oh, Cousin John!" I said. I put my face in my hands.
Cousin John spoke in a kind, level voice.

"Never mind, Lacy, I'm determined to tell you this
story because you've got a long time to live." He was put-
ing a new quid into his mouth, a small plug that made
a slight bulge in his left cheek. I fixed my eye upon it.
"A year or two before Mr. Clay died I saw him at the
National Hotel and he was in a temper when I was shown
into his room. He had a letter in his hand which he tossed
upon the table. He explained that a young kinsman of his
in Kentucky had written letters to a fancy woman, and he
said to me: 'Mr. Semmes, what is getting into these young
fellows? They treat whores like ladies and ladies like
whores. They ain't worth a damn. They do their frig-
ging with a pen!' " Cousin John rolled his quid. "Boy, you
remember that story!" He lifted his sharp eye to Charlie's
face. "I reckon you know George Posey didn't even go in
to pay his respects to your pa before he went away?"

He walked out of the room, and as I followed him
Brother Charles came up behind me, put his hand on my
shoulder; I looked into his rigid face. We emerged into the
light. Only a few hours before, Brother George had ridden away, but it was years and several lives ago. I heard
the clump of our boots and saw the afternoon filled with
weak sun as we descended the gallery stairs.

*   *   *

Cousin John and Brother Charles turned into the back
parlor. I went on into the front hall and stood by the
newel post. There was somebody at my elbow. It was
Coriolanus, and he passed on to the front door, which he
swung wide, moving against it with his foot a large conch
shell to hold it to the wall. The front steps and the yard
were covered with people. Coriolanus looked at me unseeingly and went into the front parlor. I was about to
retreat into the back hall when I looked through the door
and saw Will Lewis shaking hands with a young middle-
aged gentleman who was examining the face of a watch
which lay in the palm of his left hand. "Half an hour,"
he said. It was Captain Corse from Alexandria. Will was
pumping his hand, up and down, in the fashion of men
in that age. "Mr. McBean is late, just got here," he said.
A low buzz of voices drifted into the hall from the front
parlor, and raising my head to hear it, I caught the average
scent of many flowers which is the unnatural disguise of
death.

I felt sick and I did not know where to go. There was a
rustle of silk, and Aunt Myra and Minta Lewis came out
of the parlor, leading old Mrs. Langton who with a frilled
handkerchief was dabbing the end of her nose. Aunt Myra
saw me and came over and led me by the hand into
mother's bedroom. There were no men there, only women,

and I noticed that Mrs. Langton, as soon as she was seated, took out of a small reticule her knitting, to which she proceeded to give her placid attention.

I think Aunt Myra was called suddenly away: at any rate she left me alone in the middle of the room where I became the target of old, kindly eyes. Mrs. Langton dropped the knitting into her lap, looked around her alertly, and said to no one in particular, "A motherless boy becomes an unsatisfactory husband. My dear," she said to Minta Lewis, who was looking out of the window, "let the poor child sit down. . . . Come here," she said to me. I stood by her chair, my hand on the faded blue plush. "You have your ma's eyes." She took my hand. "I think you'd better sit over there with Jane — is that your name, honey?" She glanced at Jane who was leaning stiffly against the side of the big tester bed in the far corner of the room; but Jane only lowered her head. "Lacy, listen to me." She was oblivious of the other ladies. "Mind your pa. I take a great interest in your welfare."

"Yes, ma'm," I said but I didn't know what she was talking about. I had seen Miss Ginnie, as we called Mrs. Langton, many times since the "trouble" between John and Brother George; the families were as intimate as ever, the Langtons never having mentioned it to any of us, assuming that John's behavior had better be ignored because it could not be defended; we, for our part, and papa especially, were glad to accept that view, since John Langton's boorishness on that now famous occasion had left Brother George's conduct in a better light than it would have deserved had his opponent been an honorable man. These reflections had no place in my sensations of that room and that time: as I stood by Mrs. Langton I saw familiar faces — the fat Mrs. Broadacre and her three daughters with the vague eyes of their father; Minta Lewis, now sitting on an ottoman by the window, showing to a little boy a picture book that I had become tired of — *Picturesque Niagara* — one of the Broadacre grandchildren, I suppose—he seemed tolerant of Minta's simple delight in the pictures; and old Mrs. Gunnell, her face a mass of wrinkles, holding a black ear-trumpet to first one ear and then the other but usually at the wrong ear to catch the talk; and there was Brother George's mother, Aunt Jane Anne, we now called her, and her old maid sister, Miss Milly George Gibson who had lived with her ever since the death of old Mr. Posey years before.

Aunt Jane Anne was a little old lady, not really old, but nearly sixty, whose features, tied up in a knot by her nose, bore an expression of sustained surprise: she had not spoken since I had come into the room. I was wondering how she had taken her son's departure, whether indeed she knew he had gone, when she spoke to Mrs. Langton.

"We'd better return this evening, thank you. I can't be away overnight." She spoke in a low, sweet voice. "We'd really have to stay with Susie and the poor major. But Milly George and I, both of us really do thank you for wanting us. I declare, I don't know what people would do without kindness." She inclined her head gently, then sank into her chair as if she were frightened by the boldness of her speech.

Mrs. Langton nodded her head and smiled. She pushed me from her and cast her eyes towards Jane, who had not moved an inch. Jane's eyes were still lowered but her face held the glow that no child's face can achieve, and I noticed the regular rise and fall of her bosom as a hand touched my shoulder and I turned to look into the face of Lucy Sterrett.

"You poor lamb," Lucy said, and she stroked my head. I felt my legs shake and I knew, when she held me close, that now that she was married to my brother I was more afraid of her than ever. She was always putting her hands upon me and saying she would have a boy just like me some day. While she held me I saw the holes in the skin of her neck and the light brown hair under her ears. I was humiliated, and because I would be a gentleman when I grew up I did not know whether I ought to notice her skin and hair and the unfixed mouth, or to think twice about the weak, cold hands that touched my cheek and made it burn.

"Now stay right there, Lacy." She went to the mantel where she lifted out of a Dresden vase about half of a large cluster of violets. She shook the water from the stems. Jane moved on the bed and opened her wide eyes, and Lucy went to her and thrust the violets into her passive hands, closing the fingers upon the stems. She pushed Jane to the middle of the room where I was standing, I think, with my fascinated eyes not upon Jane but upon the violets and the white wrist under them. Lucy said to the room: "They were Mother Buchan's favorite flowers." Her tone was assertive, but meeting no resistance she continued. "It will be something for you to remember, Lacy, the last thing you did for your poor mother." She pulled Jane brusquely by the arm and said to me, "Come!"

As Jane followed Lucy she gave me over her shoulder a glance, appealing and scared, and I decided that I would follow her anywhere, and the ritual in which I was about to participate became an heroic quest. I was conscious of my hands and feet as carefully, with such concentration that I might have been walking upon eggs, I followed Lucy and Jane into the hall, where an impulse seized me and I whispered: "Sister Lucy, wait a minute."

I ran back into the room and going behind the door I took from my pocket the old strap and dropped it upon the floor out of sight, feeling great relief to be rid of that indecorous thing. I came from behind the door and I heard Mrs. Langton say: "Lucy Sterrett never had the sense the Lord gave a goose."

Aunt Jane Anne raised her head with a sweet smile, her lips parted for speech, but getting from the expression on Miss Ginnie's face the force of her remark, she fell back into her chair like a crushed paper sack. I became aware of Miss Milly George's eyes which were fixed upon me in a misty stare. In her gaze there was something secret and penetrating; and in the working mouth, framed by the almost white curls under her black coal-scuttle bonnet, there was a force wonderfully alive! I had a vision of her peeping from behind a door into a dark hall.

"Well, now," she said in a high voice. "ain't the boy flesh of his mammy's flesh and bone of her bone, and all?"

There was motion over by the side window and Minta Lewis came to me, and saying, "Lacy, I'll just go too, she looks so sweet," pushed me ahead of her into the hall where we followed Lucy and Jane into the front parlor.

Lucy and Minta left us at the threshold and walked with even steps to the coffin. They looked down into it with their heads held primly back. At the near end of the coffin, by the heaped flowers, sat Uncle Armistead dozing in his chair, his big soft black hat lying between his feet and his head sagging into his long white beard; I glanced from his little Negro, squatting behind the chair with an empty toddy glass before him on the floor, to the tuft of gray bristles on the side of his thin, hooked nose — an evil-looking mark, and I heard a voice out of the long past: at the age of ten he cursed God and his faithful wife gave up the ghost in her twenty-sixth year. The odor of the banked flowers grew stronger. In the corner beyond the coffin old Lucy Lewis sat in a low rocker, black crepe tied

around her head and round her shoulders a decent black
shawl; Coriolanus stood by her, his hands folded over his
stomach. I had no doubt that, called away, they had returned to those postures time and again. At last I gazed at
the long black repose of my mother: it rested upon wooden
trestles between the two front windows, against the white
wall, under the fading portrait of my grandfather who
stared into the far distance with dropsical eyes.

A long ray of sun, stretching from the window, threw
upon the white mantel across the room a crazy trapezoid:
it was a turbulent sunbeam and I watched the motes eddy
into the shade, and into the light, then into the mysterious
shade where they were lost. In the dim far end of the
room, near the door into the back parlor were people talking in an undertone. Captain Corse, the man who had
looked at his watch, held his chin in one hand whilst he
nodded his head.

"She just looks asleep," Lucy said to Minta.

Uncle Armistead opened his eyes. "Hanh?" he said.

"Nothing, Cousin Armistead," said Minta. She leaned
over the coffin, putting one hand upon the upturned lid.
She pursed her thick lips and blinked her round, opaque
eyes. "Folks are mighty funny about dead people." It was
a whisper into Lucy's ear. "Cousin Sally don't look dead.
I think she looks real pretty."

Lucy had moved the glass covering. She turned towards
me. I looked into her flighty blue eyes and felt that now
for the first time I wanted her to touch me, to hold me
close to her until I felt nothing of that room, which should
be transformed into a dark and secret place all my own.
She came to me and put her arm around my shoulders, and
with the other hand gathered to her Jane Posey, leading
us up to my mother. Minta stood away to make place for
us. Jane was looking down at the violets in her hand. She

suddenly held them out to me and I took them, understanding what I must do, and marveling that she had
known all along.

I looked into the coffin. The right arm rested upon the
bosom, the fingers not quite touching the small oval
portrait of my father that lay on her breast. I stuffed the
violets between the thumb and unyielding fingers, and I
marked the dark luster of eyelids in a sweet face that I
had never seen before.

As I stepped back, turning to face the cold room, I felt
a hand touch my hand: it was Jane. She gave it a little
tug, to lead me away. I halted and gripped her hand. I
could not move.

Sister Susan was standing at the door, and I noted her
right arm which she held over her bosom as mother was
holding hers: her eyes were blazing, but not at us. She
was looking at Brother Semmes who from the center of the
room stared at Jane Posey with astonished eyes, his forefinger pressed against his nose, one foot advanced. Susan
shifted her gaze to Jane, and I saw the color in Jane's face
as the fire went out of Susan's eyes: she looked at the child
with pity, and, turning, disappeared into the hall.

Jane dropped my hand and started towards the door
where Brother Semmes met the child and led her slowly
out of the room. I think this was the most desperate moment of my life. Later I faced greater terrors, but I was
ready for them; for this I had no preparation. What could
I, a boy, do to win a girl, now almost a woman, from the
attentions of my dearest brother? I had been snared, bound,
and delivered into the future. The unrecognizable woman
lying in the box, for whom I had performed the meaningless rite, was, to those foolish girls, dead in a completeness
of death that gave them an ease before it. I could not face
that death. For me my mother had merely ceased to exist

and the guilt that I had felt earlier in the day dropped from
me. What good man does not feel that he has been in at
the death of a beloved one? I could not feel it, and I was
not good, but I knew none of this then, understanding it
with the body, not the mind, and I acted out my understanding when, hating Lucy's latest embrace as we left the
parlor, I saw with excitement the face of George Posey in
the shadows of the back hall.

*   *   *

When he had come back and why, I did not learn till
later, for I was relegated again to the bedroom and the old
ladies: Lucy had pushed me into the room and disappeared, and I was well rid of my cousin Minta. Jane had
taken up her former position at the edge of the bed so
exactly that I had to look at her a second time to make
sure that she had ever left it. This time I walked straight
to her and sat at her side. The old ladies were talking but
I heard the rising bustle in the hall; I saw Coriolanus
enter the front door, followed by Tim Lewis, Henry Jackson, and three other Negro men, all in black coats and
white collars; they stopped in the hall. Cousin John
Semmes and Captain Corse were talking to Coriolanus
at the threshold; the old Negro wagged his head sorrowfully and turned again into the house.

Jane slipped her hand into mine and gazed at me out
of her doe-like eyes. I acknowledged to myself her protection. "We can't play," she had said to me that morning;
and I thought now she would never play again. For me she
had achieved that privacy of person which meant that she
was a woman, but marvelously different from other women
because she remained in my world where I could reach her:
as we sat on the high bed and my legs and feet grew numb

and her hand burned in mine, I was conscious of an even greater power than boyish love. It was a force that I could not and cannot now understand, and I see now as then I saw, there in the front parlor, the fury of Susan's glance, the astonished, mask-like trance of Semmes' gaze, and the extraordinary courtesy of his leading the child away. There are scenes that last a lifetime and remain the keys to the mystery of life: this was one of them but it survives for me through no act of understanding on my part, no judgment of motives. The meaning of what happens to us is never a phrase but lies rather in its own completeness, and the completion of that scene was the glimpse I had got of the presiding face of George Posey in the hall.

I have said that the big tester bed stood in the far corner of the room: by the head of the bed, where I could almost reach out and touch it, was a door leading into a small cabinet, my mother's dressing room. Nobody had been in it for two days. The door was open about an inch, and I rose to close it, but, my hand on the knob, I opened it wider, and turning to make sure that I was not observed by the old ladies, I looked at Jane. She got up and followed me through the door, which I closed without sound, and we were alone in the little room.

I stood a moment in the middle of the floor. A small mahogany dressing table filled the end of the narrow closet. A bracket on each side of the mirror held a candlestick, but the candles were missing, and a dirty yellow stalactite hung from each bracket. At the other end of the closet was a dresser; one of the drawers was half open and a piece of red silk spilled over upon the floor and partly covered a white satin slipper.

I had forgotten Jane and I was saying to myself that I had to go, I had to go, over and over, but I saw her standing against the wall by the door, her eyes wide and expressionless, her hands at her sides, and I said to myself, Son, I've got to go, Son, I've got to go, and I saw myself a big man in black broadcloth saying in a whisper to a lovely girl: I've got to do it, I've got to. I went to her and put my hand on her arm.

She moved her eyes to mine and I kissed her on the mouth but her face remained without expression, her arms limp, and I kissed her again, childishly without lingering, and said, "Jane, do you love me?" She looked at the floor. I came as near to her as I could, putting one arm around her, and as I kissed her cheek I laid my hand on her bosom. She said, "Don't, Lacy," but she turned her face to me and I kissed her again, and it was different. I was afraid of her as I was afraid of Lucy Sterrett, but I had done this thing myself and I could not break away from her as I could from Lucy. I had been driven into a fence corner and I had to jump over to the other side.

She said, "Do you want me to be your sweetheart, Lacy?"

"And never anybody else's," I said. She took a deep breath, and was leaning her forehead against my cheek, when the door opened.

My back was turned but I knew who it was. There was a pause, and Sister Susan closed the door behind her. At the sound of the door closing I left Jane and turned around. Jane was still standing against the wall, looking precisely as she had a few moments before, her liquid eyes fixed upon space and the ruffles of her pantalettes covering the tops of her red button shoes. Susan was looking at her with the cold compassion I had seen in her eyes when Semmes had led the child out of the parlor. Then she looked at me.

"Lacy, I want you to stay here. You come out in a minute." She took a step towards Jane.

In that strong, harassed face there was a flash of humor

as she said to both of us, or rather I think to nobody
really: "Excitement and propinquity!" She rearranged the
ribbons of Jane's bonnet and stepped back to inspect her.
"Jane, honey, you ought to have stayed at home."

Jane lowered her submissive eyes. "Yes'm," she said.
The luster of her face and the secrecy that I had sensed in
her body there on the bed fell away from her and she was
a child again. A tear ran down each cheek. "I want ma to
take me home." She recoiled from Susan and backed up
against the wall but Susan took her hand and led her to the
door where they went out without giving me a glance. The
door closed with a faint click of the latch.

I do not know what the emotion was that seized me. I
suddenly felt calm. I went to the half open drawer and
was about to open it all the way, when I took the slipper
from the floor and examined curiously the fine cross-
stitches worked by hand round its top. Still holding the
slipper I gathered up the end of the silk dress, which I
saw was a petticoat that mother had worn not a month ago,
and I buried my face in the folds and drew my breath from
the soft odors.

All this could not have lasted more than a few minutes,
yet it seemed a day and I wanted it to be longer, for at
the end, when I should get up from the floor, I knew obscurely there would be something that I did not want to
face. I was aware of my cold hands and my hands are cold,
now, after fifty years.

After fifty years I can do nothing about it nor could I
have done otherwise than I, a boy of fifteen, did then—
holding the end of a petticoat and a wrinkled slipper till
I desired to see Jane again so desperately that my hand
shook. I saw her standing over me, in these grown-up
clothes, the small feet in the satin slippers and an edge of
red below her hoops, but the hands were not hers, the

wide gold band on the long left ring-finger being too familiar; the delicate blue veins above the knuckles were on
my mother's hand. So my mother, I thought, had been like
that too, and I was terrified as the smell of the petticoat
blotted out the room.

*   *   *

In the chamber the ladies were on their feet. Jane was
standing between her mother and her aunt, Miss Milly
George, whose eyes could not focus upon you and whose
head jerked aimlessly, like a chicken pausing alertly between scratches. The only other people I could see were
Miss Ginnie and some ladies I either didn't know or knew
slightly. I knew what they were on their feet for, and panic
seized me lest I should miss it: in the home of my childhood I felt the dread of a small boy who has strayed away
at a carnival and is torn between fear of being lost and
desire to see what is there. The immense length of that
day has disembodied all its reality, and my mother had
been dead longer than I could imagine. I kept my eyes
upon Jane but she would not look at me and I burst into
tears of self-pity.

Miss Milly George twitched her nose and touched me
with her skinny hand. "I always say it's harder on chillun
than anybody, with their helplessness and all." But she
wasn't saying it to anyone. "Save your tears for the death
of your mother is what I always say."

That brought me around; I stared at her and I wondered where in her secret being she really was. Miss Ginnie had heard the remark.

"Well, Miss Gibson," she said, "that's just what he's
saved them for—the death of his poor mother." She pushed
me towards the door into the hall but we halted before a
group of men. Captain Corse came forward and shook

hands with Miss Ginnie, followed by my brothers: Charles spoke to no one but Semmes came over and asked the Posey ladies if they would come with him. There were many feet sounding in the hall and I caught the effortless penetration of Mr. McBean's Presbyterian voice rising above the low talk: "The Lord giveth and the Lord taketh away." At that moment Dr. Cartwright, the Episcopal rector, papa's spiritual adviser from the glebe near the Court House, stood in the door: the stiff reversed collar and the black pleated clerical shirt were correct enough, but I gazed at the round red face, the batting eyes, and the wide generous mouth of a pleasant worldling. He was papa's great friend—"the kind of pastor a gentleman can talk to." Papa liked Mr. McBean well enough and because of mother had given generously to his church, but he said that "McBean ought to carry a pillow around with him" because he was always ready to drop to his knees to start praying.

Dr. Cartwright looked over his shoulder, and papa appeared and came into the room on his arm. I have brought this scene into the mind's eye for many years, and I cannot believe that everybody there saw papa come in. Yet his quiet entrance had silenced them like a pistol shot. I started to run to him but something in his bearing forbade what at no other time would have been a liberty. I believe that not even God would have dared any familiarity with papa. I simply felt that this was not the time to ask for his sympathy by running to him, by reminding him of my own shaken self: his sympathy could not fail, and that was all the greater reason for not asking it then. Mr. Cartwright's arm was through his. Papa stood a little advanced, his free hand resting on the knob of his dress cane, an ebony stick gold-headed. His long black coat was wrinkled but he stood erect with all his six feet: as my eyes moved up his person I was startled by his almost snowy hair falling at the sides to his shoulders. It was only later that I knew the mystery of that surprise. I had not seen papa for the whole two years of that interminable day, and I had denied, no less than mother's life, his own, because I had allowed him just as much life as my excitement about Brother George would permit. He moved his head in the high choker collar and surveyed the room with calm gravity. The old gentleman was crushed but in his sorrow he knew what everybody else was feeling, and in his high innocence he required that they know it too and be as polite as he.

He turned his head to Mr. Cartwright, disengaged his arm, and walked slowly over to Miss Ginnie. He took her left hand and held it a moment, and bending over a little he kissed her on the forehead.

"Madam, I am obleeged to you for your kind offices," he said. Miss Ginnie, holding me a little closer to her and looking at papa with sad, intelligent eyes, said nothing. Papa moved his glance towards me. "Son, I've been looking for you. I haven't heard from you all day." He ran his long fingers through my hair, then took my hand and held it. He straightened up and surveyed the room as if he were a speaker greatly at his ease or alone in a room looking for a book that he had mislaid.

"I hope I have not neglected any of our friends," he said. He gazed about him, and, looking a little surprised, he bowed. "How-d'ye do, ma'm," he said to Mrs. Broadacre.

She came to him and putting her fingers on the hand that held the knob of the cane, lifted her face and pecked him on the cheek. "Major, you know Sally was my dearest friend. We just couldn't get here sooner. Henry was detained." She looked uneasy. "I think Henry is out in the yard."

"No, ma'm, he's been with me." Papa's eyes drooped and held a brief flicker of amusement. "He's been with me and he needed a little cheering up."

With a final glance at Mrs. Broadacre he turned his head and rested his gaze upon the Posey ladies. With deliberation he took a few steps and stood before Aunt Jane Anne. He held out his hand and she rose and timidly gave him hers.

"Mistress Posey, it was mighty brave of you ladies to undertake this long journey." He turned to Miss Milly George. "Miss Millicent, my respects to you too. I know Myra and Susan have arranged for you all to stay the night at least."

"I declare, major, you country folks are mighty kind and all. Mrs. Langton asked us to stay with her and all but we mustn't do that."

"Yes, Major Buchan," said Aunt Jane Anne, "that's so. We must get back to Georgetown. Why, there's nobody with the servants and you know how it is with servants in a town. Then there's Brother Jarman. He's been mighty poorly. I'm poorly too."

Her mouth was still open to speak, but she seemed unable to find the words. I had never seen Mr. Jarman Posey, George's uncle, and I believe that none of our family had seen him. He lived in the Posey house in a remote room and communicated with the family through the servants. Aunt Jane Anne's lips, still parted, fluttered a little, and a shy, injured expression shone in her gentle eyes. I glanced quickly at Brother Semmes. He was staring placidly at Aunt Jane Anne. I looked at Jane, and I could not look again at Semmes, but I wondered if he had noticed that neither of the Posey ladies had said a word about mother or had expressed any concern for papa's bereavement.

"Come here, child," papa said to Jane. "Come to your old uncle Lew."

Jane obediently came forward and papa bent over and kissed her ear. A few grains of dandruff fell from the white hair to his shoulders.

"She's a pretty young un," he said to Aunt Jane Anne. "A perfect little beauty — and she ain't so little, madam, now. It won't be long, it won't be long!"

Miss Milly George cocked her head. "I always say the child was Janie's afterthought. Why, Janie, you know you're old enough to be the child's grandmother and all. And all."

There was a scraping of feet on the bare floor, the first sound I had heard since papa entered the room. Papa smiled at Aunt Jane Anne while he addressed Miss Milly George.

"No, no, Miss Millicent, your sister is just old enough to be a dashing widow, a very dashing widow, ma'm," and he bowed to Aunt Jane Anne.

"Major," said Aunt Jane Anne, "it don't make any difference about the long journey." She looked gentle and weary, and I saw Miss Ginnie raise her eyebrows as if to say: Has she still got that on her mind? She went on: "We just felt so sorry for poor Susie and you know I do believe Susie herself felt sorrier for my George than she did for herself. George was mighty broken up, I tell you. Why, he —"

She took a deep breath and fell back into her chair, looking around her with startled eyes. Everybody was looking at her. Semmes was rubbing the side of his nose, looking covertly at papa.

I haven't seen our George today, ma'm," papa said. He turned and looked around him, and drawing his free hand to his breast he inclined his head and moved towards the door. He stopped half-way. He looked at me.

"Son, you will come with me." I went to him and he took my hand and led me out into the hall.

Now I felt nothing, yet the moment had come that all this waiting had been for, but it was lost in each new movement, each new step into our places in the melancholy procession. There was of course no one moment that it was all leading up to, and that piece of knowledge about life, learned that day, has permitted me to survive the disasters that overwhelmed other and better men, and to tell their story. Not even death was an instant; it too became a part of the ceaseless flow, instructing me to beware of fixing any hope, or some terrible lack of it, upon birth or death, or upon love or the giving in marriage. None of these could draw to itself all the life around it or even all the life in one person; not one of them but fell short of its occasion, warning us all to fear, not death, or love, or any ecstacy or calamity, but rather to fear our own expectancy of it, good or ill, or our own lack of preparation for these final things.

I had to learn this: papa, leading me by the hand into the yard to take his place at the rear of the coffin, behind the six Negro pallbearers, had no need to learn nor even to understand it, for to him there could have been nothing whatever to understand.

That was why, as we stood there, he could leave his place and go to old Lucy Lewis, who waited respectfully to one side, and take her brown hand to lead her into the line, and make her take her place ahead of us just behind the body of her mistress.

I looked about me, anxious to start, in the foolish delusion that people were looking at me. Over beyond the

garden, I saw Uncle Armistead walking towards the graveyard, leaning on his gnarled stick, his white beard and hair
blown by the breeze. The colored boy followed him,
stopped as his master stopped, at intervals, to rest, holding
in his hand his master's wide black hat.

Except Coriolanus the Negroes were stout men but they
had been holding their burden too long, and I saw Captain
Corse and Cousin John, who stood with the two ministers
in front of the coffin, look over our heads at the front
door. It seemed long but presently Brother Charles and his
Lucy came out and walking around the people near them
came to us, and waited behind papa. But Cousin John was
still looking at the door.

Near the door people were making way and Sister
Susan stood at the threshold, a black shawl gathered at the
neck, her head covered with a heavy black straw hat from
which fell a veil concealing her eyes and nose and mouth.
In the crowd on the porch she could not see us but at last
she lowered her head and came down the steps. The man
who came out of the door after her was not George Posey.
It was Brother Semmes.

Susan took papa's arm and I drew away and waited by
Semmes who stared at her back with his usual signs of
agitation, shifting from one foot to another and rubbing
his long, humorous nose.

Then the procession started, slowly at first and I suppose we kept a slow even pace for all the two hundred
yards up the ridge, past the garden wall, the abandoned
well, the gooseberry thicket, to the three big chestnut
trees and the low brick wall of the graveyard. We were
there so quickly I thought we must have flown. We followed the coffin through the open gate and stood before
a long wooden bench set for the immediate family before
the open grave. We sat down and looked straight ahead.
Our friends and cousins stood outside the graveyard along

the wall at our backs. The servants of the family and others from neighboring farms lined the wall to the right of the white people, forming a semi-circle around the burying.

I fixed my eye with careful concentration upon a glistening spade upon which Johnson, one of the grave diggers, was leaning by the big chestnut that shot up out of the graveyard beyond the grave; in the corner of my eye I saw Mr. Higgins, near the Negro, squatting and turning his hat round and round by its brim. His thin hair was neatly brushed over his high, flat forehead. Then I felt a hand on my shoulder.

It was Aunt Myra. She must have been delayed. Without looking I seemed to know that the bench was full: I was at one end by sister, so I got up and gave my place to my aunt, who said, "Thank you, honey," and sat down. I went towards the Negroes and sat upon the edge of a recumbent tomb, a big stone slab. There was another just like it by its side. Uncle Armistead was kneeling by it, his elbows resting upon it in the attitude of prayer. His boy sat on the wall.

I was aware that Mr. McBean's voice had been sounding and sounding — I didn't know when it had begun, and it went on and on. I was at the end of the tombstone and my eye ran down the inscription that Mr. McGovern had assigned to me as a punitive lesson earlier that year. I knew it by heart but like counting sheep in the middle of the night I spelt out every word, one after another:

MEMORI MARGARETAE NATAE FILIAE CORBIN
LEWIS GENEROSI ET UXORI FIDELI JOHANNI
BUCHAN MEDICI GENEROSI : ET NEPTIS
GEORGII WASHBURN DUCIS : AETERNITATE
AESTIMATA IN PACE REQUIESCAT INGENUA

BORN SPOTSYLVANIA COUNTY JUNE 3, 1754 O. S.
DIED FAIRFAX COUNTY DEC. 10, 1806 N. S.

Uncle Armistead suddenly said in a loud voice *A-men* but the interminable prayer continued into supplications for the divine mercy upon papa, sister, my brothers called by name, the servants, myself the motherless boy and at last the President of the United States who for some reason had suffered a loss. *A-men* muttered Uncle Armistead and I thought how easily the old gentleman keeps company with his father's grave. He leaned upon the slab as if it were the back of a pew. I raised my eyes to the six lugubrious pall-bearers lined up on the far side of the open grave. Coriolanus, his fingers interlaced, was nodding his bowed head.

A-a-men, shouted Mr. McBean in a minor key, and there was a faint shuffle in the crowd as he retired a few steps to the rear, the flesh round his high, lean cheekbones flushed from his exertion. Dr. Cartwright advanced to the end of the coffin, his fat forefinger marking a place in his prayer-book. His placid gaze ranged over the congregation; he dropped his eyes as if for a moment of silent prayer.

I looked again at Uncle Armistead: he was wiping his face with a coarse linen handkerchief, his eyes, old and vague, lifted towards Dr. Cartwright. I thought it remarkable that he and I, a nephew young enough to be his great-grandson, should be bound back, should be held in *religion* as I should say it now, to the long message of the dead. He prayed upon his father's tomb and I malingered stupidly upon his mother's grave. I found myself tracing the branches on the Tree of Life at the top of a small upright stone: the fine lines of foliage swayed over to one side in mournful abandon, stylized and looking like well-brushed hair.

> Ah lovely appearance of death
> No sight upon earth is so fair

> Not all the gay pageants that breathe
> Can with dear Molly compare

Molly Buchan, the sister I had been born too late to see, dead of a cold draft. A strip of damp lichen covered the third verse but I knew it all by rote, knew that papa had composed the lines and had stood over Henry Jackson telling him how to chisel the letters upon the freestone. . . . Why did Dr. Cartwright talk differently from Mr. McBean? His words were different, he seemed to be just a voice, in the *ore rotundo* of impersonality, no feeling but in the words themselves. I stared at his round face.

"Behold I shew you a mystery: we shall not all sleep, but we shall all be changed, in a moment, in the twinkling of an eye, at the last trump; for the trumpet shall sound and the dead shall be raised incorruptible . . ." There was a woodpecker at his work high in the chestnut tree. I lowered my face into my hands . . . "For this corruption must put on incorruption and this mortal shall have put on immortality . . ."

In the silence the woodpecker savagely jabbed the high limb, rapidly like a riveting hammer, as Mr. McBean came forward and said we should now sing Rock of Ages. A wavering cry went up and the Negro men, three on each side of the grave, tugged at the ropes and the coffin began its perilous descent. I saw the black edge sink below the clods as the hymn ended, and the Negro men toss the rope-ends into the grave and stand back in respectful postures. A long thin note hung in the air, *Let me hide myself in thee,* and the two grave-diggers, their black arms bare and glistening, came forward and with rapid, sure scoops turned the rusting earth back into the grave. I heard with wonder the crash of the first clods, then, as the work went on, the muffled thud of earth upon earth.

Then they stood away from their work, and old Coriolanus came forward with a flowery pall and carefully fitted it over the mound. When he had risen, papa rose and went to him and took him by the hand and with his left hand touched the old Negro's shoulder. He turned back to face the family, his lips softly compressed; the family got up from the bench and followed him out through the gate between the rows of relations and friends, and the procession returned upon itself, whither it had begun.

I was at Aunt Myra's side, but when we came opposite the garden I broke away and getting out of sight behind the garden I ran to the back of the house in order to be there first. On the lower back gallery at the door into the back hall, I stopped. What had I been running for? I pushed the door open and tip-toed through the hall to the door of the chamber, which was open, ran in and, reaching behind the door, picked up the old strap. As I got up I was startled. Old Mrs. Gunnell sat in mother's chair, her eyes closed; a fly was running up and down her nose. I held my breath. She moved her head and with relief I stuffed the strap into my pants pocket and went quietly out into the hall.

I looked into the hollow front parlor but avoided it. I went through the hall to the door into the back parlor. It was open, and directly across the room lay Mr. Broadacre on the long horsehair sofa, breathing stertorously, one hand dangling limp upon the bare boards. Sniffing, I caught the fumes at that distance. I entered the room.

George Posey was standing in the far corner by the window, looking towards the garden at the returning mourners. Outside the sun was high on the trees and the room was a soft shadow in which I could see the handsome profile of my brother against the fading light of the window. He had not seen me; so I touched a chair, shoving it gently a few inches upon the floor.

He turned his head and stared at me inquiringly. I waited for him to speak but he said nothing, only stared, and I wanted to leave him but I could not. I fingered the back of the chair.

"Well, you came back, didn't you, Brother George?" I couldn't help it, it was not malice; yet the devil moved my tongue.

His eyes narrowed. "Yes, I came back." He turned again to the window. He put his thumb under his chin and without looking at me or moving in the least he said, "I can't even remember their names." He turned to me once more. "I meet them but I don't know who they are," he said with a rising voice. "And by God they'll all starve to death, that's what they'll do. They do nothing but die and marry and think about the honor of Virginia." He rammed his hands into his pockets and shouted: "I want to be thrown to the hogs. I tell you I want to be thrown to the hogs!"

Mr. Broadacre suddenly sat up and rubbed his eyes. "Has somebody been speaking?" he said.

Brother George gave him a swift glance, then said to me: "Come here, Lacy." I went to him and looking into his face, which had been dim from across the room, I saw in it what can only be called fear.

"Lacy," he said in a whisper, "I am not well today. I tried to go through with it, I tried. But I couldn't." He said to me what he had said so many times, but this time without the smile, and his face was white. "You're my friend, Lacy boy."

I heard the sound of a stick on the floor. Uncle Armistead, his hat on his head, stood in the door.

"Hanh?" he said. He looked at Mr. Broadacre. "Aye God, I told Susie I wa'n't going to sleep in no upstairs room." He squinted his weak eyes at Mr. Broadacre. "Now ain't that a cur'ous thing. I thought that janetleman was Lew." He blinked his eyes at Brother George. "Who's that, son?" he said to me.

"He's Brother George," I shouted. "You know, Uncle Armistead, Susie's husband."

"Hanh?" he said. "George you say. Hanh? Had a Nigger named George once. Best Nigger I ever had. Died of cholera." He went to the sofa, and bowing to Mr. Broadacre, sat down by him. He sighed. "He means George Posey, I reckon. Old Rozier's boy. Well, Rozier Posey ain't been dead longer'n he needs to be." He laughed a thin cackle.

I shouted in his ear: "George is in this room, Uncle Armistead."

"Hanh?" he said.

Cousin John came in and glancing at George, turned his back and went to the other window by the sofa. Then I saw papa.

He surveyed the room and I noticed that his eyes rested an instant longer upon Brother George than upon anybody else. He walked to the fireplace and placing his cane in the ingle, turned round.

"Henry," he said to Mr. Broadacre, "you're feeling better but you're feeling none too well. You and your lady are staying for supper. Now don't discuss it."

He was about to sit down; his hands were on the arms of his chair; but he pushed himself up again. Without looking at Brother George, who was still at the window where the twilight was shutting out our world, papa went to the high mantel and striking a match in the back of the cold fireplace, lit a candle. He held the match burning with an oily blue flame, then tossed it into the fireplace. I smelt the sulphur. He looked up at the candle and turned away, and went over to Brother George.

"Son, I am glad to see you," he said. He extended his hand and I thought it would stay there, stretched out, forever, but at last George swiftly and awkwardly put out his hand, and the two men faced each other a long instant.

The candlelight was at papa's back but it shone full and fitfully upon Brother George's face which was white and sullen. I could not see papa's face. Brother George lowered his eyes, then raised them towards me in an unseeing stare. Papa withdrew his hand and returned to his chair, into which he dropped heavily, like a sack of bran, and sat with a meditative bow of the head. Cousin John still gazed into the rising night. Mr. Broadacre was cutting a quid from a long, dark plug. Uncle Armistead's head was in his beard and his nose vibrated with sleep.

"Lacy," papa said, "you're through school for the year, but you'll construe a little with me every day." He took his snuffbox out of his waistcoat pocket, and opening it on the palm of his hand lifted a pinch to his nose, and sneezed.

Cousin John looked at him, smiled to himself, and shook his head. Papa sat up straight.

"Henry —" but Mr. Broadacre was asleep, his mouth open and the quid a small knot in his cheek. Papa tapped the arm of his chair with his long, hairy forefinger. I started for the door.

There was Uncle Armistead's Negro. Seeing me he backed into the dark hall. He whispered, and I returned to the threshold.

"Brother George," I said in a loud voice beyond control, "Aunt Jane Anne wants to see you. She's in ma's room."

He bolted from the window like a runner who has heard the starting shot, but when he reached the door he turned to papa, his right hand lifted before him in an unfinished gesture. Without a word he backed into the hall and was gone.

Papa looked at me as he rubbed his chin.

"Son," he said, "bring me your Ovid in the morning." He motioned me to him with the long finger. I stood by the arm of his chair. "Good night, son," he said and pulled me down and kissed my cheek. He squeezed my arm. "Good night."

"Good night, papa." I walked carefully out of the room.

In the front hall there was subdued, rapid conversation, and quick footsteps. Through the moving figures I saw Coriolanus standing in the open door, a lighted lantern in his hand, and beyond him the pinched face of Blind Joe, who held in his hand Brother George's silver spurs.

I stood by the newel-post and presently Aunt Jane Anne and Miss Milly George, followed by Jane with her perpetually downcast eyes, came from mother's room into the hall. Aunt Jane Anne seemed so little to be in those enormous skirts. Her shawl was tied over her black bonnet and, but for the color, she might have been Little Red Riding Hood timidly hoping that she might soon encounter a wolf. Miss Milly George, the taller by two heads, looked round her suspiciously but suspicious of what I could not see. Jane stood behind her and I could not see her at all.

"Janie, we better hurry up, it's so far and all. George better hurry."

"Where's George?" said Aunt Jane Anne. "George!" she called in her gentle voice.

Brother George came out of the void of the front parlor and, back in the shadows, I saw Susan menaced by the dark, a specter in cloak and bonnet.

"We're ready," George said to his mother. "Susan is going too," and the corners of his mouth drew up in a half-smile. He was standing perfectly erect. His face hardened. "Damn you, Joe, where are you?" Rabbit-eyed Joe came into the hall and as he fastened the spurs to his master's boots, Sister Susan came to me and embracing me, said: "Tell papa, I can't help it. I have to go." She saw the other ladies going out to the gallery and she followed. I saw her reach out in a gesture towards Jane, but she withdrew her hand and rapidly put on her gloves.

Cousin John passed me and stood with the ladies outside the door. He offered his elbow to Aunt Jane Anne. "Allow me, madam," he said. They went down the steps.

Brother Semmes appeared out of the dark yard and tried to give his arm to Miss Milly George. "Humph," she said. "I never saw the time I needed a man. Come here to me, Jane."

But Jane did not move. Miss Milly George pinched the sides of her skirts and marched down the steps. Semmes held out his hand to Jane but she ignored it, or did not see it, and he reached for her hand and holding it gallantly high he led her down the steps. Her arms and hand were stiff and she walked as if she were going to break in two. She had not looked at me at all. Coriolanus was holding the yellow light at the open door, and the Posey ladies disappeared into the carriage.

I followed Brother George to the threshold. He stopped and put his hand upon my head.

"You're my friend, Lacy boy. Don't get into any meanness." He threw back his head and laughed, and then gave his arm to Susan; together they went down the steps.

Cousin John was looking through the pale light at Semmes and I followed his gaze. Semmes' eyes were fixed upon Susan in terrible amazement and his mouth hung open as if he had stepped barefoot upon a stingaree. I knew then he had not seen her on the gallery. She spoke to him, looking away: "Good-by, Semmes," and got into the carriage.

George slammed the carriage door and held out his hand to Semmes who took it without change of his amazed expression. George laughed.

"We'll be looking for you," he said. "I reckon you'll be cutting up your cadavers again this time next week. We'll be looking for you."

Cousin John turned his back upon him and mounted the gallery steps, standing by me, his arm round my shoulders.

"It's been a day," he said.

Together we watched Brother George vault into the saddle and saw the toss of the bay mare's head as she cantered off towards the cedared lane that we could not see. The carriage followed beyond the ring of Coriolanus' yellow light as we heard the darkness take all but the hooves and the creaking springs. The old Negro disappeared round the end of the house. I saw him no more that day.

"It ain't over yet," said Cousin John. The bracket lamp from the hall lit the oily gray hair hanging in strings about his tall collar. "He's a cur'ous fellow. Semmes thinks he understands him but he don't, any better'n we do." He studied my face. "You better come in the house." He went in and on down the hall where I heard him close the back parlor door.

But Cousin John doesn't know everything, I thought, seeing again Brother Semmes' face by the coffin and Jane's luster, the silk slipper on the floor and then, fearfully, Susan withdrawing her hand from Jane into the glove. What did she want me to tell papa? What was there to tell? That was the way those things stood with us in the

April of 1860, at the death of my mother, and I ran
down the steps and around the house in the dark, and sat
down where Jane had sat, on the big root of the sugar
tree.

Part II

THE CRISIS

THE next winter Cousin John Semmes went to Washington to live, and we stayed in his house in Alexandria, a tall three-storey red brick, on Fairfax Street near Duke in the same block with the Presbyterian Meeting House. From the top of the house where my room was, I could see over the roofs on bright days far up the river into Washington, six miles as the crow flies: the unfinished dome of the Capitol, the truncated obelisk which later became the Washington monument, and off to the right a little, the flagpole in the White House yard from which I could see, if there was a strong landward breeze, the fluttering American flag.

Whether my mother's death had matured me, or whether the long year that had gone by since her death, bringing me to the next twenty-third of May, had enlarged my observation, I do not know. But from that day, the twenty-third of May, 1861, I count myself a man, from the time I was only sixteen. And from that twenty-third of May to the twilight of July twenty-first, just two of the eight hundred and forty months of the Biblical span of life, I witnessed an accumulation of disasters that brought about in our lives changes that would otherwise have taken two generations.

I mark the beginning of my maturity with a scene, and

another marks its completion, and you will understand that
neither of them properly speaking was an experience of
my own, but rather something sheer, out of the world,
easier to bring back than the miseries and ecstasies of my
own life. To this day I can see without effort the dark
mustache of dead Mr. Jackson lying in Colonel Ellsworth's blood, the two bloods mingling there at the foot of
the stairs; Colonel Ellsworth the first and Mr. Jackson,
papa's friend, the second to fall, of the many thousands that
were soon gone.

That was the beginning. I knew I was a man when
Brother George at dusk of July twenty-first opened the
carpetbag and took out the black suit to change his clothes.

*   *   *

Even now as I lie awake early in the morning I can
bring back the sounds of that winter: old Lucy Lewis going out of the garden gate with a click, just before day,
with her basket to meet the huckster who cried his winter
vegetables into our sleep — cabbages and cauliflower, old
potatoes, onions and leeks — and the man geeing his yoke
of oxen to turn them up Duke Street. If it was cold I
would pull the covers over my eyes and count from the
last bump of the cart on the cobblestones to the first sound
of Henry Jackson's feet on the stairs. Henry tapped on the
door with his knuckle and came in and set the coal scuttle
on the hearth, and began laying the fire. I listened then for
another sound — papa shaking down the ashes in his grate
far downstairs. He would not let Henry or Coriolanus
make his fire and I am not sure that he gave orders that
mine be made; Henry, in town, had little to do, but being
a fine Negro — papa said of Coromantee stock, the best
African tribe — he was scrupulous to the last degree and
could not bear idleness. Henry got up from the grate, the

scuttle full of ashes in his hand, and without looking towards my bed always said, "Major say git up." And then
he was gone.

I knew that papa had not said anything of the kind: it
was only Henry's appeal to an authority that he was sure
would sustain him. Then the rising-bell sounded and I
heard Aunt Myra come out of the bedroom under my room
and go down the stairs, two steps and a pause, two steps
and a pause, for her rheumatism, until the parlor door
clicked behind her. I leaped from the bed, drew on my
Osnaburgs, dashed my face into the cold water, and was
dressed with the speed of a soldier. Because the halls were
empty I knew it was safe for me to slide down the banisters,
and large as I was I always did it.

Our habits are hard to remember. Perhaps it is only a
special thing, a slight alteration of our daily routine on
one morning of that winter that brings back the scene of
our morning prayers.

When I came into the parlor that morning — it was late
in January — all the family were there, in their places: all,
that is, but Brother Charles, who seldom came, and Lucy,
who never joined us but lay abed until nine and never
showed herself until dinner-time, which in those days was
at two o'clock. Papa stood with his back to the cold fireplace, in a long dressing gown and carpet slippers, holding the Prayer Book in his left hand, his long forefinger
marking the place. But for the life of me I can't remember
whether Coriolanus always stood where I saw him that
morning, to one side of papa, like him facing the room,
but turned a little towards the servants, as if he were papa's
deacon appointed to represent the divine interests of his
race. There were Lucy Lewis, Henry Jackson, and the free
Negress Lucinda, the cook, whom I did not like, but who
was there because Juniper, our old cook at Pleasant Hill,

had begged papa not to bring her to town, and of course papa, who never yielded a point of discipline, always gave in to human feeling, and he let her stay.

There was another thing that morning: Brother Charles came in and joined us as we were kneeling, or rather just as papa lowered his bulk on one knee upon the ottoman placed there for him. Brother Charles closed the door softly and knelt just inside. I am sure that Aunt Myra saw him, but she went through her set speech anyhow: "Brother Lewis, my stiffness prevents the appropriate attitude of devotion," she said sliding forward in her chair and bowing her head. But papa still looked at her expectantly for the rest of her speech, which we all knew was coming. "And you must excuse our dear Lucy, she can't be with us this morning." She had never been with us, but Aunt Myra made her persistent neglect of family prayers a daily exception and a daily reproach. From where I knelt on the far side of Aunt Myra I glanced at Brother Charles' face: it did not change, and if there was no resentment in it there was no humor either.

Charles, of course, had made Lucy come over to live in Alexandria on account of our late bereavement. Sister Susan could not leave her husband and infant, and Brother Semmes had resumed his medical studies and only rode over from Washington every fortnight or so to see how papa was. But Lucy had come with bad grace. She had lived for two years amid the official society of the capital city, and I suppose it had turned her head. Lucy's people were like ours in every respect, and I am sure I must have met some of them in my childhood, but before her connection with our family I saw no reason to observe them, and they made on me the anonymous impression that miscellaneous grown persons leave upon the mind of a child. But she was distinctly, as the country phrase went, above her raisin', and she looked upon us, upon papa particularly, as old-fashioned and provincial.

Once papa asked her if she had seen the Lacys, distant kin of ours in Washington, and she replied that she had not—that "they are not in society." And papa had said in his innocent way: "What is that? Never heard of it."

It was Brother Charles of course who, by coming over to live with us, had made the sacrifice, but from Lucy we heard nothing of that. Charles had to ride horseback eight miles to General Scott's office in Washington every morning where as a staff-officer he wrote letters and orders for "old Fuss and Feathers," as the young men in the army called the old hero. But Charles once remarked, with his own kind of innocence, that he liked it, that in Alexandria he saw a great deal more of even Susan than he had when he and Lucy were in Washington just a couple of miles from Vista Avenue in Georgetown where the Poseys lived. Susan and Lucy moved in different sets, Lucy having decided that the fashionable official life of the city comported ill with the simpler ways of her own kin; and she held a small "levee" one afternoon every week to which foreign attachés and army officers came, as well as litterateurs and journalists—among these a young man to be better known later, Henry Adams, a great snob even then, who got on Charles' nerves by pretending friendship with Rooney Lee, the colonel's son, having been with him at Harvard, and yet ridiculing him for his lack of learning. I had always thought of papa as an educated man, but Lucy didn't, and this matter of education, for her, came down to knowing things very quickly and, I suppose, just idle curiosity. Even then she must have been thinking of Charles as a dull fellow with merely correct manners who constantly confused people and disconcerted her by asking acquaintances to "look in upon us this evening"—by which he meant of course Lucy's afternoon tea; and people from the North would turn up at nine o'clock when Lucy had other engagements.

Although Lucy had set up as a minor hostess and considered her teas the scene of smart gatherings where bright worldly talk glittered over the cups, I wondered later what the poor girl found to talk about, but I never knew; we were never there, not even Susan; and I think Lucy and Susan met only once in Washington, at a wedding that had been for weeks the talk of the town and even of the surrounding towns like Alexandria which had sent their share of the wedding guests. The daughter of a rich wholesale grocer, a Miss Barker, was being married on December twentieth — the date became a landmark for another reason — and the reception was one of the few occasions on which the local society mingled with the official. The groom was a young naval officer and the bride came of a family originally of Fairfax but then of long residence in the capital. Her older sister had been a friend of Susan's, and that is why, I suppose, Susan was at the wedding; I do not know whether Brother George went, but I suppose he did, for Cousin John Semmes next day reported to papa a remark that George must have made at the wedding: "The damned old fool ought to reduce Charleston to ashes!" The damned old fool was President Buchanan.

It was after the ceremony, and the refreshments were being passed at the reception, when a group of young gentlemen headed by Mr. Lawrence Keitt of South Carolina literally burst into the front door. They were so headlong that it was said Mr. Keitt rushed into the front parlor unannounced, waving his hat, and subdued himself only when he saw in the back parlor the Presidential party, Mr. Buchanan and his niece Miss Harriet Lane; and even then his excitement impelled him to march into "the presence," and, commanding the attention of the entire room, bowed and said in his best platform manner: "Mr. President, ladies and gentlemen, I take great pleasure in announcing to you that the people of South Carolina have this day in convention assembled passed an ordinance of secession, severing the political ties that once existed between that sovereign State and the Government of the United States."

Susan said that he was about to continue, but applause from the front parlor arrested him, and when it had died away the occasion for further oratory had passed. All eyes were on the President, who was breathing heavily, his face flushed and his hands shaking; after the briefest adieus to his host and hostess he went to his carriage, and people feared that before he reached the White House he would succumb to a stroke.

It was then that George had made his remark, and from that day on the atmosphere of Washington was never the same, and the lives of even quiet people like us, in Alexandria, became expectant, we knew not of what. I only remember, of those early days of the struggle, that papa felt South Carolina ought to be suppressed but was astonished when Cousin John told him what George Posey had said. As it came out later and as I shall explain in the proper place, papa wished to see the cotton people brought to their senses, but he could not at that time make up his mind to let any of the known agencies of suppression, like the Executive department of the government, do the work.

For a month after that exciting time, a month in which events came headlong one after another, I began to observe my father more closely than ever, but to no conclusion: what I say here about the inward strain that I soon detected in his kindly old eyes is partly after-knowledge. The first time he gave warning of some unusual anxiety was on that perfectly commonplace morning during family prayers. I do not mean to say that he had not, in the month since the secession of South Carolina, spent most of his time at the newspapers, or in conversation with the citizens of Alexandria, to say nothing of his long talks with Cousin John Semmes when Cousin John came over on a Sunday. I never heard any of these talks and I only remember a remark Cousin John made to me one day after dinner: "Your pa is still living before he was born—in 1789. He thinks the government is a group of high-minded gentlemen who are trying to yield everything to one another. Damn it, Lacy, it's just men like your pa who are the glory of the Old Dominion, and the surest proof of her greatness, that are going to ruin us. They can't understand that reason and moderation haven't anything to do with the crisis. They won't let themselves see what's going on. Aye God, they'll see when Federal troops march through the State on the way to South Carolina!" But I didn't know what he was talking about, and remembered that he and papa had never agreed in politics. I let it go at that.

That morning in the front parlor it was so cold that I had to blow my fingers to keep them warm: Charles' horse, tied outside to the horseblock, stamped on the cobblestones. But papa pushed his spectacles up on the bridge of his nose and said, "We will repeat the Lord's Prayer."

And I didn't fix my mind upon it, but let it wander, so that when it was over and papa had begun to read, not from the Psalter for that day but the ordinary morning prayer, I did not notice the transition, for I could have said it by heart too. Suddenly I knew something was wrong, for Aunt Myra raised her head and opened her eyes, looking straight at papa, then lowered her glance. For when papa had read, "We thy needy creatures, render thee our humble praises for thy preservation of us from the beginning of our lives to this day," he should have continued, "Having delivered us from the dangers of the watchful Providence we owe it, that no disturbance hath come nigh our dwelling; but that we are brought to safety to the beginning of this day." But he read the alternative version: "That *notwithstanding our dangers* we are brought in safety," and so on. It was the version provided in the margin, in fine type, for the threat of calamity to the family, and even Charles as he rose to his feet and drew on his gloves looked alarmed, standing there by the door so long that papa disappeared into the back parlor before he could say his usual good-by.

I had heard papa say the day before that on the morrow Senator Davis by announcement would address the Senate in farewell, and I knew he felt that the last hope of public reconciliation was gone. But was that the real trouble? Was there something else? I cannot to this day decide just how papa looked at it: whether in his mind the domestic trials, growing out of my mother's death, were one thing, and the public crisis another. Nor can I decide in my own mind whether it was possible to distinguish the two—they worked together for a single evil, and I think the evil was the more overwhelming among us because of the way men had of seeing themselves at that time: as in all highly developed societies the line marking off the domestic from the public life was indistinct. Our domestic manners and satisfactions were as impersonal as the United States Navy, and the belief widely held today, that men may live apart from the political order, that indeed the only humane and honorable satisfactions must be gained in spite of the public order, would have astonished most men of that time as a remote fantasy, impossible of realization.

Notwithstanding our dangers, papa began that 19th day of January, 1861, as if it were like all days. For after the family had scattered — Aunt Myra to the kitchen with her keys to dispense the food for the day, Brother Charles to his duty, and the servants to the rear of the house — I went into the back parlor for the private ceremony that papa had established between us when I had entered the Academy the autumn before. He sat to the left of the fireplace in his favorite chair, the old Windsor that he had brought in from Pleasant Hill, the fire-screen shielding his face from the blaze, and his snuffbox in his hand for his first morning sneeze. As I came in he laid the box on the small table by his chair, rose to his feet, and as I stood before him he leaned over and kissed me on the forehead. Then he shook hands as he said, "God bless you, my son, in your labors of this day."

"God bless you, papa," I said. And I went quickly out of the room as papa resumed his seat and Coriolanus busied himself with a feather-duster about the fireplace.

On Saturdays I saw the two old gentlemen together in the morning, as they must have been every morning in the week. Papa would seat himself with his paper or a book, or would go over to the secretary on the other side of the fire to write his letters while Coriolanus dusted the room, set the chairs in order, and, if papa was writing, raised the Venetian blinds a little to let more light in. When this work was finished — it took only a few minutes — papa would glance up from his reading over the rims of his steel spectacles, and say, "Well, Coriolanus, your labors must have fatigued you. You'd better rest a little."

Coriolanus sat down in a small straight chair near the

hearth, but he would not have done it had the "major" not punctiliously invited him every morning. He let his head fall on his chest, and dozed with the feather-duster in his hand, as papa continued reading. In this way the two old friends enjoyed each other's company.

But this winter papa had visitors, especially after the 19th of January when not only had Mr. Davis resigned from the Senate and gone back to Mississippi, but the State of Georgia had seceded, making the states out of the Union a solid block from the Atlantic to the Mississippi River.

One Sunday afternoon early in February a group of gentlemen drove down Fairfax Street in an open carriage, and I was mildly astonished, looking out of my high window, to see them draw up at our door. The first man to alight even from that distance I recognized as Mr. John Minor Botts, a Virginia politician, portly and consequential, whose countenance nowise belied his reputation for partisanship and vituperation: his heavy features were fixed in perpetual anger. I did not know the other men, and I did not know what the visit portended, but I knew it was politics of some kind; so I ran downstairs in time to see papa greet them and usher them into the back parlor. I stood irresolute in the door and papa, seeing me, said, "Come in, son," and then to the visitors, "This is my son Lacy, gentlemen." I clicked my heels and bowed and walked quickly to the back of the room and stood by a window with my eyes fixed upon the churchyard's familiar scene.

They were all politicians, and I wondered if Cousin John, if he hadn't been kin, would have seemed like them. Two of the men I looked at narrowly, although I was never to see them again. They both had black beards covering their entire faces, clipped close and unfamiliarly neat. These men were from the North. They spoke briskly, without warmth, and yet there was something personal in their demeanors, and I noticed that when either of them spoke papa leaned forward and looked him gravely in the face — I thought in order to catch every word; for I could understand only about half of what they said. But who could remember a conversation like that, after so many years? I recall chiefly the impatient emphasis of Mr. Botts, who broke in to correct his Northern allies. "No, no! We are Union men, but you must remember that our Union sentiment is different from yours; it must be treated gently. I believe, gentlemen, whatever the State may do eventually, we can keep northern Virginia for the Union, but we must be careful!"

On the way out, the taller of the two Northerners paused at the door and as he shook hands with papa he said, "Major, I am delighted to find so many of *our* people down here." I can't remember if papa said anything, but I wish he had; it would have given me some idea of the future, of what he intended to do. I knew that papa was a strong Unionist, and had refused to attend Secession meetings in Alexandria in which Cousin John was a leader. I don't know whether papa caught the slight emphasis that the Northern gentleman put on *our:* as I thought about it I began to hear a certain unction in the echo of that one syllable, "*our* people," but if papa felt anything of the kind he took it innocently, as if it meant only people of the same politics. I am sure that the Northerner meant something else, some sympathy beyond political belief — for such, I learned later, was the mysterious power of the idea of Union among people in the North.

I suppose the talk had been about the Peace Convention that a few days before ex-President Tyler had called in Washington to meet on the very day the Confederate

Government had been organized in Montgomery, Alabama. Montgomery was only a name and the Confederate Government did not, for me, exist. At that time I had not been in Richmond and seen Mr. Jefferson's replica of the Maison Carrée—the Virginia Capitol; so the only government I knew was the collection of buildings that straggled from the Capitol to the White House, some classical, others paste-board Gothic—for that was the flimsy look they had at a distance. But it was a "government," and it was in the South, and it had been set up by Virginians: it was my distinct impression until manhood and education effaced it, that God was a Virginian who had created the world in his own image. It followed that the Government was ours too. That was the illusion of a boy, but men felt it too, with what dire consequences to their equanimity the next few months were to show: it made hard the choice of allegiance among people on both sides of the Potomac. And as for Montgomery, it was far away, more than a thousand miles, and while it was in the South, it was not Virginia, and we habitually spoke of all that country beyond the mountains, from Minnesota to the Gulf, as the "West."

The visiting politicians had been particular to inquire about the probable sentiment of our old neighborhood towards Mr. Tyler's Convention. Papa had assured them of the support of a typical community of that locality. The Convention in fact was a gesture quite after his own heart: he saw no reason why intelligent men should not meet from all parts of "our country" and compose their differences.

So the irrepressible conflict gathered in fury into April: the Peace Convention had failed; Abraham Lincoln had been inaugurated but had done nothing; the People of Virginia were in constant Convention in Richmond, behind closed doors, but the Union men still had the upper hand; and there were many persons like papa who believed that the Cotton States would be allowed to make good their separation, and relieve the "border" of the responsibility of making a decision. Only Cousin John Semmes kept saying that, by God, it was nonsense. And then one day that will never fade from my memory we heard boys shouting in the street, "Extra! Extra! Fort Sumter bombarded!" Papa sent me out into the street to get a paper, and just as I was turning back into the house I saw up Fairfax Street a company of soldiers: they were marching up King, and as I stood there the file-closers disappeared from sight. They were the Alexandria Rifles, an old military company that papa had fought with in 1812. But it was only their drill day; they were going out to a field west of town.

I was about to close the front door when I heard a voice: "Lacy, Lacy! Here we are!"

It was the voice of Brother Semmes. A carriage had pulled up in front of the house. In it were Semmes and Susan, and the colored nurse with little Jane. I went back to the sidewalk to be embraced. Susan patted my cheek, and I touched little Jane's hand.

"Well," said Semmes, looking at the copy of the *Gazette* in my hand. "I reckon you've heard the news." He looked at me with mock severity: "When do you start fighting?"

Before I could say anything Brother George had come up on the bay mare, and had leaped from the saddle. He came directly to me and put his hand on my head. He never shook hands with me. He rumpled my hair.

"You're my friend, Lacy boy!" He smiled and I smiled back at him as Semmes and Susan led the way into the house.

*   *   *

Memory is all chance, and I have learned that you remember things not because they are important; you remember the important things because they help you to fix in mind the trifles of your early life, or the trifles simply drag along with them through many years the incidents that have altered your fortunes. I suppose it was important for me to know some time that winter that Brother George controlled our family property, and had controlled it for nearly a year. When I knew this clearly I do not know, and cannot recover the gradual awareness of the fact. Doubtless it began the day of my mother's death, with Semmes' remark about "papa merely thinking those Negroes were free" — meaning Jack Lewis and his family, whom papa had certainly sent to Alexandria with manumission papers that were to be executed by Brother George. I suppose I had thought of the old horse papa had given Jack Lewis as getting his freedom at the same time.

But Brother George had sold the whole family to a dealer from Georgia — that I learned that winter from Charles, who dropped it casually, like a secret too old to be any longer kept hidden: had sold them, doubtless the horse too, and applied the couple of thousand dollars to papa's debt at a bank in Alexandria. I could not tell whether papa knew it, but everybody else in the family knew, and took sides — Cousin John Semmes against George, saying it was "a piece of damned impertinence for George Posey to mind Lew's business for him"; Brother Semmes for George, for reasons that I cannot explain but in the course of this narrative shall hope to elucidate; and Brother Charles was for him too, after some persuasion on the part of his wife. Lucy said that it was only right for George to protect the heirs by keeping the estate solvent, or words to that effect; if Lucy was ignorant of business she had a strong instinct about it. I took no sides; I learned about it

so gradually, and I was so young, that when I knew everything it was too late to judge it, and there was too much to
be said on both sides. Semmes always justified George by
saying that if papa realized that the Negroes were uselessly
eating away his substance, it was better to sell a few than to
drift into bankruptcy, which would compel him to sell
them all under the hammer. And who can say that he was
not right?

I have never been able to say to myself that George
Posey, that remarkable fellow, was not right about everything, even to the point of rectitude. I never knew him to
do a selfish thing; there were only things, like following
the family to my mother's grave, that he could not do. And
who, after that moment, could blame him for that, without
at the same time acknowledging the disinterested concern
for the welfare of us all? He cared nothing for money: if
he did, why did he give it away or spend it so lavishly?
He thought nothing of spending a hundred dollars to
charter a little steamboat to take a large party for an out-
ing at Arlington spring. People had gone there for years
at Mr. Custis' invitation; now that he was dead Colonel
Lee extended the same hospitality, only he could not send
the old Negro fiddler to entertain the company, for the fiddler, like his master, was dead too.

Some time in the summer of 1860 it had been arranged:
papa was nearly sixty-five years old, and upon representations from Brother Charles, as the eldest son, some sort of
deed of trust was given to George Posey for all the landed
property, including, besides Pleasant Hill, some two thousand "undeveloped" acres of my mother's in one of the
western counties; this put great responsibility upon
George, but it did not tax his generosity. He immediately
paid to Charles and Semmes the money equivalent to their
shares, about fifteen thousand dollars apiece, and they

signed over to him their interests in the estate. George paid
them more than the market value of the land, which was
getting lower rather than higher in our county every year.
Would he ever get his money back? Cousin John Semmes
seemed never to consider this, and as I see it now he failed
to consider it for the same reason that George was willing
to risk a loss. They were both disinterested and set in
their ideas, and the ideas clashed. Cousin John resented the
plan because it meant the breaking up of the Buchan
estate; but that meant nothing to George Posey. I think
he was convinced that it would break up sooner or later.
He would never carry on the life at Pleasant Hill; Lucy
would never permit Charles to do it; Semmes was unmarried; and I was a boy. Was he not acting in our interest?
Was he not protecting us from the consequences of our
situation, consequences that seemed inevitable to him?

And papa had virtually yielded to Brother George the
farming operations: Mr. Higgins was now under the super-
vision of a "man of business," and that man was George.
It was in further protection of the heirs, of course, that
the cultivation of the land was put upon a money basis,
for which Mr. Higgins was accountable in terms of strict
economy.

All this must be reckoned against prejudice; reckoned,
that is, against the attitude of Cousin John Semmes. There
were ways in which Cousin John was "smarter" than
George, he knew more about everything; he was better
educated; he was in fact, like my grandfather, an "elegant gentleman"; yet he saw little in George Posey but impertinence because he allowed himself to see not what
George was doing but only the way he did it. I had fre-
quently heard Cousin John say that he freed his own
few Negroes to keep from raising more Negroes to be sold
into the canebrakes of the Mississippi. If papa had faced

that, to him, dreadful phase of his position, I never knew it; but George Posey had faced it for him. To him papa's refusal to buy or sell a Negro was only a kind of fastidious self-indulgence at the expense of his posterity, who would have to sell the Negroes sooner or later, or manumit them at the cost of actually giving money away. I suppose George, in what was considered his high-handed fashion, took the first step against this family bankruptcy when he sold Jack Lewis and his family into Georgia: to have freed them, in deference to papa's wish, would have been, to George, to permit papa to rob his children in order to do what he considered humanly right. Papa could not use the Negroes; therefore they must be freed. But was not George Posey right about this? And was not papa also, in his own way, right?

Other people had to be provided for out of the estate. Susan and I would get our portions after papa's death. George had in effect lent the estate thirty thousand dollars to pay off Charles and Semmes; and if the final evaluation should be more than sixty thousand, they would get more. They would surely get it, since the estimate of sixty thousand did not include Negroes, stock, implements, to say nothing of the Pleasant Hill house and its appointments, which Brother George somewhat characteristically transposed into cash figures. It was that sort of thing of course that annoyed Cousin John and irritated papa, who could not bring himself to think of the house that Dr. Buchan had built in 1791, "for the enjoyment of the heirs forever," not, mind you, for their profit, had any money value at all. If he admitted its money value he also admitted that it might some day be sold — which was unthinkable.

In giving this account of our property I am straddling two ages. Nobody in my youth discussed money; we never

asked how much money people had; and it was a little
different, I believe, from the ordinary good breeding that
demands reticence about the cost of things. That too was
never done; but the point of the other "rule" was that it
had grown out of long habit, out of a way of seeing men
in society; it was less a rule than an actual habit of the
mind. It was significant that we always spoke of the Carters
of Ravensworth, the Carys of Vaucluse, the Buchans of
Pleasant Hill. The individual quality of a man was bound
up with his kin and the "places" where they lived; thinking of a man we could easily bring before the mind's eye
all those subtly interwoven features of his position. "Class"
consisted solely in a certain code of behavior. Even years
later I am always a little amazed to hear a man described
as the coal man or the steel man or the plate-glass man,
descriptions of people after the way they make their money,
not after their manner of life. When George began court-
ing Susan I once overheard some of the old ladies of our
neighborhood, Mrs. Langton and I think old Mrs. Gunnell, trying to "place" him, and because he lived across
the Potomac they found it a little hard: Gibson and Posey
were good names, but which Gibsons and which Poseys?
Then somebody said that George sold fish, but of course
they could have said that he sold tobacco, lumber, and
leather, as well as everything raised on the Posey land in
Charles and Anne Arundel. I remember old Mrs. Gunnell
trying to catch the talk in her ear-trumpet, and not quite
getting it. "He does something about fish?" she asked.
Cousin John Semmes always said that George would sell
anything for the pleasure of buying something else; he had
to keep moving. Even if somebody had called George the
fish man he wouldn't have cared. He would have laughed.
He had only put the Gibson Negroes in St. Mary's to fishing commercially the waters that lay by the Gibson land,

and I think he sent to market a great many oysters too.

*   *   *

When we got into the hall I lagged behind, and stood irresolute by the stairs until George had followed Susan and Semmes into the back-parlor and closed the door. The only sounds I could hear were the shouts of the news-boy, now far down the street, and, from the back-parlor, papa's voice rising and falling in an unnatural sing-song that meant he was playing with little Jane. My niece, I said; and for the first time I took it in, with the feeling that it made me a man. But I always stood away from her and I could never remember how she looked. I began counting over the people who had come — George, Susan, and Semmes, the baby and the colored nurse, Ricky some-thing they called her; and then I added big Jane whom I had not seen since Christmas. I had seen her a few times since the funeral, but never alone; I wondered if knowing that Susan was keeping us apart gave me the feelings about Jane of which, at night, I was secretly ashamed, or whether Susan understood what I felt and was exercising that pe-culiar cynicism, that vigilance and lucidity that seem to exist in women in proportion to their innocence. Per-haps it was only my size: at sixteen I had shot up to five feet ten and was strong as a mule colt.

I wanted to be alone and I had put one foot on the stairs when I heard a door close, and looking up I saw Aunt Myra in the upper hall. Presently Lucy joined her, and I heard low voices.

"No," said Lucy, "I saw them get out of the carriage. Charles didn't come."

Aunt Myra said nothing, but presently she started down the stairs in the slow one-two rhythm of her rheumatism,

and Lucy followed her. At the foot of the stairs Aunt
Myra turned to Lucy and said, "Lucy, listen to me.
There's going to be a time when Charlie will make a
habit of not coming, and it won't be his fault. You know
what is happening. You know what he will do."

I said, "What will Brother Charles do, Aunt Myra?"

She looked at me sharply. "Lacy, thank God for your
age. I wish you were even younger." She took Lucy by
the arm and led her down the hall into the back-parlor.

I was about to follow, but the knocker sounded, and
I went to the door; as I grasped the knob I heard men's
voices and when I opened the door the two men, glancing
at me, continued what they were saying while I stood
waiting for them to enter. Cousin John gave me his hand.
"Howdy, son," he said. Major Corse — he was now a major
— smiled at me and put his hand on my shoulder, but said
nothing. "Tell your pa we're here," said Cousin John.

As I went down the hall Coriolanus appeared and said
to the gentlemen, "Marse John, is you gentlemen come to
see the major?" He went to the back-parlor door. The
nurse Ricky came out with little Jane in her arms. Coriolanus stood at the threshold and said: "Marster, Marse
John and Major Corse to see you, sir." They went in and
I slid in behind them.

While the gentlemen were bowing to the ladies I went
to a window, and got in between the window and the
curtains. Children were playing among the graves. Then
I heard papa speak: I looked over my shoulder to see him
shake hands with Major Corse.

"Well, well, major," papa said, "you no sooner get
promoted than you stop wearing your uniform. Isn't this
muster day?"

Cousin John's voice was at once matter-of-fact and
ominous. "He don't know what uniform to get." Then

he seemed to be lecturing us. "If a major's uniform were the same everywhere, he could just get a major's uniform. Couldn't you, Corse?" He paused and looked at papa. "We don't live under the 'Parliament of Man, the Federation of the World.' Men don't fight yet with olive branches."

"Why, major," said Lucy, "you looked *so* handsome in your captain's uniform. I told Charles that you looked like an army officer."

"Just the militia, ma'am." He bowed slightly and sat down in a small straight chair. He opened his mouth to speak, then glanced uneasily around the room. He was a young man, not more than forty, with a tall narrow head, clear large eyes of neutral color, strong chin and small determined mouth. I traced his glance to George Posey who was sitting on a low chair behind Susan in the far corner of the room. Susan caught the glance.

"Mr. Corse," Susan said, "we are all friends here."

Papa leaned forward and tapped his knee with his forefinger. "I don't understand you, daughter. Of course we are friends. Montgomery," he said to Major Corse. "What does this mean? What is this talk about uniforms? I presume you will wear the uniform of the Alexandria Rifles? I wore it once, sir," he said gently.

Semmes rose, but a dead silence fell and he was caught there; as he sat down again he found my eye, and raised his brow inquiringly. Good God, I had left it on the newel post in the hall! How could I get through all those people to the door at the other end of the room?

"We heard the cry of the newsboy." It was Aunt Myra. "We know what it is." She looked at Lucy. Semmes said in a low voice, "Lacy, go get the paper." I walked carefully down the long room, feeling conspicuous in the silence that suddenly descended again. I left the door

open after me, and the silence accompanied me all the
way to the front hall and back again until I confronted
Semmes at the threshold. He took the paper and handed
it to papa without a word.

Papa was adjusting his spectacles with deliberation as
I scurried back to my station at the window; I turned
and looked at the room. There was a solemnity of expression and a strained ease of posture everywhere. Lucy
looked as if she were about to be reprimanded for something; Semmes was rubbing the side of his nose; Susan
had moved forward to the edge of her chair. George
Posey was letting his watch dangle on its chain, glancing
from it to papa, who I thought would never put the paper
down. George looked at me and smiled with his eyes,
then suddenly returned the watch to his pocket. I was
afraid somebody would speak, wishing at the same time
that somebody would, somebody else than papa, whose
eyes moved slowly down the page. The dying coals in the
grate settled with a thud. Everybody looked at the grate.

Papa held the paper vaguely extended; Cousin John
took it and laid it on the secretary behind papa, and said
in a low tone: "Brother Lewis, the time has come that I
have been telling you about these past six months."

So long ago that I had forgotten when, I had heard
Cousin John call papa "Brother Lewis." Papa fixed him
a moment over the rims of his spectacles, and I suppose
that reminded him to take them off, which he did with
the usual deliberation, as if he were at Pleasant Hill and
had been studying the prices of wheat and corn. But
now he looked around the room at everybody in turn,
appearing to take in the tension that held us as an astonishing mystery. He raised his brows and cleared his throat.

"Brother John," he said with a twinkle, "you had never
told me about this. You had never said that Jeff Davis

would order the reduction of a Federal fort. Myra, has John in your recollection ever said anything of the kind?"

Everybody in the room moved a little. George smiled again at me, and then at Semmes, who looked at papa with, I thought, a sort of disappointment, as if papa had not received the news as he somehow ought to have received it. Major Corse and Cousin John were solemn; but Lucy, doubtless thinking it was expected of her, laughed at papa's joke, but nobody else did, least of all Aunt Myra who looked a little vexed.

"Now Brother Lewis, you know quite well what Mr. Semmes meant. Don't you realize that it's war? Don't you know that Semmes will be in it?" But she actually looked at me. Papa saw the look; for the first time his face clouded.

"War?" he said. "How can there be a war? Why, the Federal government will reinforce the troops at Fort Sumter. Ain't any question about that. When the Federal authority is supreme in South Carolina the other Cotton States will come back one by one." The flush on his cheeks mounted to his eyes and forehead. He drew his kerchief from his sleeve and put it to his mouth, clearing his throat at the same time.

Cousin John addressed Major Corse. "Corse, will the Alexandria Rifles offer their bayonets to the Federal government?"

"No, sir," said Major Corse.

"Why not?"

"Because we feel that they might be used against our own people."

Papa looked politely at Major Corse, almost indulgently, and said, "Montgomery, we have nothing to do with this South Carolina trouble. It don't affect us at all."

I don't know what was in my mind, or why I thought

anything, but I ran into the room a few steps, and cried, "Oh, papa, but it does — it does affect us." He smiled at me and made a slight gesture with his kerchief, and I felt abashed; but Cousin John stepped forward and touched my arm.

"Lew, this boy is right. And I advise you to get out of this town as soon as you can. It's too near—well, it ain't so far from South Carolina, as you'll see."

Papa didn't look up; he seemed vastly preoccupied with his own thoughts as, with his snuffbox before him, he kept opening and closing it absently, until I was sure that he was thinking of something very far from the scene, perhaps Pleasant Hill where spring plowing was already far advanced. He surprised us; he rose to his feet and ignoring Cousin John he addressed George, the first time he had addressed him directly since that evening in the back-parlor at home after the funeral when George had stood by the window and Mr. Broadacre had dozed on the sofa. He always answered George's questions but he never asked him one.

"George," he said, "what have you to say about this? I suppose you are still a good Union man?"

George got up and pushing his chair against the wall bowed slightly to papa, then began walking up and down across the far end of the room. Once he stopped and looking at Semmes smiled broadly: "Semmes, are we good Union men?" He shifted his eyes toward papa and seemed about to speak, but he only gazed, and the perpetual smile was a little softened by the serious concentration of his chin and brow. Papa was waiting for him to speak; he suddenly sat down.

"Major," said George, "there's no discourtesy in my failure to reply. I am thinking."

Cousin John came from behind papa and walked rapidly across the room, his touseled hair framing an angry expression. Major Corse rose. When Cousin John reached the door he turned and surveyed the room.

"Well, we better leave George Posey to his thoughts. And mark ye, Lewis Buchan, your son-in-law is too damned rich for his sense of responsibility. I know you can't be bought," he said to George; "I know you're as honorable as the next one. I don't know what side you'll take, you won't take the side that offers you advantages—you'll take the side you can buy. You think you can buy anything. Come on, Corse, I have an engagement at the Marshall House." He backed out of the room.

Major Corse rose and bowed to the assemblage. "Good evening, ladies and gentlemen." His hand on the door knob, he paused. "Major Buchan, you've known me from my boyhood. I am serious, sir; we are all serious. Try to think well of us." He inclined his head and disappeared into the hall; the door closed after him.

I looked at George: he was staring at the closed door, standing perfectly erect, his hands thrust into his pockets, all that remained of his smile lingering in the wrinkles at the corners of his eyes. I asked myself: Is he angry? And I decided that he was not angry, that he was not insulted, but genuinely perplexed. His perplexity had caught him between steps as he was pacing back and forth, so that he looked coiled and as if he were about to spring. I looked at Susan: the blood had left her face, as I had seen it do when she spoke to Jim Mason about John Langton's rascality after the tournament. She rose and took a few steps towards the fireplace, turned round and faced her husband, then looked at papa.

"Mr. Posey has borne a good deal from his wife's family. Perhaps the time has come when he will not bear it any longer." Her pale face was flushed. She turned away from papa and walked slowly out of the room.

George suddenly relaxed and leaning forward a little put his hands upon the back of his chair. The perplexity had turned into amazement. He opened his mouth, but no words came, and it remained open. The dangerous ambiguity of Susan's defense of her husband had driven into retreat everybody in the room. What lay behind that speech?—what had Susan and George been saying to each other when they were alone? I decided: nothing—they had been saying nothing. If Susan had broached with him his relation to her family, it would have established it as a privacy between them, and she could not have attacked him so fiercely in the presence of others, least of all her family. I was not sure she was conscious of the full import of her words. As I heard the words again in the mind's ear, I was convinced that she intended no ambiguity whatever: she started to speak, and in simple good faith meant to rebuke her family for their treatment of a son-in-law who in his fashion had been their prop and stay; then as the words came forth they dragged with them, from some hidden depth, a judgment of George of which she herself until that moment had not been quite aware.

Aunt Myra was looking at the floor; Lucy, who had not felt the danger, caught the silence by contagion, and looked vaguely frightened; Semmes, who had got it all, looked anxiously at papa, from whom I suppose he expected relief. George by this time had fixed his gaze upon papa, and its insistence seemed to bear upon him like a demand: without moving his head he cast his eyes upon papa's face, which now held a flushed reaction from his awareness of what Susan had meant. Papa was staring at the door, but after a few moments, without change of posture, he calmly moved his eyes to George who still leaned against the chair.

"My son," he said in a tone so low I could barely hear the words, "we are devoted to you. I am still the head of the Buchan family. Young as you are, I presume you are the head of your family. We understand each other."

George moved to the center of the room, and he was, as if by virtue of motion, the old George again: he was self-possessed, he gave me the distinct impression that he had recovered his solitude, that quality that he carried always with him as a weapon equally of attack and defense. My mind went back into the parlor at Pleasant Hill that afternoon of the remarkable interview between papa and George, when George had played the old gentleman on a taut line. Now his head was thrown back and his gaze fixed papa steadily.

"Major," then he paused. "Major, I am gratified that we understand each other. Frankly, sir, I do not understand the present necessity of this conversation."

The late afternoon light had begun to fail. When I looked at papa again his face was gray. Then, unobtrusively as a shadow, a man came through the door, but after a few steps he paused, taking in the scene; I doubt if either papa or George would have noticed him. As I recognized my brother Charles I heard, about ten seconds delayed, his knock at the door, which I was certain no one else had heard, so compelling was the tension of the conflict before us. I was a little disappointed; Charles' presence would break up the tension, whose issue might have illuminated for me a great many mysteries, the meaning for instance of papa's rebuke—whether he knew everything that George had done about us.

"My son," said papa to George, "there is this necessity, that families must face the times together. The young men of my family will consult me in their politics. You will decide whether you can act as a member of my family. That," he added dryly, "is all I meant by our understanding."

George slumped a little, his chin dropped to his chest, his feet shuffled; I thought he was at last embarrassed, but his eyes blazed in the fading light, and when he turned away he would have left the room if he had not confronted Charles, who had advanced a little further from the door and was holding Lucy's hand. As for me, I lost some of my disappointment of a moment before, for indeed I had seen a small mystery, but whether I understood it then, or a little later, or only years later, I do not know. Why was it that George took everything to himself? Of course, that was a mystery that I could not solve. I suppose he had too much imagination and he could not confine the things that people said to what lay right before him, under his nose; papa's rebuke had obviously been aimed at a particular difficulty, it was only a very strong warning that he would tell his sons, without the interference of George, what course to take in the excitement of public affairs.

"It is too late to consult anybody, even you, papa." It was Charles. He looked at George. "How d'ye do, George," he said. "Excuse me, papa." He advanced and shook hands with papa. He looked at Semmes. "If I hadn't gone away when I did I would be spending the night in the old Capitol Prison."

"Oh, Charles!" Lucy cried.

"Why, son," said papa, "I don't understand you."

"My dear," Charles said to Lucy, "you will excuse us. The men had better talk this thing over."

Lucy got up, and Aunt Myra followed her without a

word. Charles watched them soberly as they disappeared and closed the door.

"George," he said, "Captain Schaeffer is in prison. Major Stone arrested him at noon, under orders from General Scott."

"Who is Captain Schaeffer?" papa asked.

George looked at papa, then at Charles, who hesitated an instant and spoke in a casual tone.

"Captain Schaeffer is the commander of the National Rifles, the company in Georgetown that George belongs to. George, you've wasted your money. Stone hunted down and disarmed half of the company, and seized the reserve arms, which are at this moment in the government arsenal."

Papa's face showed extreme perplexity as he rose and took one step forward. The young men, George no less than the others, gazed at him respectfully until, at a loss what to do on his feet, he sat down again, stiffly, holding the arms of his chair.

"What has George to do with that?" he asked.

"Major," said George, "my grandfather Gibson organized the National Rifles when Washington was a village."

Papa still gazed at him inquiringly.

Semmes said, "George contributed a good deal to refitting the company last winter." He took a long black cigar from his waistcoat pocket, bit off the end, then removed it and gestured in the direction of papa, all the while looking at George, who instantly nodded his head. Semmes continued: "Papa, the Union men resigned from the Rifles a month ago, not more'n ten or a dozen."

I suppose, son, that you resigned too?"

"Papa, I did not." He turned away and putting his arm against the mantel leaned his head against it. George backed off a few feet and sat down. Charles sat on the hair sofa where Lucy and Aunt Myra had been sitting. In these seconds of time papa had taken out his kerchief again; he drew it through one hand, and aimlessly spread it out across his knees, but soon gathered it up and stuffed it back into his sleeve and with the same motion began to tap his knee with his forefinger.

"Gentlemen," he said, "perhaps one of you will poke the fire."

Semmes turned, startled, but bent over swiftly and brought the dying coals to a feeble blaze. Everybody in the room watched him with concentration. He straightened up but kept looking at the fire with exaggerated zeal until he could no longer pretend that it needed him. He seemed to struggle with himself but quickly his eyelids drooped and he stiffened, then moved quietly towards papa, leaning over him.

"Papa, I am very sorry."

Papa's finger came to an abrupt stop in mid-air, his hand sank listlessly upon his knee. The firelight threw into relief the long nose and the wide mouth, which was set as if in pain; but as he glanced from one young man to another his eyes were bright. When nobody said anything he leaned back in his chair and gazed at the fire. He had surely heard Semmes, but he gave no sign of it. Semmes backed away and stood at the far end of the mantel.

Papa cast an inquiring glance at Charles.

"Well, sir," said Charles, "you see I had been drilling the company at night, ever since Christmas, two or three nights a week." He rose and paced back and forth, and turned again to papa. "It was perfectly regular." Papa nodded and he continued. "I didn't know it but since Mr. Lincoln's inauguration we've been under observation." He paused again as if the recital were about to reach its painful stage. And I noticed that he had said "we" meaning himself and the National Rifles, and not the United States Army, of which he was an officer. "When I returned to General Scott's office after dinner today the orderly called me aside and said that I was about to be arrested for engaging in activities hostile to the Federal government. He said General Scott was in a rage, the news of Sumter had just come over the wires, he was particularly suspicious of Virginians, being one himself." And Charles smiled, I think the second time I had seen him smile in my life.

But no one in the room smiled back at him. He immediately sobered, and composing his features tried to seem casual, but he only succeeded in being extremely formal.

"Considerations of honor will compel me to resign my commission tomorrow, and I think I had better do it by letter."

He looked at George as if he expected him to say something, and George seemed about to speak, but papa rose and glancing over his shoulder at me, said:

"Son, hand me my shawl, please."

The shawl was hanging on a hook between the near end of the mantel and the window, by papa's secretary. I lifted it from the hook and handed it to him. He drew it carefully round his shoulders.

"It is a little chilly in the halls at this season."

When he came to the door he turned, his hand on the knob, to face the young men. George had risen; he bowed his head; his lips moved, then he suddenly compressed them into silence. There was in his face at that moment a shadow, or a line, or perhaps it was only a trick of the falling dusk, that I thought was agony, or at least painful indecision.

"Father Buchan," he said, and the form of address

startled me. "We can't do anything else now. I am not choosing sides, I am chosen by circumstances. I want you to know, sir, that I do prefer the Union." He lowered his voice. "And that I do sympathize with your position."

By the time I looked at papa again he was standing straight as a bell pole. The shawl gradually slid off his shoulder to the floor as he threw his head back: the last light was full in his face, his nostrils were dilated in anger. With difficulty he held his arms at his sides. He gave George a long, fixed stare.

"I thank you, sir," he said. His mouth widened with a fierce smile, but he was no longer looking at George. "Semmes, I hope that I have your sympathy too." He backed out of the door, closed it with a firm, gentle bang; and I heard his rapid footsteps ascending the stairs. The shawl lay in a heap where it had fallen. Charles got up stiffly and recovered it, hanging it carefully over the back of a chair.

Semmes was chafing his hands in agitation.

"George," he said, "perhaps we had better reconsider our position. We can't —"

"Can't what, Semmes?" The tone was remote, and in the last minute he had become again the George that I knew: his eyes were cold and smiling.

Charles said: "George, maybe Semmes would feel better if he could explain things to papa. Papa don't know that Mr. Lincoln will ask Virginia for troops to send to Charleston. Lincoln and Seward have planned this all along, waiting for an overt act by Mr. Davis."

George seemed not to hear. He moved towards the door, then ignoring Charles, he addressed Semmes.

"Semmes, are we together in this thing or not? That's the only thing you've got to decide. Are we together?"

Semmes had been looking at him but now his face fell,

and he leaned against the mantel-shelf. Charles folded his hands and looked beyond me through the window. I said to myself: Are we together? What was together? I did not know, and I heard again: Son, I've got to go, and I decided that this time I would go with him, because it was so simple to go and to leave behind all the things that I would have to think about if I stayed. Then I thought how easy it would have been if I could have gone off with George away from the funeral, and come back to be with him in the back-parlor, and to have met with him the contempt of Cousin John, the courtesy of papa: how easy it would have been to have had all my feelings simplified, to have felt the exultation of loyalty not to myself or to all the life around me, but to one person who to my dying day will be a man always riding off somewhere. I thought I had better go up to my room, and I started for the door, but when I came to George I stopped, and he smiled at me.

"I know *we're* together, son," he said.

Semmes turned around. "Well, George, what shall we do?"

He smiled at Semmes. "I thought you'd come with me. I think we had better see Major Corse." He looked at Charles. "We can offer him our men."

"We'll *all* go to see Corse," Charles said.

George threw open the door and stood aside for Charles and Semmes to pass. Charles touched him on the arm. "After you, sir." And George led the way into the hall.

*   *   *

A few days later, after the Virginia convention had taken the State out of the Union, I was coming home from school, it must have been about four o'clock, and I saw a crowd down Washington Street gathered around the

flag-pole. The United States flag hung limp against the
pole in the windless air. I ran, and when I came to the
edge of the crowd heard the steady plunk of an ax in
an unnatural stillness. I pushed my way slowly into the
center of the ring. A young man handed the ax to a
man with gray hair, who with stiff, feeble strokes loosened
a few chips, then would have fallen had not two younger
men stepped forward to support him. There was still no
disorder, not even talk. Men quietly awaited their turns.
Just inside the circle Major Corse stood, a little aloof,
his arms folded and a vague smile lighting his eyes. He
looked at me but gave no sign of recognition. There was
a cry, "Look out!" The circle broke and scattered as the
crackling pine fell with a crash upon the cobblestones.

Before the Presidential election of 1860, only a few
months ago, supporters of the Union ticket of Bell and
Everett had erected the pole, and I believe papa contributed to it. They insisted that secession was a crime, and
continued to insist until this day, the 17th of April, when
Mr. Lincoln's proclamation reached us, calling for sev-
enty-five thousand volunteers to suppress in South Carolina
"combinations too powerful to be dealt with by the
courts"; on this day they all became violent supporters
of the crime.

All, or nearly all, but papa; for during secession week
he seldom went abroad, staying indoors and reading the
papers as never before. Cousin John Semmes came in to
sit with him in the evening, but by tacit understanding
there was no discussion of "politics." One evening, as
Cousin John was about to leave, he asked papa if he
hadn't better go back to Pleasant Hill.

"No, sir, the madness will subside."

So far as papa was concerned life went on as usual—
which meant that Coriolanus dusted the back-parlor every

morning and I went to school and at night pretended to
study my lessons. Boys of my own age, too young to volunteer in any of the militia companies, envied our older
brothers, who would surely in a few weeks go up the
river and cross the Long Bridge into Washington, and
wrest the government away from the "foreigners." We had
our own excitements, our own special and immemorial
ways of amusing ourselves; but this is not my story.

In the week after Charles had resigned his commission
he waited at home, and we understood that he could not
decide whether to join the Mt. Vernon Guards as captain
or offer his services to the Confederate government. He
was waiting, I think, for Colonel Lee to set an example
—which he did towards the end of that week by offering
himself to the State of Virginia, not to the Confederacy,
for Virginia had only declared her independence and
could not officially become a part of the Confederacy until by popular vote the Ordinance of Secession had been
confirmed; that was more than a month away. Papa said
that Colonel Lee had been "precipitate," that conserva-
tive men would not consider the state out of the Union
until the actual vote was counted, since the Ordinance
had been passed under pressure from the fire-eaters led
by Henry A. Wise, a former governor of the state whose
political ambitions had been frustrated by his failure to
get the presidential nomination in 1860. To us, the boys,
Governor Wise was already a great hero. Had he not,
when he mounted the platform to speak on the last day
of the convention, prefaced his remarks with a gesture of
the heroic order? He had drawn two horse-pistols from
inside of his coat and dramatically laid them upon the table
before him. I had heard him speak several years before,
at political meetings, with Cousin John: he was a small
man with a big forehead and a sharp, angry expression.

Charles left for Richmond early the next week, accompanied by Lucy, who was eager to go, thinking that Charles might rapidly accede to high rank and thus broaden the stage of her social operations, which had been so narrow in a family headed by an old fogey who had never heard of "society." I think Aunt Myra was divided in feeling between anxiety for Lucy's decorum and relief to be rid of her. Charles had been commissioned major in the army of Virginia, charged with the drill and organization of militia companies as they arrived from remote counties of the state. I did not see Charles and Lucy again until after the war.

You cannot imagine the rumors and alarms that filled those days, and I myself, a part of them, though a minute part, cannot recall the excitement in which we lived. The day after secession a "body of troops," which swelled in the imagination of the people of our town into an "army," passed mysteriously through Manassas Junction; and in a few days we heard that the armory at Harper's Ferry had been captured. It was a great victory, of course, and Washington would be next. But what actually came next, what seemed so important at the time of its happening, I cannot remember, though I might consult the books and bring back the true order of events. It was at about this time, perhaps a little later, we heard that Massachusetts troops, marching through Baltimore, had been mobbed by the secessionists of Maryland. It seemed for a while that perhaps papa would be right—that the madness would subside, no power being great enough to subdue the bright soldiers who paraded the streets of Alexandria the Sunday after the fall of Fort Sumter had forced Virginia into her independence.

Of course we got used to war, to what after a month of parades we thought of as war, but on that first Sunday

it was a novelty that I remember chiefly for a slight reason
—my anxiety to see Semmes and George who I knew would
be somewhere in the ranks of the Alexandria Rifles. After
the scene with papa the Sunday before neither George
nor Semmes had appeared, and we had heard only from
Susan, whose weekly letter might have been written in
times wholly lacking in agitation, it stuck so close to
family news: the Poseys were well, Aunt Jane Anne being
better after her attack of gout, Aunt Milly George as
usual, and Mr. Jarman (he never became "uncle") had
actually only yesterday (the 17th) not only emerged from
his room but had gone in the carriage up to Georgetown
Heights because he said he didn't believe the Confederate
flag was flying over the Marshall House in Alexandria;
when he saw it he got back into the carriage and told
Blind Joe to take him home, that the war was over; little
Susan was getting better of the rickets and would be
walking soon, "so efficacious has been the diet prescribed
by Dr. Burrows, of buttermilk and pot liquor"; and "my
husband is busier than ever before, his engagements de-
taining him until late at night." But there was no mention of Jane Posey, and George's "engagements" were a
mystery that papa, reading the letter to Aunt Myra, acknowledged with a brief pause.

That Sunday at dinner papa put down his knife and
fork, and addressed me: "Son, it is beyond any dispute
now that Colonel Lee has resigned from the army." We
had known it beyond dispute for several days, but papa
had not been convinced even after Charles' departure
for Richmond; he had at last faced it at the morning services at Christ Church where Miss Agnes Lee had told
Aunt Myra that her father, unwilling to fight his own
people, had become a private citizen; then old Mr. Daingerfield had shown papa the *Washington Star* of the day

before in which Lee's resignation was announced. "But," papa said, "I cannot understand Colonel Lee's reasons for assuming that he would have to fight his own people. A show of force by the government would keep all these young men from forming military companies. Lacy," and he looked at me, "I don't forbid you to go to the parade, but I want you to understand that we have nothing to do with Disunion."

That was the first time, I suppose, that papa had seemed to me to speak from a great distance, as if he were a man preoccupied with some private mystery that could not be connected with what was going on in the world. How easy to think that "a show of force" would disband the Alexandria Rifles and Mt. Vernon Guards! Where in his mind were the vast hordes of young men who were rushing to village and county town, from the river bottoms and the hills, coming with squirrel rifles, shot-guns, bowie knives, to "form military companies" in Georgia, Alabama, Mississippi, by the banks of the James, the Chattahoochee, the Tennessee? For papa, these young men did not exist; all that country from below the James to the Rio Grande was a map, and the "war" was about to be fought between the "government" and the sons of his neighbors and kin in the old Northern Neck of Virginia.

After the cloth had been removed I told papa that I did not care for any dessert, and could I be excused? He let me go, and I ran upstairs to get my jacket and cap. I remember at that moment a sense of loss as I was about to close the door behind me, and I thought I had forgotten something. I glanced about the room, in which there was never sufficient light, and the bare wall opposite me became the wall of the "boys' room" at Pleasant Hill where my double-barreled gun rested upon its pegs. I closed the door swiftly but softly, and ran as softly down the stairs and through the front door into the street where according to appointment, down on the corner, two of my friends waited for me. They were just my age, Hank Herbert was not so large as I, but Jack Armistead was taller and looked more than our age; he, of course, was a cousin, but our boyish code forbade our ever referring to it in the presence of other boys. When I approached there was no greeting — that too was an article of conduct among little savages — but Hank and Jack shifted a little their postures.

Hank said: "Old Kenny says my pa said to beat me if I talked about enlisting." Old Kenny was Mr. Kennedy, master of the Alexandria Academy. "Say, Lacy, you reckon Major Corse'd take me?" He looked about him slyly, and stuck a small plug of tobacco in the corner of his mouth.

"Hell," said Jack. "Hell, I don't want to be a private. They ain't any of the officers gentlemen but the Major, maybe a couple others."

"Major Corse ain't going to take any of us," I said. "Listen here, Jack, we got to set an example. We got to show the plain people we ain't any better'n they are." They gave me their solemn attention, and we all felt that we had already sacrificed ourselves to the glory of the Old Dominion. As we considered it, distant strains of music came to us from the south end of town. We looked all at once up Duke Street towards Washington.

"Less go," I said.

"Less go," said Hank.

"Come on," Jack said, and he pushed Hank in the back as we started at a half trot up the street.

"Say," Jack said, "Wink Broadacre's jined the Rifles only he ain't got a uniform yet."

"You say he has," I said. I hadn't seen Winston Broadacre for about three years, but I got all the news of him

I could because his superior age and achievements made him a hero to the younger generation to which I belonged. He had been at the University for two years and surprised everybody with his judicious balance of study and dissipation, excelling in both.

"Yas," Jack said, "he's a leftenant." He looked at me. "Hell, you oughta know that. Hell, didn't your brother-in-law tell Major Corse Wink had to be made an officer?"

We slowed to a walk. Hank looked worried. "Shut up, Jack, you oughtn't to be telling that."

I hadn't heard a word about it but I pretended I had. "Yas, Brother George is mighty patriotic." An embarrassed silence fell upon my companions. I had to lift it. "Well, anyhow he made all the Georgetown boys come over here and enlist, didn't he? And he give enough muskets for two companies. Ain't that patriotism?"

"It sho is," said Hank. "Look here, Lace, it's a dern shame Mr. Posey wa'n't made an officer, after all he's done. My pa says it is. He says Mr. Posey oughta been made cap'n of one of the new companies, the one with the Georgetown boys in it. . . ."

"Well," I said knowingly, "maybe Brother George don't want to be cap'n, maybe he wants to be a private."

"Huh," Jack said, "you wait and see."

As we came to the corner of Duke and Washington the sounds of the distant band were more distinct.

"Let's wait here for them to pass," I said.

"Naw," Jack said, "we better go up to Prince."

That was where the speaking was going to be. We walked fast. As we came to the end of the block the crowd thickened, mostly boys like us or Negroes who milled about in clusters; across the street there were white people only, young girls dressed in bonnets and hoops. Out in the middle of the street at the crossing of the four corners stood a wooden platform about three feet high and big enough for not more than four or five men to stand on. We looked to the left down the street: far away, probably as far as South Street near Hunting Creek we saw the head of the column with two indistinguishable flags in the lead.

It seemed a half hour before I could make out the features of the white, serious face of the leading color-bearer, a young man I had never seen; then the band struck up an air, the new tune of "The Bonny Blue Flag," and a loud hand-clapping preceded the wild cheer that I was to hear later in the dusty fields of war. The first color-bearer carried the flag of Virginia; a few paces behind him came one of the older Herbert boys, a cousin of Hank's, carrying a small replica of the flag that had been flying since Friday over the Marshall House—two horizontal bands, red and white, with, in the upper left-hand corner, a blue field containing a single white star. The first company was the Rifles, perfectly uniformed in dark blue, white shoulder belts crossed over the chest, and tall patent leather hats — they looked like pictures of soldiers in the Mexican War. After them came the Mt. Vernon Guards, similarly dressed but with different insignia. The Rifles marched across the square and formed in line facing towards the platform. The Guards turned left into Prince Street, and about-faced. The next company had only a sprinkling of uniforms, few of them matching, and the arms were muskets, shotguns, sabers, pistols, and pikes. As it came opposite us I stared at a familiar face, an officer, sword at shoulder, dressed in the new, beautiful bluish gray of the South. It was Winston Broadacre. When he came near enough to the curb for me almost to touch him, I said in a low voice that penetrated the shouts: "Hello, Wink."

He turned an impassive, grim-looking young face unseeingly in my direction. Then his eyes narrowed into a smile.

"Howdy, Lacy," he said without change of expression. As his company turned the corner to the right into Prince Street I felt tears come to my eyes, but I turned away to keep my companions from seeing until I had fought them back.

I said, "Say, I'd sho like to enlist."

"So would I," said Hank.

"I reckon I will pretty soon," Jack said. We looked at the next company. About half of the men were uniformed and I suddenly recognized them; they were the National Rifles from Georgetown. I felt a little tense. The first face my eyes fixed was the solemn features of Brother Semmes; he wore the uniform of a private in the National Rifles; and except that when he turned his head in our direction his eyelids drooped, I should not have known that he saw me. Then I noticed a difference between this company and the one that had preceded it: although half of the men were without uniforms, every man had a new shining rifle, with bayonet fixed—the muskets that Brother George had so patriotically supplied! I was looking down the ranks for Brother George when Jack whispered: "Who's that man there?" He pointed towards a man of middle height, powerfully built and of swarthy complexion, who marched with drawn sword outside the column and near its head. Before I really saw him I realized that he was the captain. I kept staring at the tinge of gray in the long hair over his ears. It astonished me; then I knew why: it had delayed my recognition of a man I had known from infancy.

"He's Mister John," I said; then, "I mean Mr. John Langton, he's our neighbor in the country."

"He's cap'n," Hank said.

I pretended not to hear, turning to look at the file closers who brought up the rear of a column that seemed to me a great army. It was about five hundred men, but that was more than twice as many as the Rifles and Guards could have mustered a week ago. Captain Langton's company halted in front of us. The four streets radiating away from the platform were now filled with soldiers standing at order-arms. The cheering subsided, and I heard the rapid clatter of hooves from the direction of Duke Street. A body of horsemen was turning into Washington; they came at a quick trot past the halted company. At the head rode Major Corse, dressed like Wink Broadacre in gray, followed by five or six dignitaries rigged out in odds and ends of military regalia. They dismounted at the platform: one man I gazed at narrowly and recognized as Cousin John: the only military touch about him was a tightly buttoned, double-breasted coat of dark blue; the buttons were silver; and he wore a soft gray hat.

Cousin John and Major Corse talked in a low tone, looking from the bunched horses to the crowd, and then at the men in the ranks. Cousin John shook his head: No, I was sure he was saying, we can't ask gentlemen to hold our horses. They had forgotten to appoint an orderly. I stepped down from the curb into the street; Jack pushed me a little in the back; "Go on," he said. I caught Cousin John's eye; he nodded and I ran forward as if I were being pursued. The gentlemen handed me their bridles: as Cousin John handed me his I looked at his horse—it was the bay mare, Queen Susie. I drew the horses together into a half circle, looking over my shoulder towards Captain Langton's company. The captain slouched with his left hand at his hip, the point of his sword resting upon the toe of his right boot, which was slightly advanced. He looked insolent, humorless, and bored. Queen Susie tossed her head, giving the bridle a stiff yank, and I knew that Brother George should have been standing in John Langton's place, and then I realized, after the diverting excitement, that in all that vast host of men—I still considered them a host—I had not seen George Posey, and that John Langton, his enemy, had marched at the head of his—George's—men. I could hardly keep my mind on the ceremonies for wondering how George's mare had got there; as Cousin John mounted the platform with professional dignity. I could not understand why he, also in his way George's enemy, should have ridden his horse. But I did know this: that George Posey was in town, and I imagined him somewhere in the crowd, a stranger here as everywhere, looking down on the ceremonies from his great height, his eyes half closed in his backward tilted head.

"Citizens of Alexandria!"—Cousin John was standing a little apart from the other men, holding his hat across his chest. "Fellow Citizens, I have the pleasure of announcing to you, under authority received by telegraph from Governor Letcher, the formation of the Seventeenth Regiment of Virginia Infantry. This regiment is at present composed of the gallant men and patriots assembled upon this occasion. Their ranks"—he paused—"their ranks, should the emergency require, will be doubled overnight!" The shouts of at least three thousand people jamming the sidewalks were so prolonged that at last Cousin John raised his hand for silence. "It is the devout and burning wish of every patriot that this cruel emergency may pass." He paused and surveyed the crowd amid whose silence a hoof on the cobblestones could have been heard a block away. His mouth widened almost into a smile, and he nodded his head slowly and repeatedly. At last, under the spell of the expert demagogue, there was laughter in the ranks which was taken up by the crowd who suddenly broke into cheers. Again Cousin John gestured, half bowing, for silence. "Now, my friends, I come to the greatest pleasure of all. I have the signal honor to present to you your neighbor, kinsman, and friend: he will be known henceforth, until the honor of further promotion, as *Colonel* Montgomery Corse, commander of the Seventeenth Virginia!" There was more cheering as Cousin John stepped back and Colonel Corse moved forward with a long sheet of paper in his hand.

He stood calm and business-like, his gray cap, trimmed with patent leather, firmly on his head. He raised the paper and began to read. I turned my back on the platform the better to manage the horses; looking between them I saw in the crowd, back against the wall of the corner house, the impassive face of Brother George surveying the scene.

". . . that our first allegiance is due to Virginia; that we will obey her commands and abide by her fortunes; that in her defense against all assailants whatsoever we are ready to risk life and all that renders life desirable. To this we pledge the faith of soldiers and the sacred affection of sons."

The silence in which the crowd had received the Colonel's speech continued: when it broke I was brought sharply out of the superior reality that George's face had created for me. I had heard again his anguish in the shadowy back-parlor—"they think of nothing but marriage and death and the honor of Virginia." You will understand, of course, that the honor of Virginia meant something to me; yet for that instant my experience had been like a dream; words that would ordinarily have moved me as it had moved the crowd, to shouts and tears, had been far away, and I knew what it was to be apart from the emotions that all men shared; I suppose I came nearer, there in the street holding his mare, to seeing the world through George Posey's eyes than I had ever come before.

Before the cheering began I fancied I had caught his eye, and a gleam of this communion flashed to me.

Before I knew it the officers were taking their horses from me. Cousin John, flushed with his exertion, said: "Lead her down to the Marshall House. George'll get her there." When I turned round to start, the fierce yells struck me: the crowd and the soldiers had melted as I slowly made way for the big mare in the direction of King Street.

*   *   *

When I came to the Marshall House the crowd was thinning away. I tied Queen Susie at the hitching-rack around on the side street, and went back to the front door where I expected to find Brother George. He was nowhere to be seen. I hesitated before I could decide to enter: I had been forbidden to go into taverns, but I re-membered it was Sunday, the bar would be closed, and I had a definite mission. (Gadsby's I think was considered a more genteel place, but one of the early Gadsbys had been a "speculator," that is, a Negro trader, and papa was dead-set against the very name. Mr. Jackson, the proprietor of the Marshall House, was an excellent man.) I walked through the front door into the dim little "office." There were some strange men leaning upon the desk, behind which, on the wall, was a rack upon which a few keys hung from wooden pegs. Against the opposite wall stood a row of big unpainted chairs flanked at each end by large brass cuspidors. Most of the chairs were occupied by men silently smoking cigars. I walked up to the desk.

"Good evening, Mr. Jackson," I said.

Mr. Jackson gave me a polite glance followed by recognition. "Lacy, what can I do for you?" I waited for the rest of what he would surely say, but got instead only an urbane stare.

"I am looking for Mr. Posey, sir."

"I expect he'll be in here in a minute." He turned away, but he too had felt his omission, and he looked at me again. He had a strong, shrewd face, partly concealed by a wide black mustache. "Son," he said, "I hope that your father is well." He paused. "I haven't seen him all this past week. I feel that people are entitled to differences of opinion." He said it coldly and turned again to the men. "By God," he said in a loud voice, "if Yankee soldiers enter this town they'll be greeted by two fourpounders from my back yard. I've got 'em covering both streets to the river."

A man in one of the chairs quickly folded his newspaper, and walked out of the hotel. All eyes followed him. "Too hot for him," one of the strange men said. I heard footsteps descending the stairs in the back of the room. It was George. He smiled at me, without speaking, walked to the desk and laid a key upon it.

"Five dollars, sir," said Mr. Jackson. George took five silver dollars out of his trousers' pocket and stacked them neatly upon the desk. He had evidently been in Alexandria for nearly a week but he had not come near us: what had he been doing? He came to me at the end of the desk.

"Semmes wants you to go over and visit us in Georgetown, Lacy," he said. I said nothing. "Your pa sent him a message."

I was bewildered. "School ain't over yet, Brother George," I said.

The front door opened. A strange man carrying a small handbag followed by Cousin John entered. There was no greeting except that George nodded to them, and Mr. Jackson moved quickly to the back of the office and opened a door into a private dining room. He waited until we had disappeared through the door, then closed it, remaining on the outside. The three men sat down round the bare table. "Be seated, son," Cousin John said. I sat down in a chair near the door, against the wall. He looked from me to the stranger, and back at me. He said to the stranger: "The boy is my kinsman. We may proceed."

George took out of a long wallet a sheaf of papers and laid them before him. The stranger produced what seemed to me an identical sheaf, handing it to Cousin John, who put on his spectacles and with pencil poised in the air looked at George. George began reading in a brisk modulated voice. "Two thousand pair of shoes." Cousin John made a mark on his paper. "Three hundred tons of super-refined powder." Cousin John checked again. "Two thousand stand of new Springfield muskets." Cousin John made his mark, and the same proceedings went on for another half hour. There was a pause at the end. George looked at the stranger. "Mr.—," he began, then glanced at me. "Well, sir," he said, "I have furnished eighty-two Enfield rifles to Company D of the new Seventeenth Virginia."

The stranger looked at Cousin John, who said: "Mr. Posey equipped these men while they were still in the National Rifles of Georgetown."

"I understand," the stranger said, "that the company was mustered in equipped. If Mr. Posey wishes to be reimbursed he will have to get the captain of that company to make requisition for a voucher."

"I'm damned if I'll do that, sir," George said.

The strange man looked taken aback; he lowered his

eyes. "Mr. Posey, I can do nothing for you. The State Treasurer will have to pass on it." He rose, and placing the handbag on the table, said: "Here are sixty-one thousand dollars in gold and gold certificates of the Federal Government. Do you wish to count it?"

George got up. Cousin John struggled to his feet and produced a small flask of whiskey. He reached for three whiskey glasses on a side table, set them in a row, and poured drinks. George raised his glass. "No, sir, it won't be necessary to count it." He put the glass down. Cousin John and the stranger tossed off their drinks.

"How much longer can you do this business?" asked the stranger.

George's cold eyes shone. "I can do it as long as the fords ain't guarded. The goods are consigned to me at Frederick, and the teams have no trouble crossing White's Ford."

The stranger said nothing. He backed away from the table, bowed, and left the room.

George turned on his heel and began to pace up and down, ignoring Cousin John and me, till at last he said: "If I hadn't told the boys to do it they wouldn't have accepted Langton as cap'n. Now, Mr. Semmes," he said looking straight at Cousin John, "do you think it right and just that I should arm John Langton's company?"

"Well, George, I reckon it ain't precisely just, sir."

Cousin John sat down and fingered the rim of his empty glass. George turned toward the door. He came back to pick up the satchel. "Lacy, I have business tonight. I may not get home till tomorrow some time. You ride Queen Susie over in the morning. Your pa will give his consent." Satchel in hand, he addressed Cousin John. "Mr. Semmes, your people are about to fight a war. They remind me of

a passel of young 'uns playing prisoners' base. Good evening, sir." And he opened the door and was gone.

I got up from my chair and moved towards the table.
Cousin John stared at the empty glass. "Well, Lacy, you
better do as George says. It would kill your pa if you
enlisted."

"Why wa'n't Brother George made cap'n, Cousin John?"

"Maybe it ain't just, but he ought to be willing to be a
private, damn it!" Cousin John hit the table with his fat
fist. "Lacy, George Posey ain't from Alexandria. The Seventeenth is the Alexandria regiment."

"Mister John ain't from Alexandria either," I said.

Cousin John gave me a shrewd glance. "But he's a
Virginian. That's the difference—he's a Virginian." He
pinched his dewlap meditatively. "Don't expect George
to come to see your pa. Your pa's Union sentiments are
embarrassing to him in this ticklish business he's doing.
Lacy, George is serving the cause as much as if he had a
musket. And it's what he likes to do. He thinks fighting is
nonsense." He got up. "Come on, let's see how your pa is."

When we came to the door, I said in a low voice:
"Cousin John, ain't Brother George one of our people?"

"Good God, boy, what a question! Go and get the mare.
If George got caught, the next place you'd see him would
be the Old Capitol Prison where his friend Schaeffer is.
Now let's go."

I went round to the hitching-rack, untied the bridle,
mounted Queen Susie, and started at a trot towards Fairfax Street. I turned down Fairfax, and in a couple of minutes I dismounted in front of our house. I looked up and
down the melancholy red brick and at the windows where
the blinds were closely drawn. I decided to wait outside
and to go in with Cousin John when he came.

*   *   *

I came to the head of the Long Bridge next evening at
sundown, and I got by the sentries without trouble: "I'm
going to visit my sister in Georgetown," I said, and the
sergeant of the picket said, "Search him," which the men
did very carelessly; and I walked the mare over the bridge.
By the time I had gone the length of Virginia Avenue
to the Water Street Bridge into Georgetown, it was nearly
dark, and, to keep from getting lost in the maze of narrow
streets, I continued along Water Street and followed it
into town, until I came to the end of Frederick Street,
where it suddenly pitches from the heights above down
to Water Street and the canal. I dismounted at the foot
of Frederick lest Queen Susie slip in ascending the steep,
cobbled grade. At the top I mounted her again, and in
two minutes I came to Vista Avenue and drew rein at the
carriage gate of the Posey house. I sat in the saddle to
listen for I know not what. I looked down the river where
a few yellow lights were slowly moving. On the Maryland
side I saw many fires, the camps of Northern soldiers.
The house before me was dark. I heard footsteps behind
the gate, then a low voice:
"Is that you, Marse Lacy?"
"Yas," I said.
"This yere's Joe," the voice said.
The gate opened towards me, I dismounted, and Blind
Joe took the bridle, and led the mare towards the stables
in the rear, and disappeared. I stood on the brick driveway
trying to hear something. Low, indistinguishable voices
came from the servants' quarters beyond the stable at the
rear of the garden. I knew that the garden ran all the way
round the other side of the house and fronted on the

street where a high stone wall shut it in. I looked up at
the rear windows; they were dark. I walked quietly over
to the garden and found myself at the entrance to a narrow path which was blocked by dense, unpruned shrubs.
The voices ceased. I had better go to the side door. I
turned to the right into the path at the side of the house
and came to the little door that the Poseys called the
"wicket." There was no knocker. I pushed on the handle,
but the door was locked. Before I knew what I was doing
I was knocking hard upon the door. There was no response.
I cried, "Sister, sister! Here I am." I waited about a minute.
"Sister!" I cried again.

It seemed an hour but it was only a few minutes before
I heard slow footsteps inside, and the key turned in the
lock. In the silence that followed the door did not open.
I said quickly, "It's Lacy Buchan." The door opened with
a squeak, and an old Negro woman said peevishly, "Whyn't
you come to de front door?" She held in her gnarled fingers
a battered tin candlestick in which the candle had almost
burned down to the socket. She turned abruptly, I entered
and closed the door. "Don't make no noise," she said.
"Ole Miss sick." Ole Miss was of course Aunt Jane Anne.
I followed the old woman up the short flight of steps into
the main hall. She disappeared in the rear of the house
where I heard her muffled feet ascending the back stairs.
I moved into the front hall where a candle was burning
weakly in a wall bracket at the foot of the main staircase.
Now where shall I go, I thought, how shall I find sister
if I can't make any noise? I was trying to think it out.
Staring at the face of old Jeremaiah Gibson in the portrait
hanging over the candle, I took in his features one by one
—the harsh, ascetic eyes, the small mouth, the bulging forehead. Well, I said to myself with serious irrelevance, the

old man will never help me. I had better go right up to
her room.

I could see that the upper hall was dark, so I seized a
candlestick on the small table near the front door, and
lit it from the candle on the wall. From the top of the
stairs, which wound round the back of the hall, the lower
hall spread before me in its mellow amplitude: the ceiling was so high that from where I stood I might have been
peering into a deep, torch-lit cavern, a bright place surrounded by darkness. It was only the fancy of a boy that
for an instant peopled the hall with gay young figures,
bright faces and laughter at the end of a soirée, saying
Good-bye, good-bye, and then I almost heard it like a voice:
Good-bye.

I started towards the front rooms: the upper hall was
heavily carpeted and I made no sound. When I had got
about halfway down the hall I heard a door open behind
me; I halted and waited for somebody to speak. There
was no voice but I knew that the door was still open. I
turned quickly and saw peeping from a door which was
open about six inches, a dim face that seemed to have no
support below it, being wedged tightly between door and
jamb. I suppose I stared back at the face, and the impropriety of my situation grew upon me, but the even greater
impropriety of speech kept me silent; I waited for the
face to utter a word or to disappear. It stared; then it suddenly withdrew and the door closed with a soft click.

The front room on the right was Aunt Jane Anne's; the
room on the left, sister's. I knocked gently upon her door. I
heard regular but quiet footsteps, broken by regular short
pauses. When there was no cessation of the steps I knocked
again. They ceased abruptly. The door opened, and sister
stood before me. Without a word she backed away; I entered and closed the door. She kissed me upon the cheek

and, though I was inches taller than she, she put her arms about my shoulders as if I were a child, and walked me over to a chair by the slow fire. She remained standing. I thought she was handsomer than I had ever seen her: she had evidently been brushing her hair, it hung down to her waist over the folds and ruffles of a white negligee. Her face was marble-white and her eyes were calm.

"How is papa?" she said.

My hands were not cold, but I held them to the fire. "Sister," I said, "who peeped at me out in the hall, I mean from the back bedroom?"

"That was Aunt Milly," she said, but she did not smile.

"Papa is well." I hoped she would say something. She sat down in a small rocker. "Papa," I said, "is well." I looked at her. "I wa'n't going to enlist, sister." She gazed at me but said nothing. She turned her eyes towards the fire, then rose and walked to the narrow door into the adjoining room, which was the nursery. Presently she came back, and I followed her steps over the worn track in the carpet that ran from the middle of the room to the nursery door. Idly my eyes traced out another worn place running from the dismal tester bed to the *prie-dieu* that stood behind me near the mantelpiece against the wall: sister, not being a Catholic, had profanely dropped her sewing upon the lectern. I was waiting for her to sit down, but she remained standing, her hands clasped before her; it was the first time I had not been able to say to sister whatever came into my mind, the first time I had no chatter, nothing being in my mind to say. She looked tired. I kept my eyes on the floor; directly I found myself tracing out still another of those confounded tracks on the carpet, this time it was over by the far front window, a short path of five or six feet, and it looked different from the others, as if the nap had just been taken off, leaving the fiber clean where the fiber of the older tracks looked faded and aged.

"How is little Jane?" I said.

Her face lighted up for a bare second. "She cries for her father." She sat down in the rocker.

"Sister," I said, "you look tired."

"I don't sleep well. Not since George went into the army."

I hardly knew what to make of that. Sister asked: "Didn't papa send any messages?"

Of course he had sent messages, but I could not remember how he had worded them; so I said bluntly: "Papa said for me to protect you."

Sister put her face into her hands. When she looked up and spoke her voice was difficult. "I need no protection, Lacy; it's papa who needs it. Poor papa—what will become of him?"

After a few months I remembered her words and knew that I had not understood them, that I had not even known there was anything to understand.

"Sister," I said suddenly, "why did Miss Milly peep out at me?"

"I don't know, Lacy, I don't know." She rocked back and forth a little. And then she said, calmly as if she were merely explaining why the Washington Monument had not been finished: "It is no wonder he is the way he is— I mean my husband, Lacy, he's so fine, but he's so violent." She pressed her eyelids with thumb and forefinger, then placed her hands in her lap. "People have got to get life where they can, that's all there is to it. That's why Aunt Milly peeps—it makes her live."

She seemed to be thinking about it, but I couldn't ask her to go on. "Lacy, hadn't you better go to bed, you know upstairs in the south bedroom; I know you're tired." I tired? I had never been tired in my life. I did not move. "Sister, Brother George ain't in the army. Mr. John Langton's cap'n of the company with the Georgetown boys in it." I don't know why I said it, but some instinct told me that she had better know. She rose and walked to the nearer window, putting a hand against the casement: a posture that she must often have taken, only now she looked at the blank, closed blinds; yet she was oblivious of them, and of her purpose in standing there.

"Then I don't know where my husband has been for a week." She had turned to face me, but now she went over to the bed and sat against it, running both hands under her smooth, loose hair. I looked again at the fire, and there was a long silence.

When she spoke again I was startled: I heard her voice like a harsh echo a few seconds after she had spoken. "When I was a girl at Pleasant Hill I couldn't have known about this." As I was taking in all that it meant, the stillness of the house was broken by the big clock in the lower back hall striking the hour: without counting the strokes I said to myself after the last one: nine.

"I thought they were just two peculiar old ladies," she said in a low, excited tone. "I was so young I couldn't know that they weren't really old. And George was so handsome and independent. He still is," she said. "But he's always living somewhere else. He never talks to me. He comes upstairs and talks to little Jane and smiles." She came over to the fire and started to sit down. She stood by the chair. "Well, Lacy, good night."

I got up and started for the door. "Come kiss me good night, Lacy."

I went back to her, then stopped to face her. "Sister, why did you send for me? I know papa didn't think of it. Why did you send for me?"

"Yes, Lacy, I sent for you," she said. "We do need protection." I continued to look at her. "They don't know—
they think nothing is happening. Why, Mr. Jarman's only
been out of the house once—last Sunday—in a year. He
walks the floor reciting his compositions." She smiled. "I
walk the floor too. I suppose we all get that way!" She
came forward and held me by the shoulders. She kissed
me. "Good night, Lacy."

There was a knock at the door, and I felt as if I had
been surprised or menaced in some way wholly unfore-
seen. Sister gazed steadily into my eyes, and without moving her gaze, she said in a slightly raised tone: "Come in,
Jane."

She kept looking at me as the doorknob moved timidly,
and I said in a flash to myself; she hasn't mentioned
Semmes! Had she thought about him? And I hadn't mentioned Jane, but that was because for some reason I had
not thought of her. The door opened and Jane, her straw-
colored hair down her back, came into the room with
short, modest steps. She saw me without surprise, then
looked inquiringly at sister.

"Jane, here's Lacy," sister said, and it would have
sounded foolish anywhere else.

"Hello," Jane said to me.

I said, "Hello, Jane." I glanced furtively and saw that
her eyes were on the floor.

"Have you done your French?" asked sister.

"Yes'm," Jane said. Her eyes were still downcast, but
there was something grown-up in her face that I had not
seen there before; it was as if her features had settled into
the mold of maturity round the chin and eyes, leaving
the mouth to be attended to later on: the mouth still
had the submissive droop, or was it the mouth? Or is it
ever any feature that means anything? I tried to think what

I meant by the submissiveness of her mouth, but I couldn't; I suppose there was something in Jane that I was trying to understand, but then I knew only that I wanted to see her alone: perhaps sister would let me walk with her to the convent next day when she went up for her music lesson. Sister was looking from me to Jane. She was taller than sister; it was only pretense that kept her a moment longer a child.

"Jane has come for her prayers," sister said, smiling at Jane.

I went to the door and turned around, ready in my embarrassment to make a bow to Jane; but she had not changed her position; so I said, "Good night," and as sister smiled at me I opened the door and went upstairs. At the door into the south bedroom, where I had stayed before, I remembered again that Susan had not mentioned Semmes. Why had I not thought of Jane? Well, I should have to get used to her in this house where people were either in rooms or about, irrevocably, to go into them. I could see Jane standing against the wall in my mother's dressing room and the satin slipper lying on its side on the floor.

*   *   *

Two days later I received a letter from papa saying that he was getting along well, but that old Lucy Lewis had been found dead in her bed, and Coriolanus and Henry had driven the body to Pleasant Hill for burial; but that he had not gone himself "which I much regret, as the respect in which Aunt Lucy was held by our family was such as to warrant the tenderest devotion to the memory of her conspicuous, if humble virtues; but the weather suddenly becoming inclement, I had to forego the duty. Your Aunt Myra leaves today for Falls Church: I allude to her depature chiefly for dear Susan's eye, since our dear daughter may wish to drive to her Uncle Armistead in what may be his last illness. I am pained, my dear son, to deepen further the melancholy of this epistle with the recital of another misfortune. Your Cousin John Semmes, according to advices just received in Alexandria, was seen yesterday on the streets of Washington and arrested by Major Stone: while I cannot condone the unlawful arrest, which was executed in contempt of a writ of *habeas corpus,* yet his pronounced secessionist activities have made him subject to this action. It appears that he must languish, in the company of other disunionists, in Fort Delaware. He was charged with smuggling materials of war from Pennsylvania into Virginia. I cannot conceive why I had not heard about this activity..." Well, papa, I said to myself, I can! Poor papa, who still thought that his neighbors alone were perversely opposing the Federal Government! I glanced again at what I had read: had Brother George been arrested too? No, I decided; we should have heard it..."I come now to a piece of news that has been received by our friends here with wild demonstrations of delight. Even my friend Daingerfield at his age was seen to jump up and down with excitement. I was dumfounded. Robert Lee has accepted the post of general-in-chief of the Army of Virginia. I had supposed his resignation from the United States Army to be a gesture of neutrality, a position with which I feel a considerable sympathy; although I felt and do still feel that in so far as one must be swayed by faction, one ought to support the authority of the Federal Government. Alas, my son, there are every day fewer and fewer of *our people* in Alexandria. Now in closing this tedious communication I must advert briefly to your present situation. I did not feel that you would enlist without my consent, yet it is my

desire to remove you from the sphere of excitement and
temptation, and the influence of your Brother. Last night
I had a painful interview with that young man. Semmes
came in a few minutes after supper. I commanded him to
resign from his company, saying that I would send in to
John Langton a request that his name be dropped from
the rolls on the ground that membership in an organization sworn to uphold disunion was inconsistent with the
views of his family. Semmes stubbornly held that he was
in favor of disunion, whereupon I said, reluctantly and
without passion, that he was no longer a son of mine. I
cannot but feel that my other son George Posey's influence
has placed Semmes in this position, although George himself seems to have reconsidered and returned to his family,
where I presume he is conducting his business as usual.
That is a mode of conduct that all men should pursue—
business as usual; our present troubles for sheer lack of
attention would subside. Give to Susan and infant my
dearest love and convey to the Posey ladies my respects.
Yrs. my son till Death do us part, L. Buchan."

I had by this time come to my own idea of George's "influence" on Semmes; it was not an influence but an exchange in which each got from the other what he could
not supply for himself. I can see George Posey from his
boyhood in the dark halls of the Posey house, then emerg-
ing into the bright light of day; you must try to imagine
him after he got outside—what could he do? His father,
old Mr. Rozier Posey, had died while he was still a small
boy: I never knew much about him but the tales of his
secrecy of action and brutality of character have done a
good deal in later years to explain the extreme refinement
of sensibility of which Aunt Jane Anne and I suppose
Jane also were the victims, and George too in his curious
way. The family did not live the normal life of their times

—that, I suppose, is what it all comes down to. Old
Mr. Posey had left the plantation, but he was a rich man,
and, in town, the family could not merge into the small
middle class of folks who were beginning to rise. The
women particularly had nothing to do. And Mr. Jarman
—many years younger than his brother—who had wanted
to be a man of letters, could not find anybody else who
wanted him to be one; so be became a recluse, a kind
of Roderick Usher, whose nerves could bear whatever
reality they received from the dormer windows at the top
of the house, which looked out upon the river. There is
much less fantasy in Poe's creation than most people think:
Usher was just like Mr. Jarman—Poe had a prophetic in-
sight—for Mr. Jarman, like Usher, had had so long an assured living that he no longer knew that it had a natural
source in human activity; and I suppose he began from his
early manhood to retire upon himself. I doubt if heredity
had anything to do with it. Aunt Jane Anne was not a
Posey, but a Gibson: she was a gentlewoman who became
in the common sense more and more "gentle" as she
got older, and ended up by not being able to entertain
longer than a minute any thought that did not concern her
health and her feelings. There was a wonderful story about
her that I picked up somewhere as a boy: how, as a young
woman, perhaps as a bride, she had been high-spirited;
how, when once late at night "Mr. Posey" had come home
intoxicated, she was ready for him: she had got the Negro
girls to sew two sheets together; she had spread the sheets
out at the top of the stairs; when "Mr. Posey" with great
effort achieved the flight, she with her own hand tripped
him with a poker, and as he lay there in a stupor, she
sewed him up in the sheets and then horse-whipped him
into sobriety. How could she have done it? Her hands

were small and waxen, her feet like birds' feet, and her voice so gentle it was a marvel that she spoke at all.

I should say that the Poseys were more refined than the Buchans, but less civilized. I never saw a letter written by George Posey; he must have written letters, but I cannot imagine them. In the sense of today nobody wrote personal letters in our time: letters conveyed the sensibility in society, the ordered life of families and neighborhoods. George Posey was a man without people or place; he had strong relationships, and he was capable of passionate feeling, but it was all personal; even his affection for his mother was personal and disordered, and it was curious to see them together: the big powerful man of action remained the mother's boy. What else could he have been? What life was there for him in the caverns of the Posey house? What life was there for him outside it? That was what, as I see it, he was trying to find out. If he had been poor, he would have gone out West; well off as he was, he might have gone West anyhow if it had not been for the "ailing mother." I never heard of his considering the West, and I am sure that he never did. He had great energy and imagination and, as Cousin John said, he had to keep moving; but where? I always come back to the horseman riding off over a precipice. It is as good a figure as any other. And that is what he gave to Semmes—mystery and imagination, the heightened vitality possessed by a man who knew no bounds. What Semmes gave to him was what he most needed but never could take: Semmes gave him first of all Susan, and then—papa being absolutely wrong about this—he tried to give him what the Poseys had lost: an idea, a cause, an action in which his personality could be extinguished, and it seemed as if George had succeeded in becoming a part of something greater than he: the Confederate cause. That afternoon in the back-parlor in Alexandria Semmes had hesitated out of consideration for papa, not in irresolution; he could wait a few days because he knew where he stood in a belief that was to him, as to thousands of young men, a religion. But George Posey had to act at once if he was to be certain of acting at all outside his own feelings; there could be no delay or he would lose hold of his purpose and be temporarily diverted, as he actually was, by the appearance of John Langton as captain of his company—a trick of fate that threw him back again into himself. In a world in which all men were like him, George would not have suffered—and he did suffer—the shock of communion with a world that he could not recover; while that world existed, its piety, its order, its elaborate rigamarole—his own forfeited heritage—teased him like a nightmare in which the dreamer dreams a dream within a dream within another dream of something that he cannot name. All violent people secretly desire to be curbed by something that they respect, so that they may become known to themselves. If I had been old enough or had had the occasion to think of it, I should have known the meaning of George Posey's refusal to attend my mother's corpse to its grave; I should have seen into his terrific joke, there at the end of that day, about Semmes' cutting up cadavers, when he wrested Susan away from her father so that he might escort his ailing mother home; I should have been less embarrassed and more illuminated by his blushing, two years before, at the behavior of the little Durham bull.

*   *   *

It was the only letter I ever received from papa, so I put it away in a bureau drawer, where years later, after they were all dead but Brother George, old Aunt Milly,

and myself, and I was living in the Posey house while I
finished my studies at the Columbian Medical College,
I found it again: a curious spark of life still glowing with
the public and private passions of its time! Old Uncle
Armistead, dead at eighty-two, saved from the new world
for which he would have had only a curse and a watering
eye: the gallant John Semmes—dead, his cynicism, his urbanity, and his kindness having rotted away in the damp
casemates of Fort Delaware: Mr. Jarman, before the war
was over, dead of a slow consumption that (who knows?)
may have hastened to its end under influences of which
we should not have credited Mr. Jarman with being
aware—the subtle pressure of near and remote changes
upon the life of the dormer rooms, like the unacknowl-
edged influence of the sun-spots on the tone of a letter or on
the feelings that one communicates in the clasp of a hand.

Well, I did go walking with Jane: one morning early
in May—it was not the first time—sister asked me to walk
up to the convent and carry Jane's music roll, and if I
cared to, she added, I might wait in the college grounds
until the lesson was over and accompany her home. You
will remember that ladies did not then go out on the
street without escort or a female companion, though it
was permissible for a lady to go abroad alone in a vehicle
driven by a servant. Why Blind Joe, who usually drove
Jane the three squares to the convent, began to have other
duties in the morning, I did not know; yet I soon saw that
Susan for a reason of her own let me see Jane two or
three times a day, and even told me to keep Jane company
in the front parlor after breakfast while she ran scales on
the harpsicord.

It had been a pleasant room and I suppose it still was,
because every morning one of the house-girls came in and
opened the blinds and dusted and swept to make it bright

for the callers that never came, but this routine attested to a more social era in the past, before the unused Victorian parlor, with its what-not loaded with bric-a-brac, had replaced the eighteenth century withdrawing room in which the ladies of the family played backgammon, whist, or cribbage all day. But that time was gone; one stepped into the parlor and was cut off from the Posey world of closed upstairs rooms, a world where people communicated only through their infirmities, in hushed voices, a world in which the social acts became privacies: the family never dined together, and while I was there that spring in the lull before the violence, Susan, Jane, and I sat at great distances from one another at the long walnut table and were waited on by two sullen Negro women who could not serve the food but merely handed it to us. Not since Brother George had sold Yellow Jim, the butler, had there been any dining service; the other Negroes had not been taught, and Susan took food grimly from the Negro women without ever correcting them. "They are not my servants," she once said to me.

Nor was Jane her daughter, yet imperceptibly all the care and education of the girl had fallen upon Susan, who, I must say, had assumed the duty with a little more than her usual intensity, saying that Aunt Jane Anne's invalidism had made her own course clear to her. But was that the reason? I doubted it. Everything I had heard or seen dated the beginning of her care from the day of my mother's funeral, when it had been obvious that at almost any moment Jane would cease to be a child: if one cared to see, as if it were a picture, the beginning of Susan's responsibility one could bring before the mind that particular moment in the old parlor at Pleasant Hill when Jane and I were turning away from the coffin of my mother, and Susan had come in to catch Semmes at the very instant he had

become for the first time aware of the whole person of Jane
—the lovely insipidity of her docile eyes, the constantly
parted lips, and the languid posture that was yet instinct
with a vitality that men paused to observe, with the remark:
"What a pretty girl!" when she was not pretty at all. It
was doubtless this vitality in the innocence of a sixteen-
year-old girl that made her attractive to men, if indeed she
was attractive to more men than Semmes and myself; for
I never saw the girl except at Pleasant Hill and in Georgetown; and I confess that in the past year I had thought to
myself more than once: "How nice it would be to be married to Brother George's sister!" Do not people fall in love
in order to share with the loved one a secret of life that
they imagine she possesses? I say "she" because women
seldom feel this secret power in men. There can be no question but that Susan had been fascinated by George's mysterious power, by his secrecy and his violence; but she
wanted not power, nor secrecy, nor violence, except in so
far as she could employ them to subdue those qualities in
George Posey. She could not have known that George was
outside life, or had a secret of life that no one had heard
of at Pleasant Hill. To Susan the life around her in childhood had been final; there could be no other, there never
had been any other way of life—which is, I suppose, a way
of saying that people living in formal societies, lacking
the historical imagination, can imagine for themselves
only a timeless existence: they themselves never had any
origin anywhere and they can have no end, but will go on
forever. When I was a small boy I used to watch my
mother wash what she called the "good china" after dinner: Coriolanus brought to the dining-room two enam-
eled basins and set them before her, and then handed to
her, a dish or a plate at a time, all the china on the table.
She washed each piece in the suds of the one basin, and

rinsed it in the clear water of the other, then wiped it dry with a little napkin. If this little ritual of utility—not very old to be sure but to my mother immemorial—had been discredited or even questioned, she would have felt that the purity of womanhood was in danger, that religion and morality were jeopardized, and that infidels had wickedly asserted that the State of Virginia (by which she meant her friends and kin) was not the direct legatee of the civilization of Greece and Rome.

In Susan too there was a great deal of this: she could not have imagined a family that did not live by rigid order wherein everything meant something, whose meaning had been long agreed upon. The Posey ladies were not eccentric, not "two peculiar old ladies," but rather excessively refined sensibilities that had let their social tradition lapse in personal self-indulgence in which the draught under the door, the light sifting through the blinds, the remote threat of rain—into which, of course, they would not have ventured—became the overwhelming concerns of life. Aunt Jane Anne drank coffee all night, and nobody had ever seen Miss Milly eat anything but overripe bananas. On the rare occasions when they came downstairs to chatter with some of the old ladies of the town, Miss Milly would vaguely sniff if money, childbirth, or poverty were mentioned, and Aunt Jane Anne could not admit that common people were real—"It is just too painful that they should exist." Once when I was a small boy a neighbor's bull had been brought to Pleasant Hill, and some young girls asked mother what he was doing there. "He's here on business," my mother said, and looking back to that remark I know that she was a person for whom her small world held life in its entirety, and for whom, through that knowledge, she knew all that was necessary of the world at large.

Some time in that first week at the Poseys, one morning, I believe, when I was with sister and we thought we heard Brother George coming up the stairs (it was only Blind Joe), she said to me: "Lacy, I might have done better to marry some plain man. Like Jim Higgins. He would have been so grateful, and I should have known every minute where he was." She smiled. "Of course when we had company he would have come in and squatted in the parlor. How droll it would have been!"

Droll indeed; but I still wonder whether she was not right. For it was impossible to communicate with the Posey family: like children playing a game, they had their fingers perpetually crossed—which permitted them to do what they pleased. I have never been able to understand how any man can be a lawyer, for the law, assuming that people act upon motives, is rational; but people never act for a reason, even a bad reason. My father was the most rational man I ever knew. Did he seem reasonable to George? George thought him willful and arbitrary because he, George, did not recognize the assumptions of the game. Papa's feeling about Negroes seemed to George foolish and sentimental. But then George was a man who received the shock of the world at the end of his nerves. As to all unprotected persons, death was horrible to him; therefore he faced it in its aspect of greatest horror—the corrupt body. And it is likely that he hated money too; therefore he spent all his time making it. There is no doubt that he loved Susan too much; by that I mean he was too personal, and with his exacerbated nerves he was constantly receiving impressions out of the chasm that yawns beneath lovers; therefore he must have had a secret brutality for her when they were alone. Excessively refined persons have a communion with the abyss; but is not civilization the agreement, slowly arrived at, to let the abyss alone?

At about this time I used to walk down to the canal, then turn into the tow-path, and follow it up to the gas works, across from which, on Washington Street, stood the old two-storey brick building that Brother George owned and in which he had his "office." The windows had been recently boarded up, after a mob had broken all the glass. Crudely painted on a plank nailed above the door were the words: "Warning to Secessionists." At Pleasant Hill or in Alexandria I should have known what a secessionist was. But here in Georgetown, knowing Brother George as I already dimly knew him, I couldn't decide the question: What is a secessionist? The building looked deserted, but on the door-sill there was a clean place where the lower edge of the door had recently scraped the debris away. Someone had been inside the building in the last few days. In the backyard lay broken tobacco hogsheads and a great heap of dark, unstripped tobacco. About a dozen oyster barrels had been pried open and the rotting oysters gave out a foul stink. I walked into the wagon yard, at the side of the building, towards the stalls of the dray horses. Under the shed were two heavy wagons in perfect repair. From the stalls I heard the stamp of a horse that startled me, and I began to retreat. Blind Joe came out of the stable. He stood looking at me curiously, without recognition.

"G'long," he said.

I think I must have been afraid of him; I neither spoke nor moved.

"G'long, my marster ain't no seecesh. He ain't in de rebel army."

"I know he ain't, Joe," I said, and laughed.

He came forward and squinted at me. "Lawdy, Marse

Lacy, I wouldn't have knowed you hyar. Is you lookin'
for de marster?"

"No," I said, and I turned on my heel and started
towards the street.

Blind Joe ran after me. "Cause if you is I knows whar
he is. Yassir, don't you tell nobody."

"Where is Marse George?" I said.

"T'other white gentleman, he was took last night, he
was took when he was trying to get back to Virginny in his
skiff."

"What white gentleman?" I was mystified.

"De one with de satchel. He come ever' night to meet
the marster." He nodded towards the upstairs rooms. "He
was took by de paterole."

Of course the town was under martial law and the ignorant darky thought the sentries scattered through the
town were the same as the patrol that rounded up wandering Negroes.

"Look here, Joe," I said, "what you doing skulking?"

"I ain't skulkin', Marse Lacy." He had that bad-dog
look in his pinched brown face. He drew his lips back.

"Joe, is Marse George here now? Don't you lie to me."
I was bigger than he was and tried to look severe.

"Naw, sir, he shore ain't, Marse Lacy, and that's de
truth. He ain't hyar in de daytime." He squinted again.
"Marse Lacy, I ain't skulkin'. De marster he give me orders
to come to de war'house to see after de horses."

I turned on my heel and went out of the yard into the
street, and then up the hill to Bridge Street to the Post
Office. In the square I saw a company of soldiers dressed
in Scotch kilts: they were lolling about in the worn grass,
smoking and chewing, a few in close huddles playing cards,
their muskets stacked along the sidewalk in a bristling row.
I gazed stupidly at the gaudy tartans above the knobby

legs and before I knew it I was angry. These men ain't Scotchmen, I said; I'm a Scot and they're my enemies. I paused at the corner of Congress Street by a group of card players and saw on their collars in gold embroidery, *79th New York*. The cheap Glengarry bonnets set off the hard, foreign faces. One man looked me over as I passed, and I thought: I am a foreigner to him.

But here are "our people," I said, thinking of poor papa who had, I was sure, made a stern ceremony of disowning his son. I hurried along to High Street and turned to the right past the Masonic Hall, and came to the corner of Vista, from which the Posey house was only about five blocks; but instead of going out Vista I kept to High Street, looking leftwards at the sun, which was still high, and I said: it couldn't be more than three o'clock. In ten minutes I had reached the Seventh Street Road, where I turned west and after two blocks I had open ground and woods on both sides, rough land fenced into small fields. The road was rising all the time; the ground to the north was still higher. I came over a little hill. A middle-aged Negro man sat on a rail fence smoking a pipe; behind him his mule, still hitched to the plow, was tied to a rail. The darky uncrossed his legs and stood before me.

"Good evening," I said. I looked around but there was not a house in sight. "Whose land is this?" I said.

"It ain't nobody's." He spat, and I thought there was a trace of insolence in his gesture. He glared at me. "It ain't nobody's. It's mine, that's whose. I's free. I's free-born." He waved his pipe in the air, and gave me a sly look. "Is you seecesh?" he said. "You talks lak it."

I turned my back on him, and crossed the road, and as I put a leg over the fence I called back, "Yes, I'm seecesh." I jumped to the ground and started up the hill to the woods. I don't know why, but I found myself turning round to look at the Negro again. I shouted, "Yes, God damn you, I am."

At the top of the hill I came to a rocky ledge upon which grew a few stunted cedars. Down the slope ahead of me I saw tall sycamores, and in the quiet air I heard running water: the creek emptying into the canal above the college. I followed the ledge to the north till I came to a clearing that revealed a little to the east the white dots of Holyrood Cemetery. To the north and west I got a long view over rolling fields that led to a brick mansion on a still higher hill: it was about a half-mile away and I suddenly recognized it—the house of Mr. James Kengla, "Cousin James" to the Poseys, who had been thrown into the Old Capitol Prison a few weeks ago. I broke into a dogtrot and I arrived winded at the last fence which I took at a vault; then I leaned against it to rest. I got my bearings: if I had stayed on High Street until it became the Tennally-town road I should have reached the entrance to the Kengla place that way. As I began the last ascent to the house I saw flying back of it the Union flag, and a little below it on a big flat rock a group of blue men looking eastward through field-glasses and waving red-and-white flags.

Fifty yards from the house ran a high box hedge that concealed the house and out-buildings and even the signal station. I thought I had better go to the house and see who was there and tell them who I was. I went through a gate in the hedge and had gone only a few steps when a harsh voice said:

"Hey, boy, where you think you're goin'?"

A soldier scrambled to his feet and raised his musket, with fixed bayonet; he was dressed in rusty blue and on his cap were the simple letters US. The Regulars, I thought, looking him over, not those foreigners from New York;

then looking down the barrel of his musket, I knew that he was an enemy too. I kept looking at him, backing away towards the house.

"Didn't I say halt?" He cocked the musket.

"No," I said. "You said where'm I goin'."

He set his lips, uncocked his musket, and seized me by the sleeve of my jacket, pushing me ahead of him around the end of the house.

"We're goin' to see the colonel," he said. When we came to the side of the enormous flat rock the top of which stood about twenty feet above us, the soldier prodded me in the butt with his bayonet. "Shinny up there," he said.

I turned on him. "Yes, God damn it, I am," I said.

He was startled. "What you say?"

I shinnied up the rock, he followed me, and we stood before a handsome officer in blue who held his field-glasses in his hand. A sergeant was still waving the signal flags though the sun was rapidly setting, and I wondered how the other station, wherever it was, could read the messages. The colonel had not looked at me. He spoke to the sentry.

"What do you want?"

The sentry stood at attention. "This boy was prowling around. Here he is, sir."

The colonel eyed me. "Well, son, you haven't any business up here."

"Yes, sir," I said.

"Where do you live?" he asked.

I was suddenly scared. "Langton's Cross Roads, sir."

He laughed. "My man," he began to the sentry, but broke off and looked at me again. "Langton's Cross Roads. Is that across the river?" I nodded. "What's your name?" he said.

"Lacy Buchan, sir."

"My God, boy!" He laughed again. "I thought I knew about Langton's Cross Roads." He hesitated, then spoke in a quiet voice. "Your brother, Captain Buchan, he's—" he hesitated again: "He was a friend of mine." He raised his glasses and said, "Here, take them. Your brother may be over there." He pointed to the south across the river. I raised the glasses and looked.

I saw first the white columns of Arlington in the shade, with the setting sun blazing in the trees above the house. Then I felt a shiver, and my hand shook. The glasses were so powerful that I could see the scarred places on a tall evergreen by the house, scars where the branches had been cut off making the trunk a slender pole: at the top, flapping against the pole, hung the same flag that flew from the roof of the Marshall House, red and white with the big star in the field of blue.

"Your brother may be there," the colonel said. He took the glasses. "That flag went up an hour ago. That's what we're signaling." He studied the flag again, then spoke to me. "If they've got five thousand men they can walk across that bridge—and who's to stop them?"

I looked at the bridge, the Long Bridge that I had crossed so many times: I saw a long line of gray soldiers on it moving rapidly into the city; but as I listened I could hear no sound, and with the naked eye I saw a lone army wagon parked, without its team, in the middle of the bridge. I turned to the colonel.

"I better be going," I said.

"Young man, I suppose you are all right." He pursed his lips. "What are you doing on this side?"

"I'm staying with my married sister in Georgetown, sir."

He came forward and took off his gauntlet. We shook hands. "Keep on staying there, my boy, till this"—he made a sweeping gesture—"is over."

I followed the gesture: from the Long Bridge it seemed but a step to the housetops of Alexandria. The Washington monument, only half done, rose in the foreground out of a sea of tents, I had almost said tombstones, they were so like the distant dots that I had glimpsed in Holyrood. Farther to the left Pennsylvania Avenue ran like a ribbon to the remote Capitol, towards which a long column crept like a moving smudge. My eyes drifted off into a scene of terror soon to be taken by the twilight. I would have stood there, rapt, forever. From below, from out of the white sea of the Federal army, came the weak, lingering notes of a bugle. The whine was taken up by another, then another, till the air was rent with brass: not a hundred yards away, under the brow of the hill, the sharp cry of a bugle brought me to myself. I turned to the colonel.

"It's supper time," he said.

I moved to the place where I had ascended the rock. The sentry had gone. I slid down on the seat of my trousers, ran round the back of the house into the lane, and by the time I had gone the half-mile to the Tenallytown Road, it was dark. Yes, God damn it, I am, I said, and I mumbled it over again. But first I've got to go walking with Jane in the morning, in the morning. Christmas day in the morning, I said to myself as my heavy bootsoles clumped upon the hard turnpike.

*   *   *

It was ten o'clock in the morning of May 7th: I know that because it was the day after the Confederate flag went up at Arlington, and the books agree that it went up on the 6th. I came out of the parlor to wait for Jane, and when she too came into the hall I started to open the front door but she said, "Wait a minute, I'll be right back," and tripped up the stairs. I said, "I'll wait for you outside."

The sunlight blinded me as I shuffled down the stone steps and went to the edge of the walk to lean against the big elm. The façade of the house was in the shade. I scanned the stonework of the first storey; as my eyes came back to the door I wondered why the house had been begun with stone and finished with brick from the second storey to the top: I wondered if old Mr. Posey had done it. But it didn't make any difference and I found myself adding, what they did—it doesn't make any difference. The door opened, and Jane came out on the stone landing, shading here eyes. As she stood there I tried to guess which steps she would come down—the steps on the lower side pointing towards Fayette Street and the convent, or the upper steps near the elm tree. She came down the steps towards me, her white fingers showing through the mitts and touching the curved iron balustrade. I stiffened as she reached the sidewalk. She stood before me as if she didn't know what to do next, with the helpless and already womanly reliance upon the nearest man, to whose will she had yielded her own. I took from her hand the music roll, and my hand tingled. She did not move.

I said, as if somebody else were saying it: "Let's go the long way"—the long way up Warren Street by the college.

She raised her eyes, blue and shining, to my eyes. Her color deepened. I touched her elbow with the tips of my fingers, and gave her a gentle push, but as we began walking I couldn't keep her step: her little red boots moved inches at a time, like a bird.

We came to the corner of Lingans Street by the schoolhouse and were about to cross over when she stopped, one foot on the curb, and turned with a glow in her face towards the river. I looked too: the wooded Virginia hills lay green before us and the great river stretched for miles to the west. I could see the flag over Arlington. The air was quiet; there was no motion in the leaves above us; there was nobody in sight.

I was standing in the gutter; she took a step backward up to the sidewalk and her eyes were higher than mine as she looked placidly but with the glow still in her face out upon the river and the Virginia hills, and back into my eyes. Then she gazed at something in the distant blue.

"I love it," she said.

I turned my head and pretended to follow her gaze. I said: "I love it too." I do not know how long we stood there but it seemed very long because I knew what was coming. I stepped up to her side but kept looking into the distance. I said, "Jane, I love you."

I thought that she had not heard me and I felt a little relieved, but she at last dropped her eyes and touched my arm.

"Lacy," she said and that was all.

She stepped off the curb and I fell in with her and almost instantly we had turned the next corner and were walking rapidly up the street. The high, damp wall of the college ran with us the three blocks to the convent wall, where we turned again, to the right, and came up before the dark, cool entrance to the convent. I went to the door and pulled the knocker, and stepped back again. A Negro maid opened the door. I handed Jane the music roll and she walked up the steps, but before she went in she turned her face to me and gave me, her lips parted and her eyes bright, a long and wondering stare. She went in and the maid closed the door.

Too late, I continued to return her gaze, but there was satisfaction in it because now, alone, I could linger upon it and see in it all that I myself felt. I wanted to lie down upon the place at the door where Jane had stood. I heard footsteps nearby and I knew that they had been sounding all the time. I adjusted my cap to my head, and faced the walker who paced in a blue uniform with a musket on his shoulder, across the street. He was just a boy, hardly older than I, with a long bony face and small eyes.

"Howdoo," he said, pleasantly.

I glared at him. He stopped and faced me.

"This ain't no war. I ain't even seen no rebels." He dropped the butt of his musket to the ground, and took out of his blouse some stringy tobacco. "I promised ma I wouldn't smoke but I didn't say nothin' about chawin'." He sucked the tobacco into a quid in the corner of his mouth. "I seen you with your girl," he said. "I got a girl at Parker's Four Corners. That's in Connettycut."

I advanced a couple of paces. "The hell you say," I shouted at him. Then I said in a low voice: "You're looking at one right now—you're looking at a rebel."

"Well, well," he said, pleased.

"Well, well," I mocked him. "Whyn't you go back to that gal, you meddling Yankee!"

He looked bewildered, and shouldering his musket started down the street, then stopped and said over his shoulder in a voice surprised and plaintive, "I ain't doing nobody any harm."

I hated the way he said har-r-r-m, and then I thought of papa who was too noble to hate anybody for the way he talked or the place he lived, but I considered how being papa's son made me what I was and that made me hate that boy. In a fury I ran along the convent wall until I came to the college gate where I sat down on a bench to wait until the college clock struck eleven. There isn't any hope, I said to myself, and I saw in the mind's eye the hordes swarming over mountain and field like ants on a soft ant-hill. An aged priest, in cassock and a flat-crowned black hat with an immense brim, came through the gate and seeing me, paused. I rose and bowed, taking off my cap; he raised his hat and said, "God bless you, my son."

His face was contorted with age and pain but his eyes were quick and bright. He moved nearer to me to make way for somebody I could not see. A squad of eight boys in blue uniform, two abreast, marched through the gate flying a small Union flag. The old gentleman watched them impassively until I saw him recoil and throw his hand up before his face. At the same instant a piece of rock hit me in the chest, and I saw several heads peering over the college wall—young faces like the faces of the soldiers—and a harsh yell, more like a jeer, followed. The boys in uniform marched down Second Street. The old priest nodded his head sorrowfully and went back into the grounds.

I suddenly said, "It's coming." In a few seconds the clock began to strike and I counted eleven. I ran fast to Third Street, turned the corner, and ran two blocks to the convent. The street was deserted. The sentry had gone. I fixed my eyes upon the door, and waited, and then I counted first a hundred, then two hundred, and began all over again up to five hundred, but Jane did not appear. The tall, heavy oaken doors might never open again: was I sure they had ever opened? I thought of the nuns whose vows forbade them to speak again, other nuns whose taking of the veil sealed their lips forever from conversation with men. But these must have been fallen women, I thought, in Protestant ignorance of the mysterious Church that never changed for peace or war. I said simply: Jane is late.

The door opened but no one came out, only the spreading wimple of a nun appearing dimly in the hall. At last Jane's back appeared in the door, and over her head I saw the nun's face, pretty and smiling. Jane backed away with a curtsy, turned and came down the steps, the nun smiling benignly until Jane handed me her music and we started down Fayette Street, the nearer way home. I turned awkwardly and raised the bill of my cap. The nun closed the door.

"That's Sister Assisi," said Jane.

I tried to adjust my steps to hers but gave it up. I looked at her slyly. Her face and eyes were suffused with a marvelous light. She tapped her feet or I should have thought she was not touching the sidewalk. She laughed and became shy again. She stopped and faced me. "Lacy, will you write to me? Sister will let me write to you, I know she will."

I said, "Yes, Jane, I will write, but we don't need to write. I am here."

"Yes. You're here." She began walking again, the shy look in her face.

"We're both here," I said. We came to the corner of Vista: it was only half a block to the house. We lingered at the corner. "Here we are," I said.

"Yes, here we both are."

The sun was hot, so I moved under a sycamore, and said, "Come over here."

"Come in under the shade?" Her voice was sweet and absent. She was looking again out over the river, and I wanted to touch the curl that hung from under the white poke-bonnet.

"Under the shade, here?" Then she looked at me and moved to my side. "What is the flag over there?" And she raised her face towards the Virginia shore.

"That's the—well, it's just the flag."

"Lacy, what is the war?" A little frown appeared under her bonnet. "Are you going to be in it?"

"I don't know," I said. Then I looked at her: "Yes—maybe."

"Has it begun? Tell me about it."

"It's begun but there's nobody been killed." I couldn't believe she knew so little. I said, "Not yet."

"Uncle Jarman said they won't fight." Then her voice was prim: "Mother has a spell if it's mentioned. Sister won't talk about it. And Aunt Milly just says, 'Thank you, honey,' when I take her bananas up to her, and closes her door." She frowned again. "Lacy, tell me about dead people."

I put my hands into my pockets and looked at the ground. In a flash I was standing in the parlor at Pleasant Hill by a little girl with violets in her hand, but I could not see her. A green leaf fluttered from the high tree and brushed Jane's shoulder, then curved to the sidewalk. She clapped her hands, bent over and picked up the leaf and gave it to me.

"Lacy," she said gaily, "let's not go in. Let's stay out here."

"Let's not go in," I said.

We started walking towards the house, silent, and we went by it and had to turn back. We went up the steps side by side and I threw open the door; we went into the hall, the door swung to, and we were in the dark. I took her hand and drew her to me and kissed her. When it was over I could see because my eyes had got used to the dark. I dropped the music roll upon the table and watched Jane as she fled up the stairs.

Part III

THE ABYSS

I lay in the dark trying to decide what time it was and what had wakened me and how long I had been asleep before. There's not a doubt in the world, I know what I am talking about, there is no way to get around it, I said; Sister never mentions Semmes but she gets letters from him and she doesn't want him to see Jane and she lets me see her even beyond propriety because she thinks it's puppy love and anyhow I can't marry her because I am only a boy. Well, it was only Mr. Jarman upstairs who had wakened me, walking up and down, he may be thinking about something yet it's easier to say he is reciting his compositions. But as I listened I heard no steps. The college clock struck three. There were voices below, in the garden or maybe back in the stable court. I got up and went to the back window and leaned over the sill. There were no voices now but I saw two men come from the stable towards the house. They stopped almost directly under my window.

"Who's that?" I said in a low voice.

One of the men moved swiftly against the wall of the house where I could no longer see him. The other raised his head.

"That you, Marse Lacy?" he whispered. "Is you awake?" It was Blind Joe. He moved uneasily on his bare feet. "Could you please sir come down hyar, sir?" he whined.

I made no reply but turned from the window and drew on my trousers and stuffed my nightshirt into them. I picked up my boots and went noiselessly out into the hall and down the two flights of stairs, then down the short flight to the wicket and out into the garden. When I reached the corner of the house the two men were flat against the back wall in the deep black. I stooped to pull on my boots. As I rose the moon came from behind a cloud in her third quarter. Blind Joe stepped out into the light. He drew his open lips tight over his teeth in an evil grin.

"Well?" I said.

The other man came forward and drew himself to his full height, placing his hands on his hips. His back was to the moon, and at first I couldn't see his face.

"You knows me all right, young marster," he said.

The voice startled me and I advanced to examine his face: his head was thrown back and he looked down at me. The voice still echoed in my ears, and I crazily thought of Brother George and how he threw his head back in that arrogant tilt. The man turned his face into the full moonlight. My mouth fell open.

"Yellow Jim!" I said. I fell back a step and stared at him.

"I come home," he said in a whisper.

I was bewildered and I said nothing, staring at Yellow Jim impotently, until it seemed that the moonlight washed all the Negro out of his face and he was a white man, and a white man too who had a right to be where he was.

"I'm glad to see you, Yellow Jim," I said aimlessly.

He didn't move. "Maybe de young marster will come to de stable," he said. He nodded his head and seemed to stand aside for me to lead the way, but I was still rooted in amazement. He moved back into the shadow of the house,

followed by Blind Joe, and I walked as quietly as I could
to the stable door, and went in. The Negro men came in
after me.

At the far end of the stable a weak light came from a
lantern hanging on a beam in the low ceiling. The carriage horses were still, but near us Queen Susie was nudg-
ing against her manger; she whinnied and gave the back
of her stall a vicious kick. That mare needs exercise, I said.
She suddenly put her head out over the gate of the stall,
and looked us over. Yellow Jim, who in the lantern light
looked Negro again, stared back at her: in his excited face
there was both recognition and fear.

He took a step and put his hand on Queen Susie's
nose. It quieted her. "Hit's been three years since me and
this mar' swapped places."

Of course I hadn't known Yellow Jim before, had seen
him once the day of the tournament, but there was a note
of self-pity in his voice that embarrassed me.

"Jim," I said severely, "why did you run off?" He looked
at me humbly, but from his open mouth no words came.
"Jim, I'll have to find Marse George and send you back."

He straightened up and looked over at Blind Joe who
was shifting from one foot to another and giving forth low
cackling sounds of delight. I said, "Shut up, Joe," and he
retreated a few steps into the background. Yellow Jim now
looked at me and in the compressed lips and in the eyes
that glared intensely I thought I saw something like
menace. Instantly it passed, and he was his humble self
again.

"Jim," I said, "why did you run off?"

He took a step forward and held his hand vaguely before
him, as he had done by the roadside that day. "Young
marster," he said, "they ain't no way for a man to change
hisself into a field hand at my age." He waited for me to

speak but there was nothing that I could say. "De colonel, he go off to be in de war in Richmond, and de overseer — you remembers de overseer, young marster?—Mr. Hinks he don't lak me nohow, so he put me in de field and I say, 'What fer you put me in de field when I been in de house?' and he give me nine lashes." He began tugging at his shirt-tail as if he were about to show me the lashes.

I turned to Blind Joe. "You fix Jim a bed somewhere." I walked towards the door and, pausing, spoke over my shoulder. "It's late. I'll see about you tomorrow, Jim." I started across the paved court. With a swift glide Yellow Jim was at my side.

"Please, young marster, you ain't goin' to send me back, is you?" He spoke in a low wheedling tone. But I could not be severe with him.

"Yellow Jim, you know I haven't anything to do with it." I spoke kindly. "Good night, Yellow Jim."

"Good night," he whispered, and gliding away disappeared towards the quarters. Now the moon had gone under a cloud and I had to hold my hand before me when I came to the corner of the house, and feel along the wall for the wicket. I took off my shoes, and opening the wicket went swiftly up the stairs.

*   *   *

Susan said to let him stay for the time being, but I went next day up to the town hall to see the marshal, who said he was perfectly willing to take charge of Jim until he could deliver him to his master, but he didn't know when that would be, in the present state of the country. So Yellow Jim settled down "at home." He went upstairs on the second day to pay his respects to Ole Miss, and before he had left her presence, Aunt Jane Anne had forgotten that he had ever been away, giving him petty orders and cau-

tioning him to be careful with her "good glassware"—
which, of course, had long ago been broken by the trifling
Negro girls. That was a house where the Negroes ran
everything that ran at all: they had their own way because
nobody but Susan gave enough attention to the practical
affairs of living to think them through. Old Atha, Aunt
Jane Anne's maid who had let me in the first night I was
there, also did the cooking, what little there was, and
supervised the two house-girls. If I asked for anything,
or even if Susan did, old Atha would say: "Naw'm, we
can't do that, I ain't heard of doin' no sich thing since I's
born."

But with Yellow Jim it was different: he put on a white
summer coat and moved around the house an eager specter
looking for things to do. He cleaned my boots and brushed
my clothes and toted upstairs the warm water for my bath.
Except for old Coriolanus I think he was the best Negro I
ever saw; he was the most refined Negro, a gentleman in
every instinct. But he was a Negro, and I am not sure that
he would have been as good as he was if his white blood,
which everybody knew about, had not been good. But
since there is difference of opinion on this question, I had
better say that white blood may have ruined poor Yellow
Jim in the end. He knew what his blood was and he had
many of the feelings of a white man that he could never
express. He had conscience and pride, and no man, whatever his hue may be, can have more. He had never, so far
as I had been able to learn, committed a single breach of
conduct. I will never forget to my dying day what he said
to Coriolanus. "I say, 'Marster, what I done?' He say, 'You
ain't done nothin',' you liquid capital, I got to have
money.' " Ninety-nine out of a hundred Negro men would
have taken it as a matter of course, and gone their way to
the new master. But Yellow Jim was humiliated; worse

than that, he was betrayed. I think he felt about it as I
should have felt: suppose papa were dead, and Brother
Semmes had acted towards me in some grievous way, as if
I were not a brother or even a member of the family? Yellow Jim had been in the full sense a member of the Posey
family, and the peculiarity of his situation as a slave had
in no wise diminished his loyalty or even his complete participation in the family life: it had rather intensified it.

I suppose Yellow Jim was with us a little more than
a week. All that time Blind Joe tormented him. "Free
Nigger now, ain't you?" Every day he would say to him,
"Marster come home tonight," and the evil grin spread
over his face. I had been making Blind Joe take the mare
out for exercise at least once a day and late one afternoon
I heard an altercation between Yellow Jim and Blind Joe
down in the stable court. I had only to look out of my
window to see and hear it all. Yellow Jim had saddled the
mare, and Blind Joe kept hollering out that the girth was
too tight—"That mar'll th'ow me shore." Yellow Jim
stepped up to loosen the girth, and Queen Susie threw
her head around and bit him savagely on the forearm.
Jim recoiled and held the place with his hand, backing
swiftly towards the stable; he emerged with a heavy buggy
whip and gave the mare a merciless beating. He quit only
when he was out of breath. He tossed the whip to one side
and stood, his hands on his hips, glaring at her. Blind Joe
mounted her and rode out through the carriage gate.

Yellow Jim had broken a "rule," but it wasn't that that
made me uneasy. When Blind Joe disappeared, Jim looked
about him stealthily, moving at last with a sidelong gait
towards the house; I heard the door into the winter
kitchen, which was in the cellar, slam after him. The
mouth, thin and sensitive, was tortured, the shoulders

humped: I should have said that he and not the mare had
received the beating.

That ought to have been ominous but was not: omens
are those signals of futurity that we recognize when the
future has already slid into the past.

I have not described the special veneration in which
Yellow Jim held the character of "Miss Jane." Jane's
nurse, who had also been Brother George's nurse, had died
when Jane was only eight or nine years old. Yellow Jim
practically became the child's nurse. He was her groom
when she rode abroad on her pony; he rode with her, a
half day's journey, down to the Posey farm in Charles;
he was her escort to school, early Mass, and confession.
When Jane received from the Sisters a medal for progress
in French, music, or drawing, although the "medal" was
only a small pewter image of Our Lord or Our Lady,
Yellow Jim talked about it for days. "Ain't nobody lak
our Jane," he would say. "Smartest little lady at the convent." Now that he was back and Jane in the interval
had become Miss Jane, he was as zealous as ever in his
devoted service. I suppose in the desperation of his un-
certainty he was compelled to assume the old security of
affection in Jane: he needed it. But it was not there. The
three years of absence had marked, as it would mark in the
life of any child, the sudden change from childhood to
maturity. Unless the objects of childish affection are
present at that time and, lingering into the new life, are
transformed, they are lost, or become strange, as if they
had belonged to another world. Yellow Jim had become a
stranger to Jane. I do not think that he quite understood
this: how could he?

We were now in the third week of May: Jim, as I say,
had been with us nearly a week: Jane and I had come back

from our morning walk to the convent. Before I could open the front door Yellow Jim pulled it open and stood aside. I saw now in his smile and his "Good mornin', Miss Jane" a self-consciousness that I had not seen before. The specter-like ease of his movements had an intensity that I have never detected in any other Negro. Jane had answered his good-morning pleasantly enough, but she drew back when he reached out to take the music roll, her light cloak, and her bonnet. She handed them to me instead, and I, embarrassed, handed them to Yellow Jim, whose eye met mine on its return from a swift glance at Jane. He lowered his eyes and backed away as we went into the parlor.

There was a chill in the room remarkable at that season, but there was no fire. Jane walked to the window. I was about to sit down but I took a step towards her.

"Are you cold?" I said.

She came away from the window and sat down at the harpsicord, then turned to me. I could see her hands trembling. I knew better than to go to her: after that other day, we had dropped back into the shyness of youth, a ritual of prudence, I had almost said decency, that very young people cling to with greater fastidiousness than the old. At least that was the way I saw it, the way I acted upon Jane's reticent withdrawal which to me seemed to say: the time has not yet come. . . . Her hand shook and her lip quivered, as she spoke.

"I'm not cold." I thought she would weep. She looked into my eyes. "I am afraid of that man," she said.

I was at first bewildered, then scared. It was almost as if she had feared something that did not exist, a ghost, or perhaps a presence in the room that I could not feel.

"*What* man?" I whispered.

"Why," she said with amazement, "why, Yellow Jim."

At my back I heard a tinkle of glass, and was about to

turn my head but Jane's eyes held mine. She was sitting rigid on the edge of the small, scrolled chair, her eyes wide-open and opaque with horror. I turned to look over my shoulder.

Yellow Jim advanced into the room with a waiter upon which stood two tall glasses. He kept his eyes fixed upon the waiter which he set down with a remark made in a thin voice.

"Hit's most too cold for sangaree but hyar 'tis."

Without removing his eyes from the waiter that now rested upon the table near the front window, he backed out of the room. I didn't see him again for more than a day—thirty-six hours exactly: he stayed away in the quarters and I didn't send for him because nobody could have sent for him. Nobody sent for a Negro under such circumstances. It is futile for me to wish that I had: it could no more have occurred to me than it could have occurred to me to wish that I were a Yankee.

When Yellow Jim's retreating steps no longer sounded in the back hall, I turned again to Jane. She had not moved: the same horrible opacity filmed the liquid blue eyes.

"Jane!" I said, and it brought her to.

Still frightened, she said, "I'm afraid of him, I don't know why I am afraid of him." She contracted her brows. "He's always handing me things!"

She rose abruptly to her feet and ran out of the room and up the front stairs.

*   *   *

The next day it rained and I stayed indoors all day, not seeing Jane the whole time and not yet thinking it remarkable that Yellow Jim had not appeared. Once I got out my mackintosh and actually put it on to start for the

city to see what was going on in the camps of the Union
soldiers, who were daily increasing by thousands till like a
flight of locusts they had covered all the lower end of
town; but it was too wet, and I gave it up for one of the
tales of Captain Marryat that had drifted downstairs from
Mr. Jarman's library: the story of Peter Simple the English
midshipman who received a memorable lesson in manners
from his grandfather the earl. It was like Hamlet's rebuke
of Polonius for his discourtesy to the players: "Use them
after your own honor and dignity." It was hard to understand, at my age, for it seemed plain that a great many
people had to be treated, not as you felt about yourself,
but as they deserved. How could you decide what people deserved? That was the trouble—you couldn't decide. So you came to believe in honor and dignity for
their own sake since all proper men knew what honor
was and could recognize dignity; but nobody knew what
human nature was or could presume to mete out justice
to others. I thought of papa down in the old house in
Alexandria thinking of his honor, which he would if necessary mention, and acting upon his dignity which he did
not know he had because he had it so perfectly. Men of
honor and dignity—where are they now? I knew gentlemen in my boyhood but I know none now, and I know
that I am not one. The classical proverb should be revised:
Non viri fortes *post* Agamemnon multi. Men of honor
and dignity! They did a great deal of injustice, but they always knew where they stood because they thought more of
their code than they did of themselves. Papa thought more
of his honor than of any of us, but he did not know that
he did, and not even Semmes, who had suffered from the
logic of honor, would have seen it so. There was nothing
personal about it, and it was adamant, but there was no
personal resentment in Semmes, and no anger; only a feel-

ing like anguish, and uneasiness for papa's own situation. That was what it came to, for Semmes, to be disowned.

At four o'clock that day, May the twenty-first, I heard people talking below me. I went out into the hall and down to the second floor which I reached in time to see Semmes' back at the threshold of sister's open door. Semmes took a step into the room, and the door was about to swing to.

"Brother Semmes!" I said in a voice too loud for that quiet hall. A door opened behind me but after so many times I no longer turned to see Miss Milly's peeping face. Semmes waited with his hand on the tarnished brass knob, the light at his back keeping his face in shadow; he wore a short, gray dressing-gown that I recognized as Brother George's. When I came to him he took my hand and then pushed me into the room by the shoulders. He had not spoken. I was about to say, Why did you come and how did you get here, when I saw sister standing over by the far front window gazing intensely down into the shady street.

Semmes closed the door and we stood there, but Susan did not move; the flicker of an eyelash acknowledged our presence but that was all. The sun came over the trees outside, it being afternoon, and pouring into the upper panes lit her acorn-colored hair with a streak of gold. A glance would have noted a woman in thought; a second look discerned the lines of muscle in her cheek, and the rapid heave of her bosom revealed agitation. I looked at Semmes: his face, since I had last seen him, had grown lean, he was white about the mouth, and his drooping eyes stared in bewilderment. He walked over to the mantel, stood a second, and sat down in a chair.

Sister turned. "How long have you been here?" she said.

"An hour," he said, surprised.

She gazed into his eyes as if she were trying to read them, then turned again to the window.

"Aren't you glad to see me, sister?" he said.

She came away from the window and stood before him. "No!" she said in a harsh tone. She walked back to the window, and a softer expression came into her eyes as she said, "Didn't you get my last letter?"

"I haven't heard from you in over a week," he said.

"Well, then," she said. She thought about it a moment. "I told you not to come here." She moved rapidly across the room to the door, seemed to listen, then came back to Semmes and sat down opposite him. Her pale face was flushed. "I won't have it—I will not have it, Semmes!" She sat back in her chair and studied his face. I could not decide just what it was that she would not have, but Semmes seemed to know; he rose and paced the floor, his finger at the side of his nose, his humorous, humorless face twitching. At last Susan said, in a calm, almost indifferent tone, "Well, have you seen her?"

Semmes halted abruptly, looked at her, and began again his measured strides.

"I'm on my way to the Valley. I've been transferred. I'm assistant-surgeon in the Thirty-third Virginia, Jackson's brigade, at Harper's Ferry. Doctors are scarce." He looked slyly at sister. "John Langton was damned glad to get rid of me. He put up my name before I could volunteer." He stopped and stared hard at sister. "He sent his regyards to George." The stare turned into a hard smile that I had not seen in my brother's face before. "Our George," he said; then, "*Your* George."

Susan dropped her hands into her lap. "Semmes!" she said.

"Semmes!" he mocked her. He stood over her. "Semmes!

Yes, I've seen her. That's what I've been doing for the last hour. I've been with her. And she says yes—she says yes she will marry me. Tomorrow." He became more matter-of-fact. "I will take her to Cousin Bruce Washburn's in Charlestown. I can see her nearly every day." He resumed his seat and there was an expression of triumph in his long face.

The flush of a moment ago had subsided from Susan's face: her gaze into Semmes' eyes was fascinated, almost charmed.

"It's indecent," she said in a low, remote voice.

"It's indecent," he repeated in his mocking tone. "It's indecent," he went on in a rising voice, "it's indecent to take Jane away from this mad-house. You're as mad as they are but you don't know it." He seemed suddenly to hear his own words. He came over to sister. "Forgive me, sister," he said.

If she had heard him, she gave no sign. "Why, she's only a child." She smiled weakly but there was a gleam of purpose in her eyes. "She's as much in love with Lacy as she is with you." She looked at me, and Semmes followed her glance.

I had been sitting on the edge of the bed. Now I stood up, with the door in the corner of my eye; but I moved to the foot of the bed and held to the tall post. Semmes' eyes drooped, and I knew that the tension had left him.

"Are you in love with Jane, Lacy?" His tone was both inquiring and incredulous. I must have blushed, for my face was hot and my hands cold. I kept listening, as if for another voice; I suppose I was trying to hear what my answer would be. I did not intend to lie, but when I spoke, the words were a lie that I see now may have hastened the enveloping destiny of all these people. I should have said, Yes, I love Jane and I think she loves me; and Semmes would have hesitated, he might have delayed his purpose, and sister would then have withheld hers. I clung to the bedpost as sister, with parted lips, looked me eagerly in the face. But I was looking at Semmes.

"No, brother," I said, "I ain't in love with Jane." I left the foot of the bed and went back and leaned against the counterpane. Susan lowered her face into her hands.

Semmes addressed her. "Is it indecent? I have everybody's consent but yours. I have George's, in this letter"—he took a folded sheet from his pocket and waved it vaguely, but Susan taking no notice of it, he thrust it back into his pocket—"and I've got Aunt Jane Anne's consent too. I went from Jane to her. Old Atha said to 'git away from hyar' when I knocked at her door, but I put my foot on the threshold and spoke directly to Aunt Jane Anne. She let me come in. It took me ten minutes to get the talk away from her 'condition.' I made the unavoidable mistake of asking after her health. Well, she said she'd been poorly ever since ma's funeral—the journey had permanently impaired her health." He paused and moved a step towards her. "Is it indecent to take Jane away from such a mother? She'll indulge herself the rest of her life because just once she did something for somebody else, for somebody who was dead. And now after all this time, when we've forgotten all about it, she kept harping on George's grief over mama's death—because it seemed he might have to think for a few hours about somebody else's mother." He paused with his mouth open ready to go on; but he suddenly shut his mouth and sat down with a sigh. "Sister, I don't understand you," he said.

"You said she gave her consent?" sister asked.

"Why, yes, she did. She said, 'Of course, my dear boy,' and then she asked, 'When?' but before I could answer her she had forgotten all about it, and was asking Atha when the priest, Father Monahan, was coming to play pinochle with her. 'Get out my new lace cap, Atha,' she said. And I excused myself." He put his hands on his knees and leaned forward. "Sister, I am going to marry Jane."

She got up and went to the wardrobe between the window and the head of the bed. She opened the door and took out a black knitted shawl, throwing it round her shoulders. As she turned back to the room she stopped at the window and looked out. She glanced at us and nodded her head towards the street.

"There's Jane now," she said. "I wonder where she's been." She pursed her lips reprovingly, as she might have done had Jane been present. Semmes was watching her intently, but she was oblivious of him, and I felt that I knew what Semmes was going to say.

"That's one reason why I'm taking Jane away."

Still sister looked out of the window as if she were alone; still Semmes kept looking at her. "Sister," he said, "Jane has been to special confession and to get Father's special blessing and a waiver of the banns in this bad time. That's why," he said almost gaily, "Father Monahan's late for pinochle!" He got up and went towards the door but I beat him there, and stood at the open door with the knob in my hand. I felt that I could not get out of that room quickly enough. Susan apparently had not heard anything. But as Semmes came to the door he glanced towards Susan's rigid figure, a frown contracting his brow in perplexity.

Then Susan turned round suddenly and sat upon the bed, her feet thrown under her in the manner of a child. There was a smile on her face, secret and certain, and I thought she looked like a woman who had drawn a good hand at whist and waited impatiently to play the cards.

"Semmes," she said in a tense but sisterly voice, "no member of our family will ever marry into the Posey family." Although the tone was kind, there was a note in it that I had not heard from her, ever, and the astonished expression that gradually spread over Semmes' face told me that he had never heard it. I backed into the hall. From downstairs I heard the rapid, soft cadences of the harpsi-cord in a familiar strain—*Flee as a Bird*—and the color-less, sweet voice of Jane rising above the mellow bass. Semmes heard it too, with a glance into the hall. He seized the doorknob, took a stride into the hall, and closed the door with a bang.

"I didn't mean to do that," he said to himself.

"No," I said listlessly.

He went down the hall to the last door, Brother George's dressing-room, and disappeared. I walked softly past Aunt Jane Anne's and Miss Milly's doors to the head of the stairs. Jane had come to a *bravura* passage, trills and arpeg-gios, that covered my creaking descent. I stood at the par-lor door waiting for the end. When it came she turned on the seat and gave me a happy smile. Her eyes were large, liquid, and blue, and she said, "Hello, Lacy."

"Hello," I said. I went into the room and sat on the edge of a rickety gilt chair, and stared at my boots.

"Are you going to marry Brother Semmes?" I said, still fixing my boots.

"Yes," she said. "You won't mind, will you, Lacy? I'll still love you too—I love both of you." She smiled.

"I thought maybe you'd marry me some time," I said, and although I had not felt much of anything, the words made me pity myself, and I felt tears coming, but I sup-pressed them.

"Oh, but you didn't ask me. Semmes did—weeks ago, when he got into the war." She looked serious. Her voice dropped to a low register, as if she feared being overheard. "Lacy, I can't stand it. I'm afraid. I'm afraid of everybody. Sister too. She gives me such strange looks!"

I could hardly believe what I heard: was this Jane, the child Jane, who in body only was a woman? She was far beyond me now. I said, "I see, Jane."

Then there were footsteps in the hall. I rose in order to retreat—why, I don't know; but retreat was cut off by Susan who stood in the door.

"Jane," she said in a harsh tone. "Jane!" She waited. Jane clasped her hands together.

"Yes'm," she said.

"Jane, you know you don't practice your music in the evening." She looked around. "Where's your embroidery?"

Jane, her hands still clasped and her eyes meekly cast down, rose and went to the embroidery frame by the front window. Her back was turned to me as she began to push the long needle through the cloth. I went by Susan into the hall, and ran up the stairs. At the top I leaned over the banister. Susan looked up at me with a smile of satisfaction. That smile frightened me. I turned away and ran to the backstairs, and up to my room where, throwing myself upon the bed, I waited for it to get dark.

*   *   *

Whether Jane saw her mother later that day I am not sure, but I suppose she did see her, because one of the things that Jane kept repeating time and again, all night, was: "Mama didn't listen to me. Mama didn't listen to me," but what it all meant was one of those mysteries that never come into the light. Perhaps Aunt Jane Anne ought to be blamed, but it would be like blaming a what-not or a piece of bric-a-brac. Doubtless we cannot help judging everybody a little, but if we judge one person we have got to judge all the others and to fix nicely the degree of personal within the common frailty, until in the end the judgments add up to a pharisaical jumble of ifs and buts. But this story is not an effort to fix blame, any more than it is a record of triumphing virtues. It is not only possible, it is necessary to say: that man is dishonest, or this other man is an honest man, for in so saying we are not judging an action or blaming or praising him for it; we are only distinguishing a quality of character. But if two honorable men kill each other—and it is possible for men of honor to kill without dishonor—and bring upon their families untold sorrows and troubles, what have we then? Who is to blame? I believe that here towards the end of my story all that one can say justly is that some of us behaved a little better than the others; but not much better. If Aunt Jane Anne had listened to Jane, would the end have been different? I doubt it; and I doubt if it would have done us any good to think better of Aunt Jane Anne.

I have already said that I went upstairs to wait for it to get dark. Why I wanted the dark no one could remember after all this time. There are days when we consciously guide the flow of being towards the night, and our suspense is a kind of listening, as if the absence of light, when it comes, will be audible just because sight and touch are frustrated. Of course this is what we all know. But how many of us know that there are times when we passionately desire to hear the night? And I think we do hear it: we hear it because our senses, not being mechanisms, actually perform the miracles of imagination that they themselves create: from our senses come the metaphors through which we know the world, and in turn our senses get knowledge of the world by means of figures of their own making. Nobody today, fifty years after these incidents, can hear the night; nobody wishes to hear it. To hear the night, and to crave its coming, one must have deep inside one's secret being a vast metaphor controlling all the rest: a belief in the innate evil of man's nature, and the need to face that evil, of which the symbol is the darkness, of which again the living image is man alone. Now that men cannot be alone, they cannot bear the dark, and they see themselves as innately good but betrayed by circumstances that render them pathetic. Perhaps some of the people in this story are to be pitied, but I cannot pity them; none of them was innately good. They were all, I think, capable of great good, but that is not the same thing as *being* good.

I suppose I wanted the night to come so that I could face a new emotion, that no doubt meant that I was no longer a boy. Children never hate; they only feel anger. Hate is of the mind, a consciousness of defeated purpose; children have no conscious purpose. I knew as night came on that I hated my brother Semmes. There may be many ways of killing time—how accurate is the common phrase! —but I knew two of them: minute activity either monotonous or surprising, but if it be the latter you will have to be borne up by some powerful excitement; or just lying on the bed and floating away into the stream of timeless images, and then suddenly you are aware of the secret feeling that all the set concentration in the world would not have let you face. It must have been about eight o'clock when without a knock the door opened a narrow crack. There was enough light, on that south side of the house, for me to distinguish my brother's face: he stepped barely over the threshold and leaned, unspeaking, against the jamb. How do I know what I should have felt had it been full daylight? He was dim, and only the configuration of person would have let me at any other time recognize him. But even without that I knew it was he, and I knew he was a stranger whom I hated for the sacrificial lie that I had told. Is not a noble liar God's own scourge? He is always believed, and his genuine disinterestedness, his repudiation of self, seems to render him exempt from all responsibility: was not his intention good? I knew that I hated Semmes, and if I had known as much as I knew a day later I should have known that my hatred was a kind of fear. My lie committed Semmes to full participation in the events directly to come. We are like children playing drop-the-handkerchief; the conventions make the emotions that we are willing to die for, as children eagerly run themselves to exhaustion round a ring.

He stood more than a minute in the door, then closed it behind him and came, softly in carpet slippers, over to the bureau where, striking a match on his slipper and watching the oily purple flame change to yellow, he lit a candle and gazed at it, his long face pale and composed. He looked as if he had been working problems in trigonometry. Without changing his posture he turned his face to me.

"You'll get like Mr. Jarman if you keep on staying in the dark," he said.

I did not move or speak. I felt that if I ever addressed my brother again I should have to tell him that I had lied; but no noble liar is noble enough to obviate the evil of his lie. He waits to confess it vindictively.

He straightened up, and said in a formal tone, "The ceremony is set for four o'clock tomorrow." There was not a breath of air in the room. The candle burnt with a straight, unwavering flame. Seconds passed. I did not answer. He backed towards the door. "It will be here, of course."

I wanted to ask him a question, and he knew that I did, for just as he reached the door he paused and raised his head inquiringly. I turned over and pushed my face into the pillow.

"Lacy," he said. I raised myself on my elbows but did not turn my head. "Lacy, I can't be here tonight." Yes, I thought, he can't be here tonight. He grasped the doorknob and said, "Yes, what about George? He can't be here. He can't get here in time." As he was about to close the door after him he said, "Lacy, Cousin John is right about George Posey. I see it now. Why is he away all the time? I've got to take Jane away from this." I still said nothing, and then Semmes must have heard the thunder of his own soliloquy echoing in his ears. With a swift awkward motion he jerked the door to after him, and I heard the first two or three steps as he went down the stairs.

I heard somebody talking downstairs; I supposed it was Semmes and Susan; and then silence, which I thought meant that Semmes had gone, but gone where for the night I could not guess, and I never knew. What difference does it make? He was running a risk coming to Georgetown at all where he knew everybody and everybody knew that he was a rebel; yet at that early stage of the conflict men passed to and fro between the lines with ease if they were cautious. But where was Brother George? Where, indeed, was he? Did sister know? I was sure that Semmes Buchan knew perfectly well where he was, and his rhetorical question: Why is he away all the time? made me feel, as I turned it over, hollow inside, and not a little glad that the candle still burned on the bureau. Semmes' moral desertion, and there is no other word for it, of his friend and brother, somewhat thickened the darkness around me, and I fixed my eyes upon the candlelight in a mesmeric stare.

*   *   *

I was not sleepy and I said, "I can't lie here forever. Semmes had been gone about an hour and the voices downstairs were persistent and unabashed and I recalled the long procession of silent evenings in that house. There would be talking for five or ten minutes, then doors would close, and silence for a while; the voices rose again. I had nothing to do with anything in that house but I saw no way of getting out of it. It must have been midnight or later when at last the talking ceased, or rather I thought it had ceased, since the rhythm of its lapse and renewal had been followed by a long silence; and going to the side window overlooking the garden I saw the blackness where had shone on the foliage a ray of light from a window in Jane's room.

It was so quiet I thought I heard water running over rocks, and I said, I must be getting sleepy after all. I pulled my jeans off over my boots, and started to unlace my boots but for some reason left them on. I walked on my toes to the bureau and taking the candle brought it over to the bed and put it on the floor, and dropped a few matches by it on the bare floor. Then I lay down on the counterpane, still hearing the running water after I closed my eyes

Sometimes when you think you are sleepy and are not, time races through you, and years that have never happened perform a whole cycle of events more complete and satisfying than a lifetime of our beginnings that have no end. The water kept running and at last I saw it through the scrub pines down back of the farm where the lane from old Mr. Woodyard's blacksmith shop drops sheer to the ford. Wolf Run! Now that I could see the water I saw myself gazing at the riffle in late evening, as I squatted on a rock with my gun across my knees. It was one of those scenes without purpose that come to you complete: you do

not know how you got there on the rock or where you are
going, and then it is dark. Doubtless there is a little conscious direction in these reveries because you always want
something to happen, you always want to be doing something, but I doubt if you ever want to hear anything. But
that is what I did—I heard something, sitting there on the
big rock, my gun, loaded, across my knees, and the clear,
black water swirling round a log and falling on a shelf of
rock a foot below. This, I said, with that double awareness
that we sustain in reverie, is only a way of hearing the
night, far off, a cry that the darkness makes, and I thought
for an instant that it was only the water getting louder,
or the water changing its tone, as if a flute had altered its
timbre from lucid trickle to the whine of the hautboy. I
saw myself looking up the opposite bank through the trees
for the panther whose scream now came with the rhythm
of breath, low on the intake but rising to a high wail with
the heave of the expulsion.

I touched my face and I was lying on the bed: my forehead was wet and I heard a door slam like a gunshot as I
slid from the bed to the floor, fumbling for the matches
that I could not find. I grabbed my jeans from the footboard, drew them on, and getting from the top bureau
drawer a navy revolver, I went out into the hall to the
head of the stairs. It was dark and silent. I was about to go
back to my room when there was a step in the hall below,
and I said, "What's that?" There was no answer. I listened.
I could just distinguish the susurration of hard breathing,
and I went rapidly down the dark, familiar stairs with the
revolver held before me. In the hall, between the doors
into Aunt Jane Anne's and Aunt Milly's rooms, I bumped
against the small table. Reaching with my left hand for a
match I lit the candle, and as the pale light filled the hall

I saw crouching, at the head of the stairs, a man, his head lowered upon his crossed arms as if he were shielding himself from an expected blow.

"Get up," I said pointing the revolver at him.

The man, his arms still over his face, pushed his back against the wall and slowly gained his feet. He dropped his hands to his sides and with a startled expression stared, not at me or at the pistol, but at the burning candle. I dropped the pistol to my side and took a step forward.

"Yellow Jim!" It was a whisper.

His muddy eyes bulged and with effort he moved them to my face, but it was only a glance; his head drooped and he began rubbing his leg nervously.

"Put your face against the wall," I said. "Hold your hands over your head." He did it, and I looked up and down the hall. In the back hall the door into Jane's room was ajar; all the others were closed; the silence was perfect for even Yellow Jim was no longer breathing hard. "Stay where you are," I said. I kept looking at Jane's door and decided that she must be with sister; so I turned to look up the front hall, and turning again to keep my eye on Yellow Jim I backed towards sister's door, and still facing Yellow Jim I tapped on her door, and waited. Yellow Jim had not moved: he might have been a dead man propped against the wall. As I waited, hearing no sound in sister's room, I gazed at the Negro, thinking perhaps he had been sent for. But why had I found him crouching? Why had he not answered me? Then I shivered a little. Where had sister been, where was she when whoever it was screamed? And where were they all now? I began to shake all over and I tapped again on the door but before I finished it Aunt Jane Anne's door opened and sister came out into the hall.

She stopped short, and frowning looked at the candle

burning on the table. Then she saw Yellow Jim, but she seemed not in the least astonished; she only looked at him curiously as if the anomaly of his presence lay solely in his being propped to the wall.

"Sister!" I said.

She was startled: she almost dropped her candlestick. As she recovered it midway to the floor, the candle went out, and the other candle threw her profile into silhouette; her mouth was compressed into a hard line. Then she turned towards me.

"She's dead," she said in a flat tone.

"Well," I said, as if I had been asked to fetch a glass of water. Then it came over me. "Dead?" I echoed her.

"I said she was dead." Sister's voice sounded almost legal, it was so controlled. "She died of fright. There's not a bruise on her."

Her hair flowed down her back, gathered at her neck with a ribbon; her white wadded silk gown was neatly folded about her waist. My God, what a woman! was all I could think to myself, but I said, "Who screamed?" I advanced towards her and the pistol caught her eye.

"I suppose you'll kill him," she said. She looked at Jim. Then she fixed me with a purposive stare. "It wasn't Aunt Milly," she said. "She's still asleep—took her sleeping draught after the excitement of Jane's betrothal." She looked down the hall at Jane's open door. "It would be Jane who screamed," she said deductively.

I walked past her towards Jane's door. She followed and I looked at her over my shoulder. When she came to Yellow Jim she walked round him as far as she could, holding to the banister. She's at least still human, I thought, as we stood at the door. She held her unlit candle. I searched my pockets and found a match and lit the candle. She made a gesture with her free hand; I stepped back;

she walked steadily into the room, throwing the door wide open.

As the light discovered the room I discerned a white body lying on the floor about three feet from the foot of the bed. Jane lay on her back as if she had been stretched out, as if, too, some one had carefully drawn her white nightgown down over her limbs. Sister knelt by her, placing the candle on the floor. The light suffused Jane's face. The mouth was open. Her skin was tight and chalky, like pressed muslin. I thought it a shame that any girl should be lying there humiliated, so young.

Sister looked up at me. "Jane is alive," she said. She began to rub her cheeks and then to chafe her hands. She rose and went to the washstand and finding only a toothbrush holder of some pink flowered pattern, she filled it from the pitcher and dashed the water into Jane's face. The prone girl did not move. "Come here, Lacy," sister said. I glanced up the hall at Yellow Jim; he had not moved either. I went in and together we lifted Jane onto the bed. She was limp as a willow and light as cork. Sister looked her over, and at the same instant we saw that the left sleeve of her nightgown was torn. Sister bent over her and turned the sleeve back, disclosing four shallow scratches about an inch apart and an inch long. She had been clawed as she had drawn away. I gazed at them with infatuated eyes, until I felt my stomach heave and I knew that I was sick.

Sister had stood back and now stared at the wounds with wide eyes, her lips closed so tight that the blood had left them.

Jane's head moved and as if in weakness fell over towards me, away from sister. She opened her eyes but I knew she saw nothing. "Mama wouldn't listen to me," she said in a normal voice that brought me to. "Mama wouldn't listen," she said.

That was all I ever knew but I suppose I could have known more; I didn't want to know any more. Didn't I know what had happened? I thought I did, and I still think what I then thought, which was what any man would have thought. I suppose Susan's continued stare ought to have started a little doubt in my mind, had I been able to take it in, but nobody at that time could have seen in sister more than agitation and horror, emotions that certainly dominated me out of all observation. As we continued to look at the poor girl I knew that here at last was the night that followed the brilliant day in May when the gay party rode away from Pleasant Hill for the gentlemen's tilt in the west meadow of Henry Broadacre, Esq., that rolled away into the distance green as the sea. I saw Brother George charging down the course, his lance perfectly balanced; only I saw him sadly astride, not Queen Susie, but the man Yellow Jim whose face was as white as his master's. And they ran over a child in white, but they left her there, and it was all over in a minute, and the tournament had been won.

Suddenly I was holding the bedpost and puking on the carpet, but before it was done with I had recovered and was looking at Susan. It was too late for astonishment; so I just watched her run her hands over the now conscious but still immobile body of Jane. She ran her hand from the girl's ankles up her legs to her thighs, and examined curiously the folds of the nightgown, till perplexity dulled her eyes, and she stood away. Then her face tightened, and she shifted her eyes in their sockets till they fixed me with a decisive glare.

"Take him up the river," she said.

"But, sister," I said, then stopped. She was looking at

me. "Yes, sister," I said. But as I backed towards the door where a few steps would bring me to Yellow Jim I was afraid, and the fear heightened my awareness of myself until I felt a design form in my head, of great cunning I thought; so I paused. I said in a low tone, "I've got to get ready." I advanced to the bed, and spoke across Jane. "I'll just lock him up for a while." Then the adventure seemed too bold. "Sister," I pleaded, "can't I get help?"

"Help?" she said, and she actually smiled briefly before she set her lips. It was the smile she had sent me from the lower hall. I could not even think of Yellow Jim at that instant. The smile had turned the world upside down. All that had happened up to that moment, even the old lady down the hall lying in death alone, could somehow come out of the life we lived; but not that smile. There was no way to take it in, no sense in it; it was like a herd of kangaroos asking to be taken as commonplace at Pleasant Hill farm. But looking at it steadily one could easily see that the smile only signaled a sudden, remarkable purpose in Susan Posey who had undoubtedly felt for Yellow Jim something like pity as she had passed him in the hall. I suppose you'll kill him—and it had been a little contemptuous of the usual violence of men. Now she commanded it.

"It'll have to be done tonight," she said. I turned again, and I wondered if this time I should get out of that room. I did, and it was with relief that I saw Yellow Jim still standing as I had left him.

"Come on, Jim," I said.

He turned around and tried to lower his arms but his face went taut with pain. An inch at a time he brought his arms down till his hands reached his shoulders, and I motioned him to the stairs. He looked bewildered, and then scared as he faced what he had to do. Still he hesitated.

"Go on," I said.

He appealed to me with his eyes, and as he went before me he murmured, " 'Scuse me, marster," for even at that, for him, terrible moment, the ultimate fear of any Negro, he was aware that he was about to precede a white man. I took the candle from the hall table. He picked his way down the stairs as if each step might be different. We came to the main hall and he knew which way to go— down the hall to the short flight of steps leading to the wicket. When he came to the steps he turned and gave me a look of mild surprise. I was not following him. I said, "Wait." There were footsteps upstairs. Susan appeared at the upper banister and said in an ordinary tone, "Send Atha up."

I nodded. I went to Yellow Jim. He led the way out through the wicket into the garden, then round the corner of the house to the door into the winter kitchen. From there through pantries and storerooms we came to the little cell surrounded by brick walls a couple of feet thick, into which the only access was a massive oaken door all studded over with spikes. In the center of the door was a small, stoutly ironed grating. It was only a little old calaboose that Mr. Rozier Posey had built to put his bad Negroes in. I held the candle to the door and turned the brass key. The door came open and Yellow Jim stepped over the threshold with a sort of briskness as he said, "Please, young marster, don't leave Jim in de dark."

I handed him the candle. "Jim," I said, "what made you do it?"

He made a motion in front of him with his hand as if he were asking for silence. "Young marster, hit just come to me. Hit come to me and 'fore I knowed it I was up them stairs and openin' de door. I didn't mean to open de old mistis's door." He ran his hand through his coarse, straight hair. "Hit come to me," he said. "I just looked in de door, then shet it. Now de old mistis daid."

"It's going to be bad for you," I said.

He looked at me humbly, then his eyes were wide with terror. "I didn't do nothin', I didn't mean to tech Miss Jane either. Hit was when she hollered. That's when I done it. Hit come over me." He gestured again, his palms extended as I had seen them by the roadside at the Court House. "I couldn't do nothin' lak that now, naw sir, young marster, 'fore God I couldn't. Hit's gone clean outen me." He touched his face to see, I am certain, if it was he and he was there. "Seem lak I couldn't do no good after I hearn Miss Jane say she's afeared of me." His tone had become manly and his posture erect. I gave him a look which he returned. I closed the cell door, turning the key and putting it in my pocket, and found my way back to the kitchen in the dark.

Fumbling at a shelf that I remembered in a corner, I found the stump of a candle, lit it, and went to a door leading to the other side of the basement. A narrow, smelly hall led a few steps to a door. I knocked. "Atha!" I said. There was no sound, but presently I heard a bed creak and then low mutterings.

"Who that?" she said.

"Miss Susie wants you," I said.

There was more mumbling, then: "Miss Susie ain't never sent fer me, she ain't sent fer me sence I's born." The door opened a crack. "G'long," she said.

"I reckon your mistis will be needing you, Atha—old mistis."

She rolled her ochreous eyeballs and said, "Yassir," but she said it insolently. I went back to the kitchen and out through the door into the court. At the corner of the house the dark figure of a man blocked my way. I stepped back and raised the pistol. The candle went out.

"Hit's me," a voice said. It was Blind Joe. But he still stood in my path.

"Get out of my way," I said in a low tone.

He moved, and then there was a leer in his voice. "You done put him in de lockup, ain't you, Marse Lacy?"

I was angry. "Go on where you belong, you black bastard."

He said nothing for a minute but I heard a whining chuckle. "I belongs to go fer de doctor. I belongs to go fer de priest. Miss Susie said so."

"How'd you know she wanted you?"

"Ain't ole Marse Rozier say, 'Joe ain't wuth a continental but lak de buzzards and de flies he's everywhar'."

I stepped forward and whispered, "Joe, where's Marse George?"

It was pitch dark but I saw his mouth stretch before I heard again his low chuckle. "Marse Lacy, now you talkin', you shore talkin' now." He moved so near he could have touched me. "I git de marster—I git him before sun tomorrow."

"Get him," I said. "Joe, you get him."

There was no answer. He disappeared on noiseless feet in the direction of the carriage entrance. I went round to the wicket and into the house. In the lower hall I stopped to light the stump, and in the light I said to myself, I've got to have help. When I reached the foot of the stairs I paused to consider the darkness of the upper hall, and the silence that I thought should not have been there. The pistol was getting heavy in my right hand. I started to lay it on the table under old Jeremiah Gibson's portrait but instead I stuck it under the waistband of my jeans, and went up the stairs. Out of Jane's room appeared old Atha, a candle in one hand and a basin of water in the other; I knew she saw me but she kept her head averted. Her face looked like wet ashes and there was drool on her lips. That Negro, I thought, will never be insolent again. Then, as if I had always assumed that Madagascar lies off the coast of South America, but now realized that it lies off west Africa, I remembered that Yellow Jim was Atha's son. She went into the back hall and down the back stairs.

I got to get away from here, I said, or I'll be seeing sister again. I went up the next flight but when I came to the door of my room I went on past it to the end of the hall where a steep flight of steps, inclosed in a narrow well, led to the fourth storey, and Mr. Jarman's apartment. The steps, so steep that my knees bumped them and I had to go up sideways, led abruptly to a door, without a landing. I knocked gently, but getting no response, lifted the latch and entered a low, narrow, dark hall, the ceiling of which sloped away on my right. On my left were two doors. I knocked at the nearest one, and prepared for a long wait. Almost instantly the door opened; I was so astonished that I lost my tongue.

"How do you do, sir," said Mr. Jarman in the most beautiful human voice I had ever heard. He had greeted me as he would have saluted a friend at a horse race. I stared at him rudely. He backed away, opening the door for me to enter. A bright lamp was burning across the room, at his back; I could not see his face. I continued to stare at him. "To what unusual amenity," said he, "am I indebted for the honor of this visit?" He made a sweeping gesture. "Enter, sir."

I walked in and turned to look at him as he closed the door.

"Mr. Jarman," I said hoarsely but the old gentleman's air, I suppose his innocence and urbanity, forbade another word. He came by me and paused a little uncertainly in the middle of the room. I glanced around. The lamp stood on a rough, unpainted table against the far wall. Under the lamp were heaped odds and ends of papers, big sheets of foolscap scribbled over, and dirty quill pens. At the far end of the table I saw a battered silver waiter piled high with eggshells, and over in the corner of the room stood, in a row, five large slopjars, the lid of each being covered with a network of intricate tatting. He looked about him apologetically.

"This," he said, "is my dormitory and my graphaecium. The lamp burns diurnally and nocturnally so that the progress of my labors will not be interrupted by the succession of days. Time—time! Our great enemy, sir." He looked at me through his steel-rimmed spectacles. "Have you read *Triumph of Time* by Shelley?"

Why had he got the title wrong? I suppose he simply couldn't let *Life* triumph!

"No, sir," I said. "I haven't read it."

He looked disappointed. "Well," he said amiably, "shall we go into the atelier?" With studied politeness he walked before me to the door into the other room, which he opened, then stood aside for me to enter. An identical lamp burned on a large square table which was littered like the other table, only there were piles of books. The walls were lined with bookcases. There were four straight chairs, each placed at a corner of the room. With a wave of his hand he pointed to a chair. I sat down as he sat diagonally across from me.

"Atelier," he said with the French pronunciation: he had said *ateleer* before. "Alas, now that Custis is dead there is none of my contemporaries to whom I can speak French. His death, sir, is a loss that I feel more keenly with each passing year." He leaned back meditatively in his chair. I observed the pallid face, the high bulging forehead under the metallic white hair, the pale blue eyes that did not focus on anything, the thin, sensual mouth, the small determined chin and the lobeless ears: the nose was small and slightly turned up—which gave him an expression of perpetual surprise. He had a look of selfish intelligence that was distinctly heightened by his attire, which was absurdly elegant: frock coat, choker collar, and black satin cravat. "My late brother was not a scholarly man. But an able man, sir, a man of large interests. It was his munificence that to a great extent has made possible the leisure of my studies, although, of course," he added, "our patrimony was comfortable." He pursed his lips, his eyes became alert, his white face glowed. "I am now engaged upon a most interesting and illuminating work, the most ambitious work of the imagination, I do dare aver, of the nineteenth century. It is nothing less than a history of the struggle of man to build civilization upon the sterile wastes of the earth after the ice age." He rose with the spring of a child, went to the table, and seized a huge scrinium from which he drew a rolled manuscript. He pulled his chair to the light, sat down, adjusted his spectacles, coughed slightly for the attention of his audience, and looked at me. "I shall read from the first chapter. My model has been Gibbon." He scanned his manuscript with deliberation. I moved forward to the edge of my chair. "I ask you, sir," he said, "to consider critically the opening sentence. It has, I have no doubt, what Dr. Johnson called the grandeur of generality." He coughed again. *"'The skin-clad remnants of humanity fearfully shivered in their caves as the ice-age drew to its tedious close.'"* He laid the manuscript in his lap. "Ah, how Custis would have liked it!" He looked off into space, smiling his perfect satisfaction with himself. "Death is indeed the sunderer," he sighed.

I almost fell out of the chair. I regained my seat, and looked at him. Death couldn't be an old lady, his sister-in-law, downstairs; death was the sunderer, or time, or our enemy. I gripped the arms of the chair.

"Mr. Jarman!" I shouted.

"Ah," he said, and glanced at me slyly. Then he gave me, over the rims of his spectacles, a long stare. He closed his mouth like a fish, hastily placed the manuscript upon the table, and settled back in his chair.

"I see that it is young Mr. Buchan to whom I owe this pleasure."

I shouted again. "She's dead!"

"Dead?" he echoed. "Yes, yes, he's dead—been dead these many years. As I say, a man of business. But we are of noble lineage and, I think it could be proved, of royal descent. You will understand that while my means of entertainment are limited by the habits of a man of letters, I wish to make your call as pleasant as possible." He smiled hospitably. "Your little niece, my grandniece, is descended from the Vyvyans of Shropshire, and through them from the Plantagenets. We count among our ancestors Philip the Third of France, Edward the Confessor, and the grandfather of George Washington." He leaned forward in his chair. "I thought that this information would give you greater relish in our society."

I rose and stood uncertainly looking at the door. He was gazing at me with surprise. "I see that you are armed," he said. "No doubt a necessary precaution in these times. The war. I assume that measures of pacification have succeeded."

I went to the door. "Good night, Mr. Jarman."

"Night?" he said. He pulled out a big silver watch. "It is, indeed. Half-past-three." He took up his manuscript, and was instantly alone. I left the door open as I went out, and found my way down the difficult stairs. I had left my candle. When I reached the second floor there was a candle burning on the table, and there were voices sounding from Aunt Jane Anne's room.

I could not hear a word, but presently the door opened and Father Monahan followed by two nuns came out into the hall. He saw me and stopped, looking sharply at the pistol handle protruding from my jeans. As the nuns receded a few steps and began to whisper, he advanced and spoke in a low tone.

"I know all about it," he said. His sharp black eyes looked into my eyes. "I've seen the Nigger Joe. You've done the right thing. Your sister's distraught. Keep the Nigger where he is."

He turned his head and gave the nuns a nod. They came forward and at the head of the stairs waited for the priest to lead the way. "That is the Mother Superior," he said to me. One of the nuns turned and looked me full in the face; she looked at Father Monahan, who said, "The Mother Superior will come for the young lady at eleven o'clock. There's no other way. The girl can never be the bride of any man."

I looked at the floor, saying to myself, Liar! But I knew that Father Monahan was not the liar. As he passed me I saw heavy beads of sweat on his forehead. He looked at me, it was man to man.

"I know you are not one of us, young man," he said. "We've got to keep life simple. That is a practical reason for saving the human soul." He put his hand on my shoulder. "God bless you, my son." He crossed himself, and the nuns crossed themselves as they followed him down the stairs.

How long Susan had been standing in the hall I do not know. There she was, at the end of the front hall, just outside her own door. To go up to my room I had to get to the stairs in the front hall, not more than ten feet from her. I pretended that I had not seen her.

"Come here, Lacy," she said in a dead voice.

As I approached her she went to the threshold of her door, then turned to face me.

"Where have you been?" She was appealing to me under the harsh tone. I could not answer her. "Did you take him up the river?" she said.

"No, sister." I hung my head.

With one step she backed into the room, seized the doorknob, and slammed the door in my face.

I grabbed the butt of the pistol, thinking it had gone off. I started back towards the stairs. There was old Atha in the hall outside her dead mistress' door. The door was standing open. I could see at the foot of the bed a tall candle burning, and a heap of white dresses hanging over the back of a chair. On a table opposite the door there was a pile of small pasteboard boxes, each tied with a string from which dangled a small card: the knicknacks that the old lady for many years had put away in boxes and labeled, so that she knew the contents of the boxes by heart, though once classified the beads and gloves and handkerchiefs never appeared again. The walls of the room were lined with chests and trunks, and unopened packages covered the mantel-shelf. That room would never change: nothing would happen in it, nobody was dead, nobody had ever lived. It must have taken all the life out of her to beat her husband when she had tripped him at the top of the stairs.

Old Atha put out her hand and touched me on the sleeve. "Marse Lacy, whar's Jim?" There was a squint in one of her eyes. Her lip trembled.

"In the cellar," I said. I started up the stairs.

"Gawd bless you, marster," she whined.

As I went into my dark room I felt that I had been blessed too much, that I was a liar and a coward, and now, God knows, falling upon the bed without even putting the pistol down, I knew that I had achieved my full measure of darkness. When I closed my eyes I was sitting on a big rock listening to the water in the run, and again I heard the panther scream.

*   *   *

I haven't slept a wink, I said, as aching in every bone I put my booted feet upon the floor and rose from the bed. I stared dully at the revolver lying on the floor. I tried to think how it had got there but gave it up and decided that I had slept a little because there were things I could not remember. I had not seen the first light of sunrise. The first sun in the last week had struck the top middle pane of the east window; now it came through the top panes of the lower sash and flooded the room. May the twenty-third, eighteen-sixty-one, I said, and at least eleven o'clock in the morning. I went over to the washstand and cupping my hands reached into the pitcher; I dashed the water over my face. Eleven o'clock in the morning, at eleven o'clock said the priest. I went to the window and looked diagonally across the court to the stable: the carriage door was closed. It is not eleven yet, I said, hearing a voice, Blind Joe's, rasping in the light morning air.

"Mistis, I didn't do no sich thing." His tone became wheedling. "No-o-o, *ma'm,* I ain't seen him a-tall."

The voice was under my window, so I put my head out and looked down. There was Blind Joe facing the house, and a woman in black crêpe, her back to me, talking to him in an undertone. There was something remark-

able about her. I thought perhaps I had not seen her before, yet she wore no hat: a strange bare-headed woman,
her hair almost white, was talking to a servant of that
house, in the back yard.

Then I understood it, but what I understood first I do
not know; whether I identified her and in that way understood that Joe had been saying he had not seen his master,
or whether what he said could have been said to one person only, to Sister Susan alone of all people under all the
circumstances of that bright morning that had risen upon
so dark a night. Like the causal priority of the chicken or
the egg, it could tease me into speculation forever. But
there it was: Blind Joe and sister talking in the back yard.
Presently he went off towards the stable and sister came
round the house. I heard the light tap of her feet on the
brick walk leading to the wicket, as I held for an instant the image of her graying hair.

I wiped my face, picked up the pistol and put it back
into the bureau drawer, drew on my jacket, and went to the
door. I stood for a while holding the doorknob. I better
see Yellow Jim, I said. In this house nobody will give him
a drink of water. But what did I care about Yellow Jim?
I had to think of something to get myself down the stairs,
and after you've told one lie it makes little difference if
you tell others, even to yourself; and I went out into the
hall and down the stairs.

On the second floor the nuns were standing in the hall
by the table, and I could hear people moving about in
Jane's room. I went quickly past the nuns, who gave no
sign of recognition, and was starting down the next flight of
stairs when I saw sister already halfway up. I retraced my
steps and stood just at the head of the stairs, waiting for her
to pass. She came by me as if I had been a lamp post, and
looking straight ahead went into Jane's room, leaving the

door ajar, where I could hear her talking to Atha; but if Jane was in there she was not talking.

I went on down the stairs and back into the dining-room. It was a strange place: the long bare table, the black chairs lining the walls, the futile elegance of the ivory wainscoting. The intended brightness of the blue walls could never get enough light from the remote side windows. Nobody had ever eaten in that room. Yet there, across the table, was Jane's place, and I heard myself saying: Will you have some gooseberry jam?

The narrow stairs down into the winter kitchen were by the dumb-waiter. I went down, and in the kitchen it was nearly as dark as night. On the table was Atha's old candlestick with a good candle in it. I lit the candle and stood listening for a sound from the stable court, but there was none. I went back through the pantries to the cala-boose. It was dead-quiet: Jim is asleep, I thought. I took the key out of my jeans and unlocked the door, holding the candle before me. Jim was sitting on a three-legged stool, his back against the brick wall. He rose to his feet.

"Sit down," I said.

He sat, trying to hold himself erect. "Marster, don't let that Nigger Joe come here no more." His eyes were half closed and he seemed to be talking to himself. "Don't let him come no more." He suddenly raised his head. "Is de marster comin'?"

"I don't know," I said. "Jim," I said in as kind a tone as I could, "it won't be Marse George. It'll be Mister Semmes."

He seemed to hear me from a distance. "Marse Semmes," he said. "Marse Semmes." He looked up at me, one gentle-man to another. "I reckon he do owe it to hisself." Then apologetically: "Hit's the Nigger in me."

The stump of candle, burnt to the wick end, lay on the

floor. I handed him Atha's candle. "Here, Jim," I said. I gave him a few matches. If he had said it was the white man in him I should have been able to take it in: I was dumbfounded. But I've got to kill him, I said, without even giving him a chance; I've got to kill him to keep Semmes from killing him. My face was hot, and I was a little queasy in the stomach, but I felt pleased with myself.

"Look here, Jim," I said in a hollow voice, "it ain't goin' to be Mister Semmes. It's got to be me. It's my fault."

He dropped his hands to his sides and turned a dazed yellow face to me. His mouth fell open. He looked me in the eyes a long minute, and sank back against the wall. I turned to go. I saw him from the corner of my eye sitting placidly with the candle in his hand.

"You better lock de door, young marster," he said.

I stopped dead, turned awkwardly and seized the door, and without looking at Jim closed it with a thud, and turned the key. I put the key back into my pocket.

Going back to the kitchen I could see the dim light from the kitchen window, so I began to run, and it is well that I did, for I heard the trot of the horses in the court, and a second later the slam of the carriage gate after the horses had reached the street. I ran up the stairs into the dining-room and out into the hall, which was empty, but I slowed to a walk, and went tiptoe to the foot of the main stairway. The front door was open. The carriage was already drawn up in front of the house, the step let down; and Joe was perched on top, not in his livery, but in a torn alpaca coat and felt hat which was crazily adorned with peacock feathers. I went to the door. Blind Joe saw me instantly. He jumped off the box, and standing on the sidewalk put his face through the bars of the iron banister.

"Marster," he whispered. "Miss Jane take de veil." He

showed his teeth like the cur that he was, and grinned.

"Shut up, God damn you," I said. "Get back on the box." He didn't move. I moved nearer to him. "Why did you lie to Miss Susie this morning? Why'd you say you hadn't seen Marse George?"

He tried to look solemn. "Marse Lacy. I ain't told no lie to Miss Susie. I ain't *seen* de marster. I sont him word." As he turned away he said, "He be here tonight."

I went back into the hall in time to confront Susan as she reached the bottom of the stairs. The black crêpe that she had on was the same that she had worn as mourning after mother's death: it just touched the edge of my mind that it was absurd to see anybody in black when the dead person had not been alive, and only the living were dead. At that instant she was a black object which acquired humanity only through the vehemence with which she moved that terrible white hair. Her face was blue-white without any light in it, like the dining-room ceiling, and her eyes looked like scratched agates. She stood at the foot of the stairs with her hands clasped before her, looking out into the street.

Without lowering her eyes she said in a casual tone, "In a few minutes I want you to let Jim out. Tell him to run away."

If I had not been able to see her I should have thought that she was a woman giving directions to a servant while her mind was on something else.

"After the vows are taken she may leave of her own will. But nobody can take her out. Do you understand, Lacy?" she said in a sweet tone. "After the final vows she can't get out at all." She turned her hardened eyes upon me. "Do you understand?" Then she said fiercely, as color came into her cheeks, "The moment she's gone you let Jim go!" There were steps in the upper hall as the nuns appeared at the head of the stairs. Susan gave them a glance, then with a swift motion she was at my side. "George will be with his mother. You take charge of Semmes." Her face was pale again. She put out her hand. "Please!"

There was just time for me to say it. "Jim won't leave." Then I whispered. "You can't get out of it."

The nuns were halfway down the stairs when Jane, leaning on Atha, came to the head of the stairs and started down, finding each step with the toe of her slippers. I fixed my eye upon the hem of her gray dress but when she came to the foot of the stairs and stopped, still on Atha's arm, I let my eye travel up to her face: it was covered with a white veil which was tied scarf-like about her neck. She pushed Atha away.

"Mama wouldn't listen to me," she said in a little voice. She moved her head around as if she were trying to see. "Where's mama?" She took a few steps towards the door. "Where's mama? Mama wouldn't listen to me," she said.

The Mother Superior came to her and took her hand, and the other nun falling in with them, they went out of the door and, turning to the right, disappeared. I stood listening. The carriage door closed, and I waited. Blind Joe said, "Giddap," and the horses moved down the street. Atha closed the door. I watched meticulously her gnarled brown hand as she released it from the knob. She raised her expressionless face.

"I ain't white folks, praise be de Lawd," she said. She disappeared into the back hall. I looked around for sister. The hall was quiet, bright, and empty. I was alone.

*   *   *

Until after dinner, I mean dinner-time, for there was no dinner, only some ham and cold biscuits that I called to Blind Joe in the back yard to bring up to me: until, I suppose, about two o'clock, I saw nobody, and heard only the vague bustle that meant that they had laid out the old lady in one of the white dresses and were taking her body down to the parlor where it would lie in the coffin until the funeral the next day. Then in her white dress hidden in the ground she would still be white—a white dot in Holyrood back of town on the hill. But as time passed I could not stand nor lie nor sit, yet was so tired that my eyeballs ached, and I kept thinking of poor sister, with her hair and eyes, and how she must at last be getting a little rest, when there was a knock at the door.

I was about to say come in, but I had a presentiment that, after all, it might not be Semmes. I walked to the door and opened it.

"Miss Susie say give her de key to de calaboose," said Blind Joe.

I took out the key. "Here," I said.

He rubbed it with his thumb and squinted at me. " 'Tain't no use. That yaller Nigger he just ain't got it in him to run away."

"No," I said, "it's no use." Blind Joe was still rubbing the key. I closed the door in his face. Well, she was not getting any rest, and the more I thought of it, I could not see how she had it coming to her. How clearly at that moment I saw it, I do not know, yet I saw it well enough to perceive that Yellow Jim had been used by us all: by Brother George, to get a bay mare and to cut a big dash among strangers; by sister, to prevent a marriage that out of some deep and, to me, barely discernible level of her being, she hated; by me even, who had lacked the imagination to take Jim the night before up the river and, instead of shooting him, to turn him loose and make him run away; and I had used him again today, boasting of my fault before him as if I expected, as I no doubt did secretly expect, him to applaud the confession; and then by Jane herself, in some obscure but still culpable motive of shallow hysteria that had impelled her to dramatize her fear of sister into the perpetual fear of women—Negro men. Where did it all end? From the bed of violets at Pleasant Hill it seemed a long road to the convent, but I think it no exaggeration to say that from that moment in the parlor over mother's coffin sister had been leading Jane there. When I denied to Semmes that I loved her, it was as good as telling sister to hasten Jane upon her way. Was she not well out of it? I looked back to her departure: her small feet, her gray dress, her heavy white veil, but that was all that I could see. I loved her and I could not remember the color of her hair.

What had we done to Yellow Jim more than we were, minute by minute, doing to ourselves? After the carriage drove away, sister, like one possessed, tried every expedient to get Jim to run away. She sent Atha down; she went down herself; she offered him money; she even threatened to add to the story of the assault the lie that Jim had deliberately entered old mistis' room intending to kill her. At intervals Blind Joe came up to report. Sister sent me word to take Jim to the town marshal as a runaway: it was fantastic. Jane was at the convent because Jim had assaulted her, and yet sister was willing to let it be known that she had let the criminal go. There was no way around it: Jim could not go.

But why didn't he go? In mid-afternoon Joe came up again. He stood at the threshold.

"He just ain't got it in him," he said. He moved into the room and lowered his voice. "And he don't need to have it in him."

I went to the window to look down into the court. There was Semmes, dismounting from Queen Susie and looking about him for Joe to take her to the stable. He was dressed all in black—black tight trousers over short boots, black sack coat, black soft hat: he looked like a respectable merchant, or his getup, I thought, would do for a wedding or a funeral or even for a man to be laid out in.

"Blood thicker'n water," Joe said. I hadn't really heard it. Semmes was leading the mare away to the stable. I turned to look at Joe's evil face. His yellow buck teeth touched his lower lip.

"Blood thicker'n water," he said.

I took a step towards him. "You ought to be whipped for that. Get out of here!"

He sidled away towards the door. "That what Jim say. I ain't said it." He grinned. "Jim say blood thicker'n water and he keep on sayin' it. I ain't said nothin'." He was out in the hall. "Jim say de marster save him when he hear de truf." He laughed like a Negro at a dice game, and disappeared.

I went to the door and closed it: why in the hell, I said, couldn't Jane have been afraid of *him*. At the washstand I dipped the washcloth into the pitcher and held it to my hot eyes. I left my face wet. The stable court was deserted.

There was a knock at the door. I knew who it was but I could not say come in; I walked as slowly as I could to the door, yet when I got there I stopped. Why didn't Jim go away? That was nothing. Why hadn't I gone away? Only because I had wanted to stay to make all the trouble I could out of my lie. There it was, plain as day, but it was too late to do anything about it. I opened the door.

Semmes was standing back in the hall with his hat held over his arm, formally, as if he were going in to a reception. The posture was so distinctive that it was only by looking at him again that I avoided saying how-do-you-do. He came into the room, the hat on his arm and the black

string tie dangling rakishly from the low collar. He did
not even look queer. As he sat down on the bed still holding the hat, he might—but for the bulge of muscle in his
clamped jaws—have been listening to a sermon.

"Where is he?" he said.

"In the cellar."

I thought if he didn't put the hat down I would take
it from him. I kept my eyes on it. I walked up to him, took
the hat, and laid it on the bureau. His arm was still raised;
he looked at it and dropped it to his leg. Then he began
to stare at me. He followed me around the room with his
eyes, which I felt on my back as I seized the hairbrush and
brushed vigorously at one spot on my head. When I turned
he was looking through me.

"Look at something else, brother," I said.

He relaxed his jaws. "Why didn't you prevent it?"

I went over to the south window, beyond the foot of
the bed, and sat on a low chair.

"Who told you?" I said.

"Sister." He got up and paced twice the length of the
room. He sat on the bed. "She was walking the floor too."
He turned his gaze upon me again: it was a speculative
stare. "Her hair is white."

"Wouldn't yours be?" I said.

After a long silence I rose and going between the bed
and the wall lay down on the bed, facing the wall. I felt
the bed move. Semmes too had lain down. The sun had
just left the south window, and time was getting on.

"Hers shouldn't be," he said reasonably. I turned over
on my back. He took my hand and gave it a squeeze. "You
were in love with her too." He let go my hand. "And I
thought you were just a boy."

"I don't know," I said. I sat up and looked down at him
over my shoulder. "Look here," I said. "Sister wanted me

to take him up the river last night. Today she was willing for him to run off. Took the key away from me." I considered the rest of it but I could not make myself say more. I felt that I had said all that I was entitled to say: it was what I had heard and seen, and it was really all that I had known: from it Semmes ought to be able to know as much as I did. He had seen the white hair. But he had a logical mind. He sat up and straightened his tie, and stood in the middle of the floor. I marveled that I had ever hated this man.

"Where's that pistol?" he said.

"There." I pointed to the bureau.

He opened the top drawer and took it out, holding it by the heavy barrel as he spun the cylinder to see that the chambers were loaded. He put it inside his coat and buttoned up the coat, and sat on the edge of the bed. He glanced out of the east window.

"It'll be dark in an hour," he said.

Nothing more was said. Towards the east in a little while the sky became black, and out of the south window I could see only a little light in the top leaves of the juniper tree that rose to the level of the sill. We were two brothers waiting in a bedroom for it to get dark. The house was so quiet I heard the front door close. Semmes looked at me. We waited. After about a quarter of an hour I decided that Father Monahan or another priest had come in, or perhaps two nuns to take the place of those already there, for the night vigil.

Somebody was knocking at the door. I had not heard footsteps.

"It's Blind Joe," I said; then, "Come in."

He opened the door but in the dusk I could not see his face. "Marster say come down to de dressin' room." And he was gone.

I leaped to the closet and got my hat and with a bound I was standing in the door. Semmes put his hat on and confronted me.

"Let me pass, Lacy," he said.

I stood there.

"Stay here!" He advanced and raised his hand as if he would push me aside.

"Make me," I said. He hesitated, then lowered his arm. I let him pass, and followed him down the stairs.

The second floor was deserted and all the doors were closed. We went into the back hall past Jane's room to the last room in the hall, and standing before the door Semmes knocked. Immediately the door came open. The bright lamp on the small table in the middle of the room blinded me as I followed Semmes in.

Brother George was standing in his shirt sleeves by the washstand behind the door. He pushed the door to, and looked at us. His black trousers were dusty and he held a towel in his hand.

"Sit down, gentlemen," he said. His cold blue eyes burned in a swarthy face, narrower than I had ever seen them; his mouth was tight.

Semmes looked at a chair and remained standing. I stood behind him. Brother George tossed the towel upon the rack, took his coat from a chair, put it on, and sat down.

"Be seated, gentlemen!" He said it sharply, and as we backed off to the chairs, he smiled at us.

We took seats, and there was a pause. Semmes put his hands upon his knees, and said, "Where'd you come from, George?"

"Lancaster, Pennsylvania," he said promptly. He rose and went to a dingy wardrobe by the washstand. Opening one of the doors, he took out a black metal box about two feet long and a foot wide; he held it a moment, put it back, and closed the door.

"Eighty thousand dollars," he said. "God damn the money." And he sat down. He contracted his brows as he stared full at the bright lamp. Well, Brother George, I thought, you're all by yourself again. He looked at Semmes, still frowning. "Otherwise I'd be in jail," he said. He got up and threw his head back, looking down at us. "I had to cheat old Cameron on the contracts to cover up the stuff I sent to Richmond. I let Governor Letcher have it at a loss." He sat down again. He looked at Semmes, then at me. "Howdy, Lacy," he said.

I looked at Semmes, who returned the look and cleared his throat. I glanced covertly at Brother George's preoccupied face: the astonishing greeting had come out of no change of expression whatever: a man who could take both views of anything.

"But, George," said Semmes, then stopped in his amazement.

George looked at him, and as he looked an expression of intense concentration spread over his face.

"We have something to attend to, haven't we, Semmes?" He looked inquiringly.

Semmes rose. "I see that we understand each other," he said.

I got up too. Brother George went to the wardrobe again, and took out two army pistols in holsters. He held one of them out to Semmes.

"I have one," said Semmes.

Before George could move I took it by the barrel and pulled it out of his hand.

"What's he got to do with it?" said George.

"I reckon he knows," Semmes said. He looked at me, and I nodded, and he nodded back. I was astonished and

I kept hearing *You were in love with her too,* as George and Semmes waited by the open door.

Out in the hall Semmes said, "I suppose there could be a reasonable doubt." George said nothing, but he turned round and waited. "Of course," said Semmes, "you've got it from Susan. You've seen her hair."

"Hair?" he said. "I didn't notice."

In the dark I could not see Semmes' face. There was no hesitation in his tread as he walked past George up the hall to the stairs. When we came to him, he did hesitate; then instead of descending the stairs he went on towards sister's room where without pause he tapped lightly upon the door. He turned and said in an ordinary tone, "Come here, George, please."

George went, and I followed; we went up to Semmes as the door opened and old Atha put her head out. Semmes pushed the door back and walked past Atha; again George and I followed. A candle was burning at each end of the mantelpiece. Sister was sitting bolt upright in a small chair, still in the black crêpe, her hands folded in her lap. Her face was in the shadow.

We stood like erect mummies looking at the child Jane who was playing with a china doll at her mother's feet. She banged the head of the doll against the bare floor.

"Papa," she said.

"Atha," said Sister in a voice like a stage direction, "go outside and close the door." Atha closed the door softly after her.

"Papa?" the child said, looking up at George, who gazed back at her gravely.

"Susan," George said, "send the child away too."

Little Jane held the doll at arm's length and dropped it. It broke evenly in two and lay there. "Papa make money, papa make money, papa make money," she chanted.

"Send little Jane away," George said. He lifted her from the floor, took her to the door, put her outside with, "Here, Atha," and closed the door. He came back to the center of the room.

Susan turned her eyes upon him, throwing her face into the candlelight. There was no expression in the face at all. Her lips were closed and her chin hung a little low, as if she had a large pebble in her mouth.

"An impressive delegation," she said. She looked at us in turn. "Armed to the teeth." She leaned forward. "Do you need the help of a woman?"

"I think we may have had all the help from you that we need." It was Semmes. Susan jerked her head towards him and leaned back in her chair. Her lips parted, and into the dry blue of her cheeks came a little flush.

"We are here," he said, "because we thought it might not be as bad as it seemed at first."

Susan looked now as she had when we came in: her hands lay in her lap, her face was white, and if she breathed it would have taken a mirror to show it.

Semmes stood over her. "Is there a reasonable doubt?" he said.

She lowered her head and studied a crack in the floor: Semmes all the time was looking at her intently, and now he backed away as if from something he feared, and feared to look away from. Suddenly she lifted her hands, turned the palms up, and examined them.

"Well!" she said, and sighing leaned back in her chair.

George came to her and touched her forehead with the tips of his fingers.

"Susan?" he said, and I thought there was a little tenderness in it. He was gazing seriously at her hair.

But he might have been putting his hand on a hitching-post: she clenched her fingers and sat like a stone, having turned her face from him into the light, which put into it the chalky blue of a cold wall. George, clenching his own fists, raised himself to his full height, and turned on his heel.

"Come on," he said to us.

He was at the door with his hand on the knob when Susan's voice came like an unknown, moving object to a little boy in the night.

"Mr. Posey," she said. I jumped as if I had been shot at. Semmes had not moved; he was still facing the door. George let go the doorknob.

"Mr. Posey, you know what a fool my brother is." She looked at Semmes. "He would have shot any man for Mrs. Stacy and now he wants to shoot a Negro for Jane Posey. Because he is a fool who happens to be a gentleman." She was a blazing fury as she rose to her feet. But her voice was low. "George Posey, if you allow my brother to shoot your brother for you, I will never see you again." She gazed into his wavering eyes.

He looked at the floor, then straightened up, and took the doorknob. He was nodding his head, and it occurred to me absurdly that he was trying to make her a bow. His head stopped moving and a small fixed smile came over his lips as he glanced from Susan to Semmes: it said, Yes, he's a fool. Susan was still looking at George. Well, why didn't she keep all of us from shooting Yellow Jim? Then I looked at her more closely. She had not moved her eyes from her husband, and in her gaze there was nothing but hate.

George was still looking contemptuously at Semmes who looked, not like a fool, but an idiot boy; his lips were working and his eyes, wide with wonder, were fixed upon Susan.

"How'd you know—Mrs. Stacy—how'd you know?" he stammered.

She sat down and clasped her hands. I had the impression that she had been in that posture all the time, that we had just entered the room.

"I know everything!" she said.

George took Semmes by the arm and led him out of the room. I followed, not glancing back, and closed the door. Atha and the child were gone. Who is to blame now, who is to blame? I said it to the tramp of our feet as we went downstairs. But it doesn't make any difference. Susan is done for anyhow.

*　　*　　*

George will be with his mother, Susan had said, when that was where she had wanted him to be, but now she wanted him to go up the river, and I had no doubt, as we went downstairs, that she would still have her way, though the way had been reversed. But it had not been reversed, really, for not being at any rate a monster until George had returned and it was too late to let Jim go, she had been only a Buchan, and to be a Buchan was to be possessed by only one idea at a time. I suppose it was not so simple as that when you came down to it except in the case of papa, whose politics had closed his eyes and whose honor accepted the results of his politics and drove him to the formal repudiation of his son. If papa had not been a Buchan there is hardly a doubt that Semmes would have been with him in Alexandria until the Seventeenth Virginia moved off to war: he would have written letters— another Buchan passion—to Jane, and Jane would have kept them in a little packet until the war was over.

There was nobody in the hall when George reached the foot of the stairs and waited for us to come to him. The parlor door was open: I walked round behind George and looked in, seeing two nuns seated impassively one on each side of the coffin and a tall candle burning at head and foot. Miss Milly sat by a lamp near the embroidery frame in a small rocker, looking down through her spectacles, which were pushed forward to the end of her nose, at her tatting: I had a quick vision of the lids of Mr. Jarman's slopjars when, moving a little nearer to the door, I saw the scholar himself. He sat on the far side of the room midway between the corpse and the light, holding up to the level of his eyes a large paper-back book.

But I was looking at Miss Milly. She raised her eyes but still looking over the rims of her glasses—although she was not standing at her door—she peeped at me, and then spoke as if I had been with her all day: of course, I had not seen her to speak to for a couple of weeks.

"And to think I slept through it all." She looked down at her tatting. "Is George out there?" she said as if she were asking if her bananas had come.

"Yes'm," I said, and as I turned round to look at George I regretted it. He looked at me or rather through, over, and around me as if I didn't exist, and he turned upon Semmes—whose mouth was still open—a malevolent glare; then he turned his eyes back to me, right *at* me this time, and walked to the parlor door. He put out his foot to step over the threshold, but withdrew it, and seemed to be studying the situation. Miss Milly looked up at him, then at her tatting, then at him again, like a fidgety, incurious pullet; but she said nothing. Mr. Jarman rose, and putting his finger in his place between the leaves of the book, held it under his arm, and advanced upon George. He bowed and held out his hand.

"Nephew," he said, "it pains me to greet you in these

melancholy circumstances." He cleared his throat. "Your mother—"

"She's dead, ain't she?" said George, looking at him as if he were a child.

Mr. Jarman's hand was still in the air when George abruptly turned away and started for the dining-room. I believe what George had said brought Semmes to himself, for he fell into step with George and we all entered the dining-room together. What a house! And what people! I did not quite mean it that way. They were excellent people, but unfortunately for Mr. Jarman's genealogical researches I felt, by this time, only a necessary relish in their society. As Brother George threw back the door to the steps down to the kitchen, I believed that he was imponderable, that I could have put my finger through him. When death could be like this, nobody was living. If they had not been of their Church, they would have thrown one another at death into the river. She's dead, ain't she. At least George Posey had spoken it in the English of a gentleman, not in Mr. Jarman's parrot English, and I did not feel tired as I shuffled sideways down the narrow stairs.

George led us in the dark to the lock-up.

"Strike a match, somebody," he said.

I got out a match and struck it on my jeans. Atha was sitting on the floor directly in front of the door. She looked up at George.

"You come to git him, marster?"

"Move over, Atha," he said.

As she struggled to get up he put out his hand, taking her by the arm, and helped her to her feet. The key was in the lock. He turned it, and stood aside. As Yellow Jim came out the match burnt my thumb; I dropped it. In the dark George said, "Go first, Jim."

Jim leading the way, we went out through the kitchen

to the stable court, then round through the carriage gate into the street, and without stopping and Jim still leading the way walked at the usual pace over to Frederick Street where we turned to the right for the bridge over the canal. In two minutes we passed over the canal and got on the tow-path which brought us quickly to the aqueduct, and from there on the tow-path might have been in deep country: on our left rose tall willows and sycamores, and in the dim light of the quarter-moon I could just discern the top of the stone wall on the land side of the canal, then suddenly round a little bend I saw on the canal's edge, below the wall, a large rock house. George tapped Jim on the shoulder, and went ahead of him.

"Step light," he said.

We did; and from there on for a mile and a half we were shadows, the more so for the noise of the river that now ran in a narrow channel through huge boulders: it was, I knew, in some places eighty feet deep. We came to a thicket that I knew by the odor of the blossoms to be locust, and George halted. He turned off the tow-path into the bushes, down the steep bank towards the river. We came to a ledge of rock, big enough to build a cabin on, jutting over the water which I could hear swirling, about ten feet below. George, at the far end of the rock, turned and said:

"We might as well stop here."

Semmes, next to the river, was facing George at about six paces; I stood a little away from Semmes near the overhanging locust leaves and Jim was between me and George standing erect and motionless, but I could not see his face. George's face received all the moonlight there was. I looked at him anxiously.

He put his right hand into his coat and took out his pistol. He touched the priming with his left thumb and light. His hands were extended a little and his head lifted.

"Is you goin' to kill me, marster?" His voice rose to a querulous scream of surprise.

"George, I thought we understood each other," Semmes said. He took out the navy revolver. Jim turned his head and looked at Semmes, and the expression I had first seen, wide eyes and open mouth, was frozen. He bent over a little and muttered, and crossed himself very slowly.

I think we must have all been staring at him. A pistol shot to my left was from Semmes' revolver. Jim dropped in a heap like a rope. He did not move.

"You God damn fool," said George.

But I was looking at Semmes. Suddenly he looked startled, fell upon his left knee and swaying slightly pitched like a sack of corn over the ledge into the river. Then I heard it, and saw, delayed, the streak of fire from George's pistol. He was saying, "I never had any idea of killing that Nigger."

He bent over Jim and felt him, rose and lifted the body with one arm; he dragged it to the edge of the rock and let it fall into the water. He turned round slowly and looked at me. As he came towards me I backed off, step for step. But he stopped. He moved his foot quickly and kicked into the river the pistol that had fallen from my hand. He took no further notice of me. He walked deliberately up the bank through the bushes and disappeared.

I went over and looked at the black water and then I was running and my shins burned from the scratches as I passed the rock house. I was running lightly, not out of breath, along the tow-path. I came to the aqueduct and to Frederick Street and crossed the canal. I could see the window panes and the color of brick when I reached Vista. "I'm back," I said, and gazed stupidly towards the east and the rising sun. I looked down the river, and kept look-

ing. Then I knew what it was. The Confederate flag over
Arlington was gone.

*   *   *

I had no trouble getting across the Long Bridge: the
Virginia side was in the Union lines. I took the back roads
along Arlington ridge, and at about seven o'clock that
morning I literally found myself on Montgomery Street in
Alexandria, so tired I could taste it, having come out of
the trance. It was ten miles in three hours over cart-road
and through the brush. Down Montgomery Street I could
see the river but I turned down Washington getting
some good for the first time out of the fresh morning air.
Far down the street, at the corner of Queen or Cameron,
I saw a group of men, but between them and me there was
nobody nor was there any sound in the air. The air was
clean and livid, and ponderable, when I came to the
corners and stepped off the curb, letting the slanting sun
strike the side of my face.

When I came up to the men they were silent: I suppose a crowd of about twenty. They did not look at one
another. There was nobody I knew. I went round them
and looked towards the river, but my eyes did not get that
far. In front of the Marshall House, facing it, stood a squad
of Union soldiers at order arms. I left the crowd at the
corner, feeling that I was being followed; taking the inside of the walk and trying to move casually, I hurried;
across the street from the inn I stood behind a lamp post,
foolishly, and waited to see what the soldiers would do.
They did nothing. One of them stared at me unseeingly.
I looked at the façade of the house.

The windows were blank, and as my eyes ran up to the
roof I saw the bare flagpole, with the ropes hanging from

the top. They began to move. The Union flag ran up and flapped weakly in the breeze. The soldiers raised their heads. One boy took off his cap and cheered feebly; then looked self-consciously at the ground. I glanced over my shoulder towards Washington Street. The crowd at the corner had disappeared.

The door of the inn stood open and a sergeant came out.

"One and two of the front rank come forward," he said in a clear voice.

The men left the ranks. I ran across the street and along the side of the building to the gate into the back yard. It was open. In the middle of the yard was a small brass cannon, newly furbished. Under the gallery an old Negro man was sitting on a box. As I went past him into the hall he did not look at me. I went through the private dining room where I saw, on the small table, the row of whisky glasses that the three men had drunk out of, now a hundred years ago. I opened the door and took one step over the threshold into the office.

One and two were just inside the front door gazing woodenly at the stairs which were concealed from me on my left. The sergeant addressed me.

"They got the blind staggers," he said, tossing his head at them. Then he shouted: "What the Goddamn hell!"

The soldiers moved carefully to a rocking-chair and leaned against it their muskets. I came out into the room, and looked towards the stairs. A pair of legs in brown pantaloons on the third step led to a body on the floor. The face was turned towards me: Mr. Jackson. In the forehead was a hole big as a biscuit cutter; from it oozed a trickle of blood down the nose to the black mustache, from which it was dripping to a wide pool on the boards. Not two feet from Mr. Jackson's head lay another: the body was stretched full length, face up—the handsomest face I had ever seen, large delicate nose, wide thin mouth, high cheekbones. I thought instantly of Brother Charles. The blue uniform was immaculate; the shoulder-straps were a colonel's; and on the belt-buckle, spelt out in full: MASSACHUSETTS. He might have been asleep, so flushed was his face, had it not been for the blood running from both ears and mingling with Mr. Jackson's blood upon the crumpled Confederate flag that lay under him. I looked at the sergeant and the sergeant looked at me.

"Colonel Ellsworth," he said. "The first to be killed by a rebel." He looked at the bodies. "I killed the rebel."

The soldiers came forward and as they stooped over the colonel's body, I ran out through the dining-room. I heard the sergeant's voice.

"Hey, you, wait a minute." And as I reached the back hall: "What the hell!"

But there were no footsteps as I stood listening by the old Negro man under the back porch.

"Where're the Confederates?" I said.

The gloomy expression under the grizzled wool did not change. "Skedaddled. Ever' last one of 'em. Yestiddy." He rose and hobbled towards a shed at the far end of the yard. "It ain't no skin off my belly," he said over his shoulder.

Free Nigger, I said, running out of the gate into the street, which was still deserted. But I better not run, I said. I tried to walk but I walked a little and ran a little till I came to Fairfax Street and turned right, and I ran all the way to Duke; but at the corner I paused. Maybe I can get upstairs without being seen, maybe papa is eating his breakfast. I'll see Coriolanus first. Then I remembered when I had last stood on that corner: where were Hank Herbert and Jack Armistead now? I walked with natural steps to the front door. I turned the knob cautiously and pushed against the door. It was locked. The garden gate, I said. But on the sidewalk I looked at the front windows. Every blind was closed. I raised my eyes. The blinds in the second and third storey windows were closed. The garden gate was half open. I went in. The side door was locked, and on the porch floor lay a rotting potato.

I went out of the gate, and round the corner up Duke Street, but I had to walk now, my feet were so heavy, and I do not know how long it took me to get to the edge of town and out into the country. I cut southwards through the fields to Cameron Run and not finding a bridge or a ford I swam it in my clothes, and clambered up the bank shocked and cool, and made my way a mile through the fields again, to the Telegraph Road that runs southwards, and came over a hill to a big tobacco barn by the road-side. A quarter of a mile away on the other side of the hill was a Negro plowing a field. I stepped over the rail fence and went into the barn. Inside it was dark and cool and empty. I pulled the door to after me. It's a good place, I said. I went to a pile of tobacco stems, smoothed them flat, and lay down. I sank lower and lower, almost to the level of the floor where Mr. Jackson and the Yankee colonel lay. That wasn't anything, I said. They didn't even know each other. That wasn't anything at all. I sank lower and lower into the dark, getting heavier all the time; then I was light and smothered as I sank into the suck of black water and didn't feel anything more.

* * *

When I awoke it was pitch dark. There was no struggle to come out of it; my mind was clear. Had Blind Joe really gone for Brother George? I better go down and see if Yellow Jim's had any water. Water, I said. I opened my mouth but my tongue was too big for it and stuck to my teeth. Both hands prickled. I rose on one elbow and touched my legs. They were sore and when I tried to move them they were stiff. I sneezed and thought it would break every bone in my body. I put my hand to the ground and felt the tobacco stems. The acrid dust filled my nostrils and I sneezed again. I tried to see around me. The long slits of light that I had seen when I came in were gone. There was a gray rectangle and I went towards it.

Outside the stars on one side of the heavens were bright but towards the southeast they were dim, with none at all on the horizon, which was pallid. I got over the rail fence, slowly, into the road and went away from the rising light. I came to a clear, sluggish branch, took off my clothes, and lay a long time under the water. My head towards the current, I let the crawfishy water run into my mouth, swallowing a little of it at a time. When I had dressed, a copper sun came up out of the road.

Six miles, I said, to the railrooad, and then eight more. When I came to the Lick Road forking to the right, I cut below it through the brush and across Long Branch to the railroad tracks, which I followed southwards for a mile to the Pohick crossing, then turned northwest along the Pohick Road and after about two miles came to a cross-road and paused to look at a big cabin on a little knoll to my right, about fifty yards from the road. There was an old man sitting on the front porch, leaning on a long stick which he held between his knees. A lively smoke rose from one of the chimneys. In the front yard there was a well. I turned into the lane. When I came to the well I stopped.

"Good morning, sir," I said to the old man.

He put his head forward and a stream of ambeer shot out of his mouth. "Good morning," he said. He looked me over. "Better come in and rest a spell. Hit's gettin' pow'ful wawm." He glanced at the sky.

"Could I get a drink, please?" I said.

He spat again. "I reckon you mought," he said. He rose and leaned on his stick. "You ain't no Yankee, air ye? I ain't goin' to have no Yankees a-drinkin' of my water. I'll 'spectorate in hit fust." He wrinkled his nose and spat out another stream.

"No, sir, I ain't a Yankee." I advanced a few steps. "I'm Major Buchan's son," I said.

He nodded his head. "I'm glad to see you, son." He waved his hand. "Ever'thing I got is yours." He hobbled down off the porch and came slowly to the well. He turned back the lid, put the bucket inside, and held the rope. "Now ain't that a coinci-dence. Hit wa'n't a week ago I seen old Squire Lewis at Tom Woodyard's and he says, says he, 'The Major's in fer a big surprise when he comes back from Alexandry. The Niggers won't work and that young Higgins is a-beatin' 'em.' That's what he said, son. Ain't nothin' to Higgins, ain't a thing to none of 'em. I knowed 'em all for yares." He rested the bucket against the lid. "Ain't no business of mine but I say what can you expect when you sign all your prop'ty away. Like the Major done. That's what I say."

He was about to lower the bucket when a common water snake of the harmless sort crawled up on the lid and, gliding off, disappeared into the well.

He arrested the descent of the bucket again.

"*I* put that snake in thar. Snakes eat frogs. When I come out o' nights to get a drink, I ain't as apt to swaller a snake as I am a frog."

There was a voice over my shoulder. "Why don't you put a hog in the well? Hogs eat snakes. You ain't so apt to swaller a hog as you air a snake. I ain't never seen no-body swaller a hog as you might say, *whole.*" The speaker was a tall sallow young man with a wry face. He looked at me, then at the old man.

"Good morning, Mr. Regan," he said cheerfully.

I looked at the old man again. It was indeed Mr. Regan. I saw him again leaning on his sassafras stick in the court house yard. The stick now was hickory. He looked at me, nodding his head towards the young man.

"Dick Dogan's a case," he said. "He's a case." He let go the rope, and faced Mr. Dogan. "Dick, how's your missus?"

"Dead," said Mr. Dogan. "Dead as a herring."

Mr. Regan looked a little taken aback. He said with dignity, "Ain't that too bad." He paused. I'll just tell Mrs. Regan to step over to see what she can do."

Mr. Dogan was looking extremely solemn. "I'm obleeged to you, Mr. Regan, but I thought you folks mought mind the chillen." He turned and called, "Come hyar." I hadn't seen them: five little children in a row, about twenty paces away, lined up like stair-steps in the order of age and staring at us woodenly.

Mr. Regan turned towards the house, followed by Mr. Dogan. I seized the rope and dropped the bucket into the well, and drew it up full. The snake was not in it. I tipped the bucket and drank till I could hold no more. As I set it down I called out, "I'm much obliged to you, Mr. Regan."

He turned around and opened his mouth. "Well, now—" but I didn't wait to hear it. I ran down to the road. It was hot and dusty as I started with a steady pace on the last stretch towards home.

* * *

At Lee Chapel I could have turned left, southwest again, direct to the Ox Road, but I kept to the Pohick Road still running northwest because at Brimstone Hill I should know how to cut through Squire Langton's woods and skirting the big house reach Pleasant Hill from the rear. Two miles brought me opposite Mr. Will Gunnell's place and I heard a loud blowing of horns and sharp pistol shots like the tattoo on a small drum. A big family coach drove out of the gate followed by mounted young men in gray uniforms throwing rice and yelling their lungs out. As the coach came by me I saw Miss Maggie Gunnell—only her name must be changed now—inside with the groom. The boys on horseback slowed down. I was past them before they saw me but one of them turned and called: "Hey, Lacy, where you going?" I did not recognize him. "Seen any Yankees?" he said. "A heap of 'em," I said. They laughed and rode back through the gate.

The color of the road had changed from the whitish gray of the soil below the fall line to the blood brown of old rusty iron. It is an old country, I thought, as my toes sank into the rusty clay, powdered by the sun; an old country, and too many people have lived in it, and raised too much tobacco and corn, and too many men and women, young and old, have died in it, and taken with them into the rusty earth their gallantry or their melancholy, their pride or their simplicity, after their humors or their condition of life; and too many people have loved the ground in which after a while they must all come to lie. I tried to think of the first man who had ever walked that road, but I could see only the face of my grandfather Buchan in the portrait hanging in the front parlor at Pleasant Hill. His black silver-buckled shoes printing the brown dust; the black stockings below the tight broadcloth knee-breeches, black too; the buff waistcoat under the bottle-green tail-coat and, impossibly high, the white linen stock rising to the pompous and kindly face that radiated the correct, habitual mixture of warmth and indifference; then, at last, over the long chestnut hair the black cocked hat, silver-buckled; and after seeing it I heard the shining silver of the shoe-buckles, the knee-buckles, the hat-buckle, like a song. But it was only a deep contrapuntal bass without any treble that I heard as we walked side by side upon the old road, cracked and burned, through the countless trees, old-field pine and blackjack, big chestnut and whitethorn locust, and I knew that our thirst was not slaked. Presently we came easily to a two-barred gate and we stopped to look over it and saw a big fat man standing in a dog-run, his hair stringy above the cold gray eyes. When we were standing on the porch and I was getting a drink from the cedar bucket he gave me a crooked stare. It is a good thing, I thought, that I have somebody to look to for guidance on this road, and then the man spoke, "The State of Virginia ain't in the Union no more. The people voted her out yestiddy. The Yankees are comin'." My grandfather and I said nothing but thank you as we turned way and, going out, leaned a while to rest upon the bars of the gate. I couldn't see anything; I heard a noise in the air, but it was only the fat man talking in a language that I could not understand. We went out of the gate, carefully replacing the bars, and went up the road a hundred yards and sat down on a pile of fence rails by the roadside to rest again and to think it over again as best we could. He didn't mean to do it, I said to my grandfather, and he said: No, it was not the intention of your brother-in-law to kill your brother. It is never, my son, his intention to do any evil but he does evil because he has not the will to do good. The only expectancy that he shares with humanity is the pursuing grave, and the thought of extinction overwhelms him because he is entirely alone. My son, in my day we were never alone, as your brother-in-law is alone. He is alone like a tornado. His one purpose is to whirl and he brushes aside the obstacles in his way. My son, you are a classical scholar and you have read the epic of Apollonius of Rhodes, the Alexandrian scholar who pieced together from many older authors the pathetic tale of Jason and Medea and the Golden Fleece. Jason was a handsome young blade of royal descent who had suffered much from a violent family in his youth, so that nothing ordinary interested him; and he called together a great party of heroes and went off after the wool of a remarkable ram; but before he could get it he had to master certain rituals, and it was there that he failed, and showed the white feather. For the king of the country where lived the golden ram commanded him to subdue a certain number of savage bulls, a feat that he at last accomplished with the aid of the king's daughter, Medea, a high-spirited girl of a more primitive society than that from which the arrogant Jason came. He married this girl and carried her and the Fleece back to Hellas, promising her great things and more particularly promising to the king her father certain favors that no man could perform. It was Jason's misfortune to care only for the Golden Fleece and the like impossible things, while at the same time getting himself involved with the humanity of others, which it was not his intention but rather of his very nature to betray. For he came to love another woman, or he thought that he did, but he was actually repudiating, as we should now say, the very meaning of human loyalties and ties. It is said by other authors than Apollonius that Jason desecrated his fathers' graves. I have no doubt that he did. And when Medea discovered his perfidy she killed her children, and went mad, becoming evil; whereas Jason caused all the evil by means of his own privation of good. He was a noble fellow in whom the patriarchal and familial loyalties had become meaningless but his human nature necessarily limited him, and he made an heroic effort to combine his love of the extraordinary and the inhuman with the ancient domestic virtues. If the Fleece had been all-sufficing would he have taken Medea with him back to Greece? My son, I do not think so, my grandfather said.

You know everything, I said. I got up from the rails and turned to bid him a somewhat formal good-bye, but he was gone, and looking up to the next bend of the road I knew that I was no longer tired. It is a good thing, I thought, because I have nobody to guide me now. My grandfather was dead—dead as a herring. I started for the bend of the road, thinking only that far.

At the bend I could see the first rise of Brimstone Hill: two miles and a half and I will be at home. The sun rested warmly upon my left cheek, and I knew that I had sat on the post-oak rails for a long time. It will not be long till I see papa. I wanted to see him so badly that I could not bear the last two miles. But I began to consider it and I decided that being a man I had better face the music and tell it. Could I tell it all? Had I the right to tell what had happened on the rocky ledge the night of May twenty-third? I said, I will tell papa first what I saw in Alexandria the next morning, and let him ask me why I was there, and little by little I can bring it out. How would I begin? It was easy enough to begin it for myself. Brother George would have done something about Yellow Jim if Susan had not threatened him: he would have turned him loose into Virginia after a formal promise that he would return to Colonel Tayloe's place in Prince William, or he might even have let him go north into Pennsylvania. It was remarkable, because he was surely convinced that Jim was guilty or, if not strictly guilty, at any rate subject to the full penalty for having entered at night his mistress's room. Jane merely added to his moral guilt, not to the technical culpability. Or again, George, if alone, might actually have killed the Negro. I thought on the whole that is what he would have done, for where there was nothing but direct action George Posey was a certain and powerful man. But there was Semmes. I knew how he got there but in spite of the simplicity of his part in it, if you looked at it logically, something remained that would always be mysterious. In one way his position was the only clear one, clearer than George's or Susan's, much clearer than mine, which was a folly that I should not have committed the next week: it was clear because in spite of his having loved the girl there was no passion in his going out to the rock with Yellow Jim. There was only logic in it. Susan had sent us out, George had gone, and I had followed, because we were each of us grinding sharp, obscure axes of passion that had nothing to do with a Negro who had been goaded by mistreatment into an unspeakable fault. That was the mystery about Semmes: he was logical. An engaged man had to see that a Negro who had insulted his affianced bride got properly killed. Logic in human conduct is the hardest thing of all to understand, and people are never more mysterious than when they are being rational. I mean rational without passion; for if you get the passion behind it then the reason is only a screen through which a sharp eye may discern what it really is that people do. And Jane? A man's woman if I ever saw one, but safe only in quiet times; a girl wholly without imagination who, in order to create excitement that she could not find in herself, imagined that because Jim was a runaway there was something sinister about him; a girl who could never have been in love and would have thrown herself about, a perpetual apple of discord, indefinitely, had not Semmes and, to her, the foolish excitement of war, made a quick marriage interesting. Of course that looks like a judgment of her: I remember Aunt Jane Anne and her boxes; Miss Milly George and her bananas; Mr. Jarman and his scrinium, to say nothing of his slopjars and his French; and then Susan who would necessarily do the child in, in order to keep any of us from marrying her, to keep us from putting what we were into the jeopardy of what the Poseys were. And Susan succeeded; she succeeded in keeping the Buchans away from the Poseys; she succeeded at the price of destroying herself. She was ruined from the moment she told George not to let *her* brother kill *his* brother. Did Jane start all this? I think not; I cannot blame her. Was it Susan's fault? I do not know. There is reason to believe that when Susan threatened her husband she signed the death-warrant of her brother. George was infuriated. He was infuriated because he had been charged with a definite responsibility, by somebody else: he had been told what to do. It was too much for him. From the minute he left Susan's bedroom I cannot believe that he meant to kill Yellow Jim. Without thinking it through he had, up to then, assumed that he would kill him, or at least he was prepared to take him out and to go through the motions of disposing of him. But there is another thing to be considered: if George had been able to step over the threshold into the room where lay his mother's corpse, it might all have turned out very differently. He was between two fires of enforced obligation, and there was one of them that was so bright, unequivocal, and compelling—his dead mother—that if for no other reason than that he would have taken Yellow Jim up the river.—The more I went over it the less sense it made. Father Monahan or Doctor Cartwright, papa's friend, would have known a great deal more about us all than any of us knew. They would have ordered and named the crime and the degree, and fixed the responsibility. If I had been able to do that I should have forgotten all these people years ago. You remember what you cannot understand. What could Father Monahan have done with George's observation after Yellow Jim had fallen and Semmes had pitched into the whirlpool? "I never had any idea of killing that Nigger." He had not said it to me. It was a discovery of himself. What could Doctor Cartwright have made of Susan's white hair? Well, he was a Virginia gentleman and he would have ignored it, reading in his good voice the prayer for that day. Only grandfather Buchan, who was dead, and Susan, who was mad, knew everything.

I came through the woods to the squire's old-field from which I could see, at the upper end, the schoolhouse a quarter of a mile away. I crossed the Ox Road and in ten minutes I had jumped Buchan's Branch that flows west into Wolf Run, and climbing the sharp ascent stood at the edge of the big, rolling south field which was nearly two hundred acres. I slid over the fence and heard voices near me to the south.

I saw first the team of white mules, then a man standing and gesticulating with his back to me. It was Mr. Higgins and I started to call him when I heard another voice.

"I am master, sir, of this plantation."

I stepped out into the plowed ground. Back in an indentation of the field stood papa in the same field attire that he had worn for years: jack-boots enclosing the worsted trousers, gray homespun jacket and black kerchief, and the wide black felt hat. His iron gray mustache drooped at the ends. In the face there was no sign of agitation. The broad mouth was composed and the dark eyes under the heavy brows gazed expectantly at Mr. Higgins.

"Ain't no question about that, major," said Mr. Higgins. "You know it ain't my fault. Hit's this hyar mite of paper." He held a folded sheet before him. "Me and Mister Semmes was playboys together and you and my pappy was playboys. Hit don't seem right for things to be like they are." He waved the paper. "Hyar's the law. Hit's the court order that Mr. Posey give me last winter."

Papa was not listening to him; with the toe of his boot he idly kicked a clod off the crest of a furrow. Beyond the white mules, which were hitched to a bull-tongue plow, stood a small horse before a new corn-planting machine. That was what it was all about, then: he had always harvested his wheat with scythe and cradle, and the hands had dropped the corn into hills. There were four or five field-hands standing respectfully in the background. Then I saw the black gelding farther back near the fence; Henry Jackson sat on the fence, the bridle dangling from his hand. Papa moved his shoulder and raised his arm, the thumb pointing upwards; he moved the thumb a little and Henry Jackson led the gelding forward. As papa put his foot into the stirrup, I walked forward but my feet seemed not to touch the ground. I opened my mouth and made the syllables:

"Papa,"

—but I could not hear the sounds. Very slowly and from an immense distance beneath me the ground began to rise, and as I watched it I thought it was a long time coming. It struck my face with a shock, and I felt hands upon my forehead, and heard my father's voice which sounded like the voice of my grandfather when we had sat upon the pile of rails.

"Henry, you will have to carry the young master up to the big house."

*   *   *

The next thing I knew it was dark and the place was strange with new odors in a room that smelled like paint, and strange noises outside; and from where I was lying propped among pillows, strange lights like little fires winked outside the window, only they were not lightning-bugs because they were too big and stationary, stretching far away up what must have been a hillside.

"What time is it?" I said to the dark room.

"Hit's nigh on to three o'clock in de mornin'," a voice said. I listened to its echo.

"Coriolanus," I said.

A match flared, and the light of two candles from a double candlestick on the mantel spread softly over the room. He brought the candles over to the nightstand by the bed, and sat down by me on a leather chair. I looked at it.

"The leather chair," I said.

He looked at me soberly, then leaned towards me and stared critically into my eyes. His old brown face wrinkled into a smile that framed the serious eyes.

"De fust time you ain't said, 'I got to tell papa,'" he said.

"The first time." I felt cool and as if I had nothing to do but lie there. "Have I been talking in my sleep?"

The smile had gone and he was sober again.

I said, "I was tired yesterday. I'll be all right today."

He poured me a glass of water from the china pitcher on the nightstand.

"I'm not thirsty," I said.

He smiled again and sat down. "You be all right," he

said. Then in a calm, ordinary tone: "Hit wa'n't yestiddy, young marster. Hit was six weeks ago day befo' yestiddy." He leaned forward again. "De young mistis been hyar two weeks."

I tried to think who the young mistis was. I looked at him.

"Miss Susie," he said.

"Miss Susie," I said.

"And de baby gyirl."

I felt a little tired, so I let my head sink into the pillows, and looked out of the window at the fires, which were dim in the growing light. The sun would be up in a little while to light the windows. "The big guest room," I said. Coriolanus nodded, and saw that I was trying to look out of the window.

"De sojers leaving this place today. They cook rations befo' sun."

It was like recognizing a tree: "Yankees," I said.

"Yankees nothin'," he said. "Confederates."

I pushed myself up on my elbow but fell back, and closed my eyes. "Confederates," I said.

In a little while I opened my eyes and it was day; the sun streamed into the windows and two young men in gray stood at the foot of the bed, their forage caps in their hands.

"Howdy, Lacy," said Wink Broadacre.

"Howdy," said Jack Armistead. "Well, we got to be goin'," he said.

"Young marster," said Coriolanus to Jack, "Marse Lacy don't know you been to see him befo'."

Jack grinned at me, and Wink came round to the side of the bed and held out his hand. "You're better," he said. We shook hands.

Jack and Wink exchanged glances. "The cap'n has put

your name on the rolls of our company," said Wink. "You're on sick furlough till you can join us." He rubbed the butt of a big horse-pistol in his belt. "We're retiring behind Bull Run. There's goin' to be a big battle soon."

My face felt hot. "Where's papa?" I said.

"The cap'n said you don't need his consent," Jack said.

"Pa said I couldn't join. When I did he didn't do anything." He grinned again. "Cousin Lewis wouldn't shake hands with me but he bowed to me yesterday. He said, 'Cousin, I don't like your uniform or any uniform.' I ain't scared of your pa or any old man now I've joined." He came to Wink's side and shook hands with me. "I'll be seein' you," he said.

"I'll be seein' you," Wink said.

"I'll be seein' you," I said as they went awkwardly out of the room and closed the door after them.

I went to sleep for a while but when I woke it was still morning; the sun made a triangle on the counterpane at my feet and Coriolanus came forward with a small waiter. I was hungry. I must have eaten in all those weeks, but the last time I remembered eating was the afternoon Blind Joe brought the ham and cold biscuits up to the south bedroom. Now I drank greedily out of a cup the hot chicken soup and ate the toasted biscuit, then drank the glass of cold buttermilk.

"De gin'ral come up to de house," Coriolanus said.

I was listening to the low rumble that rose from the east—the Ox Road. Coriolanus was listening. "They're marchin'," he said. "More'n two thousand in de brigade."

"Who's the general?" I said.

"Gin'ral Longstreet. He come up to de house and say, 'Tell the gentleman I won't disturb him.' He say thank you for de courtesies and he respect de diff'rence of opinion. He say he won't disturb de major on account of his late bereavement.''

''I was excited. ''What bereavement, Coriolanus?''

He looked at me. ''Lacy''—and to the old man I was a little boy again—''ain't no need for you to tell your pa nothin'. When he comes in to see you, don't you say nothin','' He put a hand on the edge of the bed and spoke tentatively. ''Miss Susie ain't said nothin' either.''

''How is she?'' I said.

''Po'ly,'' he said in a commonplace tone. Then: ''She come home with that bad Nigger Joe driving de keeriage. She just looked at the major on de front gallery, looked at him about five minutes. She didn't say nothin'. He didn't say nothin'. She went up to her chamber and she ain't been down since.'' He paused to take the waiter, which he placed upon the nightstand. ''Ain't nothin' nobody kin do. De major, he sont for Miss Myra to come to look after de baby gyirl, sont yestiddy. She ain't doin' anything since Marse Armistead's daid.'' He looked up at me. ''No, sir, she can't mind de child.'' He shook his head. ''I ain't never seen nothin' like Miss Susie's hair.'' He sat in the leather chair and folded his hands.

The door moved without a knock and I saw my father's clawed hand hesitate on the knob before it pushed the door wide open. When he was in he turned slowly and closed it, then turned round and assumed his full height. He looked at me from his impassive face, his eyes calm and serious. Coriolanus had risen. Papa came directly to the bed and as he let his weight down gradually upon it, he said to Coriolanus in his politest tone, ''We will excuse you for a few minutes.''

As Coriolanus went out I found myself examining my father's attire. He was dressed in his formal suit, black broadcloth coat and high white formal stock without a collar. His leg, thrown across the side of the bed, was covered with silk stocking and knee breeches. He saw me looking at him.

"My days of supervising in the field are over," he said. He leaned forward and smiled directly into my eyes. "Son, you are better." He reached for my hand and held it gently by the tips of his fingers. "We despaired of you for a while." He dropped my hand and said: "But you're a Buchan. In your long delirium you wouldn't give up." He rose and walked round the bed and sat down in the leather chair.

"I know all about it," he said.

I gave in to it and tears ran down my face. Papa watched me a few minutes, his wide, mobile mouth fixed in a half smile. "Here," he said, and taking his big kerchief out of his sleeve handed it to me. I wiped my face and gave it back to him, and he absent-mindedly stuffed it into his sleeve. I noticed a red spot in each cheek and the new sharpness of the cheekbones under the loosening flesh. His eyes looked tired, unwilling to focus upon anything. He stiffened a little, and I thought: it is only at unguarded moments that one may perceive the difference.

"Son, you are well enough for me to say it. I must impress it upon you that there is nothing that we can do, nothing whatever. We are not in a position to avenge your brother's death."

The green china clock was ticking away on the mantel. Gazing at it, I listened intently. Papa moved in his chair.

"Papa, where's Brother George?" I said.

He looked surprised: his eyes fixed me and his mouth quivered. "In Georgetown," he said. "I received a letter from him some weeks since." He drew out his kerchief and held it in his hand, twisting it round his forefinger. "A manly letter. And there was no doubt of the earnest sincerity of his expression. He said that he shot your brother in anger, and he explained everything that had led up to it. I have been particularly impressed by his contrition. He said that he had been harassed continuously by the thought that he had been betrayed by his anger, although he was not conscious of having done anything morally wrong up to that time." He looked anxious, and he raised his innocent old eyes to mine, and stuffed the handkerchief back into his sleeve. Then his eyes wandered over the room and came to rest upon the counterpane, at the spot where the sun had struck; and staring, the eyes seemed to draw back into his head, and to lose all their luster.

Brother George had been sincere—that I could not doubt, and nobody could doubt it. Across the hall from me, sister—and of this I had no doubt—was walking the floor in her white hair, looking with unrecognizing eyes at the little girl playing at her feet. Papa make money—yes, and papa had been perfectly sincere when he had said, God damn the money. He cared nothing for money but he was interested in it because he could feel only himself. The remarkable letter he had written—the very act of writing it had been appallingly too sincere. Had papa understood that? If he had, he had said nothing to show it, and now he continued to gaze at the counterpane, until suddenly, almost like a young man, he sprang to his feet, and took two steps to the foot of the bed.

"I sent my son to his death," he said in a tone that he would have used to say that he had sent Coriolanus for his snuffbox. "It was pride that made me do it." He rubbed the footboard with the palm of his hand. "It mortally injured *his* pride. That would make any man flee to the arms of the woman he loves. And it made him the extraordinary avenger of her honor. Son, he was a Buchan too." He looked at me fiercely. With a shudder I thought, Good God, what a proud old man! He moved to the door. "I am to blame for all this," he said with a little movement of his hand. "For your sister. Didn't I let her marry him? She would improve him! He is not to blame." He came back to the leather chair. He did not sit down. He leaned over the bed and kissed me on the forehead, and without a word straightened up and walked out of the room.

The door closed softly and the clock began to tick again as I pulled the quilt over my eyes to conceal, if I could, the arrogant set of the old gentleman's shoulders as he had disappeared through the door. I heard his certain footsteps on the bare stairs.

*   *   *

After Coriolanus had brought me my breakfast the next morning late, for I slept late, papa came in and, with a plain good-morning, together they walked me downstairs and out into the yard where I sat all morning under the big sugar tree by the violet bed. I sat in a rush-bottom rocking-chair, reading about Peregrine Pickle, but I put the book aside because I thought Pickle a fool. It was fine hot weather without rain. I studied with fascination the new paint on the house; the glistening white lead on the weather-boarding and the deep green of the blinds smelled strong in the heat, and I frowned a little at the unfamiliar line of the gallery—where it had been jacked up the few inches that it had lost a generation before. "Marse George done it this spring while we was away," Coriolanus said.

I went down every day after breakfast and I could not wait for the morning to come so that I might see papa, who had not visited me again. Ocassionally he put his head out of the chamber window—the chamber being mother's old bedroom that he occupied—and said, "How are you, son?" I said, "Better, thank you, sir." We had dinner together but after it was over I went up, at three, for a nap; Coriolanus brought me a light supper on the waiter; and I saw papa no more till the next morning. Every evening just at sundown I heard him come up the stairs and knock at sister's door. I heard the door open, and stay open, but there were no voices, and after a slight interval that I came to predict—I could say, now it will close—the door closed, and papa went back downstairs. One morning Coriolanus, as he handed me my breakfast, said, "De major don't sleep good. He walks out to de graveyard and sets on old Spotsy'vania mistis' grave. That's his mammy, young marster," he said as if I didn't know. I said, "What's your full name?" He said, "I was christened in de church. Jones Coriolanus Lewis." He looked up and said simply: "I don't want to live no longer than de major do. I nussed him. Ten yare older to de day."

On the sixth day after my fever had left me I walked down alone and around the yard, and stood under the thin green of the dogwood tree, looking up at the house, then off up the slope to the pink brick row of the quarters, and westward to the garden, a jungle of brambles and box, untrimmed, and to the big chestnut rising above the low brick wall of the graveyard. I thought how many processions of how many slow feet had followed the path by the garden into the brick wall. I thought how many more would follow it, I among them, and then they would follow me, and among these there would be some who would drop out one day and be followed to the grave; then the processions would go on to the end of time. The house, the big sugar tree, the back gallery, papa's affectionate glance were all that I was; under the chestnut tree was all that I would be. There was a pleasure in these sights and meditations that was new, and I thought how strange it was to be standing there in the yard.

I began to ride over the neighborhood on the black gelding, but I never went near a house; if I met a neighbor in the big road I bowed and passed on, to avoid condolences and questions; I usually rode over the place. Towards the middle of July I rode into our gate and drew rein to cool off under the scant shade of the cedars. I saw a cloud of dust nearly a mile away, southeast, this side of Yates' Road that leads down to the fords of the Occoquan and Bull Run. In a few minutes a squadron of cavalry pulled up at the gate. Under the dust their uniforms were gray. A young lieutenant cantered into the gate, held in his lathered horse and said, "Detachment of the Fourth Virginia Cavalry. Seen any Yankees on this road?" "No, I haven't seen any," I said. He stared at me. "You mean not yet," he said. He looked me over. "What is *your* regiment?" I pulled the gelding round and said over my shoulder, "Seventeenth Virginia, infantry." I started to say that I had been ill, but I spurred the gelding and I heard the squadron trot away to the south as I rode up the hill.

I turned the gelding over to Henry Jackson in the stable yard, and went towards the house. I found myself at the foot of the back gallery stairs, but I glanced up and saw myself at the door of the room that Semmes and I had shared; I came round the house and into the front door. How can I leave? I said to myself, going upstairs. In the upper hall I went out to the upper gallery. Far down the cedar lane, as far as the gate, I thought, a mile away, I saw a little cloud of dust, no bigger than a beam in the eye. One horse, I said, and went inside. I will see, I said, and I knocked on sister's door.

I knocked a second time and then turned the knob and

went in. I was ready to say something but there was no-body to speak to. My hand shook on the knob as I saw a black figure, its back to me, sitting by the side window, just opposite me, its face turned towards the garden below, its head covered by a small, tight-fitting black bonnet. I should have known only by the set of the neck, that it was a woman. She began to turn around, slowly, with no change of posture, and sitting sideways in the chair gave me a long, steady gaze.

"Sister," I said in a low voice.

The expression, or I ought to say the lack of it, for the gaze was neither indifferent nor interested, neither cold nor excited—the expression was that of a sleepy woman looking at her own powderless face in a glass. There was no flicker in the lids of the eyes as she resumed her position before the window. My eye fell upon the bed. The child was sleeping upon it. The knob felt warm to my hand as I closed the door after me. I ran down the stairs.

On the front gallery I sat down on the steps and ob-served the visitor approaching the house by the lane. A nondescript dark horse pulled a buggy up to the hitching-rack, and the driver sat a minute, his back to the house, before he stood up and, putting a foot on the front hub, lowered himself to the ground. George Posey turned and glanced at the house, then went to the horse's head and tied him to the rack. He came round to the back of the buggy and lifted out a small, square carpet-bag, with one hand, and, with the other, a flat brown telescope strapped at both ends. He looked inquiringly towards the house, but not directly at me. Gripping the baggage he passed the horseblock and the dogwood tree, heading for the end of the house and the path leading to the back gallery. When he came opposite me he stopped, still holding the bag and the telescope. He wore a long black coat and dingy trousers, and on his head a frayed stovepipe hat. I should have taken him for an itinerant apothecary.

"The Federal army will reach Centreville tonight," he said, as if he had come especially to bear the news. He walked around the house and disappeared.

From round behind the graveyard a horseman approached, that in a few seconds revealed himself as Blind Joe mounted upon the bay mare. I was not surprised; I merely said, the other time he came up the cedar lane. He dismounted by the buggy, untied the horse, and led both horses across the front yard. Without stopping or looking at me, he said, "Evenin', Marster." Then he stopped. "Hit was like a rabbit gittin' thoo de briars. De Yankees is everywhar. Marse George he almost got ketched at Mosby's Crossing. I come by de back roads from thar." He looked as if he expected me to say something. I didn't even look at him. He went round the house.

I got up but halfway to the door I looked into the front window of the chamber and saw, across the room, papa, who was standing at the window that overlooked the violet bed. I went into the hall and knocked at the door. He said come in and as I entered he said:

"Coriolanus, get—"

"Papa," I said.

He turned around and his face was flushed.

"Why has that young man done this thing to me?" he said.

*   *   *

At dawn next morning I heard a big forest tree fall, the trunk breaking the branches off the other trees with a crackling thunder. Another tree fell and I turned over in bed. Then another and still another until the entire big woods west of Wolf Run had fallen down. I put my feet upon the floor and listened. There was a lull and it began all over again. In a few minutes as I put on my clothes I ceased to hear it, being aware of it as one occasionally acknowledges after a while the presence of a storm.

Downstairs I could not find anybody, so I went to the out-kitchen where Juniper gave me my breakfast. There was now and then a clap of thunder that prolonged itself, rose and fell, but presently it was quiet again, and it was only the hot clear morning of July eighteenth, eighteen-sixty-one. As I came out of the kitchen Coriolanus and Henry Jackson closed after them the gate into the cuppen. I waited for them. Henry lingered in the background; his face was solemn and scared. Coriolanus said. "We been listenin'. Up on Burke Hill." I turned towards the house as the old Negro said, "You had your breakfast, young marster?" "Yes," I said and went round to the front of the house. I saw Mr. Higgins in the front yard and later throughout the day he seemed to be wandering around the house but I could not decide what he was doing. The morning passed; the time passed when I usually went for my ride but I didn't go; and shortly before dinner Blind Joe called up to me from the yard and said could I come see his master for a minute.

I knew where to find him, in the guest room on the back gallery; so I knocked at the door, he said, "Come in," and I opened the door and stood before him. He was sitting on the bed in his shirt sleeves. There was red mud on his boots but his face was smooth, and I saw two razors in a case on the dresser. Neither the bag nor the telescope, lying on the floor, was open. His coat lay crumpled upon a chair. He was holding the side of the bed with his hands, and leaning forward. His face was lean and composed. Without looking at me he said, "We can't go yet."

I was aware of my cunning as I answered. "Why not?" I closed the door after me and stood in the middle of the floor.

"I think she will recognize me if I can get in the room." He gave me an earnest glance. "Before she came here," he said, and looked away. "Before that she never knew me after that time. You know the time."

"Yes, I know the time."

"I had to tell her what happened. It was the next day. I told her but she was not surprised. She didn't know me." He got up and looked out of the window. "Her room faces this way too." The garden below him. "I made Dr. Burrows tell her she had to come home. She wouldn't speak to him either. When Joe told her the carriage was ready she came down to it with little Jane and got in."

"Yes," I said to his back.

He came away from the window and sat on the bed. "We can't go yet.

I was cunning again as I glanced covertly at the cold eyes in the lean face. "Why go at all?"

He raised his head quickly and gave me a puzzled stare. He got up and paced the room and I backed against the wall to let him pass. "Why," he said to himself. He was at the window again. "Because it seems like I ought to be with the men." He didn't move.

"You killed my brother," I said.

"Yes," he said in a distant voice.

"You killed him."

He sat on the bed again and began to look me over, but there was no arrogance in it, and I thought that he was actually feeling how strange it was.

"It seems like I've got to be with the men." He rose and came forward and said in a firm voice, "Not yet." He held out his hand but I couldn't take it as I moved sideways around him towards the door. His hand was still in the air, his face flushed and sad, when I closed the door.

I went back to the big guest room which was now mine, and lay on the bed, thinking it was all too late. He wanted to "go" too late. But he did want to go. When he had wanted to go he had always gone, and even stayed away. But now something more than decorum, something he did not understand, nor I, was restraining him: the mere recognition of his presence there by his wife, the woman with whom he had obscurely compounded a hideous wrong, at a depth of their natures that I neither could nor cared to see. For the first time his desire to go was not a running away, and it was too late. Then I remembered that before he had come sister had not kept the door locked. He had been recognized, but he had wanted to be recognized—too late. Was his determination to go to the army only his determination to be recognized by his wife, like his attempt to shake hands with me, or was it something better than that, something apart from his personal desperation? I did not know, and I gave it up once more, not knowing which beliefs were right and which wrong.

There was loud conversation in the front yard in which I distinguished the voice of Mr. Higgins. I went out on the upper gallery and saw about a dozen Federal soldiers, their faces, I thought, unrelievedly round and red, standing in a loose cluster by the horseblock. Directly under the gallery Mr. Higgins was arguing with the captain.

"Ain't no rebels here," he said.

"Whut?" said the captain, a handsome fat man with big blonde mustaches across a weak face. "I tink that you a big liar are."

There was no time for more words from them. George Posey came round the corner of the house in his shirt sleeves, walked up to the captain and without a word slapped his face. The astonished man held his cheek as George yanked his sword out of the scabbard, broke it across his knee, and tossed it away.

"You Dutch bastard," he said between his teeth. "Get off this place."

The captain, still holding his cheek, backed off. George advanced about ten paces towards the soldiers, stopped, folded his arms, and glared at them. I heard from them only a cackle, and they went off down the lane, dragging their muskets after them. The captain started running, but I was not interested in him. George Posey was walking slowly back whence he had come. He vanished round the corner of the house.

*   *   *

The rest of that day I did nothing, nor the next, but lie around the house avoiding George Posey and papa alike, after I had seen them pass each other in the yard, on the second day: papa gave George a bow, not distant or cold, but casual, not looking at him. I do not know how many times George came upstairs, but before the clock on the landing had struck six—this, too, on the second day—I counted four times, once before I ate my dinner alone, and three in the evening. He came upstairs, knocked at sister's door, and after a while said in a tender voice, "Susan." He waited, and I heard him go down the hall and down the stairs. In the middle of the evening, when it was so hot and still that even the insects seemed to subside a little, and the flies stuck to the wall, Mr. Higgins came to me on the porch and said that the thunder we had heard day before yesterday had been a battle on Bull Run at Blackburn's Ford and that the Yankees had been whipped but were still there. "Why are they still there then?" I said. He said that the Dutch who had come to Pleasant Hill were the rear guard because they couldn't be trusted to fight, and were scouring the roads to the southeast of Centreville where their brigade was posted.

A little later a carriage drove up, right to the front porch, and Aunt Myra stepped out with the peculiar spring that youngish old ladies have. A middle-aged Negro woman got out after her. Aunt Myra came up the steps and I embraced her, neither of us speaking: she went into papa's room, and a few minutes later I heard her, followed by the Negro woman, go up the front stairs. The hired coach with its white driver vanished into the lane.

After dark I went round to the gallery and up the stairs to Semmes' room, and lit a candle on the bureau. I had not been in that room for nearly a year. A hairbrush lay on the bureau, with some sulphur matches, and my double-barreled gun and powder horn hung from their pegs on the wall. The old brazier stood back in a far corner, some ashes from it dusting the floor. I took the gun down, laid it on the bed, and got a greased rag out of the wardrobe drawer. The papers fell out upon the floor and I left them there. I wiped off the gun and ran the rag through it with the ramrod. I put on a pair of breeches, light summer drilling, and found in the wardrobe my brown home-spun hunting jacket. I put on a gray hat that had belonged to Semmes, and picked up the gun.

The door opened. George stepped into the room. He wore a black felt hat but below it was the full, new uniform of a Confederate private. "Come on," he said.

I followed him down the steps into the yard. As he headed for the stable, I said, "Wait a minute."

"I'll get the horses," he said.

I hesitated. "I'll take the gelding."

It was a dark night and he was instantly invisible. I went

round to the front porch and peered into papa's room. A lamp on the center table was burning low. The room was empty. I went into the hall and through the door, which was ajar, and at the table I wrote, with papa's steel pen, on a scrap of paper: "Good-by, papa." I leaned the paper against the lamp and turned the wick up a little. At the door I paused, wondering why; then I thought of the old piece of strap that I had thrown behind the door.

At the stable George had a dark-lantern from which a slit of light emerged upon the gelding and the bay mare. Blind Joe, between the horses, held the bridles. The buggy horse, tied to a stall in the background, was saddled. We mounted our horses, George blew out the light, and we headed for the cuppen, Joe leading the way to put down the bars. Beyond the cuppen we went at a walk down the lane that led past the woods where I had first shot off the gun, but when we came to the edge of the big south field the lane turned west and we broke into an easy canter. At the end of the lane we halted, and Joe lowered the bars. We rode through the gap into the sandy road. As Joe replaced the bars George said, "Which way?" I said, "To the right."

On the sandy road the hooves were muffled. The saddles creaked and the buggy horse wheezed: wind-broke, I said. In half an hour the moon came up over the low pines and we slowed to a walk, and I began to look for signs. We came to a red oak thicket and I led off to the left into an ox track that the tobacco carts traversed in the fall of the year.

After about a half mile I heard water and we turned into a cowpath over a low hill into the woods, and halted at the bank of the stream. It was still dark and I wished it were later, so that a high moon would help us. I listened. A hundred feet to the west, on my right, I could·hear

Wolf Run tumbling into Bull Run: where we stood the
two streams made the Occoquan River. We were at the
foot of the shoals. I dismounted and looked at the path.
It led into the stream.

Brother George and Joe dismounted. We waded, leading the horses. We led the horses up the steep bank into
another path and mounted them. The path led along the
stream till we came to a rail fence at an open field.

"Halt!" a mild voice said.

"God-a-mighty," said Blind Joe behind us.

"Who're you?" I said.

"Ewell's brigade."

"We're Seventeenth Virginia, Longstreet's."

The man lit a pine-knot and came to the fence, the
torch in one hand, the rifle in the other. He held up the
torch and looked at us. "How do I know you are?" He
leaned his rifle against the fence. "Git off them hosses, and
you," he said to me, "you drop that shotgun." He looked
at us again. "You look all right. Whose Nigger is that?"

"Mine," said George.

The man looked at me. "Less hear you talk some."

I studied about it. " 'The curfew tolls the knell of parting day,' " I said, and laughed.

"Sounds Virginny," he said. Then: "Eddicated." He
waved the torch. "Gap up the fence a piece."

I picked up my gun and we all mounted, found the gap
and rode back to the man. "Follow your nose till you hit
a road and go to your right."

In five minutes we were at the road. Across it a fire
smoldered in the midst of sleeping men. One man sat
up. We were not challenged. We passed a long line of
wagons, the mules tethered in bunches to the fence. We
came to low fires, and here and there in the tangled vines
and pines I saw a tent.

We rode another mile and came to a big square tent, all lit up inside. Before it five or six men were standing round a lantern. We drew in our horses and I said, "Good evening."

They looked at us, and one man laughed. He came forward, a young officer in a handsome uniform, his back to the light so that I could not see his face. "What can I do for you?" he said.

George spoke up. "We're looking for our regiment, Seventeenth Virginia."

"Brigade?" said the officer.

"Longstreet," I said.

"Just a moment, gentlemen," he said, and turned round. "General," he said, "these gentlemen are looking for Longstreet's brigade."

A small man, bare-headed, with a long mustache, took a step forward. The lantern shone in his face. He cocked his head and focused his eyes upon a spot in the dark sky. He looked like a game chicken.

"Fifty yards more and take the right hand fork," he said. He raised his voice, "Why in hell, Flournoy, didn't you tell him?" But he said it humorously. "The left hand fork will take you to Jackson," he said to us. "Don't let Longstreet get you killed tomorrow. Gentlemen," he said soberly, "you arrive in the nick."

"Don't mind General Ewell," said the officer. "Good night."

"Good night, sir," I said.

We came to the fork as the moon rose over the trees, white and cold, and filled a big cornfield that had been trampled so that thousands of men could sleep. The back of my neck began to tingle as I surveyed the faces in the moonlight, white, cold and still, like the moon. Down the road at the end of the field I discerned a log cabin in which there was a light, and a light burned on the porch.

 "There," I said to George.

"Yes," he said and spurred his horse ahead of me for the first time.

At the cabin we dismounted and gave the bridles to Joe. I followed George to the porch where the men who sat near the lantern turned to look at us curiously.

"Gentlemen," said George gravely, "we are looking for the seventeenth, Colonel Corse."

At the far end of the porch a man rose and walking by the light on the near side came to the top of the steps.

"Good evening, colonel," George said.

The colonel came down, peering at us. "Colonel Corse!" I said. He had not looked at George.

"Lacy Buchan, what you doing here?" He looked angry.

"My name's on the muster-roll, company B," I said. "Leftenant Broadacre."

"You mean Captain Jones," he said in a military voice. He looked at George. "Good evening, Mr. Posey," he said, and shook hands. He gave me his hand. We were silent. "Those your horses?" He nodded his head. "You won't need 'em. Better let your man stay here all night." He turned to me. "Lacy, Broadacre's inside." In a low voice he told a man on the porch to call Lieutenant Broadacre. "He will show you where to go."

"I am not armed," said George.

"He will attend to it."

Wink Broadacre came down the steps peering through the dark. "Yes, colonel?" he said. Then he saw us. He looked from me to George, and from George to me. "My platoon. Fourth squad, number three in the rear rank."

"Howdy, Wink," I said.

He stared at me until I said: "Where's Jack?"

He turned to me a dirty face over which the skin was drawn tight around eyes that looked like jelly.

"Dead," he said. "Blackburn's Ford."

Colonel Corse glanced at him sharply. Then he said in a mild voice, "You better get some sleep." Wink Broadacre turned his eyes from me to Brother George; I followed his glance. He was staring back at Wink and I saw him, quick as an eyelash, cross himself.

As we were turning away the figure of a man came from behind us out of the dark and said to Colonel Corse, "That man ought to be shot for desertion."

I stopped dead in my tracks; so did George. He turned halfway round and looked at the man whose face was full in the lantern light, on one side, and on the other, white in the moon. His clothes were indistinguishable but his slouch was insolent, and the face held steadily towards George Posey was the face of John Langton.

George spoke. "Joe," he said to the Negro, "you look out for the horses. Don't you leave here if you have to stay a week." He glanced briefly at Langton, turned round, and we went to find our bivouac for the night.

*　　　*　　　*

It was bright day when I woke and I smelled coffee and bacon with the sharp odor of the pine needles upon which I lay. A rod away, two colored boys were stooping over a fire, one pouring the coffee into the tin cups that the other passed to the soldiers who, like me, were lying or sitting, sleepy or with serious faces, upon the ground. The sun pierced the tops of the pines. I drank a cup of coffee and ate a sliver of fat bacon that the boy handed me in the skillet. But for the sizzle of the bacon there was no sound. I looked curiously at the silent faces, then looked away because all the eyes were upon the ground. I crawled a few feet to the shallow branch and put my face into the water and drank. I looked up at the sun, then down at the water. It flows north, I said, into Bull Run.

I came back to my gun and sat by it, and the boy handed me a small pone of bread. He was a little Negro with big yellow eyes.

"Whose boy are you?" I said.

"De leftenant's, sir."

I looked again at his eyes. "I know you. Under the pavilion."

He grinned. "Yassir."

Everybody was looking at me. A voice said, "He wa'n't hyar Thursday." He was a big man with a blond, scraggy beard. He laughed and it was quiet again.

On the other side of the branch in a big rolling field a double line of men, standing in the ranks at ease, ran westwards up a slope for nearly a mile and continued into the woods at the top of the hill. Behind them at the edge of the pine woods another line, more densely brown and gray, curved away to the southwest beyond sight. I was gazing at the row of black cannon in front of the first line when Colonel Corse, followed by George Posey on the bay mare, appeared from the south across the branch. The colonel, sitting his horse, looked anxiously towards the north and cocked his head to listen. Brother George was holding his mare with a tight rein, patting her withers. His plain gray coat and the black, unbraided hat made him look younger than he was. At his waist I saw a wide leather belt and on the belt a pistol in a holster on the left side.

Another horseman appeared from the south and riding past George at a gallop drew his gray horse in sharply, so that the animal stiffened his forelegs in the soft ground.

The horseman took off his hat and cocked his head to listen. Colonel Corse looked at him.

"I can't hear anything, general," he said.

The general was a deep-chested man all in gray under the long brown hair and full brown beard. The eyes were small and the cheekbones high in a strong, poker face. He put his hat on.

"Why don't Ewell begin?" he said. All three horsemen, the officers in front and George ten paces behind them, sat like statues.

The ground quivered and instantly I was deaf. The roar mounted and died way.

The general looked at Colonel Corse. "That ain't the right direction," he said. "Rifled cannon. It's theirs." He took off his hat and fanned himself. "Colonel, how far off was that shot?"

"Five miles," said Corse.

The general nodded. "The Stone Bridge." He was listening again. "Why don't Ewell begin?"

There was another shot, like the first; then there was a punctuated roar. The men were moving about on the ground, looking westwards; getting to their feet and sitting down again. The blond-bearded man scuttled over the needles and shouted into my ear.

"Thar's a heap o' fat squirrels in them oak trees acrost the creek. Jest step over and ask Gin'ral Longstreet to let you git a brace of 'em fer dinner." He rubbed the double barrel of my gun.

"Where's the creek?" I said.

He pointed his finger towards a sycamore thicket. "You could th'ow a rock from hyar to Blackburn's Ford."

Wink Broadacre, his brown face washed, stepped out of the pines. He wore a faded blue shirt and torn gray pantaloons; on his head was a gray forage cap, over the long, black, matted hair. He paused near the dying fire. We listened to the big piles of lumber clattering to the ground from an immense height. Somebody off in the west would drop the planks, wait for them to settle, and drop another pile. Wink looked at me coldly out of his crazy eyes. He walked to the edge of the branch and leaned against a pine. "Hell," he said to himself. I went and stood by him. He gave me a glance. "His Nigger took him home on a mule," he said, "only man killed in this regiment."

The general and the colonel might have been listening to a concert. I looked at Brother George: he sat erect on the mare gazing at the backs of the officers. He looks like somebody, I thought, taking in the faces of the other horsemen. Why didn't he kill him? Why didn't he kill him on the spot? As he sat gazing, his eyes were narrow and the smile was at the corners of his mouth.

Under the rattle came the soft patter of hooves as a cavalcade drew up at the far side of the general. The men in the ranks over in the field threw hats into the air, and a harsh scream, rising to a high treble that wavered a long minute, filled the air. The staff withdrew under a large, gold-fringed stars-and-bars, and left, talking to General Longstreet, a thickset, dark little man with a short black mustache.

"General Beauregard," said Wink. "He's a foreigner."

He had big eyes and a wry mouth. He spurred his horse towards the branch and let him drink. General Longstreet and Colonel Corse followed and waited till the horse raised his head.

"General," said Beauregard, "General McDowell has diagnosed our plan of operations and appropriated it. He is attacking *our* left. The exigencies of the crisis have compelled me to move General Jackson to the support of General Bee. I shall go in person to take charge of the field. You may consult with General Johnston, who will remain at the Lewis house. Meanwhile you will make a strong demonstration at this point to prevent the further reinforcement of their column of attack."

If he had placed his hand over his breast, it would have been an oration. His voice, neither Southern nor Yankee, was modulated and clipped. He bowed to the officers and raised his forage cap; spurring his horse and holding the cap rigidly about six inches above his head, he rode off towards the belt of timber. The staff followed at a distance and the men yelled.

General Longstreet and the colonel were pointing towards the creek. The colonel lifted his hat. There was a splash in the branch, and the colonel, his mouth open, jammed the hat back upon his head: a hissing roar threw mud into my eyes and I stood in a momentary shower of rain. I wiped my face on my sleeve.

"Hell," said Wink, wiping his eyes with a spotless handkerchief.

"They've beat us to it here," said the general. He turned his horse abruptly and rode away.

George trotted to the colonel's side and together they forded the branch. Wink Broadacre moved from the tree and stood erect as the colonel faced him.

"Leftenant, you will command company B today. Form your men and file off to the left across the branch. Advance and deploy as skirmishers along the bank of the run. Your right will be at the ford. Captain Langton will be on your right and connect with it. He will give you orders as they are needed." He turned to George and said, I thought a little significantly: "An efficient officer—Langton."

Wink opened his mouth. "Fall in!" It was a tinny voice, as if a ventriloquist were talking through him. "Dress on me," he yelled. The men scrambled to their feet. My hands were numb as I picked up the shotgun. Two ranks were rapidly forming but I stared round me bewildered. The scraggy-bearded man grabbed me by the back of my jacket and pushed me ahead of him to the far end of the line. "Do what I do," he said. "Don't do nothin' I don't do." He about-faced me. "Thar," he said. He stood on my left.

The line moved and I followed the big man.

I heard a yell back of me. "Hey, George." Then: "Posey!" "George Posey!" I looked over my shoulder and met John Langton's eyes as he walked at the head of his company. The Georgetown boys, I said. George, still with the colonel, lifted his hat and smiled. "Howdy, boys," he said. Langton's dark, wooden face did not change.

We waded the branch and came out into the field as the battery fired a salvo that shook my teeth and I felt a warm trickle down the inside of my left leg. What is there to be afraid of, I said. We marched into the fringe of willows and sycamores by the creek, and halted. Across the creek somebody dropped a pile of those infernal planks: I waited for the crackle to settle. "Lay down, you damn fool," said a voice behind me. It was Wink. I dropped to my belly and saw that the other men were lying on the ground.

We were the extreme right of the company. Below me was a little hollow in which the road ran down to the ford. Across the hollow and back a little in a small clearing, Captain Langton sat on a stump, holding his sword on his knees. He got up and came to the edge of the road. "Broadacre," he said into the new silence. Wink stood up. "Broadacre, fire by squads at five-minute intervals. Let 'em know we're here." A small round-shot hit a big rock near the water and bounced up the road where it lay still and smoking. "Look at the damn thing," said Langton. Wink came back and lay down.

"Is it loaded?" said the bearded man. He tapped the butt of my gun. "It's our time to shoot in a minute." Our time to drop planks, I said, only they would not be planks so near. That's why I haven't heard them. The squad on our left, lying in single file, fired, and it was only rifles. "Get ready," said my tutor. "Where?" I said. "Don't make no difference," he said. "You ain't goin' to hit no Yanks. They's layin' in the woods on Chewning's hill. Bet they ain't a Yank nearer'n a quarter of a mile." I looked at him. "Chewning's," I said. "How you know?" "Wa'n't I raised on this hyar creek? Bet they fightin' on my farm right now by Young's branch." He held out his hand and we shook hands. "Will Dogan's the name," he said. "Any kin to Dick Dogan on the Pohick road?" "I reckon I am," he said; "he's my own baby brother." He rose to one knee and I squatted, and we fired. We lay down again.

Wink got up and went to the road. "Captain," he said. Langton rose but before he could answer, Colonel Corse and George Posey trotted down the road and drew rein by John Langton.

"Captain," the colonel said, "you may cease firing. Send out scouts across the creek to locate the Federal line. I will leave Mr. Posey here and you may report to me through him."

George gave the colonel an astonished glance. Then he watched John Langton slide on his heels down the embankment into the road.

"Report through who?" said Langton.

"Why, Mr. Posey," the colonel said.

"Where's Mr. Posey?"

The colonel stared at Langton. "Right here. This is Mr. Posey."

Langton took a step forward. "That feller? He hasn't got any name. He's just a son-of-a-bitch." He turned his back to George and looked straight at the colonel.

There was a long silence and then the colonel was saying: "Captain Langton, I put Mr. Posey on my staff for the day as a marked rebuke to you." But I wasn't looking at him. George Posey slowly drew his right leg over the rump of the mare and dropped squarely upon his feet. He looked as if he were dismounting in front of a post office, as he directed an inquiring look at John Langton whose back was still turned.

"I didn't want to do this," he said, dropping the bridle to the ground. He spoke so gently that he might have been talking to the mare.

"Brother George," I shouted and jumped into the road.

The colonel turned in his saddle and frowned. I gave him a glance. John Langton had not moved.

"Well, Colonel Corse?" he said.

I heard him without seeing him as I stared at George Posey, who was taking the pistol out of the holster and then touching with his thumb the hammer.

"Langton, you better look at me."

Langton tensed a little and moved his hand to his face; then slowly faced George Posey. George raised the pistol and shot him in the face.

He fell. I closed my eyes and turned away. I might have been alone in a meadow listening for the chatter of a creek. Then I heard the roaring guns in the west, that had made the silence. I forced my head up to look at Colonel Corse, with—on the edge of my eye—the dark heap lying on the ground.

George had replaced the pistol in the holster. He moved to Colonel Corse.

"I'd better be going," he said. Then he saw me. "Come here, Lacy."

"You'd better go, Mr. Posey," said the colonel. He took out a small tablet and writing a few words, tore off the sheet and handed it to him.

George looked at me. "For two men?" he said. The colonel nodded, and I nodded to George.

A dozen men were gazing at us from the opposite embankment, their faces interested but remote.

"Go to your places, men," the colonel said. He threw himself back in his saddle and spoke in a loud official voice. "Mr. Posey, you will surrender your weapon." He leaned forward. "Now leave," he whispered.

George mounted the mare and I vaulted up behind. As we went by the colonel George said simply, "Thank you, sir," and we rode off towards the headquarters cabin through the double ranks of soldiers whom I stared at but could not see.

The buggy horse stood forlornly at a fencepost but the gelding was gone. I slid off the rump of the mare and untied the horse. Brother George's carpetbag was strapped to the saddle-bow.

"I'll never see that Nigger again," he said.

I mounted. I turned the horse's head into the road to lead the way.

George said, "You're my friend, Lacy."

*   *   *

The sun topped the tree tops on Burke Hill and struck our backs as we came up the lane at a walk and turned, and I saw the big chestnut ahead and above, and then the low wall of the graveyard. I was leading the way and we said nothing. I regarded incuriously a wisp of smoke hanging in the air on the other side of the hill. We passed the gate into the south field, and before us a tall chimney rose, bare all the way down to the spread. I pulled the horse up and looked at it, and George went on ahead, and then stopped. He touched the mare's flank. My horse followed her although I had dropped the rein. We drew up at the end of the garden and dismounted, and gazed at the single chimney, from which protruded, like a stiff arm, the charred end of a beam. The smoke lifted weakly from the black embers into the still sunlight. There was nobody there.

I went towards the heap of fallen bricks. George followed me. We went round and stood on the stone steps. George took off his hat and crushed it in both hands, then looked at me.

"Lacy," he said quietly.

"Lacy," came the echo at my back.

Turning I saw Jim Higgins sitting on the horseblock with his hat on, in his brown shirt sleeves. "Lacy," he said softly.

I went over to him and stood before him, and after a while George came and sat by him on the block, still holding his hat in his hand. His eye followed the smoke rising into the slant sunbeams. His face was white and sober.

"Well, Jim," I said, calling him Jim for the first time.

He looked into my eyes with weary eyes that were set in a smeared face. "They come back at five o'clock this mornin'," he said. He looked at the ground. "The same ones. And a heap more besides."

George was looking at me, his face now flushed as he suffered a moment of anguish. I turned halfway round and I saw them and heard their gabbling tongues. "Our people," I said to myself. Our people. I turned to Jim Higgins trying to evade it, and suddenly said, "Where's sister?"

"Alexandry. They give 'em half an hour. Henry Jackson drove 'em," he said. "Miss Myra too and the baby girl. Them white mules." He moved a finger towards the stable. "The Dutchmen took the hosses."

I followed his gesture and gazed, without seeing it, at the stable. But I couldn't gaze forever. "Coriolanus," I said.

He glanced at the embers. "You couldn't find him."

George got up and I looked at him. It was a little darker than before.

"Mr. Higgins," he said, "you will have to tell us."

Jim Higgins rose and went back of the horseblock towards the first cedar, about six paces away.

"Come, Lacy," George said, and took me by the arm.

The top of the rough grave was like smoky iron. By it, the handle resting against the mound, lay a mattock. Jim Higgins stooped over and tossed it aside. I did not feel anything and I looked from end to end at the grave.

"Wa'n't no other way," Jim Higgins said. "The Niggers went off soon as they come. They busted all the windows out of the cabins and pulled the doors down. When they left I was by myself." He looked at George as if he owed him the explanation. "I couldn't put the major in no stall and I couldn't go for help. Hogs was loose."

I went to the cedar and sat with my back to it. George lowered himself upon one knee and crumbled the loose dirt in his hands.

"That isn't all, Mr. Higgins," he said.

Under the cedar it was almost twilight, and I saw that the smoke was no longer visible over the ruin.

"I wondered why the major didn't tell the Yankee officer he wa'n't seecesh."

George glanced up at him swiftly, then got upon his feet again. "Come, Mr. Higgins. I know it's hard." He said it kindly.

"The Yankee officer give 'em a half an hour to get out. Miss Myra was leavin'; she said to the major what a fool he was not to go." He frowned, and his lips were parted. "When the officer says I'll give you half an hour, the major looked at him. You know how the major is," he said in a pure voice. His eyes shone. "The major looked at him. He held himself up and, Mr. Posey, you know how he is when he don't like folks. Polite. That's what he was. He was polite to that Yankee. He come down to the bottom step and said, 'There is *nothing* that you can give to me, sir,' and walked back into the house."

He turned his gaze towards the ruin.

"Not *is*, Mr. Higgins," George said. "Major Buchan is dead." He studied the grave and came round to the cedar tree. "Get up, Lacy."

I got up and stood by him but he was looking at the grave again.

"When he didn't come out after half an hour, the officer waited a while and went up and knocked at the door. He went in with some of his men and they brought the major out and laid him on the grass." He reached slowly into his hip pocket. "Hyar's the rope," he said. He threw it on the ground.

George did not look at it. "Bury it, Mr. Higgins," he said. "Come, Lacy, we must be going. You did all you could, Mr. Higgins."

He took me by the arm and led me to the horses back of the garden. He unstrapped his carpetbag from the saddle-bow and laid it, with his hat, upon the ground. He opened the carpetbag and shook out the apothecary's suit. I went a few steps away to the horse while he took off the uniform and put on the suit. He closed the carpetbag and put on the hat. The uniform lay in a heap at his feet. There was a yellow glow coming over my shoulder from the west into his face. I looked away to the tall chimney, now a gently shaking blur, and down to the dark cedars. I looked again into his face and saw that the eyes were half-closed, but the head was thrown back, and he was looking at me.

"Brother George!" I said. I could not see.

I heard his voice. "Yes, Lacy."

I rubbed my eyes, went towards him. I stopped. He had not moved.

"Can't we do something?" I said.

He came to the mare and mounted her, then sat motionless in the saddle.

"I have done too much," he said.

The mare moved towards the cedars but he checked her, his head to one side as if he were trying to hear something far away.

"Brother George," I cried, "are you going to Alexandria?"

He was still listening.

"No," he said. He peered through the falling dusk, at the tangled garden, at the dim chimney, at the blank place where the cedars began. "It's not far enough." He stood up in the stirrups. "Georgetown," he said. He raised his voice. "Are you coming?"

I got on the horse and moved to his side.

"No, Brother George."

He cantered away into the dark. I waited until I no longer heard the sound of the hoofbeats on the big road. I kicked the old nag in the sides and headed back into the lane that ran by the south field. I knew then that I had to go back and finish it.

I went back and stayed until Appomattox four years later. George could not finish it; he had important things to do that I knew nothing about. As I stood by his grave in Holyrood cemetery fifty years later I remembered how

he restored his wife and small daughter and what he did
for me. What he became in himself I shall never forget.
Because of this I venerate his memory more than the
memory of any other man.

THE END

NOTE

Note on "The Migration" and "The Immortal Woman," with a Glance at Two Scenes in *The Fathers*.

The two stories that follow (pieces which might more accurately be called a chronicle and an "impression of life") were written in the early 1930s for a later purpose, of which I was not then aware. The immediate purpose of "The Migration" was to convince myself that I could master the detail of pioneer life and give it a hint of Defoe-like verisimilitude. This purpose, once realized as I think it was, encouraged me to proceed with a larger design. I felt that I could make the pioneer Elwin family one of the two main subjects of a book. The other subject was to be a settled, tidewater family in Virginia. I wrote "The Immortal Woman" in the effort to establish a fictional "point of view" towards that subject, and I decided to experiment with the most difficult of all fictional techniques: that of James' "trapped spectator." Not only is my narrator trapped; he also has never heard of the characters or their actions; and must piece the pattern together from fragmentary talk, enigmatic gestures, sudden appearances and disappearances.

The chronicle of the Elwins I reprint here only to let them bow themselves out: I will not write again about pioneers.

In "The Immortal Woman," the invalid in his wheelchair is obviously "trapped": his range of movement is limited to his front bedroom window and the door into the hall. He can hear his aunt moving about or talking and he can see passersby down in the street. On a certain day (accidentally, of course!), an old lady, Mrs. Dulany, comes to his house to discuss some sewing with his aunt, who is a seamstress. The invalid overhears the monologue of Mrs. Dulany and tries to relate it to the eccentric old lady who comes once a year to sit on a bench opposite his house. That's all there is to this story, an "impression of life"; but the narrator never quite sorts out his "impressions." This is left to the reader to do. Most of this story's few readers have not been able to decide who the old lady is, sitting on the bench across the street and rolling up pieces of yarn or string. The late Ellen Glasgow liked the "story" and considered subtle what other readers found obscure; the late Yvor Winters liked it for reasons that I never understood, for my story is even more obscure than his "The Brink of Darkness," which was published in the *Hound & Horn* at about the same time (1932-1933).

Suffice it to say that the old lady sitting on the bench is "little Jane" in *The Fathers,* and Dr. Beckitt, who came for her once in his "muddy Victoria," is Dr. Buchan, narrator of *The Fathers.* "Old Major Beckitt" is Major Lewis Buchan in *The Fathers.* In this story he has not, fortunately for me, hanged himself. I will use him as a character-in-the-round in my novel, developed far beyond the mere outline that Mrs. Dulany offers Aunt Charlotte. The young man who comes to take the old lady ("Miss Jane") away for the last time, could be her son or grandson: he is a vigorous and inferentially prosperous American. He could be George Posey's son or grandson, or my brother Benjamin.

These characters and many others besides rattled around

in my head for about three years, gradually, and I suspect without my will, making themselves available for fiction; or making themselves ready, in relation to one another, for participation in a fictional plot. I still do not know where the "plot" of *The Fathers* came from. I once thought I had found it in the court records of Fairfax County, in a deed-of-trust from my great-grandfather to one of his sons for the benefit of his daughter, my grandmother: this deed proved by inference that my great-grandfather did not wholly trust his son-in-law. There was a conflict in the family. But there are conflicts in all families. The discovery of the deed-of-trust at most actualized, gave a sort of historical reality to, a plot already forming in my mind.

There are two incidents, or rather "moments," in *The Fathers* that I may without impropriety elucidate, for the incidents have not elucidated themselves for readers in the past thirty-five years.

There is the violent scene "up the river": Yellow Jim may have raped Jane, Semmes' fianceé, though this was more plausibly Susan's invention to prevent the marriage by sending Jane to the convent. Semmes, literally applying the "code," shoots Jim. George Posey shoots Semmes. Here one remembers the Poseys' all-but-forgotten scandal: Jim is George's half-brother. George *therefore* kills his brother-in-law, who seconds before has killed his mulatto brother. George shot Semmes not in rational revenge but in instantaneous reflex action, an instinctive response to the murder of his half-brother. It is almost as if Semmes had tried to shoot him, George himself.

The other incident is the last moment of the novel, the narrator's reflections upon the departure of George Posey as the novel ends. Both George and Lacy are at Pleasant Hill after the Battle of Manassas. Lacy will return to the

Confederate Army. He says to himself, or rather the aged narrator reports what he said to himself as George rides away:

> I'll go back and finish it. I'll have to finish it because he could not finish it. It won't make any difference if I am killed. If I am killed it will be because I love him more than any man.

I wrote it very fast, without calculation, because I was convinced it would be right. Critics have wondered how Lacy could love a man who had killed his brother, run his sister crazy, and hated the life of Pleasant Hill. Lacy, scarcely more than a boy, has the instinct of survival, regardless of principle; yet at the same time "principle" is back of his decision to return to the army. He affirms the principles that George scorns, and in a sense, as his surrogate, attributes them to George. George will permit Lacy to survive in a new world in which not all the old traditions, which Lacy partly represents, are dead.

THE MIGRATION

THE MIGRATION

My name is Rhodam Elwin. I was born in Stafford County, Virginia, in sight of the Potomac River, on April 9,
1779, Old Style. I always reckon my birth Old Style. My
father had it bred into him by his father that the new way
of dating showed scant respect for the customs of our fore-
fathers, and he would never use it. My father was a remarkable man. For the instruction of his posterity I will
tell what I know of his life, and of the lives of the people
in the times that he passed through; of these I saw a great
deal. I write in the year 1851, in my seventy-second year,
in the little town of St. Joseph, Missouri, where I live with
my second son, Seaton Elwin; we came here a quarter of
a century ago from Sumner County, Tennessee. I am the
sire of twenty-six children, all but three of them sons, by
two wives of stainless purity who are both dead. Eighteen
of these children are living. I go over them one by one
to place them all; some are in Alabama, one in Arkansas,
two in Illinois, one in Indiana, and my eldest, John Robert,
lives in Kentucky. We are all over the West.

My father was born in County Antrim, Ireland in 1742,
of poor Scotch-Irish parents in the tenant class. They were,
of course, not Irish but Lowland Scots Covenanters who
had come to the North of Ireland in the reign of James

the First. My father said his great-grandfather was a Scottish laird, but I place little confidence in legendary tales. He knew, certainly, but I do not know the Christian name of his father, who died in debt to his landlord, about to be evicted, in 1755. My father was then thirteen, but having already heard stories of the opportunities for poor boys in the colonies, he made up his mind, so young, to run away at the first chance. His mother had been dead several years, and he was the last child. That is all I know of the Elwins in Ireland and, as my father always said of all pretense, of "the grandeur of it."

He made his way across the Irish Sea to Bristol where he tried to indenture himself as a servant to go to one of the colonies, that being late in 1756; but he was told by the agent that he was too young and, besides, had no trade. Only skilled artisans were taken under indenture to the tobacco colonies then, all the unskilled labor being done by the increasing hordes of Negroes sold to the planters every year. It was a good thing for him, for an indenture might have broken his great spirit of enterprise. He worked in Bristol nearly a year on the wharves, at all kinds of tasks that would give him a few pence, and then with a few pounds in his pocket he finally persuaded a kindly master of a tobacco ship to let him work his way to America. The ship sailed in October, 1757.

My father, whose name was Rhoda Elwin, possibly because his mother had wanted him to be a girl, arrived in Port Tobacco, Maryland in November. I was in the old town myself several times. It is in Charles County, on the Potomac, and in those days I know it was a great center for the tobacco trade. It never had more than two hundred white people at any time, but in the fall when the crops had been laid by, and the tobacco stripped and ready for shipment, gangs of Negroes filled the place, hauling and loading tobacco in the ships that lay like a flock of birds on the smooth tidal river.

Although father was only fifteen when he landed in Maryland, he was tall and strong, he said, and able to do hard work, but there was nothing there that he could do. Being a minor without a guardian, he was compelled to register with the parish clerk who warned him that he would have to apprentice himself in some trade. He decided to go to a larger town, and accordingly set off on foot for Annapolis.

He was apprentice to a fine cabinetmaker for six years, until his twenty-first year, and his master being a kind, liberal man, he was able to save in that time some seventy pounds sterling with which to set up for himself. He did this some time in 1765. After two years more, he had accumulated about four hundred pounds besides making some of the finest furniture in the colony — my son John Robert has a table of the Chippendale design made by his grandfather — and he purchased a Negro boy, about ten or twelve years old, for a little less than ten pounds.

He made up his mind to go to Fredericksburg, Virginia, at that time the most prosperous town in the Northern Neck, and the center of trade for the richest planters of the Old Dominion. These men, however, had little ready money, and found it easier to buy their goods of all kinds through the London merchants, who took tobacco in exchange for it.

But he did a good business for several years, until about 1770. In that year a family that had just landed in Philadelphia from Ireland came through Fredericksburg, on the way to the Carolinas to settle, and Father, being greatly taken by one of the daughters, Miss Emily Ransom, married her on the spot, while the rest of her family resumed the journey to the South. The young couple decided to

buy a farm, where the family they hoped to raise would
have a better life than their small means could provide in
the town.

I well remember hearing my father talk about buying
that farm and improving an old log house that stood on
the place but almost in ruin. The first parcel of land was
just a hundred acres some miles northeast of Fredericksburg and lying, one end of it, on the Potomac at the mouth
of Aquia Creek, the rest stretching back on a ridge that
divided Aquia from another deep creek. The creek banks
were not included, for that was the best land, which the
planters were jealous of and which they would not sell.
The house had two rooms and a loft, to which he added
a kitchen and milk-house at the rear, and it was there that
all my parents' children were born. For the family lived
on the Stafford County farm from 1770 to 1788. It was a
pretty place, and my first memory is the view of the Potomac and fishing in that great stream.

I have always regretted that I was not one of the older
children so that I might have seen more of the War of Independence that had been in progress about four years at
the time of my birth. I either remember or was told in
childhood, so that I think I remember, seeing my father,
Captain Rhoda Elwin, march through Fredericksburg at
the head of his company, which belonged to the regiment
of Colonel Theodorick Bland. That was at the end of the
war, early in 1783, I believe. My father was an enthusias-
tic supporter of the Revolution. His hatred of the established church in Virginia, to which he grudgingly paid
tithes, was backed up by a long antagonism, bred in him
for six generations, against everything British and nearly
everything that was established. For all such institutions,
he said, grew fat on the blood of the people. These notions
grew upon him the older he got, and I think it was in the

confused times after the Revolution that he became restless. I know that he hated the Constitution — another de-
vice, he thought, by which power would be made more
powerful and poverty, poorer. As a struggling boy he had
accepted his surroundings till he got a start in life, but the
start he had made was arrested by the war. He had enlisted
as a private soldier and come out a captain. The enlarged
conception of politics and men that this office afforded
seemed to add to his discontent. He wanted something better for his family.

How to get this could not be directly determined upon,
for it seemed that the best way, right after the war, was to
enlarge his farm and, if possible, buy more Negroes for the
cultivation of tobacco. The stories of fine, cheap land in
Kentucky were going around more and more in the early
1780s, but the cautious Scots blood of my father made him
slow to believe what he heard. He increased his farm to
nearly four hundred acres — a disastrous move, as events
showed, for the war had made it impossible for small men
to raise and ship tobacco at a profit, and besides he had had
no experience at it. He was in a fair way to lose all he had
made in his youth. Moreover, about 1784, he bought a
prime field-hand for about sixty pounds; this man along
with the runt, Boy Jim, as we called the first Negro my
father had bought, worked the tobacco; and my two older
brothers, John and Reuben, helped them, being eleven and
twelve years of age, just old enough to work.

Mr. Jefferson had broken down the system of entailed
property, which kept landed estates immune to suits for
debt, and so it was after the war that many planters, more
especially the young men who had just inherited land, were
eager to raise money by selling off large portions of their
plantations. That was how my father increased his holdings at small cost. Already it was being said that veterans of

the war would in due time receive bounty lands in Kentucky. On this prospect speculators appeared in nearly every county, trying to buy the future rights of ex-soldiers. My father resisted this temptation, for the price offered was never more than sixpence an acre, and he said that it was either worth a great deal more or nothing.

Meanwhile, as I began growing up I was sent to an old field school about four miles away, in the direction of Dumfries, in Prince William County, on the plantation of a Colonel Thornton, a fine, generous, and dignified man who aroused in me both fear and respect. The teacher at this school, which was attended by some dozen children of both sexes, including Colonel Thornton's own children, was a youth of about twenty who taught us to read and write, and to cipher. There were no classes; every pupil went ahead as fast as he could; and I made rapid progress. This was due in large part to the aid of my mother, who had got of her father a good education before her family left Ireland. He had been a "meenister" of the kirk who became a Methodist, deciding that his true mission, as well as the improvement of his worldly affairs, lay in the colonies. My father had little schooling, but could read and write, and Colonel Thornton said he had strong natural judgment—which no doubt was exercised all the better for his independence of spirit and the simple, though unexpressed, belief that he was the inferior of no man.

For some reason, against my father's wishes, my mother always opposed my attendance at Colonel Thornton's school. As I became smarter and more knowing I began to see why. We were different from all other people in our neighborhood, and as I look back upon that time I can see why this was so. My father had been a follower of the "mechanick arts," and although in breeding and in early condition he differed nowhit from many rich merchants in

Dumfries, Alexandria, and Fredericksburg, he was never-theless set apart, artisans in Virginia not being sufficiently numerous to form a class and make an impression upon the life of the people. My mother, whose people had never been in trade or worked with their hands, but had been landowners in Scotland before they went to northern Ire-land, was impatient of this circumstance. I remember we were at a county horse race, to which the families of ex-officers might go without being conspicuous, and I heard something she said. A fine lady sat near us, dressed in silk, her hair powdered, and she bowed indifferently. My mother said, "A true powderhead that can't spell her name or do the rule of three." It was the Scots bluestocking in her, and that I think is what has made us a great people, strong and self-reliant, and different from the English strain that takes things as they are.

Well, you will understand that my mother always con-ducted herself with natural perspicuity, and cared nothing for ostentation. She was thinking mostly of her children, I am convinced, and wanted them to have absolute freedom of movement and choice — which was a remote prospect in Virginia at that day. Our exceptional position, however, was recognized at least tacitly. My father's word was sought even by the quality people, in political matters, but these folks, being bound together by ties of blood for a hundred years, lived to themselves, and we had only our restricted family life. The other class of people, whose ancestors had been there as long as those of the gentry, were already beginning to be called "poor white," and the Negroes added "trash"—a class that had no education and lived on sour ground in the back country away from the rivers and creeks.

It was the remains of feudalism in Virginia that my father came more and more to dislike, and that finally determined him to move to a newer country. Yet he did not wish to begin at the bottom, but desired to save something from twenty-five years of labor. This notion kept him from choosing Kentucky as his immediate aim. Men who could take to the West large gangs of Negroes had good prospects of setting up in fine style, but without the Negroes there was no way of profiting by the possession of even large tracts of land.

Because of the Western boom, land prices in Tidewater Virginia were very low, but he decided to sell out, and to move to North Carolina, a state less ridden by aristocratical habits and traditions. He selected Edgecombe County, that being new country but still near enough to the seacoast to ship tobacco from in case he there found it profitable. Land was very cheap; for the money he got out of the Stafford farm he was able to buy nearly a thousand acres in the Halifax district of Edgecombe, more than a hundred acres of which had been improved — that is, cleared — and about twenty acres of new ground with the stumps in it that had raised only one crop. My father's title to bounty land for his war service was in the hands of lawyers, who, he knew, would try to cheat him if possible; I think at this time he had almost given up hope of getting it.

Thus in 1788, it must have been in the autumn, we had our household goods ready, and the journey to Carolina began. My eldest brother Reuben, just seventeen years old and very restless, had begged his parents' consent to strike out for himself, and when we left he turned west to the Valley of Virginia. I was a small boy and I never saw him again. He has been dead since about 1840, but he did well, for after trying various trades he accumulated a fine property in Botetourt County, marrying a woman of noble character and of some fortune; and his son John is now a member of the Supreme Court of the State of Virginia, a Christian gentleman and distinguished lawyer.

We set out with three yoke of oxen to the three wagons carrying our goods, and with four horses to the big wagon in which the family rode; my father led the procession on horseback. We were three weeks on the way.

Although my father was disappointed in the quality of the land in North Carolina, he could do nothing but settle on it. On this place there was a tumble-down cabin left by some early pioneer, which we rebuilt, adding another crib alongside and making a covered dog-run in the middle. The Negro men, Boy Jim and Willie, were put to work riving out boards for the roof, not only of the cabin but of the corncrib, and other outbuildings. And they also cleared a little new ground, with the help of brother John, who was now fifteen. By early spring the place was in fair shape and ready for a crop. In the fashion usual with children I saw the world from that farm, and began to feel I had always been there and would live there forever.

John and I slept in one loft and our four sisters in the other loft above the kitchen, that being the warmer of the two, and Mammy and Pappy slept in one of the big rooms downstairs. Mammy did all the cooking, for the Negroes too, in the enormous kitchen fireplace in which a good-sized man could stand up, and the little girls milked the cows and churned, and fed the chickens. My eldest sister, Emily, now sixteen, was a great comfort to her mother, doing most of the spinning and weaving, and she was mighty handy too with the needle; she was occupied constantly in spinning, weaving, and sewing. Nearly everything was made on the place, even our hats which Mammy made out of animal skins that we trapped or bought at the store in Halifax where the hunters traded in their pelts for supplies. By the time Emily married William Maxey in 1793 little sister Drusilla was big enough to take her place. That was fifty-eight years ago, but I still remember how Emily looked on her wedding day, with black hair and dark eyes

like her Scotch mother, and a sharp tongue for the piney
woods boys who had tried to make up to her at Sunday
meetings.

I was sure we would live there forever. Our farm was
three miles from the Roanoke River on a big creek that
emptied into that stream, and all the people roundabout
were like us, Scotch-Irish, high-minded and God-fearing
families who put Christian character and kindness before
rank and position. We were about thirty miles from Williamston, in Martin County, the largest town in the region,
at the head of tidewater in the Roanoke; below Williamston, along the river and the creeks, but less numerous than
in the Virginian Tidewater, stood the mansions of the low-
country gentry. Their daughters, lacking the strong faces
with high cheek bones and ruddy color of our girls, still
had a conspicuous delicacy of feature, the result of exces-
sive luxury and idleness. These young women were beautiful and ignorant, and had neither the strong sense nor the
education of our girls; but the young planters, though they
were effeminate looking, were highly educated men, most
of them having been to school in England.

The war feeling still lingered in Carolina at this time.
Every man of the military age was enrolled, and companies
organized in all the counties were required to muster so
many days in every year, armed and equipped as the law
directed. My father, having been a captain, was made a
lieutenant-colonel of the militia; so he appeared only at
regimental musters. Early in the day the boys, white and
black, would repair to the place of rendezvous to witness
the arrival of the different companies. It was a beautiful
sight to see them coming in from the different points of the
compass, with their guns gleaming brightly in the sun, the
officers richly dressed, with cocked hats, nodding plumes,
drums beating, fifes playing, colors waving in the breeze,

and all falling into line as they came up. In my childish opinion there would be enough men there to conquer the world.

I was never allowed to go to the village alone; it was eight miles from the farm; but on court days my father usually went on horseback and John and I, riding double on old Nag, followed him. Sometimes the women-folks came in the wagon behind four horses—carriages were rare in our neighborhood—and spent the day "visiting" with their friends in the public square. They made small purchases of trinkets and mysterious objects highly valuable to the ladies.

I used to go to the store, which was the bartering place and the tavern all in one, and watch the customers coming and going, and hear them argue about goods and prices. I would take my seat at the door to watch for witches as they passed along the road. We could tell a witch as far as we could see one. When they came to town they always appeared in the form of little old women with bright scarlet cloaks and hoods drawn over the head so as nearly to conceal the face. If they were very much bent with age and shaking a little with palsy, so much the better witch. They generally supported themselves each with a long staff that they held in the hand a little above the middle. Their skin, where it could be seen, was like old parchment; their eyes black and restless. They came to town, as they said, to buy a little tea, chocolate, tobacco, or snuff; but we knew this was a pretext. They were really bent on mischief of some kind. He who pointed his finger at one of them, or in any way offended her, was a doomed boy! In less than a week he would be attacked by some strange disease that no doctor in the world could cure. When the doctor bled him his blood would run out black. These were the terrible witches, according to our belief, that took men out of their beds at night and rode them to the desolate place where they danced around a tree that had been struck by lightning.

Perhaps a gang of Guinea Negroes just off the slave ships would be driven by on the way to their owner's farm, and we had great fear of them. They were nearly always large of stature and perfectly black. The other Negroes who had been longer in the country or born here and considered themselves highly civilized, looked upon the new black men with scorn and contempt, and with intense hatred and fear which they instilled into the little white boys also. They believed the Guineas to be in close league with the Evil One, and that when they chose to do so, they could make a mixture of noxious herbs, roots, and poisonous reptiles, and lay it under the doorsill of another Negro against whom they had a grudge, which would sooner or later induce death unless counteracted by some more powerful conjure. Many Negroes died of this affliction, so deeply did it prey upon their simple minds. And it brought amongst us a set of white imposters, the patent-medicine men with their shows, who professed to have a remedy to relieve the effects of conjuring, and this killed many Negroes likewise. All the Negroes even then wore or carried charms, usually a rabbit's foot, and they would never venture forth without a charm, particularly after nightfall. A big black Guinea Nigger would often pass with a little Nigger on his back, on the way to the fields, of course, but we knew better. He was taking the child to some hidden place to devour it. A Guinea Nigger liked nothing better to eat than babies.

Never a court day on which we did not eat the finest oysters. The dealers could always count on five or six hundred people at such times; so they started from Williamston, the head of salt water, in their carts the night before. Each dealer had a plank table set up for his customers to eat from. With each portion, usually a couple of dozen, he offered white wheaten bread, cider vinegar, salt, and pepper. The oysters were near absolute freshness and beyond comparison the best I ever ate. Herring and shad we had in great profusion — I became expert at salting and smoking these delicate fish — but I preferred fresh oysters out of the shell. My father was very fond of them, and often went in among the carts to feast upon them, sampling one here and there until he found a run of them having the right flavor to his taste. Or he went over to the store, where men of his age met to talk politics. My father never drank beer; he said it was bad for his liver; but he took rum toddies in the winter and juleps, rum juleps, in hot weather, and when he left town to gather us up for home he usually took a large stirrup cup, rum and cider mixed as a strong, invigorating punch.

In all my boyhood I remember nothing better than fishing and berrying. The woods teemed with chincapins, wild grapes, huckleberries, and huge blackberries that grow on poor soil. After an evening eating my fill of all these I would come back and wallow in the straw stack till it was time to get in the wood for the supper fire. That was one of my chores — that and keeping the water buckets on the back porch full. The Negro men never did such frivolous work, but were always at the real work of the farm. I do not recall when it began, but I do know that from the time I was fifteen at most my father never did any rough work. Niggers' work became well defined, and all the kinds of work that each person was supposed to do. No one worked on Saturday evening — evening began then right after dinner — and so Boy Jim and I went fishing in the big creek where the little-mouth bass were thick as leaves — only Boy Jim called them trouts.

He always said he could smell the fish when the breeze

came to us off the creek. He always knew where to go. About this time my father had bought a Negro woman about thirty-five years of age who became Boy Jim's "wife," and Boy Jim affected to believe or really did believe that Mariah had been purchased for his happiness alone. One day as we set out for the creek he sniffed the wind and said: "Seems like I cain't smell 'em like I could before Marster give me that 'oman. Naw, sah, I cain't smell 'em no more." He shook his head sadly over the baleful effects of matrimony.

No one paid much attention to the morality of Negroes in those days, though my mother, and I think most Methodists, believed that they had souls which must be saved. I have never been able to make up my mind about this. It is true that in the last fifty years the Negro race has improved, and religion has done them much good. And it has done us good too. Our Lord and Savior Jesus Christ has smiled upon us, and redeemed us from the coarse times of those old days at the end of the last century. Chastity is valued more highly among plain people, and the speech and manners of all men have improved. In the 1790s, coarse words for nature were in use, and although I think the present age somewhat squeamish I cannot but see the greater delicacy of feeling everywhere.

It was expected that boys at the youngest possible age should know women, and I knew them like other boys by the time I was fourteen. My father's views on the subject were simple and direct. Never take the maidenhead of a young lady whose family might conceivably be friends of your own family, and if possible never touch a virgin at all. This principle kept boys from marrying beneath them after foolishly imagining they were in love with some trollop; everything was set apart properly and understood. Most

boys were young scapegraces, but I do not think we had
need to be as bad as we were.

For some time after we went to Carolina there was no
school nearby. My mother taught me mostly out of religious books — Bunyan and Fox's "Book of Martyrs" I
remember vividly. Though well-educated for a woman of
that time, she knew no Latin, and she constantly said that I
must be a polished gentleman when I grew up and be able
to read the Classics. So, around '93 or '94, a wandering
Irishman came to our section and the families thereabouts
got up a school which he taught for five years with great
success. He was a learned man but given too much to rum,
a bottle of which he kept hidden in his desk in the log
schoolhouse. We sat around the iron stove — a great curiosity at that time, bought at the common expense — on
rough benches, all of us reading at the top of our voices.
We were allowed to chew in school after we were fourteen; we spat on the stove and liked to hear it sizzle. In the
first six months I had mastered the Latin grammar and by
the time I was seventeen I could read anything in Latin at
sight. But I never studied Greek.

The families that supported the school all lived in that
neighborhood, were mostly new people like ourselves and
formed, with us, a close community that intermarriage was
already making one family. There were the Wilkersons and
the Maxeys, families not more than twenty years out of
Ireland; but the Jarvis Peirce family were Puritans who
had drifted down from Massachusetts. My sister Emily
had married William Maxey in 1793; now my younger
sister Drusilla married his brother Walter Maxey in 1797.
Henry Wilkerson had two children, Phoebe and John, and
John wedded my sister Josephine in her fifteenth year.

After these weddings there was the charivari — only we

called it "chivaree" — and the boys came demanding gifts
from the bridegroom, which was usually liquor or the
money to buy a barrel of beer. On such a night the older
gentlemen of the neighborhood held a more decorous sym-
posium — I do not remember seeing whiskey in those days;
West India rum was the universal beverage of the spiritu-
ous variety. These gentlemen took their glasses — mixed,
stirred, and tasted; then dropped in another lump of sugar,
poured in a little more water, and then a little more of
something else; then, taking up something like a baby's
shoe, grated it — nutmeg, of course — into the glasses till
they became fragrant. They seated themselves, and sipped
and talked and talked and sipped in a way that was very
pleasant to see.

At this time, about 1797, I was eighteen, and very knowing, so that I remember distinctly that the older men were
talking land all the time. The westward boom was at its
height; both Kentucky and Tennessee had become States
in the last few years; and this kept driving down the price
of land along the seaboard. Whole counties east of us, but
for the largest landowners who could not sell at any price,
were being depopulated, and the people were going west by
thousands. My father had at last got his bounty claim cer-
tified, but at some loss, due to the lawyers and his removal
to North Carolina. It was arranged by means of some kind
of trade that his land should lie in Tennessee, the former
western domain of North Carolina, as Kentucky was the
former territory of Virginia. At first he was disappointed;
"Kentucky" was a magic word conjuring up Paradise;
thousands of emigrants passed by the most fertile acres only
to get inferior land on the edge of the Blue Grass. But, seeing this matter truly, my father, upon further inquiry, decided that he was well off.

His parcel was a little over three thousand acres lying in

Sumner County, Tennessee near the Kentucky line, one of
the garden spots of the world, as we were told, and it truly
turned out to be. The Wilkersons, the Maxeys, and the
Peirces were all for going west with us, and although they
could expect to buy only as much land as the sale of their
present Carolina holdings would permit, the excitement of
the trip and the enthusiasm for the unseen new country
worked vigorously in their minds, and they decided to go.
Along with many men of his time my father felt that he
some day wanted thousands of acres. These acres were in
the habit of receding the nearer he came to them. I know
how he felt because I too contracted that fever and have
never been able wholly to conquer it. I mean the desire to
go on and on to new land.

So he agreed to sell six hundred and forty acres of his
bounty claim to each of the families of Peirce, Maxey, and
Wilkerson, at twenty-five cents an acre. (Though we had
begun to reckon prices in dollars, our current change was
largely British money, shillings and pence.) There was a
great deal of wisdom in this. He felt that he needed more
Negroes for the expedition and to get set up properly, but
the lawyers had consumed so much that the sale of the
Edgecombe farm left nearly nothing. After buying two
more Negroes, making five all told, he had not over four
hundred dollars when we were ready to start. It was agreed
that he should take first choice in the Sumner County land,
the others to draw lots for their portions. Old Uncle William Maxey, as we called the father-in-law of my two
older sisters, had three Negroes, and was pretty well off for
the journey; but the Wilkersons and Peirces had no Negroes; and so close run were they by necessity that they
decided to burn their log houses in order to get the nails for
use in the West, all manufactured articles there, as we
heard, being scarce and high.

Early in April, 1798, all four families were ready to set out for the Cumberland country. It was a large cavalcade, each family being a group or company in what formed a kind of regiment; strict order was to be preserved. For our part, we had six large wagons drawn by oxen, eight head of horses and three cows. My father had been chosen to lead. I can see him now, erect on his horse in a tight homespun jacket and buckskin breeches, his heavy black felt hat cocked neatly in military style; he carried in saddle holsters two large horse-pistols, loaded but not primed. Brother John and I rode in the rear.

It was agreed that all should leave their old homes the same day, in the morning, and meet at a deserted Episcopal church that stood in a forest of pines, and there encamp the first night. There were many of these deserted churches in Virginia and the Carolinas at that time.

Early in the April of 1798; according to appointment, all bade adieu to their old and kind friends, the scenes of early life, some of the graves of their fathers, and many objects besides around which memory will linger, and turned their faces towards the setting sun. It was a time of great tenderness of feeling; many, in taking leave, would not venture to speak; a tender embrace, a silent tear, a pressure of the hand in many cases would be all. But few of the aged men and women now living do not remember such parting scenes. In those early times the emigrants that left Carolina and Virginia to settle in Kentucky or Tennessee hardly expected ever again to see those from whom they parted, nor was there any hope in those who were advanced in years. They parted much as do those who part at the grave.

The children and the Negroes kept up their spirits by thinking and talking about Cumberland — the name of the

beautiful new world we were to find at the end of our journey. We loved to hear the word pronounced, and on the
journey towards it if a stranger asked us to what parts we
were on our way we answered proudly, "To Cumberland."
We lost a little heart when we were told there were no herring, chincapins, huckleberries, or pine knots to kindle fires
with, in all that beautiful country. The Negroes made a
serious matter of the pine knots, and thought the lack of
these a great drawback on any country however blest in
other respects — even on Cumberland itself.

We took the direction from Halifax down to lower
Edgecombe and crossed the Tar River at Tarboro on a long
narrow bridge. The water under the bridge was still, black,
and deep, and so dangerous looking I was glad we were
safely by it. Then I remember Hillboro, a village in Orange
County, and Guilford Court House where my father had
fought in the battle seventeen years before, but of which
there were no traces but a few cannon-scarred trees.

Some days after passing the battlefield I loitered behind
the wagons, and upon catching up I found them all stopped
on an elevated stretch of road. I asked the cause, and was
shown what seemed to be a light blue cloud lying far away
to the west on the verge of the horizon. It was to our young
eyes a vision of beauty. In its vast outline not a rent or fis-
sure could be seen. I gazed at it with mingled wonder and
fear. So this, then, was the famous Blue Ridge about which
we had heard so many tales and beyond which lay the land
of our homes forever. Could wagons and teams ascend per-
pendicular walls or scale the clouds?

We went on and soon came near the base of the conical
peak of Pilot Mountain in Surry County, around whose
high summit some marvelling chap had seen shapes like
men with wings flying in the clear blue sky. This was some-

thing to study about, and for many years the younger people talked about it, so deeply did it haunt our recollections.

As we approached the Blue Ridge it seemed to rise higher and higher towards the zenith like a gathering storm. At length we pitched our tents at its base. In vain we tried to believe that this was the same calm mountain that we had seen many days before. The vast masses of rock piled up in wild confusion. The sharp summits beaten and cracked by storms, the deep ravines worn in its side by descending torrents, bore no resemblance to the blue cloud of our first view which by distance had indeed been enchanted.

For some reason it was decided not to follow the Carolina road across the mountains to Jonesboro, but to cross farther north into Virginia, at a place, I think, called Ward's Gap. We reconnoitered the pass, and the ascent began. We took out the oxen, which were good for long regular pulls, and put the horses to the wagons because they were more responsive to unusual demands. In rough steep places we often had eight horses to a wagon and a man at each wheel to help turn it. When a few yards had been gained, these men, called scotchers, dropped a large stone behind each wheel to save what ground the great effort had won. In bad places we did well sometimes to make two miles in a day.

When we had crossed the great ridge we were in Virginia, and we made for the town of Abingdon which nestled between high ranges running northeast and southwest — the gateway to the Western States for the early ministries of Christianity bearing the Word to the new country. We had got to this place — the name Abingdon even now haunts my ears — and although my mother had been ill with a deep cold she seemed to be getting better.

But only a day out of Abingdon she grew worse, and we began to fear that she could not finish the journey. I remember her pale and sorrowful face as she lay on her bed in the wagon, and her uncomplaining suffering as we moved over the uneven road. Then she died, and we halted for two days to make her a coffin and take the body to Abingdon, where it found a lonely grave.

I remember Bean's Station in East Tennessee, where the first white child west of the Ridge had been born. We were keeping steadily down the valley of the Holston River towards the Wilderness, an upland waste between Knoxville and Nashville and a hundred miles broad. It lay on the Cumberland Mountain between the Clinch River, which flowed into the Tennessee, and the Caney Fork, a tributary of the Cumberland River. It was necessary for the emigrants to get up food far ahead, as there were no stations on the Wilderness Road, and to forage for the animals lest they should not find much of the wild pea-vine that grew in such profusion in the low country.

After two days in the Wilderness we were descending a long hill, not far from a place now called Crab Orchard, and came at dusk to a pretty stream where we camped that night. It was called Daddy's Creek, a beautiful and romantic spot, and I began to understand why the Indians had fought so bitterly for that country. The hill we had passed over was called Spencer's Hill after an early hunter of that name, who with a man named Holiday had crossed the mountains and gone near where Nashville now stands. We knew his story — how a hunter, not knowing he was in the country, saw his huge footprints in the snow, became frightened, and reported the country full of giants; how Holiday lost his knife, and Spencer broke his in two and gave him half when they parted; and how, after he had finished his cabin, and fenced his little field, when on the way back home to bring his wife and children to the beautiful country he had found for them, he was killed by the Indians on the hill that bears his name.

The Indian troubles in that part of the West were nearly over; yet we heard stories of isolated outrages that made us apprehensive, especially in the Wilderness, whose ownership had been long disputed between Indian and white. At Daddy's Creek camp, at twilight, a lone Indian came to sell us fresh-killed venison, and said he was a "good Injun." Uncle William Maxey was very suspicious of him, but at last the other men decided that if the Indian would stay with us all night, there would be no danger, since he could not get back to his companions and plot a massacre. The Indian stayed, and made no effort to escape after we were asleep, and left us next morning very pleased. We heard no more of Indians on the whole journey.

When we had crossed the Wilderness and were within thirty miles of Nashville, a party of three elegantly dressed gentlemen overtook us, and seeing so large a cavalcade of settlers, one of them began conversing with my father and urging him to settle south of Nashville in what he called "the Dutch River Country." My father heard him out very politely but remained unconvinced. After the gentlemen had gone he said that they were land speculators who, by offering advantageous trades to the settlers, soon took away all they had.

We were now in what was then called West Tennessee, but soon to be known as Middle Tennessee, after the western region nearer the Mississippi had been settled. And we were rapidly approaching Nashville, which we reached early in June after more than two months on the road. Doubtless I was expecting to see a town like those on the seaboard, settled and fixed-looking, but as we came to the south bank of the Cumberland, and I looked across that deep, slow-moving stream, I saw some twenty or thirty houses, mostly log houses but a few of them clapboarded and perhaps one or two of brick, straggling away from the waterfront as if they had been set up at random in a great hurry and only for a few days. We were ferried across the river, at a good price for each of the ten or a dozen trips, and I saw how it was that the ferrymen in the West were the first men to get rich: This one was slow and unaccommodating, independent as a hog on ice. We stayed in Nashville that night and the next while my father had his patent papers examined by the land office and a surveyor appointed to accompany him to his land, which he was told lay to the northeast about thirty miles — another journey, before we could say we were there, of two days.

Hundreds of people came through the town every week. The craze for "Kentucky land" having to some extent given way to a better view of the western country, Tennessee was filling up fast, largely with families from North Carolina who brought with them very few slaves. I remember my father saying then, and I knew it was true even later, that there were four times as many Negroes in Kentucky as in Tennessee. He seemed to like this feature of Tennessee, and although we were still in the shadow of my mother's death, which bore its weight especially upon my father, we felt increasingly excited as we hourly reduced the miles to the new plantation. As we went slowly away from Nashville I did not know that I should see the town again only after ten years. I remember it seemed to my boyish perception that the tavern-keepers and the few traders in sugar and whiskey were the only permanent settlers, all the rest being Virginia lawyers with a great air of gentility, and land sharks with as great an air of benevolence.

About sundown of the second day out of town the surveyor called us to a halt, and said the tract of land lay along Station Camp Creek that we could see away in a rolling valley at a distance of about a mile. It was a lovely prospect, and yet it looked like other scenes that I knew, like other land that might be owned by other people. I felt a little dazed, and I could not think. The young children were suddenly quiet. My sister Emily's oldest, just four, asked: "Mammy, is this Cumber-land?" And I said to myself, This is Cumberland. We went on down the hill and camped by the creek, a deep stream broken at intervals by riffles and banked on both sides by tall sycamores and willows, with thick canebrakes here and there running off into the higher ground.

It was sobering to think that here we were, for better or for worse, in Cumberland, where now at last we should live forever. For some reason we broke our habit of cooking supper by families, and of pitching our tents by families, and all ate together by a big fire. The children threw cane stalks into the blaze, and the cane joints being hollow, full of air but air-tight, they crackled and sometimes blew up with a report loud as a pistol. It is mighty strange how people together will be moved by something trivial. It was the exploding cane that loosed our tongues, and the laughter of the children, and I knew before we had fairly seen it that we were reconciled to the land.

Somebody started singing, and nigger Willie got out his fiddle. Sister Emily and little Phoebe Wilkerson, who was about twelve years old, sang very prettily all the old songs. Emily had learned the old ballads from our mother and Willie scraped off the jigs and reels in a way to set everybody's feet going. It was indeed a special occasion, for old Henry Wilkerson, a religious man, made no objection. I remember one of the old favorites:

O wha will shoe my bonny foot
  And wha will glove my hand?
And wha will bind my middle jimp
  Wi' a lang, lang linen band?

When Phoebe had sung a little, Emily took it up, and then
it would go the round till even the old men got off their
dignity and began singing, and the old women too, for I
remember old Aunt Phoebe Wilkerson, Henry Wilkerson's
mother and the grandmother of my brother-in-law, John
— how she would take her cob pipe out of her mouth and
sing in a high cracked voice:

O he's gane up yon high high hill,
  I wat he gaed wi' sorrow —
And in a den spied nine armed men,
  In the dowie houmns of Yarrow.

It was too late to make much of a crop that summer, but
we burnt off two big canebrakes and about seventy acres of
wild grass to put corn in, to carry us over the next winter.
This crop was raised in common by us all, and it was
planted while we were still in our tents. My father chose
the tract of land lying along the creek, as he was entitled
to do by agreement; the Maxey tract touched the creek at
one point; but the Wilkersons and the Peirces had to take
high ground where they dug wells before they built cabins.
Our Negroes and the two Maxey Negroes were lent them
for the purpose, and towards the end of the summer every
family in this way, by common effort, had ready for the
winter a one-room hewn-log crib in which seven or eight
people had to sleep in great congestion. Our own family
lived this way until the next autumn, when we added another crib in the old style, with a dog-run between. In the

next two or three years we had added upper rooms and an ell, and built two Negro cabins.

I was now, in about the year 1800, a tall strong lad of twenty-one, and because my father was still a vigorous man of fifty-eight — six-foot-two in his bare feet, with coal-black hair, large cold gray eyes, and an iron jaw — I felt that I would be a mere boy for years to come, and I grew restless, desiring to strike out in some way for myself. My brother John at this time decided to go to Kentucky, signing away his claim to our father's estate in consideration of one of the new Negro men, bought just before we left Edgecombe, and the sum of five hundred dollars to be paid to him gradually as the farm could make it. My father had married again, his wife being the widow Thomas, who had four children, and this I believe prompted brother John to leave more than anything else; for our stepmother in some roundabout way was kin to the Wilkersons and brother John conceived the notion that that family in time would get all our land by marriage and undue influence. I was sorry to see John go; I had for him a great affection. I had known only slightly my eldest brother Reuben and he had left us early to remain in Virginia. John was killed at the battle of New Orleans in the War of 1812.

Time passed and to make it profitable I got up a school which I taught for eight years, and had at various times as many as thirty scholars. At the outset of this undertaking the great religious revival of 1800 came on, and gave a more religious hue to education. I myself was affected by it, and a wonderful effect it had towards improving our lives. The West was a godless country; but the Lord stepped in when we needed Him and lifted us up. We had always had religious training; my father believed that a man's duty lay in two things — fear of God and the honorable improvement of man's earthly state; and twice a day, at daybreak and at bedtime, the family and the Negroes were assembled for prayer.

It was in the spring of 1801 that the great camp meeting was held in Logan County, Kentucky, about forty miles from our farm. We went to it, all of us, all our family community but the Peirces, who were Calvinists, along with more than fifteen thousand other people. It was like a great army, covering hundreds of acres. This was the first time I had seen the jerks, and though I derived great spiritual benefit from the mighty sermons of many godly preachers, I looked upon this jerking exercise with astonishment. Many fell down under the burden of sin, as men slain in battle, and lay for hours in a nearly breathless and motionless state, sometimes for a moment reviving with symptoms of life, giving deep groans or piercing shrieks; and thus did they obtain deliverance from evil. Two or three of my particular acquaintance were struck down, and I patiently sat by one whom I knew to be a careless sinner, critically observing the contortions as they seized him. At one moment being still as death, he would begin to jerk in one arm, gradually and at regular intervals, till the motion spread over his entire body which heaved violently in all directions as if he were trying to tear himself apart. A grove of saplings had been cut down breast-high, and at each post a zealous Christian took his station, so that when the time came he would have something to jerk by. At these posts pretty girls and sober matrons waited, and it was wonderful to see my sister Emily Maxey jerk and kick so powerfully that the earth under her feet looked like a hitching place for horses in fly time.

Our lives were full; our large family connection numbered some forty people, not counting the Peirces, who were not yet intermarried with us; and we were enjoying a prosperity that we had never known. Our crops were enormous — eighty to ninety bushels of corn to the acre, against sixty, the best we had ever done in Edgecombe; we raised wheat and rye in large quantities. The Maxeys set up a still-house over a big cold spring on their land, and made a fine whisky, later known as Bourbon, out of a corn, barley, and rye mash. We fed most of our corn to the hogs, of which we had large droves. Every year the hog-drovers came through to take them to the East or to the new cotton country in the South; they sewed up the eyes of the hogs to keep them from running off into the fence-less country, and drove them for hundreds of miles in that way. But we raised no tobacco, and to that my father as-cribed his prosperous turn in affairs.

We had come to the year 1806, and for some time I had been keeping company with Miss Phoebe Wilkerson, the sister of John who had married my sister Josephine, and so, on June twentieth of that year we were married, and I took her to live in our family. She was the only wife I could have found to please my stepmother, who was hard to please, for Phoebe was her distant cousin. Our first child, a son whom we named John Robert, John for my brother and Robert for a dead brother of Phoebe's, was born in Nashville on June 10, 1808, whilst we were in town for a few weeks on business.

In the ten years that had gone by since I had been there, the town had changed wonderfully. There were not more than six thousand people, but the constant bustle, the com-ing and going, the sudden appearance and disappearance of strangers who had tarried there a few days, gave the town an air of being a city. The new brick buildings along the waterfront, which was piled high with barrels of salt pork and lard, of whiskey and corn, and smaller quantities of to-bacco, tended to give the scene a stability that impressed me greatly. We had friends there, and I call to mind one family whom we had known in Carolina, a family that in origin was like us in every respect, who now had a coach and four horses, and lived just out of town in a large brick plantation house amid a swarm of Negroes. The ladies came to town in flowered silk, the men of the family in tall hats and lace shirts; an outrider preceded the coach upon which was engraved a coat of arms. It was plain that the rich in the West had a desire to look richer than rich people in the East, for in a new country positions had to be maintained by appearance, at least for a time. It was commonly said that a prominent young lawyer of the town — Andrew Jackson, who was to be heard from later — had crossed the mountains in broadcloth, on horseback, with a Negro at his heels, but without a penny in his purse; and it turned out to be good business. He was already a rich man. I came to have a great reverence for him, but my father looked at him askance as a man who did one thing and talked another, and who was in all respects above his raising.

Now that the West had been conquered by the Scotch-Irish, and the Indians north of Alabama driven out or subdued, the Tidewater Virginians were coming in in great numbers. They had lived in Virginia more than a hundred years before they found the curiosity to climb to the top of the Blue Ridge, and to look westward; but looking was all that they did. They waited for men of my own blood to plunge into the wildernesses: Boone, the Lewises, and the Seviers, though it is true that John Sevier, while not a Tidewater baron, was French, and Isaac Shelby was of English origin. Now the younger sons or the broken-down heads of the Tidewater families got into their coaches, and their ladies constantly in silk dresses and French shoes, drove politely into the new country to ruin that land also with tobacco.

At about this time, when the War of 1812 was coming

on, Uncle William Maxey died, and the two boys, who had married my sisters, sold off their land, paying my father what was due him, and set out for the new cotton country in Alabama Territory. Our first ten years in Tennessee had been quiet; now it was known that the whole strip of country along the Kentucky border was great tobacco land; and another wave of settlers, not pioneers seeking new homes, but gentry bent on perpetuating their wealth, flooded the country. Men became restless again. William Maxey said the country was "filling up with tobacco-makers and Baptists" — the latter being, with some notable exceptions, however, the poor whites who follow blindly in the wake of any shift of population. I said good-bye to my dear sisters Emily and Drusilla, and I never saw them again. In my time and generation we were always saying good-bye, and the times we had together were not long enough to permit us to forget the sadness of family divisions and their farewells.

By the year 1816 my father was seventy-four, and I took over the farm, and managed it, and did very well. I now had six children, for my faithful consort had borne me nearly a child a year since we were wed. But I was convinced that the property would be left to my stepmother; what brother John had foretold was coming true. At this time the Peirces entered our family connection. My niece, Sally Wilkerson, who had been born a few weeks after our arrival in Tennessee in 1798 — daughter of John Wilkerson and my sister Josephine — was, in 1818, twenty years old; old Jarvis Peirce, twice a widower in his forty-eighth year, and still a dour old Puritan for all his long absence from New England, succeeded in winning this young girl. The ground, not only the earth but the rock-bottom of our lives, was shifting a little every day. The Peirces and the Wilkersons would never buy a Negro, and now in 1819 they had heard that the Illinois Territory had come in as a

Free State, after a severe struggle of the pro-slavery ma-
jority there to set aside the Ordinance of 1787 by which
Virginia, then the proprietor of all the Northwest Territory, had abolished slavery in the new country. Slavery had
been kept out by one vote, and old Jarvis Peirce regretted
that he had not been there to cast it. These two families, in
the summer of 1819 set out for Illinois, having sold their
quarter-sections at a good profit to the tobacco planters,
paying my father the original price of twenty-five cents an
acre, and keeping the difference.

Our community was broken up. My father was getting
old. About sundown of August 23, 1820, he took a fit of
coughing, followed by hard breathing. We got in the doctor, who bled him, and the Methodist exhorter, Mr. Doug-
lass, who prayed over him continuously for eight hours,
until at last he died, being then in his seventy-eighth year
and very feeble. I will always remember the last thing he
did and his last words. He called in Boy Jim, the first
Negro he owned, and his wife Mariah, and said, "By my
written will you are now free. Jim, take this old coat, and
go over to Nashville, and take the fifty dollars I have left
you, get you an old plug and a hack, and the fine coat with
brass buttons will get all the tobacco-makers riding behind
you." The old coat was the uniform he had worn as a captain in the Revolution. He asked for my son, John Robert:
"Chew tobacco if you will but never grow it." In a little
while he died. His thousand-acre farm went to his wife,
and on his tombstone, by the Methodist meeting-house
down on the creek, we carved by his express desire:

> Farewell my wife and children all
> I am gone away beyond recall
> Ask not for me it is in vain
> You call me to your side again.

THE IMMORTAL
WOMAN

THE IMMORTAL WOMAN

We never knew why she came but it was always in October when the warm days were few. The fallen leaves under the thick shade stuck to the damp sidewalk that the sun could not dry. It was usually the last of October. We wondered how long she had been here, a round little old lady in black holding her head up on the left side and leaning on a heavy black cane. When I saw her I thought, she has already passed several times. Then I remembered that was last year or two years ago. It got so that when I saw her for the first time in the fall, I said, It is another year. My aunt says she came every fall for fifteen years, but I know it was only in the last four or five that she took to walking with a cane. Stringy, dead-looking grey hair fringed the edge of the small black hat that she wore close to her temples, and her thick glasses gave her eyes a fixed stare. She walked steadily to the corner by the grey brick house, crossed the street to the green bench by the college gate, and sat down facing the house. Her clothes were always the same, and it is hard to remember what she wore. She seemed to sink into the faded anonymity of the old street.

Only the leaves have renewed themselves here since I was a boy. On our side there are tall trees, sugar maples

351

and sycamores, from the far corner, which is out of sight, down to the old square house where stands, heaving up the bricks in the walk, a giant oak; across the street runs the high wall of the old College. The same damp trickle has held to the wall the same patch of grey moss as long as I can remember. Early in the morning, and more distinctly in the fall, you can hear if you listen closely the clatter of the main street down by the Potomac, a low hum of noise that seems to bring with it the smell of the fishmarket. At noon there is a moment, filled always with surprise, when the sunlight falls quietly through the trees.

We see few people. Nothing happens. We never visit and no one comes to our house. I think that none of our neighbors ought to be living here. I suppose the trees know what was here, and what it was, but no one knows who planted the trees. They know something that we never hear, and they contain years that we cannot see. On the third of every month Mr. Higgins comes to collect the rent. "It's a fact now. Mark my word. It won't be five years till there's Niggers in all these houses."

There is the old brick house on the corner across from the College gate. I see first the wall running out of the side of the house down the side street. It encloses the garden, and midway along it opens, or opened once, an iron gate now a rusty green. I have never seen inside. The dull slate roof, cracked everywhere and littered over with twigs and leaves, slopes front and back; at each end, wide apart and perilously tall, two slender chimneys rise. Six windows stretch across the front of each of the three stories. In the exact center of the house stands the door; it opens into the second floor at the end of two curved flights of stone steps, one on each side. It is a double door, two plain panels with small tarnished brass knobs set in a carved, but very simply carved, frame that is arched over by a fan-light of many small panes. Some of the panes are broken, and the paint is peeling off the door. The house must have been built before this country was a nation, when there was no city east of the creek and Georgetown was a town in the Proprietary Colony of Maryland.

From my window I could just see the old lady where she sat on the green bench, day after day, and towards noon I got so that I began to look for the large white-haired man in blue serge, who came to take her away. A black derby high on his head gave him a little more than his real height, and although he must have been past seventy he was heavy and of powerful frame — the sort of man you would like to see on a big bay horse, cantering down a quiet street and, without changing pace or his own expression, gravely lifting his hat to the ladies as he passed. He never spoke to the old lady but with great simplicity removed his hat, holding it across his chest while she rose; then they started off, the old lady keeping an even distance in the rear. I am sure that in all these years he never uttered a word, but the old lady talked constantly, not to her husband but as if his presence made it easier for her to talk to herself. The large man — I am certain of this too — never once looked at the old house.

And not more than twice did he fail to come for her. The first time must have been five or six years ago, when a tall very old man, who looked tall at any rate because his knees were so long, drove up in a muddy Victoria. A doctor, I am certain; his white hair flowed over his shrunken shoulders; he wore a wrinkled Prince Albert and a shining stove-pipe hat, and he held a gold-headed cane. As the carriage slowed down he moved as though he were about to get out; but he thought better of it and the old lady, old but many years younger than he, climbed slowly in. The Negro boy driver turned — I remember he had on a greasy linen duster and a colorless felt hat decorated with a rooster's tail — and, with a solemn face, distinctly said, "Good mornin', Miss Jane." She nodded. The old doctor leaned forward and kissed her and they began talking; I could hear nothing they said. Without raising his voice, the old gentleman talked more and more vehemently, pointing towards the upper windows of the house, alternately pointing and rubbing the side of his long white nose with the knob of his cane. At last she nodded, as if she had at last got a difficulty out of her mind — as if to say, Yes, that's it, I remember now. The old doctor spoke to the boy, who pulled up the reins and drove briskly down the street.

The old house has not been occupied for years. Aunt Charlotte says that people lived in it when we first came here. There were no children, and I never looked much at the place. It is too elegant for poor people, and too large; too shabby, in too shabby a neighborhood, for the rich. Aunt Charlotte cannot distinctly remember the last tenants; they lived there less than a year. But the house looked shut up even then, and quite untouched, as if it were going its own way. Every year it seems to settle a little more into the ground. The windows look dimmer, defying the light to disturb the perfect shadows within.

Further than "Miss Jane" we never knew the names of any of the people who came back to look at the house, though I must have seen the old lady and her husband, the vigorous western man, thirty or forty times a year for ten years — the time I've been an invalid — and my aunt, sewing at her machine every morning in the other front room across the hall, watched them come and go a good

five years longer. You have understood that Aunt Charlotte is a sempstress. She had been a clerk in the Patent
Office — snapped rubber bands around papers and en-
velopes, whose purpose and destiny she did not know,
from nine to five — until I came back from overseas, para-
lyzed. We are Pennsylvania people from a small town,
Greencastle, who came here, my father and mother and
Aunt Charlotte, her sister, to go into the government
service, when I was a child; my parents are dead. I went
from the high school to the war, but when I was eleven
or twelve I spent many afternoons at the Smithsonian and
wandered over to the Fisheries and the Army Medical Mu-
seum where they keep South American mummies and wax
representations of diseases, and monsters in jars. We are the
only members of our family left in Georgetown. We never
hear from our relatives and we are poor.

I will never forget how the old lady nodded to the doctor, as if but for a slight piece of information she knew all
that the house contained; and how he nodded in return,
affectionately but a little absently, not thinking very much
about the house. He must have known all the people
there long ago, but he had not lived there. It was that, I
think, more than the old lady's coming and going that
started me to thinking about her. I began to wonder
where she lived, and where I myself should live since this
town is not my home; and then too I ask Aunt Charlotte
where the people are who ought to be living in the
square house. I don't think she quite knows what I mean.
She says the neighbors all came after they left, and they
either forget or never knew the name. My aunt is very
busy and lately she has got so much fashionable patronage
that she seems a little giddy, as giddy as an anxious old
maid could ever be.

But she does good work and somehow the ladies who go to F Street have decided that a shabby street in Georgetown is the place to go. There is Mrs. Ritter, she comes in a Cadillac, I don't know where she is from; she talks about her parties, sometimes as if she and Aunt Charlotte were really together and the parties weren't hers, but one day she said, "I just hate poor people." But Aunt Charlotte is so innocent. The senator's daughters are pretty and they don't know what they want, and they are afraid to let a sewing-woman tell them. I fall into these currents of life around me, and I like to think how far away they run. When a car drives up or the knocker sounds, I roll my chair to the window and look out. I roll over to the door, open it, get behind it and wait for the lady to begin talking.

There is old Mrs. Dulany and, come to think of it, it must have been old Mrs. Dulany who lives down near the Tenallytown Road who got all these people coming to our house.

"No, don't thank me. My dear, I don't know any of them. I just told Mrs. Roberts you did splendid plain sewing, and I reckon she told some one else who told all the others."

Every spring, every fall, Mrs. Dulany comes three or four times to have some old silk dresses made over or a new black voile. She says, "My dear, I don't know them at all."

Her right eye suddenly squints, and that side of her face twitches spasmodically until she holds it a moment with her hand. Then she talks on. Sometimes I go into the sewing-room when she is there. "Mr. Hermann, you are looking better this spring." Or "this fall" — as it happens. She always says that, and you feel a great kindness. She gives Aunt Charlotte minute directions about a skirt. "It don't make much difference how I look, I'm gettin' so old."

When I wish to compose myself I close my eyes, and I can hear Mrs. Dulany's voice. It is a little cracked for she must be nearly eighty, but the tone is at once sharp and fluent, and what she says is neither memorable nor foolish. She must have come in one day while I was dozing. I felt that she was there though she had not spoken, and I was startled at thinking that I knew what she was going to say.

"Well, Miss Charlotte, maybe you think this street has always been just like it is."

As I looked across the hall Mrs. Dulany was bending a little forward, whether to see what Aunt Charlotte was doing or in some inner excitement I could not tell. The mid-morning light fell on the heap of scraps, the odds and ends of muslin and silk, velvet and bits of thread, that covered the big table where Aunt Charlotte with her aimless patience was picking about here and there. Mrs. Dulany had spoken; my aunt looked up, her eyes blank, like a surprised beetle.

"Yes'm, only I tell John it ain't as bad as it might be if my work took me out."

Thinking the talk would go on that way I wheeled my chair back to the window — and yet I felt illuminated and pleased. The sun was just over the College wall. It struck me full in the face. It was time to put up the window and let the warm air come in. This is my greatest pleasure. The light shakes the big sycamore leaves, and the sycamore balls in the sudden heat burst, and fall softly to the ground. It is wonderful to watch the rays of sun lift the branch by my window at least a foot higher than it seems to be in the evening shade. There is a faint crackle in the air as the night mist from the river steams up out of the leaves. I knew that when I leaned over the sill I should see the old lady.

She was coming slowly up the street, head and shoulders hidden by a tree, and it struck me for the first time how she walked — as if she were being propelled from the outside, by a force that she neither knew nor could control — like the dressmaker's form in the sewing-room, moving with an even glide — a slightly stooped form for old ladies' fittings. And with a start I thought how curious it was that she needed a cane. She put little weight upon it, and at regular short intervals jabbed the rubber ferule noiselessly against the bricks as if indeed that were her way of testing her distance from the ground.

There are some things we know so little about; yet I suppose I looked at the old lady with new eyes because a tone or a phrase in what Mrs. Dulany had said put something into my mind . . . I reckon you think this street has always been just like it is . . . I cannot remember what I thought she really meant, or whether I thought about it at that moment. There are times when my sight grows dim and my head whirls; I grip the wheels of my chair, move a few feet very rapidly; objects begin to reappear. I think I know things only in action; there are the surprising and intolerable crises that a trivial act of will dissipates as breath a soapbubble — those harassing swivets of the mind. I tell Aunt Charlotte that if one must be an invalid one must have a wheeled chair, not to go anywhere in but to give one something to do. I can only say that going over to the window and seeing the old lady float by was my way of understanding what Mrs. Dulany had said.

To understand even a little of what one sees one must at every moment understand more than there is to be understood, or looked at another way, a great deal less. I

see, of course, very little. When I remember that the old
lady stopped coming by at last, in a way that told me she
would not come again, I thought how foolish it was to
say that she had always looked this way or had done this
or carried that. It takes years to understand the easy
things: I recall the exhilaration I felt swarming over my
face and eyes when I suddenly and definitely knew that
no two days are alike, no person the same two days running. There was the beach down on the bay that I had
been to as a child, where the shallow utmost reach of the
surf deposited at each thrust a thin filament of sand, but
never at the same place twice over.

I do know, of course, that the old lady held her head
up a little to the left, as if she were about to sniff, that she
wore black worsted mittens, and carried a black reticule
that sagged under the weight of shapeless objects: the crazy
stare through the thick rimless glasses and the apparently
useless cane completed the miscellany of her appearance,
one's sense of animated odds and ends. I thought she
might fall apart, or go up in a wisp of smoke. She had
merely been put together by all past generations, and she
saw no need of doing anything about it; I mean that she
could not have known that she had a self. The gliding ease
of her step, the unshakable regularity of her habits, had
all the perfection of an untested desire. I felt, as she passed
that last time, though I did not know then it was the last,
that she was as perfect as a tornado, as terrible, with the
same suffocating vortex inside.

I am trying, I suppose, to see what she really looked
like. I cannot imagine a picture of her. Could she have
sat every day for a photograph, for a whole year, always
on the same plate, one image upon another, there would
have appeared an outline indistinct as a distant shadow,
or perhaps one should say that her picture would have

been like a whisper in an empty room. Just nothing, in the sense that impalpable fear is nothing: precisely nothing at all. And then I suddenly knew that I had been hearing the voice all this time, the words from the sewing-room forming a single moment with the image in the street.

*   *   *

". . . I knew them all of course, I knew them because old Cousin John Gibson, that was the father of the girls, and my own father were second cousins. And I knew Cousin Georgiana too, his wife. We used to go up there when I was a little girl and I knew them that way, but all the girls were young ladies, too old for me to be intimate with and too young to be married and have children my age. My mother said Cousin Georgiana paid a heavy price for not having any boys. That was why the family broke up. Of the four girls, only one, Mary Anne, made a good match, a Federal naval officer. Old Cousin John, their father, said a Yankee and a rebel looked about the same to him. I reckon he was right about it for that Yankee, such a handsome young gentleman, was the only good husband any of them got."

"Yes'm, that's what papa said, the rebel soldiers that come to Greencastle was mighty well-behaved, didn't steal a thing. I'll just baste this hem so you won't have to try on the skirt again."

"Yes, I don't like to stand on my feet . . . That Yankee officer bought out the shares of the other sisters — that was after the War and their father was dead — in the land down in St. Mary's. It was the worst thing they could have done. There was Anna; she never married, I reckon I ought to go to see her, she's ninety at least, lived on charity for forty years in the Home for Incurables ever since her mother died. Susan married my cousin on my mother's side, Captain Charles Sterrett. He warn't much force. Aunt Martha, the old Negro woman who nursed the girls, helped them, but Cousin Charlie always said: Hadn't the white folks supported her before the war? Just like *he'd* done it. Cousin Lottie I knew best; she married a clerk at Beckitt and Wylie's, a nice deserving young man, only we never knew where he came from — old Major Beckitt said it was all nonsense, folks had to live, and the boy was well-mannered and industrious. But that boy took to drinking, and Cousin Lottie supported her family with her needle. Mama said it wasn't right for old Cousin John to leave the land to the girls after they'd been raised in town. Once I heard Mama talking to somebody, that Cousin John had an awful temper, and hit Cousin Georgiana on the head with a tin cup. After that she was never the same. One time she got the old gentleman when he was very intoxicated, sewed him up in two stout linen sheets and horsewhipped him till he was sober. She was never the same after that and he wasn't either. He never touched another drop. They never said much about that tin cup, but after he was dead and buried, and Cousin Georgiana and Anna were living alone in the old house towards the end of the war, Mama showed me the place where she'd whipped him at the top of the stairs. She had one sheet already spread out; he was so unsteady she tripped him with a poker. When he fell he went right to sleep, then the old lady started sewing the other sheet over him. Mama would whisper just as we came to the old lady's door, 'Who would think she could have done it?' And Cousin John left the house to his sister, when he should have left it to the girls — his sister Anne, the one that married old Mr. Posey . . .''

*   *   *

When she had got to the corner she stood for an instant on the curb; and looking at her, listening to the voice from the depths of the old house, I could see her incline her head from one side to the other and gaze, rather slyly, up and down the street. I saw her peering cautiously out of a door into a dark hall. With sudden speed she sailed across the street. I suppose she really looked like that at that moment. I see her in four or five distinct scenes, imperishable glimpses, but I know that each of these scenes is composed of many particles of memory, all of them striving day and night to come together and to take form. Before she had quite sat down on the bench she began to take odd pieces of string out of the reticule, laying them across her knees — she was too round to have a lap — and after a brief pause began tying the ends together and winding it into a ball. She rolled steadily and expertly, her hands on her knees; she raised the ball to the level of her eyes, winding all the time, back and forth from her eyes to her knees. In a little while she rested. She looked around with jerks of her head, but the head had a different focus from the eyes. Like a chicken pausing alertly between scratches. I suppose she was watching the house.

The sun always fell on her back, throwing the side of her face into a luminous shadow in the middle of which, from the temple to the chin, ran an almost straight line. It made her features thinner and younger. I had to look away. There was a firm and delicate line imbedded in the shapeless flesh. A group of students passed on their way to the College gate. A handsome boy in a bright green sweater looked back at her fumbling with her bits of string, and smiled.

I never wished to speak a word to that old lady. I try to think that after my first real awareness of her I never wanted to see her again. I could not help it — wheeling myself over to the window. I said to myself, It is to get the morning sun. It was to see the old lady. I have seen people as they ought not to be; I have seen whining monsters with only half a face, and I myself am not as I ought to be. That is different. Something will hit you, the will of God, and you're no good for the rest of your life. The old lady was as good as she had ever been; she sagged a little, I think, in her whole being, but like the old house she was, all of her, there, in a kind of perfection that I had not known before. The house stood facing her, not a stick of it changed I am certain for a hundred and fifty years. I can imagine the windows every year getting smaller, sealing up the shadows until at last there will be one great impenetrable shadow within.

*   *   *

". . . and when the war was over Cousin Anne and her husband moved up from Prince William and took possession of the house. Cousin Anne you see was much older than her brother who'd left her the place, and Mr. Posey was younger than she but still older than his brother-in-law. Their children were all grown up. Mama didn't go much to the house after they came, but I did. I was often in the old garden. On my way home from my music lesson at the Convent I had to pass the garden gate. Cousin Anne would lean out like she'd been waiting: 'Come in, child, and have some cake.' She would take my hand and give me a sharp look. She was tall and thin and her nose tied her face up in a knot. I remember how the garden looked in the spring. We sat at a rickety little table under the back gallery. Cousin Anne poured half water and half sweet wine into tall glasses. She would say, 'Honey, give your Cousin George some sangaree.' Cousin George was Mr. Posey. I took it to him where he sat at the other

end of the porch. 'Little Nellie, she shakes like jelly,' he
said, never taking the frown off his face, and that was his
way of thanking me . . ."

*   *   *

I am now sure that I never wanted to see the inside of
the house. I cannot help feeling for it a certain respect.
It carries itself well. All effort is over and it is superior
to anything its imagination might teach it to do. But it
is, in its composure, a little menacing. Like the island of
Sinbad the Sailor, it is sudden and angry with an incal-
culable life of its own. I always take my "walks" in the
afternoon the year round; being down there with the old
house, or with the old lady, myself with one of them, I
should feel secure; I should have a single problem, and its
simplicity would leave open the space between the street
and my room. But to be there with them together, the
old lady and the old house — that is to be entirely alone,
with my watch ticking on my wrist, and arrested in time.
I should have my own darkness inside, my own angry
perfection, and I should no longer be able to say: The
student going into the gate is returning from the movies
to his room in Carroll Hall. There would be the student,
the gate, and my watch ticking; then my watch ticking
alone.

*   *   *

". . . only I didn't shake because I was frail. That was all
I ever heard him say. Old Mr. Posey sat in a big arm-
chair with horsehair upholstery, his knees wide apart and
the black trousers tight on his heavy limbs. He wore a
faded bottle-green coat with tails, and a loose black stock
round his neck. There he sat frowning, picking his teeth
with a gold toothpick that folded like a knife into a small

carved ivory handle. I always wanted to touch it but I
was afraid to ask him. Cousin Anne colored a tumbler
of water with a little wine for me. We just sat there. She
rocked vigorously in her chair, then abruptly stopped, as
if she'd thought of something. At the end of the garden
by the stables was a big sycamore and along the wall by
the street ran a high box hedge — it was dug up and sold
years ago. On the other side round the kitchen and the
quarters, bushes of flowering quince grew in huge clusters. Only there was never any cake and at home we
never called him Cousin George. He was Mr. Posey. They
say he was in a rage all his life. That was peculiar and
there was something else . . ."

*   *   *

I have never believed that anger has anything in it
that one can touch and see; it is different from love which
is always physical and so knows where to stop, at the end
of familiar things. Aunt Charlotte I think never had any
feeling about anything; she does not know one person
from another; she has felt neither anger nor love. There
is anxiety, but that is kindness and kindness is not love.
This is a neighborhood of strangers. Like me, I suppose
they have all felt that it is not innocent enough, a place
that knows more than we can ever know, knows it all in
a way that we cannot understand. It is absurd to say that
an old house is angry. We get used to absurdity. To say
that of the house seems to me as ordinary as saying that
it is placed among unfamiliar things. We make it angry;
a new house built in another town makes it angry. It
must have once loved familiar things. As I looked down
at the old lady making her balls of twine, I thought how
furious she was, but then she could not know she was
furious. With incredible fury she wound up the twine

as if it were the last of familiar things; furiously she placed her forefinger against the side of her nose, taking in deep breaths; then she resumed her work with new fury.

*　　　*　　　*

". . . and it was even more peculiar. There were Jane and Sarah Georgiana, or Sally George we called her, and it was Sally George who married Mr. Broadwater and went to the Southwest. They took Jane's meals up to her room; she never came out. There were Little George and Uncle Rozier, the two boys, and I expect Cousin Anne called her son uncle because Little George had a son; he had married one of old Major Beckitt's girls and gone out West. I never saw him in my life; he couldn't get along with his father so he went West. West was a word you heard all the time. Hundreds of people were going West. It seemed so far away. The land flowing with milk and honey, old Major Beckitt said sarcastically, but it did seem to flow because Little George made money out of that land he and Mr. Ben Tayloe had bought in the West before the war, and he sent money home. Then he sent his wife and child, a little girl, Little Jane we called her, named after her Aunt Jane, he sent them home to visit. After that visit Little George sent no more money back home, and before long they shut up the house, had to I reckon. Went up to Rockville and died there about the time I was grown. Later Uncle Rozier went West too. I saw him many times, it's right strange how you remember things. I can see him in the front hall coming down the wide white stairway in his carpet-slippers — I remember that because he was such a large man, six feet four they said, and he walked so quietly I noticed his feet. He was different from his father, had the sanguine tem-

perament, but he swore every breath no matter who was
present. I think it was this same day. He put his huge
hand on my head and shook me. 'By God, she's a pretty
young un.' Then he gave me a nickel. Old Aunt Martha
who sat in the back hall with a white cap and apron on
— she was too old and fat to work so she answered the
front doorbell that rang about twice a week — she whispered, 'Don't you be scared, honey, they ain't no harm
in Marse Rozier.' She laughed and showed her big eye-
teeth, all she had left, hanging down over her lower lip.
The old hall was always dark. I could never see the faces
in the frames on the wall opposite the stairs. They were
Gibsons. You know the first Gibson was a dwarf. I think
of those times, how I'm the only one of their kin left here.
Jane died while Little George's wife and daughter were
here on that visit. Doctor Lacy Beckitt, one of the major's
boys, waited on her till she died. They said she just died,
but don't crazy people live just as long as other people?
Longer. Nobody saw her laid out. She was foolish about
her little niece Jane, I reckon because she was her name-
sake. All morning she sat alone in her room and after
dinner she peeped out into the dim hall, and called Little
Jane. Little Jane went upstairs for her daily present.
Jane cut up old newspapers into strips like ribbons all day
long, and laid them in rows and piles. 'Here's your present for today, child' — handing her some paper strips.
She never spoke above a whisper; no one saw her smile;
she was very gentle. When she got a new dress she cut it
right up into scraps — 'They might come in handy,'
she'd say. She tied strings round empty boxes, they found
hundreds of them in her wardrobe after she died. She
saved tinfoil and bits of thread, and made balls of twine.
Sometimes I think the old house is waiting to be taken
away too, and nobody will ever look inside again who

knew what happened there. Not, my dear, that anything
really happened . . ."

"That's what I tell my nephew, folks work so hard but
don't never get anything out of it. Like carrying water
uphill in a leaky bucket."

*   *   *

When Aunt Charlotte broke the silence I knew that I
had heard everything that Mrs. Dulany had said: I was
brought up sharply against the innocence of my poor
aunt, who had heard not a word of it, I mean really
heard it. And yet I was convinced that Mrs. Dulany herself, could the question have entered her mind, would
have seen nothing that was not perfectly plain. I knew,
however, that as Aunt Charlotte spoke Mrs. Dulany was
squinting her eye, and her face was twitching. These mysteries are understood in our bodies, not in the mind. I
thought I understood that too: when the umbrella-mender
cries out in the street I feel restless, even a little exposed,
and thinking suddenly that my bureau needs tidying
up I wheel myself over to it and find myself brushing my
hair.

That, too, must be a kind of anger. I looked out of the
window. The old lady was tying up the ends of her
strings to start a new ball. The air was still and warm and I
knew it was almost noon. A coal truck pounded by on
the cobblestones, leaving the noonday suspense deeper
than before. I had seen into the old house, and there
was the old lady, that cavernous bird of passage, across
the street. Damnation had read itself out to me. I remembered the elderly gentleman who had come for her in the
spattered carriage, and I wanted him to come again today.
I found myself saying, Little Jane. There was the solemn
Negro boy. Good mornin', Miss Jane. I suddenly thought,

Doctor Beckitt, who knew the room in which the crazy woman had died. The old doctor whose carriage might have become his grave. I suppose I wanted Miss Jane to die, but I found myself wishing for her a distant grave, or perhaps — and I think this was it — a moving grave that would bring her back to the old grey house in Indian summer after the morning light of autumn had begun shaking the leaves. Though I knew it was impossible, I could not bear to think of her dying in the old house. I saw her consumed by the rage of the invisible fire within. I kept thinking, foolishly enough, that she might be saved. But she had no place to die. She could neither die nor live.

The young man was coming rapidly down the street. He looked like a tower of new brick. He was all of six feet; his head, arms, legs moved all together. His clothes seemed carefully impersonal and subdued. He must have stepped out of a fashionable hotel. He wore thick glasses and looked occasionally up, then down, to satisfy himself that there was no obstacle in his way. He wore one glove; the other he carried in his bare hand. He walked quickly and deliberately and he scarcely touched the ground.

He was leaning over the old lady, kissing her, his arms at his side. She put both arms round his neck, and kissed him again and again. He withdrew at last. He sat down beside her. Neither spoke. The old lady fumbled with her bag and relaxed with a sigh. He rose, and standing with his legs slightly apart, the backs of his hands on his hips, he looked up at the house.

Still looking up, and I thought gradually tenser and more alert, he rocked on the balls of his feet. He stood suddenly still. He rubbed his bare fist slowly in the palm of his gloved hand. He turned abruptly, as if everything were quite clear, took her by the arm, tenderly, pulling her to her feet. The sun from over the wall lit up her face. I could see that she was in tears. He took her cane, a little awkwardly. She leaned heavily on his arm; they started slowly up the street. He hesitated as if he were about to speak, but thought better of it, smiled, and led the old lady on her way. I never saw her again.

OTHER LOUISIANA PAPERPACKS IN LITERATURE

I'll Take My Stand: The South and the Agrarian Tradition
Twelve Southerners

Gentleman in a Dustcoat: A Biography of John Crowe Ransom
Thomas Daniel Young

Helping Muriel Make It Through the Night Stories by
Lee Zacharias

Lanterns on the Levee: Recollections of a Planter's Son
William Alexander Percy

Bricks Without Straw Albion Tourgée. Edited by Otto H. Olsen

The Federalist Literary Mind: Selections from the *Monthly*
Anthology and Boston Review, **1803–1811, Including**
Documents Relating to the Boston Athenaeum Edited by
Lewis P. Simpson

Cabin Road John Faulkner

William Faulkner of Oxford Edited by James W. Webb and
A. Wigfall Green

The Mind and Art of Henry Miller William A. Gordon

A Bibliographical Guide to the Study of Southern Literature
Edited by Louis D. Rubin, Jr.

The Fugitive Group: A Literary History Louise Cowan

The World's Body John Crowe Ransom

My Mark Twain: Reminiscences and Criticisms
William Dean Howells

The Clairvoyant Eye: The Poetry and Poetics of Wallace Stevens
Joseph N. Riddel

Rhetoric and Criticism Marie Hochmuth Nichols

Freudianism and the Literary Mind Frederick J. Hoffman

Who's Who in Faulkner Margaret P. Ford and Suzanne Kincaid

George W. Cable: A Biography Arlin Turner

POETRY

Why God Permits Evil Miller Williams

Pro Musica Antiqua O. B. Hardison, Jr.

The Fabulous Beasts Joyce Carol Oates

Relativity: A Point of View Kelly Cherry

Round and Round: A Triptych Dabney Stuart

Halfway from Hoxie Miller Williams

Land Diving Robert Morgan

Keeping Time Judith Moffett

The Private Life Lisel Mueller

Walking Out Betty Adcock

River: A Poem Fred Chappell

Watch for the Fox William Mills

Giraffe Stanley Plumly

A Circle of Stone Miller Williams